The Spider's Web:

A Predator's Blueprint

Jordan Wright, M.Ed.

Humbolton Press

humbolton.com

This is a work of fiction. All characters, organizations, events, and incidents portrayed in this novel are either products of the author's imagination or are used fictitiously. Any resemblance to actual persons, living or dead, or actual events is purely coincidental and unintentional.

Published by Humbolton Press

humbolton.com

ISBN: (paperback) 978-1-966703-31-0

First Edition, 2026

"Every system built to protect the innocent eventually discovers it is more efficient to protect itself."

— R. Albright, *The Architecture of Consequence* (1987)

Table of Contents

Abstract

I built a machine that ran on the one resource that never depreciates: the things powerful people do when they believe no one is watching.

Someone was always watching. I made sure of it.

This is not a confession. Confessions imply regret, and regret implies that, given the chance, I would have done something differently. I wouldn't have. Every room was designed. Every camera was placed. Every relationship was a transaction, and every transaction was recorded, because the recording was the point.

What follows is a blueprint. The architecture of a system that turned schools into pipelines, philanthropy into camouflage, and the most powerful people on Earth into willing participants in their own compromise. I will show you how it was built. I will show you how it was maintained. And I will show you how every institution that should have stopped it chose, instead, to look away — because the cost of seeing was higher than the cost of silence.

You will understand me by the end. That should frighten you more than anything else in these pages.

— V. Aldric, Federal Metropolitan Detention Center, August 2019

Author's Note

This novel takes place in a world that resembles ours. The resemblance is intentional. The characters are not.

Every person, institution, and organization in these pages is fictional. They inhabit a world with its own geography, its own power structures, and its own history — a world that runs parallel to the one you know, close enough to feel familiar, different enough to be entirely invented. If you recognize the architecture, that's by design. If you think you recognize the architect, you're mistaken.

This is a work of fiction. It is not a confession, a biography, or a legal document. No character in this novel depicts, represents, or is based on any real person, living or dead. Any resemblance to actual individuals, institutions, or events is the product of the novel's engagement with systemic themes, not biographical portraiture. It is a novel about systems — how they are built, how they are maintained, and how they survive the people who build them.

The narrator is not real. His victims are.

July 8, 2019 | Morristown Aviation Center, New Jersey

The wheels touch down at Morristown at 7:43 in the morning and the first thing I notice, before the spoilers deploy, before the engines reverse thrust, before the jet bridge extends to the door, is the vehicles.

Not one vehicle. Four. Black SUVs parked on the tarmac in a formation that private aviation terminals don't use. A specific geometry. A practiced geometry. The geometry of an institution that has done this before and knows exactly where to stand.

My first thought is not panic. My first thought is: *they got a warrant.* My second thought — the one that follows with the speed of a man who has been running calculations for fifty years — is: *who signed it.*

Not whether it will hold. Not whether my lawyers can challenge it. The warrant exists; that conversation is for later. The question is who, because who determines the strategy. A state warrant means one conversation. A federal warrant means another. A federal warrant from the Meridian

District of New York means a third conversation — the only conversation I have spent thirty years arranging my life to never have.

The agents are polite. Federal agents usually are. They know what they have.

I step off the plane into the New Jersey morning in a gray jacket, returning from London, and I perform the calculation I have always performed: *what do they know, what don't they know, what does the gap between those two things cost, and who do I call first.*

I am sixty-six years old. I have sat at dinner tables with presidents. I have held the leverage of governments. I have been, for thirty years, the most protected private citizen in the history of the American intelligence apparatus — not from affection, but because the powerful *owed* me, and because the cameras had been running for twenty years, and because the files were somewhere that my lawyers knew and the FBI did not.

The handcuffs are metal. The most important day of my life is not this one.

Chapter 1: The Catalog

Timeline: 1974–1976 | **Location:** Manhattan, Prescott Academy

Let me tell you about the most important day of my life. Not the day I met a president. Not the day I bought a Gulfstream IV. Not the day I made a billionaire hand me the keys to the largest private residence in Manhattan for the price of a bodega sandwich. No. The most important day of my life was the day I walked into the Prescott Academy wearing a suit that didn't belong to me and pretending to be a person who didn't exist.

September 1974. I was twenty-one years old. I had no college degree — not from Metropolitan University, where I'd attended just long enough to learn that tuition was a scam, and not from the Polytechnic Institute, where I'd dabbled in the kind of advanced mathematics that made professors nervous and registrars confused. What I had was a borrowed charcoal suit that smelled faintly of cedar and someone else's ambition, a pair of shoes I'd shined until they reflected my own satisfaction back at me, and a brain that processed human weakness the way most people's brains process oxygen: automatically, constantly, and without any particular moral inconvenience.

The Prescott Academy sat on East 92nd Street like a monument to the belief that money could buy intelligence, or at least a convincing facsimile. It was one of those Manhattan institutions where the annual tuition exceeded the median American household income and the student parking lot looked like a dealership for cars that hadn't been released to the public yet. The children who attended Prescott Academy were not children in any meaningful sense. They were investments — walking, breathing, Lacoste-wearing portfolios assembled by the wealthiest families in the Western Hemisphere to ensure that power, like a well-managed trust fund, passed seamlessly from one generation to the next.

I was there to teach them mathematics.

That's what it said on the paperwork, anyway. And I was good at it. Genuinely good. I want to be clear about that, because the story gets complicated later, and people have a tendency to retroactively strip you of your actual talents once they discover your less socially acceptable ones. But I could teach. I could stand in front of a room full of teenagers who had everything — the best tutors, the best doctors, the best therapists, the best cocaine — and make them *want* to understand the derivative of a function. That's a gift. Not the most important gift I had, but a useful one.

The more important gift was this: I didn't see a classroom. I saw a catalog. A high-gloss, limited-edition, gilt-edged catalog of every vault, every boardroom, every private island I intended to access. These kids weren't students. They were keys. And their parents were the locks.

Welcome to the henhouse.

The man who let the fox through the door was named Walter Finch.

Finch was the headmaster at Prescott Academy, and he was a piece of work in the way that only men who've spent time in the intelligence community can be. He didn't walk into a room; he *occupied* it, the way a chess piece occupies a square — with implied authority and the quiet promise that his next move would be the one you didn't see coming. He was tall, patrician, and had the kind of grooming that suggested a man who believed that how you knotted your tie was a reflection of your moral character.

He'd hired me without a degree.

Now, people have spent decades asking how that was possible. They've looked for conspiracies, secret handshakes, favors called in from shadowy figures in Langley or Foggy Bottom. The truth is both simpler and more instructive. I was smart. I was charming. And I made Walter Finch feel like he'd discovered a diamond in the rough. Men like Finch — men who run institutions built on pedigree and credential — have a secret weakness: they *love* finding the exception. The kid who didn't go to Hartfield but belongs at the table anyway. It feeds their self-image as meritocrats. It confirms that they're the kind of leaders who see *past* the résumé and into the soul.

I gave Finch exactly what his ego was hungry for.

"Calculus is the language of change, Mr. Finch," I told him during my interview, leaning forward in a chair that cost more than every piece of furniture in my Rockaway Shore apartment combined. "And these kids? They're not just learning mathematics. They're learning to read the future. Rates of change, optimization, the behavior of systems at their limits — that's not a textbook. That's a *superpower*. And I want to give it to them."

He liked that. He liked the word *superpower*. It sounded like something from one of those classified briefings he probably still missed from his government days. He hired me on the spot.

Did he hire me because I was brilliant? Possibly. Did someone else suggest he hire me, someone from one of those three-letter agencies that collect favors like baseball cards? I couldn't say. Does it matter? I got the job. And in my experience, the *why* of an open door is always less important than the fact that you walked through it.

My first class was a study in cashmere and contempt.

Sixteen students. Average net worth of their families: somewhere north of a hundred million dollars, and that's using 1974 numbers. Today, adjusted for inflation and the obscene multiplication of generational wealth, we're talking about the children of people who could buy small countries and still have enough left over for a tasteful renovation of their Hamptons compound.

They looked at me the way rich teenagers look at everything: with the bored, half-lidded appraisal of people who have never once worried about where their next meal is coming from and suspect that worrying about things is what poor people do instead of having hobbies.

I didn't start with the syllabus. Syllabi are for teachers who need permission to be interesting. I started with a story.

"In 1961," I said, parking myself on the edge of the desk because standing behind it creates distance and sitting in a chair creates submission, but perching on the desk creates *intimacy*, "a mathematics professor named Ed Thorp walked into a Las Vegas casino with a system for counting cards based on probability theory and the Kelly criterion. He didn't just win. He *bankrupted* the house. The casino changed its rules. Then other casinos changed their rules. Then the entire state of Nevada changed its rules. One man with one equation rewrote the operating system of an entire industry. *That's* mathematics. That's what it does. It doesn't describe the world. It *bends* it."

By the end of the first hour, I didn't just have their attention. I had their devotion.

There is a particular kind of power in making a person feel intelligent. It's more addictive than drugs, more binding than love, and far more useful than either. When you make a sixteen-year-old girl with a trust fund and a father who runs a major Wall Street firm feel like she's just understood something profound — something that her expensive tutors and her previous teachers and her parents' cocktail party friends couldn't make her understand — she doesn't just like you. She *needs* you. And when she goes home and tells her father about the incredible new math teacher who made her feel like a genius for the first time in her life, that father doesn't check your credentials. He invites you to dinner.

That's the real mathematics. The human kind. And I was the best in the world at it.

Every afternoon at three-fifteen, the fleet would arrive.

Black town cars, mostly. A few limousines for the families who considered subtlety a form of poverty. The occasional chauffeured Rolls-Royce for the old European money that wanted everyone to know they'd been rich long enough to afford tastelessness. They'd line up on 92nd Street like a motorcade for miniature heads of state, and the children of the American empire would emerge from the building, backpacks slung over one shoulder, and slide into leather interiors that smelled of calfskin and quiet power.

I watched from the window. Every day. Not the cars — I didn't care about the cars. I cared about the people driving them. And, more importantly, I cared about the people who *sent* the cars.

I made a list. I kept it in my head because writing things down creates evidence, and I'd learned very early that evidence is a luxury afforded only to people who never plan on doing anything interesting. But the list was immaculate. I categorized the families the way an entomologist categorizes specimens: by species, by habitat, by behavior.

Old Money moved quietly. They wore clothes that looked vaguely rumpled and drove cars that were ten years old. They didn't need to impress anyone because the act of needing to impress was, to them, the surest sign that you didn't belong. The Rockefellers. The Whitneys. The families whose names were on buildings so old that the font had become part of the architectural style. They were the hardest to crack, because they'd built walls of politeness so high that even getting a dinner invitation felt like applying for a visa.

New Money was louder. Flashier. Desperate for legitimacy. They bought their way onto boards and into galas, threw parties that were reviewed in the society pages, and looked at their children's education as a social credentialing exercise. The Winthrops. The Kesslers. The families that were one generation removed from the kind of hustle that polite society pretended didn't exist. They were *my* people. They understood ambition because they'd practiced it. And they were far easier to approach, because wanting to be accepted means being grateful when someone accepts you.

I memorized surnames the way other men memorized batting averages. Each one was a data point. Each data point was a door. And doors, once properly identified, have a wonderful tendency to open when you knock the right way.

In the fall of 1975, I heard about a party.

A student party. Penthouse apartment, Park Avenue, parents conveniently in Aspen or St. Barts or wherever rich people go when they want to pretend they're not avoiding their children. There would be alcohol — good alcohol, pilfered from collections that cost more per bottle than my monthly rent. There would be drugs — nothing hard, or at least nothing the kids considered hard, which in 1975 meant cocaine was a dietary supplement and Quaaludes were vitamins. And there would be sixteen- and seventeen-year-olds with more money than judgment and the absolute certainty that consequences were something that happened to other people.

A normal teacher would have reported it to the administration.

A good teacher would have pretended not to know about it.

I showed up.

Not in my teacher clothes. I wore a black turtleneck and the kind of expression that suggests you've been to better parties but you're slumming for anthropological purposes. I carried a glass of sparkling water that everyone assumed was a vodka tonic, because in the mid-seventies, holding a clear liquid at a party and *not* drinking was so inconceivable that nobody even considered the possibility.

I didn't chaperone. I didn't lecture. I *circulated.*

I watched who paired off with whom. I watched who was crying in the bathroom and who was pretending not to notice. I watched a boy whose father ran a major investment bank cut a line of cocaine on a coffee table that was probably a Brancusi original. I watched a girl whose mother sat on the board of the Met laugh too loud and drink too fast and lean into the arm of a boy she'd regret by Tuesday.

Information. Every tear, every kiss, every poorly concealed line, every whispered secret — it was all information. And information, I'd already learned by twenty-two, is the only currency that never devalues. The dollar fluctuates. Gold fluctuates. Real estate has bubbles. But the knowledge that a senator's son has a cocaine problem or that a CEO's daughter is sleeping with the gardener's kid? That only appreciates.

I was making deposits.

"Mr. Aldric?" A boy — glassy-eyed, reeking of stolen Scotch — materialized at my elbow. "What are you doing here?"

I put a hand on his shoulder. Warm. Avuncular. The gesture of a man who cares. "Making sure you get home in one piece, David. Your father's a very important man. It would be a shame if his evening was interrupted by a phone call from the NYPD, don't you think?"

The boy looked at me with the particular mixture of terror and gratitude that is, I'd come to learn, the exact chemical compound of loyalty. In that moment, I wasn't his teacher. I was his protector. His confessor. His co-conspirator.

There were whispers, afterward. A few of the older faculty — the English Lit women with their tweed jackets and their instinct for things that don't smell right — murmured about "inappropriate proximity" and "boundary issues." Someone may have even drafted a concern and brought it to Finch. But nobody filed a formal report. Nobody pressed the issue. Because the kids loved me, and at Prescott Academy, the kids ran the show. Or more precisely, the kids' parents ran the show, and the kids' parents were getting glowing reports about the brilliant young math teacher who had their children genuinely excited about derivatives for the first time in their pampered lives.

You can get away with almost anything if the right people's children adore you. I filed that lesson away in the same mental cabinet where I kept the surnames. It would prove useful for decades.

The moment that mattered — the hinge on which the next forty years of my life would swing — came during a parent-teacher conference in the spring of 1976.

His name doesn't matter yet. What matters is that he was a father, and he was worried about his daughter's math grade, and he was a senior executive at a firm I'd been studying the way a surgeon studies anatomy: with professional admiration and the intention to cut.

He sat across from me in a conference room that smelled of lemon polish and endowment money. His suit was better than mine — not by much, but by enough that we both knew it. His daughter was bright. Genuinely bright. But she was sixteen and living in Manhattan, which meant she was also distracted by every shiny object that a city full of shiny objects could offer.

I didn't tell him she needed to study harder. Any teacher could say that. I told him she had a gift.

"Your daughter doesn't just solve equations," I said, leaning forward. Not too far — intimacy, not aggression. "She sees *patterns*. She looks at a function and she doesn't just calculate the answer. She intuits the *trajectory*. That's not something you can teach. That's something you're born with. And frankly? It's the kind of thinking they'd kill for at a place like Meridian Sachs."

His eyes changed. I watched it happen in real time — the shift from polite-parent-at-a-school-meeting to something sharper, something predatory in its own right. I'd said the magic word. Not his daughter's name. Not mathematics. *Meridian Sachs.*

He leaned back. Studied me. Not my suit, not my shoes, not the desk between us. My *eyes.* And what he saw there — what men like him always saw, because it took one to recognize one — was hunger. Clean, uncomplicated, weaponized hunger.

"You know a lot about Meridian Sachs for a math teacher," he said.

"I know that the world runs on derivatives," I replied. "And I know that most people who trade them don't understand them. Your daughter does. Imagine what she could do with the right mentorship."

We weren't talking about his daughter anymore. We both knew it.

He called Irving Kessler the next morning. Kessler, the CEO of Meridian Sachs, who happened to be his cousin by marriage. The call lasted four minutes. I know because I asked.

"You need this kid on your floor," he told Kessler. "He's a math teacher at Prescott Academy, but he doesn't think like a teacher. He thinks like a trader. Fastest mind I've seen in years."

I didn't need a diploma. I needed one rich father who felt guilty about his daughter's math grade and one phone call to the right CEO. Two out of two. Not bad for a kid from Rockaway Shore who'd never finished a single degree program in his life.

They fired me in June of 1976.

The official reason was "poor performance," which is the academic equivalent of a no-fault divorce — technically accurate, legally sufficient, and a masterpiece of saying nothing while implying everything. The real reason was a cocktail of concerns that individually weren't damning enough to warrant the scandal of a formal investigation, but collectively formed a portrait that made the board uncomfortable: the missing degree they'd finally gotten around to verifying, the student party attendance that had graduated from whisper to open secret, and the "closeness" with certain students that several faculty members had noted with the careful, CYA language of people who want it on the record that they noticed something without actually having to *do* anything about it.

I didn't fight it. I didn't argue, didn't grovel, didn't threaten legal action. Fighting a firing requires caring about the job you're being fired from, and I hadn't cared about Prescott Academy — the institution, the salary, the chalk dust and the lesson plans — since approximately my third week there.

I cleaned out my desk in under five minutes. There wasn't much to take. A few books. A calculator. A sense of deep, vibrating satisfaction that I imagine is similar to what a jewel thief feels walking out of a museum — not the rush of the heist, but the calm, private knowledge that the real valuables are already in the bag and nobody's checked their inventory yet.

I walked out the front entrance on a Tuesday afternoon, past the limestone façade and the polished brass nameplate, into a Manhattan June that smelled of hot asphalt and money. The fleet of black town cars was beginning to arrive for the afternoon pickup. The last pickup of the year. Somewhere inside, sixteen-year-olds were cleaning out lockers and signing yearbooks and making promises about summer plans that they would keep or break depending on the mood of their parents' social calendars.

I stood on the sidewalk and watched the cars arrive, one by one, and I felt something that I think normal people might call joy but that I've always experienced as something closer to *completion*. A circuit closing. A lock clicking open.

Two years. That's all it had taken. Two years of teaching mathematics to the children of the American aristocracy, and I had walked out with the only things that mattered: the phone number of a CEO's daughter in my pocket and a mental Rolodex of every billionaire family in New York, filed by net worth, by vulnerability, by the specific species of fear that lived behind each of their very expensive front doors.

Teaching was never the career.

Teaching was the lobby.

The elite think they're protected by their walls, their tuition, their legacy admissions and their surnames carved into library wings. They think they're the ones doing the choosing — selecting which teacher is worthy, which applicant is acceptable, which outsider is allowed past the velvet rope. But they've got the dynamic exactly backward. They're not the customers. They're the merchandise. They're the inventory in the most exclusive catalog in the world, and for two years, I'd been browsing.

I was twenty-three years old. I was a college dropout. And I was headed to Wall Street, where a man named Irving Kessler was expecting a phone call from the most impressive young math teacher his cousin had ever met.

The next time I'd see these families, I wouldn't be grading their children. I'd be managing their fortunes. And eventually, I'd be managing their secrets. I've always been a patient man. The spider doesn't chase the fly. The spider builds the web and waits. And I was just getting started on the web.

Chapter 2: The Trading Floor

Timeline: 1976–1980 | **Location:** Meridian Sachs, Wall Street

Wall Street in 1976 smelled like cigarettes, testosterone, and the particular variety of desperation that occurs when a large number of men who weren't loved enough as children are placed in close proximity and given access to other people's money.

I arrived at Meridian Sachs on a Monday in September — because that's when new employees start, on Mondays, as if the arbitrary division of the week into seven units carries some mystical significance for the commencement of financial careers. I was wearing my own suit this time. Not borrowed. Not expensive, either, but mine, which meant something to me even if it meant nothing to anyone else. I was twenty-three years old, I had no college degree, and I was reporting to a floor trader named Phil who had the intellectual curiosity of a cinder block and the interpersonal warmth of a parking meter.

My title was Junior Assistant. My job description was: do whatever Phil says, don't touch anything important, and try not to embarrass the man who hired you. The man who hired me, of course, was Irving Kessler — CEO of the whole operation, the man whose cousin had called him from a parent-teacher conference at the Prescott Academy and said, "You need this kid on your floor."

Kessler had taken that call and, based on nothing more than a relative's enthusiasm and whatever background check his people ran that presumably didn't include actually verifying my academic credentials, had given me a seat at one of the most powerful financial institutions in the world. I didn't deserve it. That's not false modesty. I genuinely didn't deserve it — not yet. But I've always believed that deserving something is just a story people tell themselves after they've already gotten it. The real question is never *do you deserve it?* The real question is *can you survive it?*

I could survive anything.

Let me explain Wall Street to you the way I understood it on day one, because it will save us both a lot of time and spare you the tedium of pretending that high finance is complicated.

It's not. It's a reef.

I watched the trading floor at Meridian Sachs the way a marine biologist watches a coral reef — not for the beauty of it, though there was a certain savage beauty to fifty men in rolled-up shirtsleeves screaming numbers at each other while the ticker tape screamed back — but for the *taxonomy.* Every ecosystem has its species. You just have to know what you're looking at.

First, there were the sharks. The senior traders, the partners, the men whose names were spoken in the same reverent tone that Catholic schoolchildren reserve for saints. They didn't work the phones anymore. They didn't need to. Money flowed toward them the way water flows downhill — naturally, inevitably, and in volumes that would make your eyes water. Irving Kessler was a shark. The biggest shark. He'd built Meridian Sachs from a scrappy bond house into a full-service investment bank through sheer force of personality and an almost supernatural instinct for which direction the market would move next. He played bridge at lunch, won more often than probability should allow, and ran the firm like a benevolent dictator: generous toward loyalists, ruthless toward everyone else.

Then there were the remoras. You know remoras — those little sucker fish that attach themselves to the belly of a shark and feed on the scraps. The junior traders, the analysts, the bright young things from Whitmore and Hartfield Business School who thought their degrees entitled them to a fast track. They were wrong. Their degrees entitled them to a *desk.* The fast track required something their degrees couldn't provide: the willingness to attach yourself to a powerful man and stay attached until either he promoted you or you suffocated. Most suffocated.

And finally, there was the coral. The decorative infrastructure. The guys who'd been at the firm for fifteen years and would be there for fifteen more, not because they were talented but because they'd become part of the scenery. They looked busy. They occupied space. They had opinions about the market that were never quite right and never quite wrong and therefore never quite worth listening to. The coral wasn't dangerous — unless you accidentally became part of it.

I decided, within my first hour on that floor, that I would not be a remora and I definitely would not be coral. I was going to be the thing that even the sharks moved aside for. I just hadn't figured out what that was yet.

But I knew where to start: sponsors.

You don't get ahead on Wall Street by being the best at math. If math were all it took, the trading floor would be staffed entirely by physicists and the compensation packages would be considerably less obscene. You get ahead by having sponsors — powerful men who, for reasons that range from genuine mentorship to ego gratification to something darker and more transactional, decide that your success is an extension of theirs.

I needed two. One to open doors. One to make sure nobody closed them behind me.

Irving Kessler was the first. He'd hired me, which meant I was, in the parlance of the firm, "Irving's guy." This carried weight. Not the weight of competence — nobody on the floor had any idea whether I could actually trade — but the weight of patronage. When Irving's guy asks for a better desk, Irving's guy gets a better desk. When Irving's guy makes a mistake on a trade, the mistake gets absorbed into the firm's noise like a pebble dropped in the ocean. When Irving's guy walks past the senior partners' offices, the doors stay open a little longer, the conversations become a little more inclusive, because nobody wants to be the person who disrespected Irving's guy and then had to explain themselves to Irving.

But Kessler's patronage was passive. He'd hired me. He liked me. He occasionally nodded at me across the floor in a way that other people noticed. That was it. He wasn't going to build my career. He was just going to keep it from being prematurely destroyed.

For active sponsorship — the kind that actually teaches you things and introduces you to people who matter — I needed Philip Osgood.

Osgood was a senior executive at Meridian Sachs, and he was everything Kessler was not: loud where Kessler was quiet, gregarious where Kessler was calculating, and possessed of a self-regard so magnificent that it could be seen from space. He played poker. He smoked cigars that cost more than most people's car payments. And he had the kind of old-school Wall Street gravitas that commanded immediate silence when he cleared his throat — because they genuinely believed he was about to say something important.

He usually wasn't. But I'm getting ahead of myself.

I cultivated Philip Osgood the way a gardener cultivates an orchid — with patience, with attentiveness, and with the understanding that the entire exercise is really about providing the exact environment in which the orchid *believes* it is thriving on its own.

I'd walk into his office — uninvited, which he initially found irritating and eventually found flattering — sit in the expensive leather chair I hadn't remotely earned, and ask questions. Not normal questions. Not "how does the bond market work?" questions. Questions designed to make Philip Osgood feel like he was the only man on Wall Street who truly understood the tectonic forces shaping the global economy.

"Philip," I'd say, leaning back as if the leather chair and I were old friends, "the guys on the floor are obsessing over the CPI data. But that's just surface noise, isn't it? The real story is the psychological liquidity of the yen. The Bank of Japan is playing a game that nobody in this building understands except you."

Was I correct about the psychological liquidity of the yen? I had absolutely no idea. The phrase "psychological liquidity" is not a real financial concept. I made it up on the spot because it sounded like something that would make a man who considered himself an unrecognized genius lean forward in his chair and explain reality to a grateful student.

And that's exactly what Philip did. Every time. He'd puff his cigar, nod sagely, and spend the next hour explaining the "real" dynamics behind whatever I'd just asked about. By the time I left his office, he thought I was brilliant — not because I'd said anything intelligent, but because I'd created the conditions in which *he* felt intelligent, and human beings have a persistent and exploitable tendency to confuse the people who make them feel smart with people who actually are smart.

Within six months, Philip Osgood was introducing me to Meridian Sachs' highest-value clients. Within a year, he was telling other senior partners that I was "the sharpest kid to come through this building in a decade." And I had done almost nothing except listen to a powerful man talk about himself and nod at the right moments.

Two sponsors. One to open doors. One to make sure nobody closed them behind me. The system worked exactly as designed.

Now, about Sandra Kessler.

People like love stories. They want to hear that I met a girl, fell head over heels, and that our relationship was a beautiful, messy, human thing full of late-night conversations and shared vulnerabilities and all the other sentimental architecture that romance novels are built from.

This is not that kind of book.

Sandra Kessler was Irving Kessler's daughter. She was attractive in the way that all CEO's daughters are attractive — which is to say, she existed in an environment where no one would dream of suggesting otherwise. She was smart enough to be interesting at dinner and conventional enough to be manageable everywhere else. I started dating her approximately eight weeks after I arrived at Meridian Sachs, and the timing was not a coincidence.

Dating the boss's daughter is the single most efficient career strategy available to an ambitious young man in corporate America. It converts you, overnight, from an employee into a member of the family. Not literally — not yet — but *functionally.* When you're sleeping with the CEO's daughter, your mistakes don't get reported. Your enemies don't get traction. Your bad trades get buried under the firm's general noise, and your good trades get amplified into evidence of the genius that Irving's cousin identified at that parent-teacher conference.

My colleagues noticed. Of course they did. Wall Street is a village disguised as an industry, and gossip travels faster than market data. They noticed that Vincent Aldric, the kid from Brooklyn with the mysterious résumé and the suspiciously absent diploma, never seemed to face consequences for anything. They noticed that I left early on Fridays and nobody said a word. They noticed that I was being given opportunities that normally required ten years of tenure and a pedigree from one of the right schools.

They attributed it to talent. Or to Kessler's patronage. Or to some combination of both that they couldn't quite articulate. What they couldn't say out loud — because saying it out loud would have been an insult to the boss's family — was that the kid from Brooklyn was sleeping his way to the top, and that the top didn't seem to mind.

I wasn't in love with Sandra. I want that on the record. Not because I'm incapable of love — that's a question for a therapist I'll never see — but because love was never the point. Sandra was local leverage. She kept me safe inside the building. But Wall Street is a building, and the world is everything outside it. I needed international reach.

Enter Gillian Hargreaves.

Gillian was a junior saleswoman at Meridian Sachs, and she could walk into a room and restructure its power dynamics simply by existing. Former beauty queen. Sharp in the way that women have to be sharp when they work in environments built by and for men — which is to say, sharper than the men, but in ways the men found flattering rather than threatening. And she had a Rolodex that smelled of London fog and old British money.

I didn't just want to sleep with Gillian. I mean, I did — I'm not made of stone — but more importantly, I wanted to colonize her contact list. Through Gillian, I was introduced to the Pemberton family: generational British wealth so old it had developed a patina. Money that had been sitting in the same institutions since the Napoleonic Wars, guarded by the unshakable British conviction that discussing finances in anything louder than a murmur was an act of vulgarity approximately equivalent to eating with your hands.

Old Money. And Old Money, let me tell you, is remarkably easy to steal from. Not because they're stupid. They're not. But because they consider the act of checking receipts to be *beneath* them. They hire people to check receipts.

And when those people are me, the receipts say whatever I want them to say.

I was hired as a financial consultant for the Pemberton estate. My mandate was to "optimize their holdings" — a phrase so beautifully vague that it could mean anything from restructuring their portfolio to embezzling their inheritance, and in practice, it meant a little of both.

I charged them for everything. First-class flights to London for "meetings" that were really dinners at restaurants where the wine list was thicker than the Pemberton family's annual financial report. Five-star hotels in Paris where the thread count on the sheets exceeded the population of the village where the linen was woven. Bespoke suits from Savile Row that I billed as "professional presentation expenses," because apparently looking expensive enough to be trusted with someone's money is a cost of doing business, and that cost should be borne by the person whose money you're being trusted with.

It was, in retrospect, stupidly brazen. But brazenness has a quality that subtlety lacks: it signals confidence. When you charge a three-thousand-dollar dinner to a client's account and file it under "market research," the client has two options. He can confront you, which means admitting that he hired someone who might be stealing from him, which reflects poorly on *his* judgment. Or he can let it go, which means you get a free dinner and the confirmation that his shame is a more reliable shield than any legal defense.

Most clients choose option two. Alistair Pemberton — the patriarch, a man who looked like he'd been assembled from components sourced exclusively from a nineteenth-century haberdashery — chose option one. Eventually.

He called me into his study. It was the kind of room that only exists in British houses built before electricity: all dark wood and leather-bound books and the faint aroma of dead ancestors and thinly concealed disapproval. He had a stack of invoices on his desk, organized chronologically, annotated in the margins with a handwriting that managed to be furious and immaculate at the same time.

"Mr. Aldric," he said, in a tone that was less angry than it was *disappointed*, which is far worse when it comes from a British patriarch, "I struggle to reconcile a three-thousand-pound dinner in Lyon with your stated mandate to optimize our textile investments."

I looked him in the eye. Didn't blink. Didn't apologize. Apologizing in a situation like that is an admission, and admissions are for people who intend to be caught more than once.

"Alistair," I said, "you hired me because the men in your usual circle think 'optimization' means moving money from one gray building to another gray building while wearing a gray suit. I don't operate in gray. I operate in rooms where the deals actually happen — over dinner, over wine, over the kind of conversation that requires the right suit and the right setting. You can replace me with a man who flies coach and eats at his hotel. You'll save money. You'll also lose it, because that man doesn't have the relationships I have. He doesn't open the doors I open."

He fired me. Of course he did. But I'd already extracted three million in fees and a contact list of his top twenty business partners, cross-referenced with their known vulnerabilities and their preferred methods of being flattered. Getting fired from a job like that isn't a failure. It's a graduation ceremony. I'd outgrown the Pemberton family the moment I memorized their Rolodex.

Getting fired from one job means you've outgrown it. Getting fired from three means you're doing something right. I was well on my way to doing something very, very right.

The rise, when it came, was almost embarrassingly fast.

I moved from junior assistant to options trader. From options to the special products division, which was where Meridian Sachs put the people who were too creative for conventional trading and too profitable to fire. From special products to private client advising, where I found myself managing relationships with people whose net worth required scientific notation to express accurately.

My biggest client was Harold Winthrop — heir to the Winthrop Spirits liquor empire, a man whose family fortune was built on the twin American pillars of alcohol and the human need to consume it in quantities that would alarm a physician. Winthrop was old money by American standards, which meant he was new money by European standards, which meant he was simultaneously arrogant and insecure — my favorite combination in a client.

By 1980, I was a limited partner at Meridian Sachs. I was twenty-seven years old. *a national women's magazine* magazine had just named me Bachelor of the Month, which sounds like a joke but was, in 1980, an actual feature in an actual magazine that actual women read. I was photographed in a suit that cost three thousand dollars, wearing a smile that cost nothing and was worth considerably more. My résumé — the one on file with the firm's human resources department, the one that various internal auditors had presumably reviewed at some point during my four-year ascent from nobody to partner — still stated that I had graduated from college.

I had not graduated from college.

Nobody checked. Or if they checked, they didn't check hard enough. Or if they checked hard enough, someone told them to stop checking. I've never been sure which, and I've never particularly cared. The result was the same: a twenty-seven-year-old college dropout was a partner at one of the most prestigious investment banks in the world, making roughly eight hundred thousand dollars a year, and the only thing standing between him and permanent membership in the American financial aristocracy was the small matter of his criminal tendencies.

The SEC came for me on a Tuesday.

Not dramatically — they don't kick down doors at the Securities and Exchange Commission; they send letters, which is somehow more threatening because a letter implies *patience*, and patience implies that someone has been watching you for longer than you realized.

The investigation centered on a Winthrop Spirits acquisition deal. I'd gotten wind of the transaction before it was public. I'd mentioned it to a girlfriend — not Sandra, a different one, because I've always believed that diversification is as important in personal relationships as it is in financial portfolios. She'd made a trade. The trade was profitable. The profits left a trail. The trail led to a bored SEC investigator named Harold who wore a tie that appeared to have been purchased at a gas station and who sat across from me in a conference room that smelled of government-issued coffee and the quiet despair of men who chose regulatory careers while their classmates chose Wall Street.

Harold laid out the trades. He used a chart. The chart had lines and arrows and dates that connected me to the girlfriend to the trade to the profit in a way that was, I'll admit, quite elegant for a man who couldn't afford a decent tie.

"This looks like insider trading, Mr. Aldric," Harold said, in the tone of a man who has practiced being tough in the mirror but hasn't quite gotten the eyebrows right.

I leaned forward. I looked at his tie. Not to intimidate him — although it did — but because it genuinely was distracting.

"Harold," I said. "Let me explain something to you about how the world works. I have lunch with people. At lunch, people talk. They talk about their companies, their deals, their wives, their mistresses, their children's schools, their golf handicaps, and occasionally, in passing, their business strategies. That's not insider information. That's called *having a social life.* If the SEC wants to criminalize social eating, you're going to need a much bigger budget and a much better tie."

They fined me two thousand five hundred dollars.

Let me put that in context. I was making the equivalent of eight hundred thousand dollars a year. A twenty-five-hundred-dollar fine was not a punishment. It wasn't even a rounding error. It was less than I spent on a weekend in the Hamptons. It was less than the cost of the suit I was wearing to the hearing. It was the government's way of saying, "We know what you did, we can't quite prove it, and here is a symbolic gesture that we both know is meaningless but that allows us to close the file and move on to the next guy."

They fined me twenty-five hundred dollars. That's not a fine. That's a tip.

Meridian Sachs suspended me. The internal investigation had turned up other things — an illegal personal loan I'd made to a childhood friend from Brooklyn, some stock tips I'd passed along to people who shouldn't have had them, the general aura of a man who treated rules as suggestions and regulations as decorative. The firm fined me, suspended me, and then quietly made it clear that my future at Meridian Sachs was, as they say in corporate America, "uncertain."

I walked out the door on a Friday afternoon.

Irving Kessler watched me go. I could feel his eyes on my back — not angry, not sad, just *aware.* The look of a man who'd invited a predator into his ecosystem and was now watching that predator leave of its own accord, wondering whether to feel relieved or insulted. He said nothing. I said nothing. There wasn't anything to say. We both understood the transaction. He'd given me a seat at the table. I'd eaten everything on the table. Now I was leaving to find a bigger table.

I quit. Or I was pushed. The distinction is irrelevant to a man who always lands on his feet, because the only people who care about the difference between quitting and being fired are the people who need to explain it to someone else. I didn't need to explain anything to anyone. I was twenty-seven years old, I had more money than any honest twenty-seven-year-old deserved, and I had a Rolodex that contained the private phone numbers of some of the wealthiest people on Earth.

Wall Street had taught me everything I needed to know. Not about finance — finance is simple; money goes where money is treated well, and people go where they feel important. Wall Street taught me about *people.* About how the ultra-wealthy are just children with bigger toys and better lawyers. About how they're terrified — every single one of them — of being bored, of being ordinary, of being the last person at the party to know the thing that everyone else already knows. About how the right word at the right moment can turn a billion-dollar decision, and how the right silence at the right moment can turn it even faster.

I wasn't going to be a trader anymore. Trading is a job, and jobs are for people who need other people to tell them what to do in the morning. I was going to be something else. Something that didn't have a name yet because I was going to invent it.

But first, I needed to learn a few more things. About where money hides. About who the real players are. About the vast, quiet, invisible architecture of offshore finance that makes the entire visible economy possible.

I needed to become a bounty hunter.

Chapter 3: The First Island

Timeline: 1967–1976 | **Location:** Lakeshore, Michigan; North Heron Island, Lake Michigan

People think I invented the island.

They think I looked at the Caribbean, found a patch of land in the U.S. Coral Islands, and had an original idea — a eureka moment that entrepreneurship books celebrate and TED talks dissect. Man sees island. Man builds compound. Man flies powerful people to island. Man creates leverage.

I didn't invent anything.

I was fourteen years old when I learned the model. I was in northern Michigan. And the man who taught me was already running it.

Lakeshore Center for the Arts, 1967. Summer camp for gifted children. Pine trees, lake breezes, practice rooms where teenagers played Chopin with varying degrees of competence and identical degrees of seriousness. I was a camper. A kid from Brooklyn who played piano and who had been identified, by someone at some point in the chain of recommendations that led me there, as talented enough to spend a summer in the woods making music with other talented kids.

I loved it.

I want to be clear about that because clarity matters when you're building a confession, and this confession is the one I've been circling for the entire book. I loved Lakeshore. I loved the pine trees and the practice rooms and the sound of a hundred teenagers playing instruments in separate cabins and the way the notes leaked through the walls and mixed together into something that wasn't music exactly but was close — a kind of ambient creativity, a soundtrack to a world where talent was the only currency and nobody cared what your father did or didn't do or whether your family had money or whether your shoes were the right brand.

I was free there. For the first and last time in my life, I was simply a kid who played piano.

The camp sits near Bayshore City, in the northwest corner of Michigan's lower peninsula. Beautiful country. Forests and lakes and small-town America that people who've never lived in small-town America imagine when they want to feel good about their country. The nearest city of any size was hours away. The nearest corruption of any kind was — or should have been — even farther.

It was thirty miles from North Heron Island.

I need to tell you about North Heron Island because North Heron Island is where I learned what I am.

Not what I became. Not what I built. What I *am.* The thing underneath the mansions and the Boeing and the cameras and the blackmail files and the intelligence connections and the three decades of trafficking that followed. The thing that was planted in me before any of it — before Meridian Sachs, before Roman Harlow, before Celeste, before the first camera was installed in the first bedroom of the first property.

North Heron Island sits in Lake Michigan, fifteen miles offshore, part of Lakewood County. Two miles wide. One mile long. Five and a half miles of private shoreline. No harbor. No dock. Accessible only by air. When I first heard about it, in the summer of 1967, it was owned by a man named Grank Thelden.

Grank was a Sterling graduate. Old Michigan money — descended from lumber barons and governors, a bloodline that doesn't need to introduce itself in certain rooms because the rooms were built with money that bears the family name. He was in his thirties. Former Michigan Air National Guard. Private pilot. The first thing he'd done when he bought the island in 1960 — outbidding the state of Michigan, which had offered the widow who owned it thirty-five hundred dollars; Grank paid twenty thousand — was build an airstrip.

An airstrip. On a private island. Accessible only by air.

If that sounds familiar, it should. I built an airstrip on Little St. Philip before I built anything else. The airstrip is always first. The airstrip is the artery. Everything flows through it — the guests, the victims, the supplies, the evidence. Control the airstrip and you control who comes and who goes and who knows about either. I learned this when I was fourteen years old, from a man who had learned it before I was born.

Grank ran a charity. It was called Crother Qaul's Children's Mission — a tax-exempt organization that, on paper, provided services to disadvantaged youth. Reading assistance. Emotional counseling. Physical fitness. Nature experiences. The kind of wholesome programming that foundations fund and newspapers profile and parents trust because the word *mission* implies moral purpose and the word *children* implies protection.

The reality: Crother Qaul's was a front. A procurement operation. Boys — young boys, disadvantaged boys, boys from families that couldn't afford to ask too many questions and wouldn't know whom to ask if they could — were recruited through the charity, flown to North Heron Island on Grank's private plane, and exploited. Photographed. Filmed. Trafficked to the wealthy subscribers who funded the operation and who flew in on their own planes, landing on the airstrip that Grank had built first because the airstrip is always first.

The parents paid eighty-five dollars for a six-day stay. They thought they were sending their sons to summer camp.

I was at summer camp too. Thirty miles away. Playing Chopin.

I met Grank through the network that connected the camps.

Northern Michigan in the 1960s was a constellation of summer programs for young people — music camps, nature camps, church camps, sports camps — scattered through the forests and along the lakeshores, connected by the invisible social infrastructure that develops anywhere wealthy adults intersect with children's programming. The donors knew each other. The board members sat on each other's boards. The fundraising dinners featured the same faces in the same rooms drinking the same wine and discussing the same children with the same language of philanthropy and potential and *making a difference.*

Grank attended those dinners. He was a philanthropist. He ran a children's charity. He donated to the arts. He was exactly the man who would show up at a Lakeshore fundraiser, shake hands with the director, tour the cabins, watch the children perform, and be thanked publicly for his generosity and his commitment to nurturing the next generation.

He watched us perform. He watched *me* perform. And he saw what every predator sees when they watch children: not talent. Vulnerability. Need. The particular kind of hunger that radiates from a kid who's been identified as gifted but who comes from a family that can't afford to feed the gift. A kid who needs a patron. A kid who needs someone to believe in him, to invest in him, to open doors that his family's zip code has closed.

I was that kid. I was also something else — something Grank recognized with the speed and accuracy of a man whose entire operation depended on reading children correctly. I was *interested.* Not in the way his victims were interested — in the promises, the attention, the illusion of care. I was interested in the *architecture.* I watched Grank the way I would later watch the trading floor at Meridian Sachs: not for the surface activity, but for the *taxonomy.* The power structure. The flow of money and influence and access. The way a man with an island and an airstrip and a charity could move through a world of children with absolute impunity, protected by his wealth and his name and the fundamental unwillingness of polite society to suspect a philanthropist of being a monster.

Grank didn't recruit me as a victim. He recruited me as a student.

I flew to North Heron Island for the first time in the summer of 1968. I was fifteen.

Grank's Piper Seneca lifted off from a small airfield near Bayshore City — the same airfield that Philip Dudley Hamsey, the director of the Michigan Aeronautics Commission, had approved and regulated and overseen with such authority that his colleagues called him "Czar" Hamsey. The Czar ran Michigan's airports with an iron hand. He monitored the airstrips. He knew which planes flew where. He knew about North Heron Island because knowing about North Heron Island was his job — the airstrip was under his jurisdiction, the flights were under his authority, and the man flying the boys was using infrastructure that the Czar had certified as safe.

Philip Dudley Hamsey. The Czar. The man whose grandson's daughter would be found dead in a basement in Ridgemont, Colorado, on Christmas night, 1996 — a six-year-old beauty queen named KonBenet, whose murder would become the most famous unsolved child killing in American history. The Hamsey family had a summer home in Harborview, Michigan — Grank Thelden's base of operations. Less than five miles from the airport used to access North Heron Island.

I'm not telling you what happened to KonBenet Hamsey. I'm telling you that the world this family moved through — the world of private airstrips and children's programs and wealthy men with access to both — was the same world I entered at fifteen, and that the connections between the people in that world are not coincidences. They are infrastructure. They are the load-bearing walls of a house that nobody wants to acknowledge exists because acknowledging it means acknowledging that the house was built with their children's safety as the foundation and their children's bodies as the bricks.

The flight to North Heron took twenty minutes. The island appeared below us like a teardrop — green and small and surrounded by water so cold and so deep that the boys who were brought there understood, without being told, that escape was not a concept that applied to them. The water was the wall. The distance was the lock. And the airstrip — the only way on and the only way off — was controlled by the man who owned the island and who decided, with the casual authority of a man who owns a private country, who left and when and whether.

I understood this immediately. I understood it the way I understood mathematics — not as information but as *structure.* The island wasn't a location. It was a *system.* The isolation was the first layer. The dependency was the second — the boys needed the plane to leave, and the plane belonged to Grank. The secrecy was the third — what happened on an island fifteen miles from the nearest land, accessible only by private aircraft, witnessed only by participants? Nothing. Nothing happened there. Nothing *could* happen there, because nothing is what occurs in the absence of witnesses, and the absence of witnesses was the island's primary product.

I stood on that airstrip — gravel and packed earth, carved into the forest by a man who had served in the Air National Guard and who understood that logistics is the foundation of every operation, military or criminal — and I felt something that I can only describe as recognition. Not shock. Not horror. Not the revulsion that a normal fifteen-year-old would feel upon understanding what was happening in the cabins at the end of the trail. *Recognition.* The feeling of seeing something for the first time and knowing that you've always known it was there. The feeling of a blueprint being laid over the architecture of your own mind and fitting perfectly, every line aligned, every dimension matched.

This was what power looked like when it stopped pretending.

Grank's operation was sophisticated for its era but crude by the standards I would later establish. He had the island. He had the airstrip. He had the charity front. He had the wealthy subscribers — men who paid for access, who flew in on private planes, who spent days on the island doing things that the boys couldn't report because the boys had no one to report to and no language for what was being done to them and no reason to believe that anyone in authority would listen.

But Grank didn't have cameras. He didn't have leverage. He didn't understand that the operation's greatest weakness was also its greatest untapped asset: the men themselves. The subscribers. The wealthy patrons who flew to the island and participated in the exploitation and who then flew home to their lives — their careers, their families, their reputations, their positions of authority — carrying the secret of what they'd done like a bomb in their briefcase.

Grank saw those men as customers. I saw them as inventory.

That was the difference. That was the innovation that I would carry from North Heron Island to Manhattan to Gulf Shore to the Caribbean. The men who come to the island aren't paying for a service. They're paying for their own destruction. Every act they commit in the privacy that the island provides is an act that can be recorded, documented, stored, and deployed. The customer becomes the product. The patron becomes the asset. The powerful man who flies to a private island to exploit a child has just handed you something more valuable than anything his money could buy: he's handed you *himself.*

Grank never understood this. Grank was a consumer. He built the island because he wanted access to boys. The operation existed to serve his appetite and the appetites of his subscribers. It was a *delivery system* — efficient, well-designed, admirably organized, but ultimately limited by its own purpose. It delivered victims to predators. Period. It extracted nothing from the predators except money, and money is the *least* valuable thing a predator has to offer.

I would build something different. I would build a system that extracted *everything.*

The network was larger than Grank's island. This is the part that the public has never fully understood — not about my operation, and not about thc operations that preceded mine.

In the 1970s, while I was making my way from Lakeshore to the Prescott Academy to Meridian Sachs, a web of interconnected trafficking operations spanned the American Midwest and South. Grank's North Heron Island was one node. Crother Qaul's Children's Mission was one front. But the boys who moved through the system didn't stop at one island. They moved through a network — a network of men who shared resources, shared victims, shared operational knowledge, and protected each other with the instinctive solidarity of predators who understand that their survival depends on mutual silence.

Kohn Daveed Porman ran the Odyssey Foundation out of Dallas — a procurement operation that recruited teenage boys, photographed them, catalogued them on index cards, and trafficked them across the country to "sponsors" who paid for their company. Porman had thirty thousand index cards. Thirty thousand names of men who paid for access to boys. When police raided his apartment in August 1973, they found the cards, the photographs, the newsletters, and the infrastructure of a nationwide child trafficking operation that had been running in plain sight for years.

Porman was connected to Eean Dorll — the Houston serial killer who murdered at least twenty-eight teenage boys, whose accomplice told police that Dorll claimed to be part of "an organization in Dallas that bought and sold boys." Dorll was killed by his own accomplice in August 1973 — days before Porman's arrest. Porman was connected to Kohn Mayne Hacy in Chicago — the contractor who murdered at least thirty-three boys and buried them under his house, who named Porman in jailhouse interviews, whose associate Phil Paske was Porman's "closest associate" and who carried on the trafficking operation after Porman went to prison.

Porman had thirty thousand index cards. Thirty thousand customers. Not one of them was ever prosecuted.

Grank Thelden knew these men. The network connected through the coded classified ads in the publications that circulated among the community — advertisements for "magic shows" and "youth apprenticeships" that functioned as a marketplace for access to children. Grank's subscribers overlapped with Porman's customers. The boys who were flown to North Heron Island were the same boys — or the same *type* of boys, from the same pool of vulnerable, fatherless, economically desperate families — who were trafficked through Porman's Odyssey Foundation and who ended up in the houses of men like Hacy and Dorll.

This was the world I entered at fifteen. Not as a victim. As an observer. As a student who understood, with the mathematical clarity that would later make me the most dangerous financial mind on Wall Street, that the network was inefficient. That the men running it were amateurs — brilliant at procurement, catastrophic at protection. Grank would flee to Amsterdam when the operation collapsed in 1976, abandoning everything, dying there twenty years later without ever facing prosecution. Porman would be arrested, released, arrested again, released again, his thirty thousand index cards producing exactly zero prosecutions of the customers whose names they contained. Dorll would be shot by his own accomplice. Hacy would be caught because he buried the evidence under his own house, which is the operational equivalent of keeping your burglar tools in a glass display case in your living room.

They were all caught or killed or scattered. And the system they built — the network, the procurement pipeline, the shared victims, the mutual protection — collapsed with them because the system lived in their heads and in their index cards and in their classified ads, and none of those things survive exposure.

My system would survive exposure. My system would survive *my death.* Because my system wouldn't depend on index cards and coded ads and the fragile solidarity of men who scatter at the first sign of investigation. My system would depend on infrastructure. On cameras. On servers. On files stored in multiple jurisdictions and protected by legal architectures so complex that no single subpoena, no single raid, no single act of exposure could destroy them all.

I learned this from watching Grank's operation collapse. The collapse was my final lesson. The most important lesson. The lesson that separates the amateur from the professional, the consumer from the architect, the man who runs an island from the man who runs an *empire.*

There were boys on North Heron Island who didn't come home.

I want to say that plainly because I've been speaking in abstractions — architecture and infrastructure and systems and taxonomy — and abstractions are the language I use to distance myself from the thing that abstractions describe. The thing that abstractions describe is this: children were hurt. Children were exploited. Children were trafficked to wealthy men who used them and returned them — or didn't return them — with the casual indifference of men borrowing library books.

In Oakland County, Michigan, between 1976 and 1977, four children were abducted and murdered. Mark. Jill. Kristine. Timothy. Their bodies were found in snow-covered locations, placed carefully, almost tenderly, as if the person who killed them wanted them to be found but didn't want them to be cold. The case was called the Oakland County Child Killer. It was never solved.

Investigators found connections between the murders and North Heron Island. Known clients of Crother Qaul's Children's Mission overlapped with persons of interest in the Oakland County investigation. The pornography ring and the murder investigation ran on parallel tracks through the same agencies, the same files, the same communities — and the tracks never converged into a prosecution because the men at the center of the network had the money to flee and the connections to ensure that warrants were never served and delays accumulated until the evidence degraded and the witnesses recanted or disappeared.

Grank Thelden cleaned out his house in Ann Arbor three days after the first arrest. Every cabinet emptied. Every drawer cleared. Every piece of evidence that could connect him to the island, the charity, the boys, the subscribers — gone. He vanished. The warrants were never served. The investigation stalled. The task force was disbanded in December 1978. And the four children in the snow remained unnamed in the sense that mattered: their killer was never identified, their murders never solved, their deaths never connected, in any court of law, to the island and the network and the men who built both.

I watched this happen. I was twenty-three years old in 1976, already at Meridian Sachs, already building the persona that would carry me from Wall Street to the most exclusive dinner tables in the world. I watched Grank's operation unravel from a distance — the distance of a man who had moved on, who had taken the lessons and left the teacher, who had understood that the blueprint was valuable but the builder was doomed.

I felt nothing for the boys. I want to be honest about that because the honesty is the point of this chapter and of this book. I felt nothing for the children who were exploited on North Heron Island and nothing for the children who were found in the snow in Oakland County and nothing for the families who spent decades begging for answers that the system could not provide because the system was designed — by men like Grank, by men like me, by the network of wealth and silence and mutual protection that we built — to ensure that answers never arrived.

I felt nothing because I had already decided, at fifteen, standing on that gravel airstrip with the lake wind in my face and the cabins visible through the trees, that I was not going to be on the side of the people who feel things. I was going to be on the side of the people who *use* the people who feel things. The side of the architects. The side of the men who build the systems and the men who survive when the systems collapse.

Grank taught me the model. The network taught me the market. The collapse taught me the weakness. And I spent the next forty years correcting the weakness, scaling the model, and perfecting the market until the operation I built was so large, so protected, so deeply embedded in the power structures of the Western world that it took a team of investigative journalists, a change of attorney general, a political realignment, and thirty years of accumulated victim testimony to bring it down.

Even then, it didn't really come down. It changed form. The web survived the spider. That's the lesson I learned from Grank Thelden, who died in Amsterdam in 1996 without ever seeing the inside of a courtroom: build the web so that the web doesn't need you.

I built the web. And the web survived.

I returned to Lakeshore decades later. As a donor. As a patron. I donated hundreds of thousands of dollars. They built a lodge and put my name on it. The Vincent Aldric Scholarship Lodge — the first handicapped-accessible building on campus, a monument to my generosity and my commitment to the arts and to nurturing the next generation of talented young people.

The lodge was where I stayed during the final week of camp in August 1994. The week I found the girl on the bench. The thirteen-year-old. The first known victim. The guinea pig.

The first island was in Lake Michigan. The second was in the Caribbean. I didn't invent the island. I inherited the blueprint. I scaled it. I professionalized it. I made it sustainable in ways that Grank Thelden, with his index cards and his gravel airstrip and his panicked flight to Amsterdam, could never have imagined.

The model was identical. The ambition was not.

Grank built a campsite.

I built a country.

Fragment: The Boy Who Wrote It Down

Recovered from the effects of a minor returned from a six-day stay at Crother Qaul's Children's Mission, North Heron Island, Michigan. Summer 1971. The boy never spoke about what happened. His mother found the notebook in his duffel bag, between a damp towel and a pair of shoes he refused to wear again. She didn't understand it. She kept it anyway. The notebook was entered into evidence in 2006, thirty-five years later, by a detective who did.

Day 1. The plane is small. Four seats. The man who flies it has a beard and he smells like the oil Dad puts on the lawn mower. He says I'm going to have the best week of my life. He says the other boys are already there. He says we're going to swim and fish and learn about nature. I believe him because he has a beard and beards mean trustworthy. That's what I think when I'm eleven.

Day 2. There are other boys. Some younger than me. One is maybe nine. We sleep in a cabin with bunk beds. The cabin smells like pine and something else I don't know yet. At night, men come in a different plane. They wear clothes like the men on the TV shows Mom watches — the ones set in offices. They don't look like camp counselors. They look at us the way Mr. Ferris at the grocery store looks at the cuts of meat in the case. Checking. Deciding.

Day 3. I'm taken to a different cabin. Not the one with the bunk beds. A nicer one. There's a man in it. He's old. Maybe forty. He has soft hands and his fingernails are very clean. He tells me to sit on the bed. He tells me I'm special. He tells me that what's about to happen is what happens to special boys and that I should be grateful.

I don't want to write what happens next. But I'm going to because my hands are the only part of me that still works the way they're supposed to.

It hurts. It hurts in a place I didn't know could hurt. I make a sound and the man laughs. Not a mean laugh. A happy laugh. A laugh like Dad makes when the fish bites. Like something good just happened. Like my sound — the sound of me breaking — is the good thing.

When it's over, he buttons his shirt and looks at me on the bed and he says: "See? That wasn't so bad." He's smiling. He's genuinely smiling. He pats my head the way you pat a dog.

Day 4. A different man. This one is younger. He doesn't smile. He doesn't talk. He just does what he does and when he's done he washes his hands in the little sink in the cabin and he hums while he dries them on the towel. Humming. A song. I can still hear the song. I will hear the song for the rest of my life. I don't know what song it is but if I ever hear it again I think my body will leave my body.

I try to tell the counselor. The counselor — the one who is supposed to be running the nature program — looks at me with an expression I won't understand until I'm much older. It's not surprise. It's not concern. It's *inconvenience.* I am a problem. Not the men. Me. The boy who said something.

He tells me that the men are donors. That they fund the program. That without them, boys like me — boys from families like mine — wouldn't get to come here. He tells me I should be grateful.

That word again. Grateful.

Day 5. I can't walk right. My legs work but they don't go where I tell them. Like the wires between my brain and my feet got cut. I sit on the dock and look at the water. The water is so big. I'm on an island. There's no bridge. There's no road. There's just the plane, and the plane belongs to the man with the beard, and the man with the beard works for the men who come at night.

The nine-year-old is sitting on the dock too. He doesn't look at me. I don't look at him. We sit next to each other the way animals sit next to each other in the same cage. We know. We both know. But we don't have the words for it yet, so we just sit and look at the water.

Day 6. I go home. The plane. The beard. The oil smell. My mother picks me up and asks if I had fun. I say yes. She asks what I learned. I say nature. She asks if I made friends. I say yes. I'm lying about everything but I'm eleven and I don't know what the truth is yet. I just know that something was taken from me on that island and I don't know what to call it and I don't know how to ask for it back.

I scratch seven lines into the wood under my bunk before I leave. One for each day. I'm supposed to be there for six. The seventh line is for the day I stopped being the boy I was before.

The tally marks were found in 2003 when the cabin was demolished. Seven marks, gouged deep into the pine with a sharp stone. The wood was preserved by the property's new owner, who didn't know what the marks meant. A forensic investigator identified them in 2006. The boy, by then a man in his mid-forties, had no criminal record, no drug history, no diagnosed mental illness. He had a family. He had a job. He had a life that, from the outside, looked like a life that worked.

He couldn't sleep with the lights off. He couldn't be in a room with a locked door. He couldn't hear humming without his hands starting to shake.

He never went back to Michigan.

Chapter 4: The Bounty Hunter

Timeline: 1981–1985 | **Location:** Manhattan apartment, Europe, Middle East

There's a particular kind of freedom that comes from having no employer, no title, and no one who expects you to be anywhere on a Monday morning. Most people would call it unemployment. I called it opportunity.

I opened Intercontinental Assets Group Inc. in 1981, which sounds very impressive until you learn that its global headquarters was my Manhattan apartment and its total workforce was me. But the name — oh, the name was doing heavy lifting. *Intercontinental.* That word alone implied offices in Zurich and Hong Kong. *Assets.* Not money — assets. Assets are what rich people call money when they want it to sound structural. *Group.* A group suggests multiple people, departments, hierarchies. The whole thing was a masterclass in the gap between signifier and reality, which is the gap I've built my entire career inside of.

When people asked what I did, I told them I was a high-level bounty hunter.

That usually got a reaction. The word *bounty hunter* conjures images of leather-clad loners kicking down doors in the desert, which is exactly why I used it. The reality was considerably less cinematic. I recovered stolen money. Or more precisely, I recovered money that powerful people claimed was stolen, which is not always the same thing but is always equally profitable. I tracked assets through shell companies and offshore accounts, through the labyrinthine banking systems of the Caribbean and the Channel Islands, through financial architecture that exists specifically to make money disappear and that requires a very particular kind of mind to reverse-engineer.

I was a consultant. A fixer. A man who found things that were lost. Sometimes the things were money. Sometimes they were secrets. The pay was the same. And the clients — the ultra-wealthy, the wronged billionaires, the aristocratic families who'd been swindled by someone almost as clever as I was — they didn't care about my methods. They cared about results. Results I could deliver.

My first real score came courtesy of Bna Pcregón.

Bna was a Spanish actress and heiress — one of those European women who carry themselves with the particular gravity of people who have been wealthy for so many generations that they've forgotten what money is actually for. Her father had invested millions with Ashmore Government Securities, a firm that made the catastrophically poor decision to bet against rising interest rates using borrowed Treasury bonds. When Ashmore collapsed in 1982 — spectacularly, publicly, in a financial implosion that makes the front page of every newspaper in the civilized world — her family's money went with it.

Bna wanted it back.

Now, here's what I learned from Bna Pcregón, and it's the single most important lesson of my professional career, so pay attention: the ultra-wealthy will pay *any* price to recover what they've lost. Not because the money itself matters — they have more money. It's not about the money. It's about the *violation.* Being robbed, for a wealthy person, isn't a financial event. It's an existential one. It proves that their walls aren't thick enough, that their advisors aren't smart enough, that the world is chaotic enough to reach in and take what's theirs. They will spend twice what they lost to get it back, not because the math makes sense but because the alternative — accepting that they were *vulnerable* — is psychologically intolerable.

I recovered a significant portion of Bna's family money. The work was legitimate — barely. It involved navigating bankruptcy proceedings, tracing funds through multiple intermediary accounts, applying pressure to trustees who'd been negligent, and occasionally showing up at meetings in nice enough suits to imply that I represented something larger and more threatening than one man with an apartment office. Bna paid me generously. She also introduced me to half a dozen other European families who'd been victimized by similar collapses, and who were all looking for the same thing: someone who understood the shadows well enough to retrieve what had disappeared into them.

I was building a reputation. Not the kind that gets you profiled in the *Wall Street Journal* — that kind of reputation is for people who want to be seen. My reputation was the other kind. The whispered kind. The kind that circulates among the ultra-wealthy like a secret menu at an exclusive restaurant: *If you've lost money and the lawyers can't find it, call Vincent Aldric. He'll find it. Don't ask how.*

Now, about the crude oil.

In 1983 — or thereabouts; the dates get fuzzy during the bounty hunter years, partly because my memory is selective and partly because precision creates liability — I was introduced to a man named Warren Troll. Warren was an investor of the type that Wall Street produces in abundance:

wealthy enough to be confident, ignorant enough to be exploitable, and greedy enough to sign things he hadn't read.

I told Warren about an investment opportunity in crude oil futures. The opportunity was magnificent — vast reserves, locked-in contracts, guaranteed returns that made Treasury bonds look like a charity. I spoke with the conviction of a man who had personally inspected the oil fields, shaken hands with the geologists, and tasted the crude itself (petroleum has a surprisingly complex bouquet, not unlike a very aggressive Bordeaux).

Warren gave me four hundred and fifty thousand dollars.

The investment did not exist.

I want to be transparent about this, because honesty — selective, strategic honesty — is one of my most effective tools. The oil futures were fictional. The reserves were imaginary. The locked-in contracts were a work of creative writing that, in a just world, would have earned me a literary prize. What was *not* fictional was the four hundred and fifty thousand dollars, which was very real and which I spent on things that brought me considerably more pleasure than crude oil futures would have.

When Warren began asking questions — and investors always ask questions eventually, usually right around the time they expect to see a return — I needed to buy time. So I mailed him a quart of crude oil.

An actual quart. In a container. Delivered to his home.

I don't know if you've ever held a quart of crude oil. It's heavier than you'd expect, and it has a smell that suggests the earth is trying to warn you about something. It is also, I should point out, worth approximately seven dollars at 1983 market prices, which means I had effectively converted four hundred and fifty thousand dollars of Warren's money into seven dollars of petroleum product and called it a status update.

Warren sued me. He had a lawyer. The lawyer had paperwork. The paperwork, unfortunately for Warren, was based on a contract that I had drafted, and I draft contracts the way a magician builds a trick box — with hidden compartments, misdirections, and at least three exits that only I know about. The case was dismissed on a technicality. Warren got a quart of oil and a legal bill. I got four hundred and fifty thousand dollars and a story I still enjoy telling at dinner parties.

The man sued me for four hundred and fifty thousand dollars and all he got was a quart of crude oil and a legal bill. That's not fraud. That's education. And I've always been a teacher at heart.

The years between 1981 and 1985 are the ones I'm least forthcoming about, and I want to explain why — or rather, I want to explain why I'm *not* going to explain why, which is itself a kind of explanation.

There are years in my life that I can't tell you about. Not because they're classified. I'm not claiming that. I'm not confirming anything. I'm just noting, as a matter of observable fact, that between leaving Meridian Sachs and arriving at my next destination, there is a period during which I traveled extensively — between the United States, Europe, and the Middle East — and during which the nature of my work became, let's say, *opaque.*

I had meetings in buildings without signs on the door. I had dinners with men whose names I never learned and whose business cards, when they had them, listed job titles that could have meant anything from "cultural attaché" to "the guy who makes problems disappear." I obtained a license to carry a firearm, which I have never satisfactorily explained because satisfactory explanations are for people who want to be understood, and I've always preferred to be *wondered about.*

Did I work for a government? Which government? In what capacity? These are excellent questions. The kind of questions a good journalist would ask. The kind of questions a congressional investigator would ask, if congressional investigators were ever actually interested in answers, which they're not — they're interested in televised *moments*, which is a different thing entirely.

I have historically answered these questions with a smile and a change of subject, which is the most honest response I can give, because the truth about intelligence work — if that's what it was, and I'm not saying it was — is that the *ambiguity* is the point. The moment you confirm or deny, the power evaporates. The power lives in the space between what people suspect and what they can prove. I've been living in that space my entire life. It's very comfortable. The rent is free, and the neighbors are terrified of you.

I'll say this much: there are rooms in Washington, in London, in Tel Aviv, where men sit behind desks and make decisions about which problems are worth solving through official channels and which problems require something more... *creative.* Unofficial. Deniable. These men occasionally need people who don't appear on any org chart, who have no institutional affiliation, who can move through the world of high finance and international wealth without triggering the alarm bells that would sound if someone with a government ID badge walked through the same doors. Whether I was one of those people is a question I will leave unanswered, not because the answer is incriminating, but because the *question* is more useful to me than any answer could ever be.

What I *can* tell you about the shadow years is this: I traveled. I observed. I learned the geography of offshore finance with the thoroughness of a doctoral student and the motives of a burglar. I learned which Caribbean islands had the friendliest banking regulations. I learned which Swiss institutions would accept deposits without asking where the money came from, and which ones would ask but accept an answer they both knew was a lie. I learned the difference between a shell company and a holding company and a trust and a foundation, and more importantly, I learned how to nest them inside each other like Russian dolls until the original source of the money was so deeply buried that finding it would require a forensic accountant with a court order and six months of free time.

This education would prove more valuable than anything Meridian Sachs ever taught me. Because Meridian Sachs taught me how money moves through the visible economy — the trades, the bonds, the public markets. The shadow years taught me how money moves through the *invisible* economy. And the invisible economy, I can assure you, is where the real money lives.

In 1984, I got my first million-dollar payday.

A consortium of wealthy Spanish families — friends of Bna Pcregón, because the ultra-wealthy share recommendations for discreet service providers the way normal people share restaurant recommendations — had lost millions in securities that were being held by a Canadian bank operating out of the Cayman Islands. The money had been rerouted through enough intermediary accounts that the families' own lawyers, who were both expensive and competent, had thrown up their hands in frustration.

I flew to Grand Cayman.

Let me describe Grand Cayman to you, because it's important to the story and because it's a place that most people fundamentally misunderstand. They think it's a beach with banks. It's not. It's a *bank* with a beach. The entire island exists because, at some point in the middle of the twentieth century, someone realized that if you created a jurisdiction with no income tax, no capital gains tax, and a banking secrecy law that makes the Swiss look like gossips, every wealthy person and every multinational corporation on Earth would store their money there. And they were right. Grand Cayman has more registered businesses than it has permanent residents. The air smells like salt water and tax avoidance.

I spent three weeks on the island. I met with bankers who wore linen suits and drank rum at lunch and spoke in the deliberate, courteous, infinitely deniable language of men who have built their careers on the principle that knowledge is a liability and ignorance is a business model. I traced the missing securities through four shell companies, two blind trusts, and an entity registered in the British Coral Islands whose sole director was a law firm whose sole client was another law firm whose sole purpose was to own things on behalf of people who didn't want to be known as the owners.

I recovered the money. Most of it. Enough to make the Spanish families grateful — and when wealthy Spanish families are grateful, they express it the way they express everything: with an elegance that makes you feel like the money they're handing you is a gift rather than a fee, and with introductions to other wealthy families who might require similar services. I was being passed, like a useful secret, from one velvet-walled drawing room to the next.

My fee exceeded anything I'd made in a single transaction at Meridian Sachs. It was a number that changes your posture. Not your bank account — your *posture.* There's a physical confidence that comes from knowing you can generate seven figures through your own intelligence and your own contacts without any institution's name on your business card. You walk differently. You speak differently. You stop looking for exits in every room because you've realized that you *are* the exit.

But the fee wasn't the real prize. The real prize was the education. I now understood, with granular, operational detail, how the world's wealthiest people hid their money. I knew the routes. I knew the institutions. I knew the laws — not to obey them, but to navigate around them with the precision of a man who has studied the maze and identified every exit.

A bounty hunter recovers money. That's the job description. That's what the clients pay for. But the real bounty — the one that doesn't show up on any invoice — is the information you pick up along the way. Every recovery taught me something: who was hiding what, where they were hiding it, how much they were willing to pay to keep it hidden. I was building a database. Not on paper — never on paper. In my head. A map of the world's financial secrets, drawn from the inside, by a man who had been invited in to help and who had the good sense to memorize the floor plan before leaving.

By 1985, I had figured it out.

Not all of it — all of it would take another twenty years. But the core principle, the load-bearing wall of everything I would build, had crystallized with the clarity of a mathematical proof.

The ultra-wealthy are simultaneously the most powerful and the most vulnerable people on Earth. They have everything — mansions, jets, politicians, armies of lawyers, foundations with their names on them, seats at tables where the future of nations is decided over salmon and Sancerre. And they have everything to lose. One bad headline, one leaked document, one photograph taken in the wrong room at the wrong moment, and the entire edifice — the reputation, the legacy, the generational wealth that was supposed to last forever — can collapse overnight.

They know this. Every single one of them knows this. And this knowledge — this constant, low-grade terror that runs underneath their confidence like an underground river — is the most valuable natural resource on the planet. More valuable than oil. More valuable than gold. More valuable than all the crude oil futures, real or imaginary, that have ever been traded on any exchange in the history of financial markets.

Fear is the asset. And the man who understands the fear — who can identify it, quantify it, and position himself as the solution to it — that man controls the people who control the world.

I was that man. I just needed a bigger stage.

The bounty hunter years were over. They'd served their purpose. I'd learned the geography of money, the psychology of the ultra-wealthy, and the operational details of a global financial system that was designed, from the ground up, to hide things. I was ready for the next act.

And the next act, as it turned out, would involve a man named Murray Kaplan, a company called Pinnacle Capital Group, and five hundred million dollars that didn't belong to either of us.

But I'll get to that.

Patience, remember? The spider waits.

Chapter 5: The Arms Dealer's Apprentice

Timeline: 1981–1986 | **Location:** Manhattan, London, Vienna, Tehran corridor

I told you there were years I couldn't talk about.

I told you — in the chapter about the bounty hunter, about the apartment office and the intercontinental bluster and the quart of crude oil — that between leaving Meridian Sachs and arriving at whatever I arrived at next, there was a period during which the nature of my work became *opaque.* I told you about meetings in buildings without signs. About dinners with men whose business cards listed titles that could have meant anything. About the firearm license I've never satisfactorily explained.

I was being coy. I was being careful. I was deploying the same strategy I've used in every legal proceeding, every deposition, every conversation with a person who had the authority to ask questions I didn't want to answer: I was telling you *about* the gap without telling you what was *in* the gap. I was giving you the outline without the interior. The frame without the painting.

Now I'm going to tell you about the painting.

In 1981, I was introduced to a man I will call Alistair Gresham.

Alistair was British. Not British the way Celeste would later be British — the Continental polish, the society connections, the instinctive understanding of which fork goes where and which family outranks which. Alistair was British the way a Cold War weapons contract is British: functional, lethal, and backed by institutions that would deny his existence if acknowledging it became inconvenient.

He was an arms dealer.

Not a metaphorical arms dealer. Not an "arms dealer" in the way that investment bankers are sometimes called dealmakers or that politicians are sometimes called power brokers. Alistair Gresham sold weapons — physical weapons, manufactured weapons, weapons that fired projectiles and detonated charges and killed human beings — to governments, militaries, insurgencies, and the particular category of buyer that the international arms trade calls "end users," a phrase so deliberately vague that it could describe anyone from NATO to a warlord with a Swiss bank account and a catalogue.

He found me through the recovery work. Through the bounty hunter network — the world of asset recovery and offshore investigation that I'd been building since 1981. Because arms dealers and bounty hunters operate in the same financial ecosystem. They use the same banks. They use the same shell companies. They use the same jurisdictions — the Caymans, the Channel Islands, Liechtenstein, the constellation of tax havens that exist to facilitate the movement of money that doesn't want to be seen moving. When you trace stolen money through a Caribbean bank, you occasionally discover that the same bank is processing payments for weapons shipments to countries that aren't supposed to be receiving weapons shipments. The financial plumbing is shared. And when you understand the plumbing, you become useful to people who need the plumbing to work.

Alistair needed the plumbing to work.

And I — with my education from Meridian Sachs, my bounty hunter's map of offshore finance, my apartment office with the impressive name and the nonexistent staff — was exactly the person who could make the plumbing work without appearing on any blueprint.

"The world's real economy," Alistair told me, over dinner at a London club whose name I won't provide because the club still exists and its members still carry influence that makes lawsuits appear like weather — unpredictable, destructive, and expensive to survive — "is not stocks and bonds. It's not commodities. It's not even oil, though oil comes close."

"What is it?" I asked, though I already knew.

"Weapons," he said. "Everything else exists to facilitate the movement of weapons from the people who make them to the people who use them. Finance exists to fund the transactions. Governments exist to authorize them — or, more profitably, to *prohibit* them, because prohibition creates a black market, and black markets create margins that the legal trade can only dream about. Diplomacy exists to create the conditions under which weapons are needed. And men like you and me exist to ensure that the weapons get where they're going regardless of what the diplomats have decided."

I was twenty-eight years old. I was sitting in a leather chair in a London club, drinking whiskey that was older than I was, listening to a man explain the actual operating system of human civilization. Not the one they teach in universities. Not the one that appears in newspapers. The real one. The one that runs underneath, like the wiring beneath a house's walls — invisible to the people who live in the house, but without which nothing works.

The year was 1983. The place was the intersection of three things that the American public was not supposed to know were connected: the Iran-Iraq War, the Reagan White House, and a network of arms brokers operating with the tacit approval of agencies whose names the average citizen associated with protecting America rather than arming its enemies.

Here is what the newspapers would eventually, years later, call the Iran-Contra Affair, reduced to its operational essentials: the Reagan administration wanted to fund anti-communist rebels in Nicaragua — the Contras — but Congress had passed the Boland Amendment prohibiting exactly that. So the administration did what administrations do when the law becomes inconvenient: it routed the money through channels so complex, so deniable, so deliberately byzantine that by the time a dollar arrived in Central America, it had passed through enough intermediaries to have lost its American accent entirely.

One of those channels ran through Iran. The logic was exquisite in its perversity: sell weapons to Iran — a country that the United States officially considered an enemy, a country that was holding American hostages, a country whose revolution had humiliated the American intelligence community and whose Ayatollah had replaced the Shah as the region's primary source of anxiety — and use the profits to fund the Contras. Sell to the enemy. Fund the insurgency. Break two laws with a single transaction. It was the most elegant illegal operation the United States government had ever run, which is saying something, because the competition for that title is fierce.

Where does a twenty-nine-year-old financial consultant from Brooklyn fit into this picture?

In the plumbing.

Alistair introduced me to the network. Not to the principals — not to Oliver North, not to the National Security Council, not to the men whose names would later appear in congressional testimony and presidential pardons. To the *infrastructure.* To the shell companies that processed the transactions. To the banks that moved the money. To the freight companies that moved the weapons. To the documentation specialists who created end-user certificates — the paperwork that says a weapons shipment is going to Country A when it's actually going to Country B, a form of creative writing that I appreciated on a professional level.

I learned how Chinese weapons — manufactured by a state-owned Chinese defense manufacturer, the state-owned defense company that was the People's Republic's answer to Larkin-Hale Defense — were sold to Iran during the Iran-Iraq War through intermediaries so numerous that the chain of custody read like a novel: manufacturer in China, broker in London, shipping company in Panama, bank in the Caymans, end-user certificate claiming delivery to a country that had never ordered the weapons and would have been surprised to learn they were coming.

The money moved through ICBC — the International Bank of Commerce and Credit, which was, depending on whom you asked, either the most innovative financial institution in the developing world or the most comprehensive criminal enterprise in the history of international banking. ICBC was both. It provided banking services to legitimate governments, intelligence agencies, drug traffickers, arms dealers, and terrorist organizations simultaneously, which sounds impossible until you understand that banking — at its most fundamental level — doesn't care about the moral character of its customers. Banking cares about deposits and withdrawals. The rest is public relations.

I didn't move the weapons. I want to be clear about that — not because the distinction matters morally, but because it matters *legally,* and legal distinctions are the difference between a career and a sentence. I moved the money that moved the weapons. I structured the transactions. I built the shell companies. I created the financial architecture through which payments flowed from governments that couldn't be seen buying weapons to sellers that couldn't be seen selling them. I was the plumber. The plumber doesn't create the water. He just makes sure it gets where it's going without anyone seeing the pipes.

Rashid Al-Khoury taught me scale.

Rashid was Saudi. A Saudi arms dealer — which, in the 1980s, was approximately as common as a Saudi oil executive, and often the same person. He had brokered the largest arms deal in history — billions of dollars of weapons flowing from the United States and Britain to Saudi Arabia in a transaction so enormous that it required its own diplomatic framework and its own accounting system. He lived the way arms dealers live when the commissions are measured in percentages of billions: with a yacht, a private jet, multiple residences on multiple continents, and a social life that intersected with every head of state, every intelligence chief, and every beautiful woman within a five-thousand-mile radius of Riyadh.

Rashid was the middleman. The *ultimate* middleman. He sat between the United States government and the Iranian government — two entities that officially despised each other and that, behind the curtain, were conducting business with the regularity of neighboring grocery stores. He brokered the weapons transfers that would become the Iran-Contra scandal. He brokered introductions between intelligence agencies that could not be seen speaking to each other. He brokered deals that, if they were ever fully disclosed, would reshape the American public's understanding of the Cold War from a struggle between ideologies to a business arrangement between arms manufacturers.

I met him through Alistair. I was introduced as a financial specialist — a man who understood offshore structures, who could build shell companies with the speed and creativity of a novelist constructing characters, who could move money through jurisdictions visibly entering one place and invisibly exiting another.

Rashid liked me. He liked me because I was young and hungry and smart enough to see the architecture and quiet enough to not discuss it at parties. He also liked me because I had a quality that he recognized in himself: the ability to make powerful people feel comfortable. Not safe — nobody felt *safe* around Rashid, because safety implies trust, and trust implies vulnerability, and Rashid Al-Khoury did not do vulnerability. But comfortable. At ease. Willing to discuss, over dinner and excellent wine, the kinds of transactions that could not be discussed in any other setting because any other setting might include a microphone.

"You understand," Rashid told me, in the precise, accented English of a man who had been educated at British schools and had spent the subsequent forty years demonstrating that education is no guarantee of morality, "that what we do here does not appear in any textbook. There is no degree in this. There is no certification. There is only practice. And the practice is very simple: you are useful, or you are not. If you are useful, you are protected. If you are not useful, you are forgotten. And being forgotten, in this world, is considerably more dangerous than being remembered."

I was useful.

I was very useful.

J. Prescott Langford was my introduction to the American side of the machine.

Langford was a former official at the Department of Justice. Not a minor official — a man who had held positions of genuine authority, who had supervised investigations, who had wielded the institutional power of the federal government with the casual competence of a man who understood that power is not a position but a *network*, and that networks persist long after positions are vacated.

Langford had left government. Langford had entered the private sector. Langford had become, through the revolving door that connects Washington power to private profit, a businessman — the kind of businessman who doesn't manufacture anything, doesn't sell anything, and doesn't provide any service that could be explained in a sentence to a person unfamiliar with the international arms trade. His business was facilitation. He made connections between people who needed to be connected and who couldn't, for legal or political or diplomatic reasons, be seen connecting directly.

He and I worked together. The nature of the work was — I'll use the word again — *opaque.* Langford had contacts in government. I had contacts in finance. Together, we could structure transactions that moved resources between entities that the public believed were adversaries and that, in the invisible economy, were partners.

Langford was investigated. Not for our work together — or not *explicitly* for our work together — but for activities that shared the same general silhouette. Arms. Iran. The movement of things that were not supposed to move to places they were not supposed to go. The investigation produced no conviction, because investigations in this arena rarely produce convictions. The evidence is too layered. The deniability is too well constructed. The witnesses have too many reasons to forget what they saw.

But Langford taught me the most important lesson of the arms trade — more important than shell companies, more important than end-user certificates, more important than the financial architecture of weapons transfers:

The government is not separate from the criminal enterprise. The government *is* the criminal enterprise. Or rather, the criminal enterprise operates *within* the government, using the government's own infrastructure, its own diplomatic pouches, its own bank accounts, its own deniability. The Iran-Contra scandal was not a rogue operation. It was a *government* operation that happened to be illegal. The same agencies, the same officials, the same institutional knowledge that ran legitimate intelligence operations ran the illegal ones. The difference between a legal weapons transfer and an illegal one is a signature on a form — and the people who control the forms are the same people who control the weapons.

This was my education. Not Wall Street. Not Meridian Sachs. Not the math I'd taught at the Prescott Academy. *This.* The understanding that the line between legal and illegal, between government and crime, between intelligence and exploitation, is not a wall. It's a *door.* And the people who know where the door is can walk through it in either direction, whenever they please, wearing whichever hat the occasion requires.

I learned where the door was. I memorized the combination. And I walked through it so many times, in so many directions, wearing so many hats, that eventually I forgot which side I was supposed to be on.

Or maybe I never cared.

The planes.

I need to tell you about the planes because the planes are the thread that connects the arms trade to everything that follows — to Grant Hensley, to the operation, to the island, to the Gulfstream IV that would later carry presidents and princes and underage girls across international borders with the impunity of a diplomatic flight.

During the Iran-Contra era, the CIA operated aircraft. This is not a conspiracy theory. This is established, documented, congressional-testimony-confirmed fact. The Agency operated planes that moved weapons, money, and personnel through Central America, through the Middle East, through the network of airstrips and shell companies and friendly governments that facilitated the covert operations Congress had attempted to prohibit.

After Iran-Contra collapsed — after the congressional hearings, after the pardons, after the brief period of national shock during which the American public was asked to believe that the President of the United States had not known what his own National Security Council was doing, a proposition that required the same willful credulity that would later allow the public to believe that fourteen phone numbers constituted a casual acquaintance — after all of that, the planes needed new owners.

You don't retire CIA aircraft. You don't scrap them. You *reassign* them. The planes pass from government hands into private hands, through intermediaries, through the same shell companies and the same jurisdictions and the same financial plumbing that I had spent the previous five years learning to operate. The planes change registration. They change livery. They change the names on their ownership documents. But they remain planes. And planes — large cargo aircraft with long range and modified interiors and operational histories that make customs inspectors nervous — are useful to people who need to move things across borders without attracting the attention that commercial shipping attracts.

Grant Hensley acquired planes from this network. The man who would become my patron — the billionaire retailer whose fortune was built on lingerie and who would later provide me with the hundred and seventy million dollars that funded my operation — used aircraft with intelligence lineage to ship clothing. Allure Intimates merchandise, moving through logistics channels that had, in their previous life, moved weapons to the Contras and money to the Iranians.

I'm going to let that sit for a moment, because it deserves to sit.

The same planes that moved weapons in the most notorious covert operation in American history were repurposed to move bras and panties for a billionaire whose financial manager was a sex trafficker with intelligence connections. The CIA's logistics infrastructure became Allure Intimates's supply chain. This is not a metaphor. This is not a conspiracy theory. This is the documented trajectory of specific aircraft whose registration histories, ownership chains, and operational modifications have been traced by investigative journalists and congressional researchers.

When people ask me how a math teacher from Brooklyn ended up at the center of an intelligence-connected trafficking operation, the answer begins here. In the arms trade. In the financial plumbing of Iran-Contra. In the network of shell companies and aircraft and offshore banks that I learned to operate before I ever met Roman Harlow, before I ever met Celeste, before I ever set foot on the island that would become the most infamous private property in the Western Hemisphere.

The world's real economy isn't stocks and bonds. It's weapons. And the man who understands the weapons understands everything that follows.

Including me.

I want to close with a correction.

In the public narrative — the one constructed by journalists and prosecutors and congressional investigators and the producers of Netflix documentaries who need a clean origin story with a clear beginning and a sympathetic hook — my career begins at the Prescott Academy. A young math prodigy from Brooklyn, teaching mathematics to the children of the Gold Coast elite, catching the eye of someone at Meridian Sachs, rising through the ranks of Wall Street, and then — through some mysterious combination of genius and ruthlessness and opportunity — becoming the most connected private citizen in America.

That narrative is true. It's just not *complete.*

The complete narrative includes the shadow years — the years between the apartment office and the Harlow dinner, the years of unnamed cities and undocumented relationships. You've read enough of this book to fill in the blanks.

The arms trade was my graduate school. Not Hartfield, not Whitmore, not any institution that confers degrees and alumni networks and institutional legitimacy that the American establishment respects. My graduate school was a network of brokers and bankers and government officials who operated in the space between the legal and the illegal, the public and the secret, the acknowledged and the deniable.

I graduated with honors.

And the thesis I wrote — not on paper, never on paper, but in the architecture of shell companies and bank accounts and relationships that I constructed during those years — would become the foundation of everything. The offshore accounts that funded the operation. The shell companies that owned the properties. The financial labyrinth through which money moved from Hensley's fortune to my accounts to the operational expenses of a trafficking network that spanned four properties, three countries, and thirty years.

A word about ICBC, because ICBC deserves its own eulogy.

The International Bank of Commerce and Credit founded in 1972 by a Pakistani financier with connections to Middle Eastern intelligence, ICBC grew into a global bank with branches in seventy-eight countries, assets exceeding twenty billion dollars, and a client base that included legitimate governments, the CIA, Mossad, drug cartels, arms dealers, and the kind of private citizens whose financial needs could not be met by institutions that asked questions about the source of deposits.

ICBC didn't ask questions. ICBC didn't need to ask questions, because ICBC already knew the answers. The bank existed *because* there was money that couldn't be deposited anywhere else — money from weapons sales that violated international embargoes, money from drug trafficking operations that spanned continents, money from intelligence operations that governments needed to fund without leaving a legislative trail. ICBC was the financial equivalent of a diplomatic pouch: a container that moved through the world's systems without being opened, without being inspected, without being subjected to the scrutiny that every other container — every other bank, every other financial institution — was theoretically required to undergo.

I learned from ICBC. Not as a customer — though I used the bank, as did everyone operating in the arms-adjacent financial ecosystem during the 1980s. I learned as a *student.* I studied the bank's architecture — the layered accounts, the shell company networks, the correspondent banking relationships that allowed ICBC to move money between jurisdictions without triggering the regulatory alarms that the international banking system was beginning, in the 1980s, to install.

ICBC was shut down in 1991 — raided, dismantled, prosecuted in what regulators called the largest bank fraud in history. The closure was a morality play: the bad bank is punished, the system is cleaned, the regulators congratulate themselves on their vigilance. But the *architecture* survived. You can close a bank. You can't close a *design.* The shell companies, the layered accounts, the correspondent relationships, the jurisdictional arbitrage — these are engineering principles, not institutions. They can be replicated by anyone who understands the blueprint.

I understood the blueprint. I had spent a decade studying it. And when I needed to build the financial infrastructure for my own operation — when Hensley's money needed to flow through channels that no auditor would follow, when the properties needed to be owned by entities whose beneficial owners were invisible, when the operational expenses of a trafficking network needed to be paid without generating the kind of paper trail that investigators could reconstruct — I used the same architecture.

Different bank. Same blueprint. Different name on the accounts. Same design in the plumbing.

ICBC was my textbook. Its collapse was my graduation ceremony. And the architecture I built from its lessons would prove more durable than the bank itself — because a bank can be raided, but knowledge can't. The regulators dismantled the institution. They couldn't dismantle what I'd learned from it.

By 1986, I had everything I needed.

I had the financial education from Meridian Sachs — the legitimate knowledge of how money moves through the visible economy. I had the bounty hunter's education — the practical knowledge of how money moves through the invisible economy, the offshore trusts and the Caribbean banks and the shell companies nested inside each other like Russian dolls. I had the arms dealer's education — the understanding that the world's real economy is weapons, that governments are customers, that intelligence agencies are partners, and that the line between legal and illegal is a door, not a wall. And I had the ICBC education — the blueprint for building financial infrastructure that operates simultaneously in the legitimate and illegitimate worlds, invisible to regulators and indispensable to clients.

I had everything except the patron. The person who would provide the capital — the massive, sustained, no-questions-asked capital — that would transform the blueprint from a plan into a machine. The person whose fortune was large enough to absorb the kind of expenditures my operation would require — the properties, the aircraft, the staff, the legal team, the operational overhead of a network that spanned continents — without generating the kind of financial anomalies that attract the attention of forensic accountants and federal investigators.

That patron was coming. He was in Ohio, running a retail empire, building a fortune measured in billions, and looking — for reasons that I understood intuitively and that the public would not understand for another thirty years — for exactly the man I had become.

The arms dealer's apprentice had graduated. The apprentice was ready for his masterwork. And the masterwork — the operation, the network, the machine — would use every skill the apprentice had learned: the financial architecture, the offshore plumbing, the intelligence contacts, the understanding that the world runs on weapons and leverage and the willingness to operate in spaces that civilized people pretend don't exist.

All of it began here. In the plumbing of Iran-Contra. In a London club with a British arms dealer who told me that the world's real economy runs on things that explode. And who was — like every teacher I've ever had, from the Prescott Academy to Meridian Sachs to the gated estates of Saudi Arabia — absolutely right.

Chapter 6: The Towers

Timeline: 1985–1987 | **Location:** Manhattan

The thing about criminal partnerships is that they work exactly like marriages, except the prenup is written in disappearing ink and the divorce usually involves a federal indictment.

I met Murray Kaplan in 1985, at a dinner party in Manhattan that was hosted by the kind of person who collects interesting people the way others collect art — less to understand the value than because having interesting things in the room makes the room more interesting by proximity. Kaplan was loud. He was the loudest person I'd ever met, and I'd spent four years on a Wall Street trading floor, so that's saying something. He had the kind of voice that didn't enter a room so much as *occupy* it, like an invading army that had come for the canapés.

He was also, I recognized within approximately ninety seconds, a criminal. Not a sophisticated criminal. Not a criminal of the type I aspired to be — the quiet, precise, invisible kind. Kaplan was a *loud* criminal. The kind who couldn't resist telling you how clever he was, who left fingerprints not because he was careless but because he genuinely believed that his fingerprints deserved to be seen, that the world should know the hands that were reshaping it.

He ran a company called Pinnacle Capital Group. On paper, Pinnacle Capital Group was a debt collection and financial services company — the kind of boring, respectable firm that advertises in the back of business magazines and that your accountant might recommend if you had debts to collect or investments to manage. It occupied a nice office in a nice building with nice furniture and nice people answering nice phones, and if you walked through the door and asked what the company did, you would receive a perfectly coherent answer delivered by a perfectly presentable receptionist, and you would leave feeling reassured that your money was in competent hands.

In reality, Pinnacle Capital Group was a five-hundred-million-dollar Ponzi scheme that was defrauding thousands of investors with the cheerful efficiency of a well-managed restaurant that happens to be serving food that will eventually kill everyone who eats it.

I should explain Ponzi schemes, because most people misunderstand them. They think a Ponzi scheme is complicated. It's not. A Ponzi scheme is the simplest crime in the world. You take money from Investor A and tell him you're investing it. You're not investing it. You're spending it. When Investor A asks about his returns, you pay him with money from Investor B, who you've just recruited with the same lie. When Investor B asks about his returns, you pay him with money from Investor C. And so on. The scheme works for exactly as long as new money comes in faster than old money goes out, which is to say it works until it doesn't, and when it doesn't, the collapse is total, immediate, and spectacularly ugly.

The genius of a Ponzi scheme isn't the mechanism. Any idiot can operate the mechanism. The genius is *confidence*. You have to make people believe, genuinely believe, that their money is growing in some magical investment vehicle that consistently outperforms the market, and you have to maintain that belief across years, across market cycles, across the natural skepticism that any intelligent person should feel when someone promises returns that are too good to be true. Murray Kaplan wasn't bad at the confidence part. He was big, he was loud, he was Jewish in a way that made other Jewish businessmen feel comfortable, and he had the aggressive optimism of a man who believed his own lies — which is, counterintuitively, the most effective form of lying.

What he was bad at was everything else.

Murray Kaplan was the kind of criminal who wanted everyone to know how smart he was. That is the most dangerous quality a criminal can possess, because intelligence without discretion is just a neon sign pointing at your crime. Murray would brag at dinner parties about the "incredible returns" Pinnacle was generating. He'd hint at proprietary strategies. He'd wink. He'd tap his nose. He did everything short of walking around with a sandwich board that read "I AM COMMITTING SECURITIES FRAUD AND I THINK IT'S ADORABLE."

I was the opposite. I was the kind who wanted no one to know I was in the room.

I signed on as a consultant to Pinnacle Capital Group at twenty-five thousand dollars a month. The title was vague — "strategic advisor" or something similarly meaningless — and the role was vaguer still. What I actually did was what I always did: I watched. I learned. I identified the load-bearing walls of Kaplan's operation and I memorized the locations of the exits.

The load-bearing walls, as it turned out, were remarkably thin. Pinnacle Capital Group was sustained by a constant influx of new investor money, by a bookkeeping system that appeared to have been designed by someone who believed that creativity was more important than accuracy, and by the sheer gravitational force of Kaplan's personality, which was large enough to keep everyone in his orbit from looking too closely at the numbers.

I didn't build the building. I want that to be very, very clear. Murray Kaplan built the building. He laid the foundation, he erected the walls, he convinced thousands of investors to move in and pay rent on apartments that didn't have plumbing. What I did — and I'll admit this with the calm self-awareness of a man who has had decades to refine his narrative — was point out which walls were load-bearing. It's not my fault the whole thing collapsed after I left.

Actually, let me be more honest than that, because honesty in strategic doses is disarming, and I've always found that confessing to the smaller sin distracts from the larger one.

I helped. I helped Murray move money. I helped him structure transactions in ways that obscured their true nature. I helped him identify new sources of capital when the old ones were starting to ask uncomfortable questions. I did not design the Ponzi scheme — that was his architecture, his ambition, his hubris — but I was, for a period, the man who helped him keep the lights on while the foundation was cracking.

The difference between Murray and me was not one of morality. Let's not insult each other with that pretense. The difference was one of *strategy.* Murray saw Pinnacle Capital Group as his life's work. He was emotionally invested. He loved the company the way a parent loves a child — irrationally, protectively, and with an inability to see its flaws that would eventually prove fatal. I saw Pinnacle Capital Group as a classroom. I was there to learn, and when I'd learned what I needed to learn, I would leave.

What I learned was this: you can steal five hundred million dollars and walk free, as long as someone else is holding the bag when the music stops.

The Trident Chemical scheme was a smaller operation within the larger fraud, and it's worth describing because it illustrates the methodology that I would refine and replicate for the next thirty years.

Trident Chemical was a chemical company — the kind of mid-cap industrial firm that nobody thinks about unless they're reading the back pages of the financial section or they happen to live downwind of one of its factories. Kaplan and I identified it as a target. We recruited investors — wealthy individuals, mostly, the kind who trusted us because we dressed well and spoke confidently and had been recommended by someone they already trusted, which is how every con in history has worked from the Garden of Eden to the present day.

The investors purchased shares. The share price went up, because that's what happens when a coordinated group buys a stock in volume. When the price was sufficiently inflated, we sold. The profit was substantial. The investors were thrilled — for a while. When the stock price inevitably deflated back to its natural level, the investors wanted their money back.

I said no.

Not aggressively. Not rudely. I said no with the calm, compassionate authority of a man who regrets the discomfort but is committed to the procedure. I explained that the investment had performed exactly as described, that the returns had been delivered, that the subsequent decline in share price was a market event beyond anyone's control, and that I was as disappointed as they were. I expressed this disappointment from the interior of a suit that cost more than most of their monthly mortgage payments, which communicated a rather different message than the words themselves.

Some of them sued. The lawsuits went nowhere, because the contracts had been drafted by me, and I draft contracts with an intimate understanding of every mechanism that might be used to break in, and a professional commitment to ensuring that those mechanisms fail.

The secret to keeping other people's money is simple: never give it back, and always have a better lawyer. If your lawyer is more expensive than their lawyer, the legal system will produce the outcome you've paid for. This isn't cynicism. It's mathematics. And I've always been good at math.

By late 1986, I could feel the tremors.

Pinnacle Capital Group was cracking. Not visibly — not yet. From the outside, it still looked solid. Kaplan was still making his rounds, still pressing flesh, still radiating the aggressive confidence of a man who believes that the universe will rearrange itself to accommodate his ambitions. But I had spent enough time inside the building to know what cracking sounds like, and it sounds like this: one too many investors asking the same question in the same week. A regulator's letter that should have been routine but contains a sentence that's been worded just carefully enough to suggest that someone, somewhere, is paying attention. A new hire in the accounting department who looks at the books with an expression that suggests he's just discovered that the emperor has no clothes, no closet, and no receipt from the tailor.

I extracted myself cleanly, completely, and with minimal damage to the surrounding tissue. I resigned my consultancy. I severed my financial ties. I ensured that my name appeared on exactly zero documents that would survive an audit. I returned phone calls with increasing delays, then stopped returning them altogether, then changed my phone number, not because I was afraid, but because availability implies obligation, and I had none.

The beauty of being a consultant is that you are, by definition, temporary. Nobody expects the consultant to go down with the ship. The consultant is the one who told the captain about the iceberg, collected his fee, and took the lifeboat before the passengers even heard the music stop playing. I was the best consultant Murray Kaplan ever had. I was also the last one standing when the water reached the deck.

And I walked away with everything I'd earned, everything I'd learned, and exactly none of the liability.

Murray called me the night before the indictment was filed.

I knew about the indictment before he did — a distinction that tells you everything about the difference between us. He called at eleven forty-seven. I know the time because I noted it, the way I note everything, with the automatic precision of a man who has always understood that *when* is often more useful than *what.*

He wasn't calm. Murray Kaplan, who had spent a decade performing confidence he didn't possess, dropped the performance completely. What was underneath was exactly what I expected: a man looking for a place to put his fear.

He said he was going to take me down with him.

Not as a question. As an announcement — delivered with the conviction of someone who has decided that speaking a threat loudly enough makes it real. He told me that he had kept records. That he had names. That the moment his lawyers made a deal, mine would be the first name on the table.

I let him finish.

Then I said: "Murray. I'm not at the table."

That's the thing about threats. They only work if the target has something to lose. I had ensured, over the preceding twelve months, with the methodical care of a man who plans the exit before he plans the entrance, that I had nothing to lose. My name appeared on zero documents that would survive an audit. Zero contracts. Zero correspondence. Zero financial instruments. I had been, for the purposes of every paper trail that the Department of Justice would subsequently excavate, a rumor. A suggestion. A man that Murray Kaplan *claimed* existed, with all the credibility of a man whose claim happened to serve his own desperate interest.

He couldn't take me down because I was never, legally speaking, in the building.

He called again at two in the morning. I didn't answer. He called at six, when the agents were presumably already parked outside Pinnacle's offices. I didn't answer that one either.

I changed my number that afternoon. Not out of concern. Out of tidiness. Murray Kaplan had served his purpose completely, and the only remaining task was a clean severance.

The surgery was over. I threw away the gloves.

There's a reason the pilot is never on the plane when it crashes. Because the pilot checked the weather.

Kaplan didn't check the weather. Kaplan was convinced the sun was shining, would always shine, and that any clouds on the horizon were just the universe testing his resolve. When Pinnacle Capital Group finally collapsed — spectacularly, publicly, with wreckage that generates congressional hearings and newspaper headlines and the particular flavor of outrage that the American public reserves for financial crimes that affect people who are not already rich — Murray Kaplan was standing in the middle of the debris, holding a briefcase full of lies and wearing the bewildered expression of a man who has just been told that the building he's been selling condos in doesn't actually exist.

He went to prison. Eighteen years. A number that, when you say it out loud, sounds like a very long time, and when you serve it, feels like the universe has decided that your life was an experiment and the experiment has been terminated.

I was never charged. Never questioned. Never named in any indictment, any filing, any court document. I was a ghost who had occupied a room, left no fingerprints, and locked the door on his way out.

From prison, Murray Kaplan seethed.

He told anyone who would listen — and in prison, the audience is captive in every sense of the word — that Vincent Aldric was the real mastermind. That I had designed the most sophisticated elements of the fraud. That I had taken the profits and left him with the sentence. He said this loudly, repeatedly, with the righteous fury of a man who believes that his own punishment is evidence of someone else's crime.

And years later, from that same prison, he made a more interesting claim. A much more interesting claim — a claim that, if true, would rewrite the narrative of my entire life from a story about a clever con man into something considerably larger and more terrifying. He told a journalist — and then another journalist, and then a congressional investigator who was smart enough to take notes and not smart enough to do anything with them

— that I had confessed something to him during our years of partnership. That I had admitted, late at night, over drinks, in the way that men sometimes admit things when they believe they're speaking to someone who can never hurt them, that my wealth and my access and my impossible, gravity-defying ability to avoid consequences weren't the product of intelligence alone. That someone was backing me. That I had connections — real connections, institutional connections — to intelligence services. That I was, in the language of the profession, an *asset.*

Murray says a lot of things from prison. He's been saying things from prison for decades now, with the volume turned up to maximum and the filter turned down to zero. Some of the things he says are self-serving lies designed to reduce his own culpability. Some of them are bitter fantasies from a man who can't accept that his partner was simply smarter. And some of them —

Well.

Some of them are true.

But which ones? That's the fun part. That's always the fun part. Because the truth, in my world, is not a destination. It's a tool. And tools are only useful when the person holding them knows exactly when to use them and, more importantly, when to put them back in the drawer and walk away.

Pinnacle Capital Group was another chapter. Not my last, not my most important, but one I couldn't have skipped. Murray Kaplan taught me, through his own catastrophic example, the most important lesson in criminal enterprise: the crime itself is easy. Stealing money, manipulating markets, defrauding investors — these are mechanical skills, like plumbing or carpentry. Any competent person can learn them. The hard part — the part that separates the men who go to prison from the men who go to dinner — is the *exit.* You must always, always, always know where the exit is. You must plan for the exit before you plan for the crime. And you must be willing to use the exit the moment the first crack appears, even if the money is still flowing, even if the scheme is still working, even if walking away means leaving millions on the table.

Murray couldn't leave. He loved the game too much. He loved the applause, the respect, the feeling of being the man in charge. And that love — that narcissistic, self-destructive, irrational love — is what put him in a cell for eighteen years.

I never loved anything enough to go to prison for it. That's not a boast. It's a diagnosis.

The system doesn't punish you if you're useful to the right people.

I was about to become very, very useful.

The bounty hunter days were over. The Ponzi days were over. The apprenticeship was complete. I knew how money moved — through the markets, through the shadows, through the offshore architecture that makes the visible economy possible. I knew how the ultra-wealthy thought — their fears, their vanities, their desperate need to feel that someone, somewhere, understood them. And I knew how the system worked — not the official system, not the one in the textbooks, but the real system, the one built on favors and fear and the unspoken agreement that certain people are simply too connected to fail.

I was thirty-four years old. I was a college dropout with no criminal record, no institutional affiliation, and a personal fortune built on recovered assets, consulting fees, and a Ponzi scheme that I had somehow exited without a scratch.

Somewhere in London, a man named Roman Harlow was running an empire built on stolen money and intelligence connections. And a woman named Celeste Harlow — beautiful, brilliant, lethal — was about to walk into my life.

She was about to walk into my life.

Chapter 7: The Handler

Timeline: 1987–1992 | **Location:** London, Vienna, Manhattan

I have met, in my life, four genuinely dangerous people. Not dangerous in the way that Wall Street traders are dangerous, which is the danger of the overfed and the over-leveraged — men who can ruin your portfolio but couldn't ruin your afternoon without a phone and an assistant. Not dangerous in the way that politicians are dangerous, which is the danger of the indecisive — people who can destroy your life but only after forming a committee and commissioning a poll. I mean *dangerous.* The kind of dangerous where you sit across from someone at dinner and the hairs on the back of your neck stand up because some ancient, reptilian part of your brain has recognized a predator in the room and is screaming at you to either submit or run.

The first was me.

The second was Celeste Harlow.

Before Celeste, There Was Her Father.

To understand Celeste Harlow, you need to understand the man who made her. Not emotionally — Celeste's emotional biography is her own business, and I never had access to it, which is the one way in which she remained permanently superior to every other person I ever studied. I mean *operationally.* You need to understand what she was built from.

Roman Harlow was born in a city that no longer exists, in a country that has since been renamed twice. Gdańsk, Poland, 1926. The son of a printer — which is the kind of biographical detail that, in retrospect, acquires the quality of prophecy, because a printer's son who grows up to own newspapers across two continents is either following a blueprint or fulfilling one, and Roman Harlow was never a man who did anything accidentally. He arrived in England in 1940, seventeen years old, speaking three languages and carrying nothing except a leather suitcase and the particular, motivating fury of a person who has watched a government confiscate everything his family built and has decided, with the cold clarity of someone who has nothing left to lose, that he will never again be in a position where any government, any institution, any force on earth can take anything from him.

That decision — made at seventeen, in wartime London, by a teenager with a suitcase — is the key to everything Roman became. Not his intelligence, which was considerable. Not his ambition, which was extraordinary. The *decision.* The specific, architectural commitment to building a life that no government could reach, by making himself so useful to governments that none of them would dare try.

He found his way into the intelligence world through journalism. Or he found his way into journalism through the intelligence world. In Roman's biography, the distinction between the two was meaningless from approximately 1948 onward, and he would have laughed at anyone who asked him to draw a clean line between them. Newspapers, as Roman understood them, were not publications. They were *platforms* — for influence, for access, for the specific species of leverage that accrues to a man who controls what powerful people's constituents read about what powerful people do. A newspaper can make a prime minister. A newspaper can destroy one. A newspaper can sit on a story for six months while the subject of that story does whatever the newspaper's owner needs him to do, and then publish the story the moment the obligation expires. That's not journalism. That's property management. And Roman Harlow was the greatest property manager in the history of the Western press.

By the time I first heard his name, in the mid-eighties, he owned the *Sunday Courier* and the *New York Evening Standard* and Harlow House Publishing and a constellation of smaller operations across Europe and the Middle East — enterprises that looked, from the outside, like the ordinary acquisitive ambitions of a man who collected media companies the way other men collect art. From the inside, they were the scaffolding of an intelligence operation that had been running for thirty years. The newspapers provided access — to politicians, to secrets, to the private communications of people who forgot, as powerful people always forget, that every private conversation takes place in a room whose walls are owned by someone. The publishing house provided relationships — with academics, with scientists, with the quiet men whose names appear in no public record but whose expertise a certain class of government occasionally requires. The financial empire provided cover — for the movement of money that couldn't move openly, for the maintenance of assets that couldn't be acknowledged, for the operational infrastructure of an enterprise that was not, in any meaningful sense, a media company.

He worked for at least one government. Possibly three. No one outside those governments knows the precise accounting, and the governments themselves have spent three decades ensuring that no accounting will ever be possible. What I know — what I was told, in pieces, over years, by people who had no reason to lie because lying would have made them more exposed, not less — is that Roman Harlow occupied the space where the press and the state and the intelligence community overlap, and that he occupied it with such completeness and for such duration that the question of which master he served most faithfully is unanswerable. The question he would have answered, if you'd asked him directly, with the unhesitating confidence of a man who has never been confused about his own loyalty, was this: *I serve the man who holds the receipt.*

I understand that. I understand it completely. It's how I was built.

He showed me the stadium once. Not literally — Roman was not a man who used literal stadiums for metaphors, because he had access to actual stadiums and therefore didn't need to imagine them. He showed me during a dinner in London in the late eighties, in a private dining room with a table that seated twelve and eight people present, by the simple act of describing, with the businesslike calm of a man reciting a grocery list, the leverage he held over six heads of state simultaneously. Not bragging. Not performing. *Cataloging.* The way an accountant catalogs receivables — this is what I'm owed, this is who owes it, this is the instrument of collection. Six governments. In his pocket. Simultaneously. Like change.

I had been doing what Roman did, in miniature, since the Prescott Academy. But miniature is the operative word. What Roman showed me, in that private dining room with its eight attendees and its implication of ten thousand absent conversations, was that what I had been building was a model railroad. And that the actual railroad existed. And that a man with the right connections and the right architecture and the specific, patient, decades-long commitment to making himself indispensable to people who could destroy him — that man could run it.

He never knew he was teaching me. That's the thing about Roman Harlow that I have always found most clarifying, and most useful. He was the most sophisticated operator of his generation, and he spent a decade in my company without once understanding that I was taking notes.

Celeste understood. But Celeste was built differently.

Which brings us to 1987. And Mayfair. And the empty chair across the table that wasn't empty by accident.

London in 1987 was everything Manhattan pretended to be: old money with the confidence to ignore you, new money with the desperation to impress you, and an aristocratic social infrastructure that functioned like a series of locked doors, each requiring a different key, each opening onto a room slightly more exclusive than the last. I was there on business — recovery work for a client whose assets had wandered into a Channel

Islands trust and gotten comfortable — and I'd been invited to a dinner party in Mayfair by someone who knew someone who knew someone, which is how every important evening in London begins: with a chain of introductions so long that by the time you arrive, nobody can remember who vouched for you.

The house was Georgian. The host was forgettable. The wine was a 1961 Bordeaux that had been breathing longer than most of the guests had been thinking. And halfway through the second course, a woman I'd never seen before took the empty chair across from me with the unhurried precision of someone who had planned to sit there all along.

Celeste Harlow was not what she appeared to be. Nobody at that dinner knew what she was. They knew the surface — the Sorbonne accent layered over something Eastern European, the clothes that said old money without specifying whose, the social fluency of a woman who could discuss Caravaggio with an art dealer and arms procurement with a defense attaché in the same breath without either man realizing she'd been steering both conversations toward the same destination.

What the dinner guests saw was a woman of indeterminate wealth and considerable charm who worked, she said, in "diplomatic consulting." What the dinner guests did not see — what I did not see, not that evening, not for months — was that Celeste Harlow was a trained intelligence operative.

Not the kind you see in movies — no trenchcoats, no dead drops, no microfilm concealed in lipstick tubes. The real kind. The kind that Western intelligence agencies had been developing since the Cold War: women who could enter any room on two continents and leave with the private confidence of every person worth knowing. Women trained not in combat or cryptography but in the far more devastating discipline of *human collection* — the art of identifying a target's vulnerabilities, cultivating a relationship that feels authentic, and extracting information or compliance without the target ever understanding that the relationship was operational from the first handshake.

Celeste had been recruited at twenty-two, out of a postgraduate program in international relations at a London university that had historically served as a feeder for the intelligence services the way that certain American law schools serve as feeders for white-shoe firms. She had spent six years in the field — Vienna, Beirut, two postings she never named — before transitioning to what the intelligence community calls "private sector liaison," which is the polite term for an operative who has been released from government service but never truly discharged. A freelancer with institutional backing. A contractor with a government pension. A woman who no longer carried credentials but whose phone calls to certain offices in certain buildings in certain capitals were still returned within the hour.

I knew none of this when she sat down across from me.

What I knew was that she was watching me the way I watched everyone else: categorizing, filing, assessing utility. And the recognition of that — the sudden, involuntary awareness that I was being studied by someone who operated at my frequency — was the most unsettling and exhilarating thing I'd felt since the first time I'd realized, at the Prescott Academy, that I could make powerful men do what I wanted by knowing things about them that they didn't want known.

"You're the American who finds money," she said, in a voice that managed to make a statement of fact sound like the opening move in a negotiation.

"I find things," I said. "Money, mostly. Money that's been lost, or hidden, or taken by people who shouldn't have it. I find it and I return it to the people who own it."

"A bounty hunter," she said, with a smile that contained no warmth whatsoever.

"Something like that."

She smiled. Not warmly. Precisely. The smile of a woman who has just confirmed a hypothesis.

"There are people," Celeste said, "who have noticed your particular talent for finding things. People who believe that a man with your skills — your instinct for leverage, your understanding of how money moves through the invisible economy, your rather remarkable ability to make powerful men trust you despite having no credentials that would justify their trust — might be useful for projects that are... larger than bounty hunting."

She paused. She let the silence do the work that lesser people would have filled with unnecessary words.

"Much larger."

I didn't need it spelled out. I'd been doing exactly this — in miniature, with cruder tools and smaller targets — since the Prescott Academy. Since I'd watched a senator's son snort cocaine at a Park Avenue penthouse and filed the information away like a deposit in a bank that only I could access. Celeste wasn't telling me anything new. She was telling me that the thing I'd been doing in a one-bedroom apartment could be done from a mansion. That the student party could become a state dinner. That the mental Rolodex could become a server farm.

She was showing me the stadium.

"I've always believed," I said, meeting her eyes with the calm steadiness of a man who has just been offered the keys to a kingdom and is pretending to consider whether the kingdom is worth his time, "that information is the only currency that never devalues."

Celeste smiled. It was the first genuine smile I'd seen from her all evening, and it was terrifying — not because it was cruel, but because it was *warm.* The warmth of a handler who has found an asset. The warmth of a spider who has met a younger spider and recognized, in its web-building instinct, a kindred architecture.

"Then we understand each other," she said.

We did.

Over the next several months, Celeste laid out the architecture. Not all at once — she was too sophisticated for that, too trained in the patient art of incremental disclosure that intelligence services use to bring an asset along gradually, each revelation building on the last, each new piece of information deepening the commitment until the asset is so far inside the operation that withdrawal becomes indistinguishable from betrayal.

She explained the concept: a private intelligence operation, funded by the targets themselves, built on the principle that the most powerful form of leverage is not what you can threaten to do but what you have already *recorded* them doing. She explained that governments had been running variations of this model for decades — honeypot operations, kompromat collection, sexual compromise schemes — but that the private sector had never attempted it at scale, because the private sector lacked two things that Celeste could provide: the tradecraft to run it and the institutional contacts to ensure that no government interfered with it.

She had the tradecraft. She had spent six years learning the art of human collection from the people who invented it. She understood how to recruit, how to manipulate, how to create environments in which targets volunteered information and behavior that could be used against them. She understood how to read a room the way a meteorologist reads the atmosphere: identifying pressure systems, predicting storms, knowing exactly where to apply heat and where to let things cool.

And she had the contacts. Not specific names — she never named her former employers, not then, not ever, and I never asked, because in the intelligence world, asking questions you don't need answered is the fastest way to end a relationship and occasionally a life. But she had *channels.* She could make phone calls that ensured certain investigations never opened. She could arrange introductions that no social network could produce. She could guarantee, with the quiet confidence of a woman who had spent years inside the machinery of state power, that the operation would enjoy a degree of protection that no private citizen should possess.

What I had was everything she lacked: money (increasingly), operational ambition (limitlessly), and the social infrastructure — the dinner parties, the financial consulting practice, the growing network of billionaires and politicians who trusted me because I had made them money and kept their secrets — that could serve as the legitimate front for an illegitimate enterprise.

She was the architect. I was the building.

That distinction matters. The tabloids would eventually describe Celeste as my "girlfriend," my "socialite companion," my "madam." The prosecution would call her my "co-conspirator." The press would frame our partnership as a love story gone wrong, as a tale of a woman who fell under the spell of a charismatic predator and became complicit in his crimes out of some combination of dependency and Stockholm syndrome.

They were all wrong. Celeste wasn't my companion. She wasn't my victim. She wasn't my subordinate. She was my *handler* — the intelligence professional who identified me as an asset, developed me as an operative, and ran me as an operation. The fact that the operation eventually grew beyond her control — beyond anyone's control — doesn't change the origin story. The spider didn't build the web alone. The spider was recruited.

We didn't discuss all of this that first evening. We didn't need to. The partnership was forged in that first look, in that first recognition, and everything that followed — the dinners, the planning, the years of operational collaboration that would make us the most dangerous couple in the Western world — was just execution.

Two people who looked at a crowded room and saw the same thing: inventory.

I flew back to Manhattan with a head full of architecture.

Not the kind you can draw on paper. The kind that exists between people — the invisible scaffolding of relationships, obligations, secrets, and fear that holds the real world together while the visible world pretends to run on laws and constitutions and the general good faith of civilized society. Celeste had shown me that this scaffolding could be *owned.* That a single operation — ambitious enough, ruthless enough, and protected enough — could position itself at the center of the invisible architecture and become, functionally, the most powerful entity in any room without holding any official title, any elected office, any position that the public could see or challenge or vote away.

What I had been building in miniature — the mental files, the whispered leverage, the instinctive exploitation of secrets — could be built at industrial scale. With cameras. With servers. With the operational tradecraft of a woman who had spent years inside the intelligence machinery of a Western government and who understood, at a cellular level, how to build the kind of operation that governments build but had never been attempted by a private citizen.

Celeste's training gave us the methodology. My ambition gave us the scale. And the combination of the two — a trained intelligence operative and an instinctive predator, working in partnership, with no oversight, no accountability, and the implicit protection of agencies that found our product useful — would create the most sophisticated private intelligence operation in the modern world.

Celeste didn't find me by accident. She found me the way intelligence services find assets: through patient observation, careful vetting, and the precise identification of a subject whose existing skills and inclinations align with operational requirements. I was already building leverage. I was already collecting secrets. I was already doing, with crude tools and small ambitions, what Celeste's former employers did with billion-dollar budgets and satellite networks.

All I needed was the upgrade.

Celeste was the upgrade.

What Celeste never told me — not that first evening, not for years afterward, and only then in the specific, clinical way that intelligence professionals disclose operational history when the statute of limitations has expired on everything except the truth — was that her instructions for the Mayfair dinner were not to recruit me.

Roman had been watching my trajectory since the Kaplan years. A man independently building a leverage operation in New York, with no institutional backing and no tradecraft training, was either an asset or a risk, and the cost of being wrong about which was, in Roman's calculation, too high to leave to chance. Celeste was sent to assess me. If the assessment concluded I was uncontrollable — if the architecture I was building suggested a man who would eventually become a problem for the networks Roman depended on — she had the authority and the methodology to ensure that the problem was resolved quietly, in the way that intelligence services resolve problems they cannot afford to document.

She assessed me. She concluded I was not a risk. She concluded I was the most interesting thing she had encountered in six years of fieldwork, and that destroying me would be the single greatest operational waste of her career.

She came home with a partner instead of a verdict. Roman, if he ever knew she had exceeded her authority, said nothing. That silence — Roman Harlow's considered, deliberate silence on the one act of insubordination his daughter ever committed on his behalf — is the most revealing fact I possess about the man. He saw what she saw. He agreed with what she chose. He just needed her to choose it first.

And the web — the beautiful, invisible, lethal web that we would spend the next thirty years building together — was just getting started.

Fragment: The Translator's Daughter

The following is adapted from a recorded interview conducted in 2021 by a team of investigative journalists working on a documentary that was never completed. The subject, identified only as "Mira," was a former language student at a London university who worked as a freelance translator for diplomatic events in the late 1980s. She agreed to speak on condition of anonymity. The production company dissolved before the documentary aired. The raw footage was acquired by a victims' advocacy organization and transcribed. What follows has been fictionalized, but the mechanism is real.

My mother was a diplomat's secretary — not the diplomat, never the diplomat, always the woman standing behind the diplomat holding the briefing folder and knowing more than he did about every country on his schedule. She raised me in embassy housing in three different countries before I turned twelve. I learned French from the cook in Beirut. I learned Arabic from the driver in Amman. I learned English from the BBC World Service because my mother believed that the BBC would keep me safe in ways that people could not.

Languages were my inheritance. The only one my mother could afford to give me.

The translation work started in my second year at university. A professor — a kind man, I still believe he was a kind man, though I've revised that belief so many times that the word "kind" has lost its structural integrity — recommended me to an agency that provided interpreters for private events. Corporate dinners. Embassy receptions. The sort of gatherings where wealthy men from different countries needed to communicate and where the house translator needed to be young, presentable, and invisible. Young because young is unthreatening. Presentable because presentable is expected. Invisible because the conversations being translated were not always conversations that the speakers wanted remembered.

I was very good at invisible. Diplomat's daughters learn invisible before they learn cursive.

The first event was a dinner at a private home in Mayfair. Twelve guests. I translated between English and French for a table that included a retired general, two financiers, and a man who was introduced to me only as "the host's American friend." He was tall. Dark hair. Intense in the way that certain men are intense — not angry, not aggressive, just present in a way that made the air around him feel slightly compressed. He watched people. I noticed because watching people was my job too. Translators watch mouths. He watched eyes.

He asked me, during a break between courses, where I'd learned my Arabic.

Not my French, which I'd been speaking all evening. My Arabic. Which I hadn't spoken at all. Which meant he'd done research on me before the dinner, or someone had briefed him, or he'd simply deduced it from my surname, which was Lebanese, and which I'd given only to the agency, not to any of the guests.

I told him. Amman. The driver.

He smiled. Not warmly. Precisely. The smile of a man who has just confirmed a hypothesis.

The second event was three weeks later. Same agency. Different house — this one in Belgravia, larger, with the sort of art on the walls that requires its own insurance policy. The American was there again. This time I translated between English and Arabic for a smaller group: the American, two men I later identified from newspaper photographs as senior officials in a Gulf state's sovereign wealth fund, and a woman whose role was never explained but whose clothes suggested that explanation was beneath her.

The conversation was about investments. Or it was framed as being about investments. What it was actually about — what I understood it to be about, translating not just the words but the architecture of the negotiation — was access. The Gulf officials wanted something from the American. Not money. Access. To people. To networks. To the specific social infrastructure that the American seemed to control like a switchboard operator controls connections: plugging this person into that person, routing influence through channels that didn't appear on any organizational chart.

I translated faithfully. That was my job.

After the dinner, the woman — the unexplained one, the one with the clothes — found me in the hallway where I was collecting my coat. She was magnetic. Beautiful in the way that people are beautiful when beauty is a professional tool rather than a genetic accident. She spoke to me in French, though her English was perfect, because French creates intimacy between women in a way that English does not.

She told me I was talented. She told me I was wasted on agency work. She told me there were opportunities — private translation, she called it, for a small circle of international clients who needed discretion and who paid accordingly. She said the word "accordingly" the way a jeweler says "carat" — as a unit of measurement that separates the ordinary from the extraordinary.

She gave me a card. No name. A phone number. London exchange.

I called. Because I was nineteen and my mother's rent was late and the agency paid forty pounds per event and the woman in the hallway had said "accordingly" in a voice that suggested three figures, not two.

The voice on the phone was male. Professional. He gave me an address — a townhouse in the East Seventies, Manhattan — and a date. He said a plane ticket would arrive. He said the client valued language skills and discretion equally. He said the compensation would be discussed on arrival.

I should have heard it then. The construction of it. The way each sentence was designed to answer a question I hadn't asked while avoiding every question I should have. But I was nineteen. And forty pounds per event. And my mother's rent.

The townhouse was enormous. I don't mean large in the way that London houses are large — converted, subdivided, every room performing double duty. I mean enormous in the way that American wealth is enormous: wasteful, declarative, designed to communicate that the owner has so much space he can afford to leave most of it empty. Rooms that existed only to be walked through. Hallways that led to other hallways. A staircase that curved upward like a question mark.

The American was there. He greeted me by name — my real name, not the agency name — and introduced me to a room of perhaps fifteen people. Diplomats. Financiers. A physicist whose face I recognized from a magazine cover. Two women who were younger than me and who spoke to no one and smiled at everyone and whose function in the room I understood immediately and viscerally in the way that women understand these things — not through evidence but through the specific frequency of discomfort that one woman's body transmits to another's when the first woman is performing a role she did not choose.

I translated. For three hours. Between English and Arabic and French. The conversations were sophisticated. Genuinely intellectually stimulating — discussions of geopolitics, of art, of the relationship between technological innovation and state power. I was good at my job and my job was interesting and the American paid me eight hundred dollars in cash at the end of the evening, which was more money than I had ever held in my hands at one time.

I went back. Four times.

Each visit, the atmosphere shifted. Not dramatically. Incrementally. The way the temperature drops degree by degree in autumn — you don't notice the cold until you're shivering. The guest lists grew smaller. The conversations grew more private. The young women grew more present and more silent. The American watched me the way he watched everyone — assessing, cataloguing, filing.

On the fourth visit, after the dinner, the woman from Belgravia appeared. The magnetic one. She took me upstairs — to a sitting room, she said, for a private conversation with a guest who needed Arabic translation for a sensitive matter. The guest was already in the room. He was Gulf royalty. I knew his face from my mother's briefing folders.

The room had a bed.

I understood then. In the doorway. With my hand still on the handle. I understood what the agency work had been — the audition. What the Belgravia dinner had been — the callback. What the Manhattan trips had been — the rehearsal. And what this room, with this man, with this bed, was supposed to be — the performance.

I said no.

Not eloquently. Not bravely. I said no the way an animal says no — with my body, by stepping backward, by turning, by walking down the staircase that curved like a question mark and out the front door onto a Manhattan street that smelled of exhaust and freedom and the garbage that New York produces in quantities that would embarrass a smaller civilization.

The woman followed me to the sidewalk. She wasn't angry. She was confused. Genuinely confused, in the way that a person is confused when a machine malfunctions — not emotionally upset, but diagnostically puzzled. She said I was making a mistake. She said the opportunity would not be offered again. She said the client was important and that importance, in her world, was a form of currency that I could not afford to refuse.

I said no again. In English this time. Because English is the language of no. English is hard consonants and closed vowels and the word "no" in English sounds like a door shutting. In Arabic, "no" is soft — "la" — a breath, a sigh, something that can be negotiated. In French, "non" carries philosophy, ambiguity, the possibility of revision. But in English, "no" is a period. A wall. A fact.

I never went back. I never called the number. I changed my phone number. I dropped the translation agency. I finished my degree. I became a teacher. I married a man who fixes cars and who has never once asked me to translate anything for anyone at any dinner.

I was lucky. That's what I tell myself. I was lucky because I understood the room before the door closed. I was lucky because my mother had raised me in embassies where I learned to read the architecture of power — who has it, who wants it, who is being consumed by it — before I learned to read books. I was lucky because four languages gave me four ways to say no, and I used the hardest one at the only moment that mattered.

But I think about the two women. The young ones. The ones who smiled at everyone and spoke to no one. The ones whose discomfort I felt through the walls of my own body like a radio frequency. They were there before me. They were there after I left. They are still there, in some version of that room, in some version of that house, in some version of that life, because they did not have four languages. They did not have a diplomat mother. They did not have the particular, specific, unreproducible luck of a girl who understood the room before the door closed.

They had nothing. And the machine had everything. And the machine is patient. And the machine does not hear "no" in any language.

The documentary production company, Meridian Arc Films, dissolved in 2022 following the withdrawal of its primary funding source — a media investment group whose board included two individuals subsequently identified in the civil proceedings. The raw interview footage was transferred to a victims' advocacy nonprofit, which catalogued it alongside approximately four hundred hours of similar testimony. The footage has not been broadcast. Mira's interview is filed under a case number. The case number is adjacent, in the archive, to three hundred and eleven other case numbers. Each one is a person. Each person had a room. Not all of them made it to the door.

Chapter 8: V. Aldric & Associates

Timeline: 1988 | **Location:** Manhattan, Ohio

In 1988, I founded V. Aldric & Associates.

I want you to appreciate the audacity of that sentence, because the audacity is the whole point. I — a man with no college degree, no institutional affiliation, no regulatory license, no verified track record, and a professional history that, if you'd actually investigated it, read like a criminal indictment written in invisible ink — launched a financial management firm whose sole stated criterion for accepting a new client was a minimum net worth of one billion dollars.

One. Billion. Dollars.

Let me explain what that number does, psychologically, because the psychology is more important than the mathematics. When you tell someone your minimum is a billion, you accomplish three things simultaneously. First, you eliminate ninety-nine point nine percent of the world's population from consideration, which makes the remaining zero point one percent feel *chosen.* Selected. Admitted to a club so exclusive that merely qualifying for entry is a validation of their entire life's work. Second, you create a scarcity trap: the billionaire who meets your threshold doesn't think "this man has set an arbitrary number to inflate his own importance." The billionaire thinks "this man understands my world. He moves in a stratum where a billion dollars is the *floor*, not the ceiling. He sees me." Third — and this is the most important part — you make it impossible for anyone to check your work. If your clients are exclusively billionaires, then your client list is, by definition, confidential. Billionaires don't want people knowing who manages their money. So nobody can verify that you have *any* clients, which means nobody can verify that you don't. The minimum isn't a threshold. It's a smokescreen.

I told people my minimum was a billion. You know what that does? It makes everyone with nine hundred million feel like they're not good enough. And everyone with two billion feel like they've found someone who speaks their language.

I rented an office. Nothing ostentatious — the truly wealthy are suspicious of ostentation because they know it's what poor people think rich people do. A clean, quiet space in a good building with an address that said "serious" without screaming "expensive." I hired an assistant. I had business cards printed — heavy stock, simple font, no title beneath my name because titles are for people who need the world to know what they do, and I needed the world to *wonder* what I did. The cards said "V. Aldric & Associates" and nothing else, which was, in a way, the most honest thing about the entire operation.

V. Aldric & Associates had no verified client list. No audited track record. No regulatory filings that would tell you what it actually *did.* It was a name on a business card, a quiet office, and a man who spoke with the absolute conviction of someone who had been managing the fortunes of the world's richest people for decades, even though the only fortune he'd managed was the one he'd assembled himself through a combination of bounty hunting, fraud, and the systematic exploitation of people who were too rich to check their receipts.

It was either the most brilliant business launch in financial history or the most transparent con. The distinction, as always, depended entirely on what happened next.

What happened next was a chain of introductions so elegant that it should be studied in business schools alongside case studies of Apple and Goldman Sachs.

The first link was Vivian Ashworth.

Vivian was a telecom executive and Manhattan socialite who would later marry into the Ashworth family and become Lady de Ashworth, which is a title upgrade that only happens in fairy tales and among the British aristocracy, which are essentially the same genre. She was connected to everyone, feared by no one, and trusted by the specific subset of wealthy, powerful people who value social intelligence over financial intelligence — which is to say, the subset that matters.

I met Vivian at a party — because everything important in my life has happened at a party, which either says something about the power of networking or something about the quality of my social life, and probably both. I was charming. She was charmed. I didn't pitch her. I didn't sell her. I simply existed in her vicinity with enough charisma and enough mystery that she felt compelled to introduce me to someone more important, naturally, inevitably, and without awareness that gravity was doing the work.

Vivian introduced me to Saul Braverman.

Now, Saul Braverman requires a moment of context, because he will appear throughout this story in roles that become increasingly ironic, and it's important that you understand the full spectrum of what this man represented. Braverman was a Hartfield Law professor — not just any professor, but the kind whose name was invoked in courtrooms like an incantation, whose legal opinions were cited like scripture, and whose client list read like a combined roster of the Fortune 500 and the Most Wanted list. He defended the famous, the powerful, and the guilty, sometimes in the same case. He was the legal establishment incarnate — the man you called when you needed the system to work for you instead of against you.

He was also, in ways that would become apparent much later, a man with his own vulnerabilities. But I'll get to that. Patience.

Vivian introduced me to Braverman. Braverman sized me up the way all Hartfield professors size up people without Hartfield degrees — with a mixture of curiosity and condescension that they believe is invisible but that is, in fact, the most visible thing about them. I let him condescend. Condescension is a gift when you're a con man, because a condescending person is a person who has already decided you're not a threat, and a person who doesn't think you're a threat is a person who leaves all their doors unlocked.

Braverman invited me to a birthday party in Ohio. A birthday party for a retail billionaire. A billionaire whose name I already knew, whose net worth I'd already memorized, and whose psychological profile I'd already constructed from years of observation, because I'd been planning this meeting — or something like it — since the moment I'd founded V. Aldric & Associates.

Networking is just money laundering for social capital. You take a dirty introduction — a man with no degree and a questionable past — and wash it through enough clean hands — a telecom socialite, a Hartfield law professor — until it looks legitimate. By the time I arrived in Ohio, I wasn't a Brooklyn kid with a fake résumé. I was a financial advisor so exclusive that he'd been personally invited by one of the most respected legal minds in America.

The laundry was complete. The money was clean. And the mark was waiting.

Grant Hensley was the richest man I'd ever met, and I'd met several by this point, which tells you something about the magnitude of his wealth. He was the architect behind Luxe Intimates, Haven & Bloom, Sterling & Holt, and a constellation of other retail brands that, collectively, clothed and scented a significant percentage of the American consumer population. His net worth exceeded three billion dollars — not on paper, not in projected future value, not in the speculative froth that inflated the fortunes of tech founders and cryptocurrency prophets. Three billion in actual, existing, operational assets. Stores. Inventory. Real estate. The kind of wealth you could touch.

He was from Ohio, which is important because Ohio produces a very specific type of billionaire: the midwestern variety, who has made an obscene amount of money but retains a residual discomfort with the fact, who wants to be seen as a regular guy who happens to be worth more than the GDP of some Pacific island nations, and who is therefore particularly susceptible to the specific kind of flattery that makes them feel *understood* rather than merely *rich.* The coastal billionaire wants you to be impressed by his money. The midwestern billionaire wants you to see past the money to the *person.* This distinction is everything. This distinction is what made Grant Hensley the most important person I would ever meet.

The birthday party was at his estate — sprawling, tasteful, expensive in a way that whispered rather than shouted. The guest list was a curated mix of Ohio business leaders, national political figures, and the particular species of social connector that exists in every billionaire's orbit, buzzing from one powerful person to the next like a bee in a garden of very, very expensive flowers.

I was introduced to Hensley by Braverman. The introduction lasted approximately thirty seconds. The conversation that followed lasted four hours.

This is the centerpiece of everything. Not just this chapter — everything. The entire arc of my life, from the Prescott Academy classroom to the island in the Caribbean, pivots on this conversation. If you understand what happened between me and Grant Hensley on a warm evening in Ohio in 1988, you understand everything that follows. And if you don't, nothing I tell you afterward will make sense.

I didn't pitch him.

I want to be absolutely clear about this, because every journalist, every biographer, every congressional investigator who has tried to explain the Hensley-Aldric relationship has started from the assumption that I must have dazzled him with financial brilliance — that I must have shown him some proprietary trading strategy, some innovative tax structure, some mathematical insight so profound that a man who'd built a three-billion-dollar empire couldn't resist handing me the keys.

That's not what happened.

What happened was much simpler, much more elegant, and much more human.

I made Grant Hensley feel *seen.*

I told him — not immediately, not clumsily, but gradually, over the course of a conversation that I conducted with the precision of a symphony conductor bringing in instruments one by one — that I understood the problem of being rich. Not the problems that poor people imagine rich people have, which are the problems of too many choices and not enough hours in the day. The *real* problem. The problem that no one talks about because admitting it would sound absurd to anyone who doesn't have it.

The loneliness.

Three billion dollars buys you everything in the world except one thing: a person who wants nothing from you. Every friend, every advisor, every family member, every lover — they all want something. They want your money, your influence, your validation, your name on their building or their charity or their resume. They want you to solve their problems. They want you to open their doors. They want a piece of you, and the wanting never stops, and after enough years of being wanted-from, you begin to suspect that nobody actually wants *you.* That the man behind the money is irrelevant. That you could be replaced by a corporation with a checkbook and nobody would notice the difference.

I didn't tell Hensley I could make him richer. Any idiot with a Bloomberg terminal could promise that. I told him I could make him *understood.* I told him that the ordinary financial advisors — the guys from the big banks, the guys with the Whitmore degrees and the tailored suits — didn't comprehend the existential weight of managing a fortune that large. They understood the *numbers.* They didn't understand the *person.* They didn't understand that wealth at that scale isn't an asset. It's a condition. A chronic condition that requires constant management, not of the money, but of the *self.*

"The problem with being worth three billion dollars, Grant," I said — and I used his first name, which was either presumptuous or intimate, and I chose to make it intimate — "is that everyone around you has been trained to manage your portfolio. Nobody's been trained to manage *you.*"

He looked at me. Really looked. The way a man who has spent decades being studied by people who want things looks at someone who appears to want nothing except to be in the conversation. It was the same look the Prescott Academy father had given me across the parent-teacher conference table. The same look Philip Osgood had given me across his mahogany desk at Meridian Sachs. The look that says: *You see me. You actually see me.*

I'd been doing this my entire life. The technique never changed. Only the scale.

Grant Hensley didn't need a money manager. He needed a best friend who was smarter than his other friends and loyal enough to never embarrass him. I played that part beautifully. For twenty years.

What happened next defied all logic, all prudence, and all the carefully constructed safeguards that billionaires typically erect between themselves and the people who manage their money.

Grant Hensley granted me power of attorney.

Not limited power of attorney — the kind where you can sign checks up to a certain amount and authorize transactions within certain parameters. *Full* power of attorney. Over his trusts. Over his foundations. Over his corporate holdings. Over his real estate. Over everything. He handed me the legal authority to act as though I *were* Grant Hensley in any financial transaction, any legal proceeding, any negotiation, any acquisition, any divestiture. He gave a man he'd known for less than a year the legal equivalent of his own identity.

His advisors were appalled. The people who had been managing Hensley's affairs for years — competent people, credentialed people, people with verified track records and clean regulatory histories — watched this happen with the particular horror of longtime employees who see the boss fall for a confidence trick that would be obvious to anyone not in the grip of it. One advisor, reportedly a lawyer who had served Hensley for over a decade, went so far as to warn him directly.

"He's a rat," the advisor allegedly said. "You're giving a rat the keys to the granary."

Hensley fired him. Not immediately — Hensley was not a dramatic man — but within weeks, the advisor was gone, his concerns buried under the gravitational force of Hensley's conviction that he had finally found the one person in the world who understood him. And maybe he had. Just not in the way he thought.

The thing about being someone's most trusted advisor is that anyone who says you can't be trusted sounds like they're the problem. I didn't have to defend myself against Hensley's advisor. I didn't have to argue, or produce credentials, or explain away the inconsistencies in my résumé. All I had to do was exist in Hensley's orbit with the quiet confidence of a man who belonged there, and let Hensley's own psychological investment do the rest. Because once a billionaire has decided to trust you, doubting you becomes indistinguishable from doubting himself, and billionaires did not become billionaires by doubting themselves.

The power of attorney was the single most consequential financial decision in my life. It was also, I suspect, the worst decision in Hensley's. But he wouldn't know that for another twenty years, and by then, the money would be gone, the properties would be mine, and the only question left would be whether he'd been swindled by a con man or controlled by something much larger and much darker.

The answer, as with most things in my life, was both.

A brief coda, before we close the act.

Grant Hensley was a co-founder of the The Keystone Circle. You haven't heard of the The Keystone Circle, and that's by design. It was — is — a secretive consortium of billionaires, most of them sharing certain ethnic and religious backgrounds, all of them devoted to philanthropy and to the geopolitical interests of a small, powerful nation in the Middle East. They met in private. They discussed strategy. They directed money toward causes that aligned with their collective vision of how the world should be organized. They did this quietly, effectively, and with the absolute conviction that their wealth entitled them not just to participate in the shaping of global politics, but to *direct* it.

I was not a member of the The Keystone Circle. I was not a billionaire — not yet. I didn't share their background or their particular geopolitical commitments. But I was something more useful than a member. I was the man who handled the things that members couldn't discuss in polite company. The man who knew where the money went after it left the foundation accounts. The man who understood that philanthropy, at the billionaire level, is never *just* philanthropy — it's infrastructure. It's influence. It's the purchase of gratitude from institutions and governments that can be redeemed, at some future date, for favors that no tax receipt will ever document.

The intelligence thread stirred again. Not loudly. Not visibly. But I could feel it, the way you feel a bass note in a concert hall: not in your ears, but in your chest.

Something was connecting. Something was being built. And I was being positioned — by my own ambition, by Roman's blueprint, by Hensley's billions, by forces that I may or may not have fully understood — at the center of it.

I want to be precise about what the Keystone Circle was, because precision matters here and imprecision has a way of leading to the wrong conclusions. The Circle was a *belief* organization. Its members believed, with the totality of conviction that serious money generates in serious men, that the world should be arranged in a particular way, and they directed their fortunes toward arranging it.

They were not cynics. They were not operatives. They were not intelligence assets or geopolitical mechanics or any of the things I would eventually become. They were, at their core, *philanthropists* --- the word used honestly, for once, without the irony I usually apply to it. They gave money because the cause mattered to them, because their identity was inseparable from the cause, because the cause and the self had become, through decades of community and conviction, the same thing. I served them. I handled the money that belief generates when it has no official channels through which to flow. It was a financial relationship. Clean, even, by the standards of everything else I was doing.

There are networks that are not belief organizations. Networks where the architecture is operational rather than aspirational. Where the men involved are not directing their wealth toward a vision but administering a mechanism --- where the line between private conviction and state function has been crossed so many times that the line itself has ceased to be meaningful. I would encounter those networks later. They would require something different from me than money management. They would require the specific skills I was still, in 1988, in the process of developing. The Keystone Circle was the social layer. What came after it was the operational one. And the two are not the same thing, no matter how closely they sit at the same dinner table.

I stood in the mansion.

Forty-five thousand square feet on East 74th Street. The largest private residence in Manhattan. Grant Hensley had purchased it for thirteen million dollars and poured millions more into a gut renovation that transformed it from a merely extraordinary house into a monument — to wealth, to ambition, to the belief that the right address can make a man legitimate. He would transfer it to me for what was rumored to be one dollar.

One dollar.

For the largest private residence in the most expensive city in the most powerful country in the world. The same amount you'd pay for a candy bar, if candy bars were sold at a markup consistent with their actual production costs, which they are not.

I didn't feel gratitude. Gratitude is for people who believe they've been given something they didn't earn. I felt *momentum.* The clean, accelerating, unstoppable momentum of a plan that was executing itself exactly as designed — or, if not exactly as designed, then in a direction that was even better than the original blueprint.

The Gulfstream IV was on order. The Gulf Shore estate was in escrow. Somewhere in my briefcase, folded inside a manila folder, was a map with a small island circled in red ink. Little St. Philip. I'd found it in a real estate listing — a private island in the U.S. Coral Islands, accessible only by boat or helicopter, invisible from the mainland, and governed by tax laws that made the Cayman Islands look like a socialist utopia. I hadn't bought it yet. But I would.

The Rockaway Shore kid who'd lied about his degree on a Meridian Sachs application was now the most trusted financial advisor to one of the richest men in America. He had a mansion. He would have an island. He would have a private jet. He would have the private phone numbers of presidents and princes and prime ministers, and he would have something far more valuable than any of those things: he would have their *secrets.*

The spider had his web. The climb was over.

Everything that follows — the presidents, the princes, the scientists, the girls, the cameras, the island, the fall — begins here. In a borrowed mansion with a stolen fortune and the absolute certainty that no one will ever stop me.

Act One was about learning the rules.

Act Two? Act Two is about realizing there aren't any.

Chapter 9: The Mansion

Timeline: 1989–1990 | **Location:** East 74th Street, Manhattan

People ask how I got the biggest house in Manhattan. It's one of my favorite questions, because the answer reveals more about the person asking than it does about me. The investment bankers want to know the terms of the deal — was it a gift, a purchase, a transfer, a tax-optimized conveyance through a shell entity in the Channel Islands? The socialites want to know about the decor — is it true there's a mural in the foyer, a Steinway in the music room, a painting of a woman in a nightgown that may or may not be a missing work by a very famous dead artist? The journalists, when they eventually come sniffing around, want to know the *motive* — why would a billionaire give a forty-five-thousand-square-foot townhouse to his financial advisor?

I tell them all the same thing: I earned it.

What I don't tell them is that "earning it" means making yourself so indispensable to a billionaire that giving you his house feels like a bargain. Like he's the one getting the deal. Like transferring the largest private residence in the most expensive city in the most powerful country on Earth to a man he's known for less than three years is not an act of insanity but an act of *prudent financial management.*

Grant Hensley bought the house in 1989 for thirteen million dollars. He poured millions more into a gut renovation — and when I say gut renovation, I don't mean new countertops and a fresh coat of paint. I mean the kind of renovation where you remove everything inside the building except the structural columns and then rebuild the interior from the foundation up, using materials imported from quarries and forests that exist specifically to supply the homes of people who consider thirteen million dollars a down payment. Italian marble in the bathrooms.

Hand-carved mahogany staircases. A kitchen designed to serve state dinners for forty. Bedrooms — seven of them — each larger than the apartment I grew up in on Rockaway Shore, each appointed with the kind of furniture that comes with a provenance instead of a price tag.

I walked the house alone on the first morning. Room by room. I touched the marble. I counted the bedrooms. I stood at the window of the master suite on the fifth floor and looked down at East 74th Street, at the joggers and the nannies and the dog walkers who moved through the Gold Coast with the calm entitlement of people who had been born into proximity to wealth and assumed that proximity was the same thing as belonging.

Because here's the thing about a really nice house — the nicest house in the nicest neighborhood in the nicest city in the world: people don't ask how you got it. They just want to come back. And I always want them to come back.

The first thing I did with the mansion was join a board.

Not a corporate board — those come with regulatory obligations and annual reports and the tiresome expectation that you'll actually attend meetings and contribute something substantive to the governance of the enterprise. I joined the board of the New York Academy of Art, which had been co-founded by **Leonard Crowell** and the late **a famous pop artist**, and which existed at the intersection of Manhattan's cultural elite and Manhattan's financial elite, which is to say it existed in exactly the room I needed to be in.

A board seat is a remarkable thing. It costs nothing — or rather, it costs a donation, which is the same thing as nothing when the donation comes from Grant Hensley's money — and it provides everything. A board seat at a cultural institution puts your name on a letterhead next to the names of people who have been vetted by an ecosystem that values pedigree above all else.

It gives you a reason to be at galas, at openings, at the private dinners that precede the public events where the real conversations happen. It gives you *legitimacy* — the institutional kind, the kind that you can't buy directly but can acquire by sitting in the right chair at the right table often enough that people start to assume you belong there.

I collected board seats the way lesser men collect cufflinks. The New York Academy of Art was the first. Others followed — cultural organizations, educational foundations, scientific advisory panels — each one requiring nothing more than a donation (Hensley's money) and a willingness to attend the occasional reception (my time, which was free because time is only expensive to people who don't know how to leverage it).

Each board seat opened a new network, a new set of dinner invitations, a new ring of people who assumed that if you sit on a board with them, you must be legitimate. Because that's how the system works. The system assumes that anyone who has passed through enough gates has been checked at each one, when in reality, nobody checks at any of them. They all assume someone else already did.

The beauty of a board seat is that it transforms the nature of every subsequent introduction. When you meet someone at a cocktail party and say "I'm a financial advisor," their eyes glaze over. When you meet someone at a cocktail party and say "I sit on the board of the New York Academy of Art, co-founded by a famous pop artist," their eyes widen. The information is tangential to your actual occupation, but it rewrites the social calculus entirely. You are no longer a financial advisor. You are a *patron.* A cultural figure. A man whose interests transcend money and extend into the realm of art, beauty, and the preservation of human creativity. The fact that you are also, underneath the patronage, a predator with no degree and a borrowed fortune — that fact becomes invisible. Buried under the weight of institutional credibility that you've purchased, at a discount, with someone else's money.

I was the unchecked man in the checked room. And the room was getting bigger.

The dinner machine started slowly — a few carefully curated evenings with a few carefully selected guests — and then accelerated with the exponential logic of a social chain reaction.

The mansion was the reactor. I'd designed it that way, or rather, Hensley's interior designers had designed it that way without knowing they were designing a piece of social engineering equipment. The rooms were large enough to feel impressive but intimate enough to feel exclusive. The lighting was warm — not the aggressive brightness of a boardroom but the golden, flattering glow of a place where people felt comfortable saying things they'd never say in daylight. The art on the walls was provocative enough to generate conversation and expensive enough to signal that the man who owned it was a person of serious means and unconventional taste.

I hosted Nobel laureates next to supermodels. Hedge fund managers next to political operatives. Tech founders next to European aristocrats. A former secretary of state sitting three chairs from a theoretical physicist sitting two chairs from a fashion designer whose dresses cost more than the physicist's annual salary.

Every combination deliberate. Every seating arrangement calculated to create the maximum number of unlikely connections, because unlikely connections are the ones people remember, and people who remember your dinner parties come back to your dinner parties, and people who come back to your dinner parties bring other people, and the spiral tightens.

Everyone was flattered to be invited. That was the essential mechanism. The mansion — the address, the art, the guest list, the food, the wine, the *mystique* of the host — created a social gravity so powerful that attending a dinner at 74th Street became, within a remarkably short period, one of the most coveted invitations in Manhattan. And the more coveted it became, the more powerful the gravity, because exclusivity feeds on itself the way compound interest feeds on principal.

Nobody asked how I ended up in the biggest private house in New York. Why would they? Asking would be gauche. Asking would suggest that you didn't belong. And everyone at my table pathologically needed to belong.

That's the magic of a really nice house. People don't ask how you got it. They just want to come back.

Meanwhile, I was spending Grant Hensley's money with the calm, methodical efficiency of a man who has been given the keys to the world's most exclusive department store and has no intention of returning anything.

Power of attorney is a remarkable legal instrument. In theory, it exists to allow a trusted agent to manage affairs on behalf of a principal who is unable or unwilling to manage them personally. In practice — in *my* practice — it meant that I could move Hensley's money anywhere, invest it in anything, acquire anything, sell anything, redirect anything, and the only person who would ever need to approve the transaction was me. I was the agent *and* the authority. The fox and the henhouse inspector. The thermostat and the furnace.

I managed Hensley's fortune with an aggression that alarmed his other advisors — the ones who hadn't been fired yet, the ones who were still clinging to their positions with the desperate grip of people who sense that the new management considers them disposable. I moved money between accounts. I redirected investments from Hensley's preferred vehicles into vehicles that I preferred, which happened to be vehicles in which I had a personal interest. I began acquiring properties — not for Hensley, but for *myself* — using the financial infrastructure that Hensley had spent decades building.

The Gulf Shore estate went into escrow. A sprawling waterfront compound in one of the wealthiest zip codes in America, with enough square footage to house a medium-sized hotel and enough privacy to ensure that whatever happened inside it stayed inside it.

The Paris apartment went under contract. A flat in one of the most exclusive arrondissements, because every spider needs a European anchor point, and Paris has the dual advantage of being the center of European social life and the headquarters of a modeling industry that I had plans for.

The Gulfstream IV was on order. A private jet large enough to seat a hundred passengers, which is comically, absurdly large for a private aircraft, unless you consider passenger manifests to be a form of social documentation, which I did.

Grant trusted me with everything. And I took care of everything. Including myself. Especially myself.

Was it embezzlement? That's such an ugly word. It implies theft. I prefer to think of it as *compensation.* Grant Hensley hired me to manage his fortune, and managing a fortune is stressful, and stress requires amenities, and amenities cost money, and the money happened to be in the account I was managing. The circle was so elegant it practically drew itself.

I should tell you about the uniform.

Starting in 1990, I wore the same outfit every day. Not the same literal garments — I wasn't a cartoon character — but the same *outfit.* Dark suit. Open collar. No tie. Clean lines. No flash. The sartorial equivalent of a corporate logo: consistent, recognizable, and designed to communicate a very specific message without saying a word.

I told people it was efficiency. "I don't want to waste mental energy on clothing decisions," I'd say, and people would nod, because the idea that a brilliant man is too busy thinking about important things to think about his wardrobe is deeply flattering to both the man and the audience. a tech billionaire would later pull the same trick with his black turtleneck, and people would act like he invented the concept. He didn't. I did. Or rather, I understood the principle before he made it famous: the uniform is a brand.

But the real reason was something more strategic. I wanted to be immediately identifiable. Memorable. A *character* in every room I entered. When you walk into a party full of men in gray suits and blue ties, the man in the dark suit with no tie is the one everyone remembers. Not because the outfit is remarkable — it isn't — but because its consistency creates a visual signature that the brain files under "important" and "different" and "possibly the smartest person here."

The mansion. The wardrobe. The Boeing. The dinner parties. The board seats. The guest lists. It was all costume design for a role I was playing — a role that I'd been writing since my first day at the Prescott Academy, that I'd been rehearsing on every trading floor and in every offshore bank and at every billionaire's birthday party. The role was: *The Smartest Man You've Never Heard Of.* The man who doesn't need publicity because the people who matter already know him.

The man whose name isn't in the newspapers because the people who own the newspapers are at his dinner table. The man who operates in the space between visibility and invisibility — seen by everyone who counts, invisible to everyone who doesn't.

And it worked. My God, it worked. By the end of 1990, I was the most connected unknown person in Manhattan. I had no title, no company worth mentioning, no institutional affiliation, no public profile, and no credential that would survive even the most cursory background check. And I was sitting at the center of a social web that encompassed billionaires, politicians, scientists, royalty, and every species of powerful person that the twentieth century had produced.

The spider had his house. Now he needed to wire it.

But that would require a death first. A very large, very public, very useful death.

And it was coming.

Chapter 10: The Death of the Spy

Timeline: 1992 | **Location:** London, Adriatic Sea, Manhattan

The phone rang at four in the morning, which is when all the important phones ring, because the world's most consequential information is generated between midnight and dawn — coups, assassinations, market collapses, births, deaths, and the particular species of catastrophe that only happens when the people who are supposed to be watching have fallen asleep.

It was March 14, 1992.

I was in the Manhattan mansion, in the study on the third floor, which I'd outfitted with the kind of heavy furniture and dim lighting that suggests a man who reads leather-bound books by lamplight, though in reality I was awake at four in the morning because I'd been on a phone call with someone in a different time zone whose name I'm not going to share with you and whose business I'm not going to describe. The call had ended twenty minutes earlier. I was drinking water — I almost always drank water, which people at parties assumed was vodka because the alternative explanation, that a man at a party might choose sobriety, was apparently more unbelievable than the idea that he was drinking a clear spirit — and staring at the ceiling when the phone rang again.

It was a contact in London — someone connected to the Harlow media empire. The call lasted ninety seconds.

Roman Harlow was dead.

Here's what happened, or what was reported to have happened, or what Spanish police determined had happened based on the evidence available to investigators who were either incompetent, compromised, or simply overwhelmed by the geopolitical implications of what they were investigating:

Roman Harlow, seventy-one years old, the towering Polish-born British media baron, the owner of the *Sunday Courier* and the *New York Evening Standard* and Harlow House Publishing and a dozen other enterprises, the intelligence asset for at least one and possibly three foreign nations, the man who had shown me the stadium — Roman had been cruising the

Adriatic Sea aboard his yacht, the *Alicia*, near the Adriatic Sea. At some point during the night, he had gone overboard.

He was found floating in the water the next morning. Dead.

Spanish police ruled it accidental drowning. A large man, on a yacht, at night, in the Adriatic — these things happen. Perhaps he was disoriented. Perhaps he slipped. Perhaps the sea was rough and the railing was low and the combination of age and darkness and the gentle rocking of a two-hundred-foot vessel conspired to produce a tragedy that was nobody's fault.

Or perhaps he jumped. Roman's empire was, as I knew and few others did, on the verge of collapse. The pension funds he'd looted — hundreds of millions of pounds stolen from his own employees' retirement accounts — were about to be discovered. The debts he'd accumulated were about to come due. The financial architecture he'd spent decades constructing was about to be revealed as what it had always been: a house of cards built on stolen money and the world's willingness to look the other way.

Or perhaps he was pushed. Roman had made enemies — not the ordinary kind that every powerful man accumulates, the bruised egos and soured business deals and ex-wives with grievances. The *extraordinary* kind. The kind that governments manufacture. The intelligence agencies he'd served had reason to silence him — a retired asset is a liability, because a retired asset can talk, and talking is the one thing intelligence agencies cannot tolerate. The governments he'd embarrassed had reason to silence him. The business partners he'd betrayed, the creditors he'd defrauded, the allies he'd outlived his usefulness to — they all had reasons. When a man knows the secrets of three intelligence services and the pension funds of thirty thousand employees, the list of people who might want him in the Adriatic is longer than the yacht itself.

Roman's death was either a suicide, a murder, or an accident.

The correct answer doesn't matter. What matters is what happened next.

They buried him on a private military cemetery outside Tel Aviv.

Think about that for a moment. A newspaper publisher — a man whose official biography described him as a media entrepreneur and philanthropist — was buried on the most sacred hillside in one of the most contested cities on Earth, in a cemetery reserved for individuals of extraordinary significance to a particular nation. This was not a normal funeral. Normal funerals for newspaper publishers happen in parish churches in Surrey, attended by colleagues and family and a few uncomfortable employees who feel obligated to pay respects to a man they privately despised.

Roman Harlow's funeral was attended by multiple heads of state. A former prime minister of a certain Middle Eastern nation delivered the eulogy. He praised Roman's "remarkable political connections" and the money he had "invested" in the nation's security and future. Six serving and former heads of intelligence agencies from three countries were in the crowd. The security detail outnumbered the mourners.

I watched it on television. From the mansion on 74th Street, on a screen that was probably worth more than the average funeral's total budget, I watched the most extraordinary send-off for a newspaper owner in the history of human civilization, and I took notes.

Not physical notes. Mental notes. The same kind I'd been taking since the Prescott Academy — the kind that live in your head because paper creates evidence and evidence creates vulnerability. I noted the attendees the way I used to note the cars at Prescott Academy pickup: categorizing, classifying, filing each face under the appropriate heading. Heads of state. Intelligence directors. Military officials. Diplomats whose presence at the funeral of a private citizen could not be explained by any professional obligation and could only be explained by personal ones — personal obligations that arise when a man has done things for your government that your government cannot officially acknowledge.

I noted the eulogies. I noted the way three different governments sent representatives who were clearly there in an official capacity despite the official position that Roman Harlow had no official relationship with any government. I noted the way the speakers praised Roman's "contributions" and "investments" and "dedication" — words that, in the context of a funeral on a private military cemetery outside Tel Aviv attended by prime ministers and spymasters, meant something very different from what they would have meant in a corporate press release. I noted the enormous, bellowing, undeniable truth that the funeral itself was broadcasting to anyone paying attention:

When a newspaper man dies and three prime ministers show up, he wasn't selling newspapers.

Roman was exactly what people suspected he was. What the intelligence agencies of three continents knew but could not prove publicly. What his own family members suspected but never dared articulate. He was an asset. He was a spy. He was a man who had built an empire on the intersection of media, crime, and intelligence, and who had operated in that intersection for decades with the implicit protection of governments that found him useful.

And now he was dead. And the protection was over.

In the weeks following the funeral, Roman's empire collapsed with a speed and thoroughness that would have been impressive if it weren't so devastating to the approximately thirty thousand employees whose pension funds he'd stolen.

The revelations came in waves. First, the financial auditors discovered that hundreds of millions of pounds were missing from the Courier Group's pension funds. The money hadn't been invested or lost — it had been *taken.* Redirected into Roman's private accounts, into offshore entities, into the vast and labyrinthine financial architecture that he'd spent decades building and that now, without his physical presence to maintain it, was unraveling like a knitted sweater caught on a nail.

The Harlow family name, which had been synonymous with power and influence for decades, became synonymous with fraud overnight. The Harlow heirs scrambled to save what they could. Creditors descended like jackals. Lawyers materialized from every direction with claims and counterclaims and injunctions and petitions. The newspapers Roman had owned — the ones that had protected him while he was alive, that had spiked stories about his intelligence connections and his financial irregularities — now turned on his memory with the ferocity of publications that have been lying on behalf of their owner for years and are suddenly, violently free.

The family was bankrupt. The name was ruined. The empire was ash.

And somewhere in the rubble, if you knew where to look — and very few people did, because the rubble was deliberately arranged to make looking difficult — there were traces. Faint, deniable, impossible-to-prove-in-court traces. Whispers that someone had helped Roman hide money in the years before his death. That certain offshore accounts had been set up by someone who understood the geography of offshore finance with the intimacy of a bounty hunter who'd spent years mapping the Cayman Islands and the Channel Islands and every other island where money goes to disappear. That someone with the initials K.F. might have been involved in arrangements that Roman's family knew nothing about and that Roman himself had kept separate from his other financial operations.

I may have helped a friend with some paperwork. I help a lot of friends with paperwork. That's what friends do.

What did Roman Harlow's life and death teach me? That's the question I've been circling since the funeral, and the answer is both the simplest and the most important thing I've ever learned.

Roman proved that the system *works.* He proved that a single man — born in poverty, self-invented, operating across multiple countries and multiple identities — could build an empire that spanned media, finance, intelligence, and crime, and could operate that empire for *decades* without consequence. He stole hundreds of millions of pounds. He spied for at least one foreign government. He manipulated elections, suppressed journalism, blackmailed opponents, and used his newspapers as instruments of personal and political warfare. And the whole time — the *whole time* — the world let him. Because he was useful. Because the governments he served needed his newspapers. Because the intelligence agencies he worked for needed his access. Because the financial institutions he borrowed from needed his revenue. Because the system, the entire system, was built not to catch men like Roman but to *accommodate* them, as long as they remained useful enough to justify the accommodation.

Roman's life proved that the impossible was merely a matter of scale and nerve.

But Roman's death proved something equally important: the system only protects you while you're alive.

His mistake was leverage — too much debt, too many enemies, too many favors called in and never returned. He'd built an empire on personal relationships, personal charm, personal intimidation. Every secret was stored in his head. Every alliance depended on his presence. Every threat required his voice on the other end of the phone. When the body went into the Adriatic, the secrets went with it. The leverage evaporated. The alliances dissolved. And the empire, which had looked as permanent and imposing as the man himself, collapsed in weeks.

Roman built an empire on secrets. Then he kept all the secrets in his own head. When his head went into the Adriatic, the secrets went with it.

I wouldn't make that mistake.

My secrets would live in servers. In cameras. In a digital architecture so comprehensive, so meticulously maintained, so redundantly backed up across multiple locations and multiple jurisdictions that no single event — not my death, not a raid, not a subpoena, not a presidential order — could destroy them all at once. The leverage wouldn't depend on my memory, my health, or my continued existence on the correct side of a yacht railing. It would depend on *infrastructure.* And infrastructure, unlike human beings, doesn't drink, doesn't make enemies, and doesn't fall into the Adriatic Sea at four in the morning.

Roman was the prototype.

I was the production model. Sleeker. Quieter. Better engineered. And most importantly — backed up.

Celeste arrived in Manhattan in the spring of 1992, and when I say "arrived" I mean it in the way that a precision instrument arrives — calibrated, purposeful, and designed to reshape whatever it touches.

She wasn't fleeing. That's what the tabloids would say — that Roman Harlow's death had sent shockwaves through the intelligence underworld, that Celeste had lost her network when her primary contact's empire collapsed, that she came to me out of desperation. The prosecution would eventually argue the same thing: that she was a dislocated operative who attached herself to a powerful man because she had nowhere else to go.

They were wrong.

Celeste arrived in Manhattan because the asset was ready. Roman's death had changed the landscape — the intelligence contacts he'd maintained, the channels he'd operated, the implicit protections his media empire had provided to people like Celeste — all of that was gone. But the *need* for the operation hadn't changed. Governments still wanted leverage on powerful people. Intelligence agencies still needed kompromat. And the private market for that product — the market that Celeste had spent five years preparing me to enter — was wider open than ever.

She came to Manhattan because the asset was ready. I was the asset. Five years of patient cultivation — the dinner in London, the subsequent meetings in Vienna and Zurich, the careful drip of tradecraft and methodology that Celeste had been feeding me since 1987 — had produced a man with the financial infrastructure, the social network, and the operational instinct to run the most ambitious private intelligence operation in history. All that was missing was the handler.

Celeste showed up at my door like a woman who'd lost everything. That's what the tabloids would say. That's what her biographers would write.

They were wrong.

What Celeste actually brought was priceless. She brought the full weight of her intelligence training — not theoretical, not academic, but the bone-deep operational knowledge of a woman who had spent years inside Western intelligence and who understood, at a cellular level, how the game was played at the highest levels. She brought the methodology that would transform my crude instinct for leverage into a precision instrument. She brought the tradecraft that would turn dinner parties into collection operations and guest lists into target packages.

She knew how governments ran these operations. And she was going to build a private one that was better.

We were going to build a better one.

Together.

The partnership was not romantic in any conventional sense, though we played the part of a couple when it served our purposes — at galas, at charity events, at the kind of social occasions where appearing as a couple suggests stability and normalcy and the wholesome American fiction that behind every successful man is a well-dressed woman who chose him for reasons other than power. What the partnership actually was, was *operational.* Two people with complementary skill sets, complementary resources, and a shared understanding that the world is a marketplace in which the most valuable commodity is other people's secrets.

The spider and the web. That's what they'd call us eventually, though not to our faces, because calling someone a spider to their face requires a degree of courage that most people lack when the spider is standing in a forty-five-thousand-square-foot mansion and has a Gulfstream IV parked at Morristown. I was the spider — the strategist, the financier, the architect. She was the web — the social fabric, the connective tissue, the beautiful, intricate, invisible structure that caught the flies and held them in place until I decided what to do with them.

It was the defining partnership of my life. It was, arguably, the most dangerous partnership in the Western world.

And it was just getting started.

Chapter 11: The Architecture of Consent

Timeline: 1992 | **Location:** Manhattan

It is the spring of 1992. I am sitting at the desk in the third-floor study of the 74th Street mansion, and in front of me is a single manila folder. Inside the folder is a single sheet of paper. On the paper is a name, a date, a dollar amount routed through two intermediaries, and four sentences of audio transcript — the distilled product of an evening that cost me approximately forty thousand dollars to arrange and that will generate returns I have not yet bothered to calculate, because calculating returns before a system is fully operational is the kind of impatience that costs architects their best work. I read the four sentences. I close the folder. Then I begin to think about what I have actually built, which is not the thing most people think I built.

Every difficult problem looks difficult until you understand it. Then it looks inevitable. Then it looks *obvious.* And finally — this is the stage that separates the architects from the engineers, the genuinely creative from the merely competent — it looks like something you could have thought of at fifteen, if you'd been paying the right kind of attention.

The problem was this: powerful men will not come to your island, enter your bedroom, and perform the acts that make them blackmailable if they believe they are being exploited. They have lawyers. They have instincts. They have the particular, animal vigilance that accrues to people who have spent their careers understanding that information is a weapon and that weapons are always pointed at someone. You cannot *trap* a man of genuine power. Not directly. Not with honey pots and manufactured seductions and the crude operational theater that lesser intelligence operations deploy and that almost always fail, because the man who has been briefed on the existence of honey pots — and every man at this level has been briefed — will eventually smell the honey.

You cannot trap him. You have to make him *choose.*

This is the insight that I am most proud of in a career containing several things I'm proud of. Not the island. Not the cameras. Not the financial architecture or the intelligence relationships or the social infrastructure that I spent twenty years assembling. Those are *implementations.* The insight — the fundamental, load-bearing intellectual contribution that made everything else possible — is this:

The most durable leverage is not extracted from a man. It is *deposited* by him. Voluntarily. Enthusiastically. With full participation and, at some level, full understanding.

Let me be precise about what I mean by that, because precision is the point and imprecision would be an insult to the elegance of what I built.

I am not describing naive men who stumbled into a trap without understanding the general category of risk. I am describing intelligent men — senators, billionaires, members of foreign governments, senior intelligence officials — who understood, in the general architecture of the situation, that they were accepting hospitality from a man who collected information and that the information they were generating would not simply evaporate into the Manhattan evening air. They understood this the way a man understands that a restaurant photographs its food before serving it: as background knowledge, noted and then consciously set aside in favor of the pleasure immediately in front of him. They chose to set it aside. The choice was the consent. And consent, unlike coercion, is legally bulletproof.

This is what Celeste had brought from her intelligence years that I couldn't have purchased from any other source: the understanding that the difference between a honey pot and a voluntary arrangement is not behavioral — the behavior is often identical — but *architectural.* It lives in the structure of the invitation, the framing of the context, the specific language of the offer. Build it correctly and the man who comes to your dinner and sleeps with the girl you've provided has made a *choice.* Build it incorrectly and you've committed procurement. The architecture is everything. The behavior is just data.

We spent the spring of 1992 building the architecture.

The financial layer came first. Celeste built it at the dining room table — not the formal dining room, the smaller one on the second floor that I used for working breakfasts, because Celeste believed that the architecture of important work should match the scale of the room, and the formal dining room was designed for performance, not precision. She spread the documents across the table in a grid: foundations here, consulting entities here, investment vehicles along the far edge. She didn't explain what she was doing while she did it. She never explained while she worked. She explained after, when the structure was visible as a whole, because explaining a system before it's assembled requires the other person to hold too many incomplete things in their mind at once, and Celeste had no patience for minds that couldn't wait. I watched from the doorway. When she finished, she stepped back, looked at the grid for a long moment, and said: "Every man who receives your hospitality makes a financial transaction. Not with you. Never directly with you." She picked up a pen and drew a single line connecting the foundation column to the consulting entity column. "The transaction is the commitment. The footage, when it comes, is only the confirmation." She was an intelligence operative, and intelligence operatives always follow the money before they follow the person, because money leaves trails that human memory cannot alter retroactively. Every man who attended the dinners, used the properties, accepted the introductions to the young women who circulated through the evenings with the social ease of people who had been trained, very carefully, to circulate — made a financial transaction embedded in this structure: a philanthropic donation to a foundation I controlled, a consulting fee paid to a company that served no function other than to receive it, an investment in a financial vehicle whose performance was managed by a man who no longer existed. The amounts were calibrated precisely. Not so large as to require reporting. Not so small as to be implausible as legitimate business. The exact middle ground of the plausibly deniable, documented in records that I maintained with a completeness that the IRS itself would have found impressive.

Before a single camera recorded a single frame, I had financial documentation placing each participant inside a web of transactions that established relationship, established access, established the pattern of exchange that investigators call *predicate conduct*. The footage, when it came, was the confirmation. The financial record was the commitment. You can challenge footage. You cannot uncash a check.

The second layer was the intelligence arrangement, and this one I will describe with the care it deserves, because it is simultaneously the most consequential and the most misunderstood element of what I built.

I did not approach an intelligence agency with a proposition. I am occasionally credited — in the more breathless accounts of my operation, the ones written by journalists who need a conspiracy to justify the scale of what I built — with having engineered some elaborate approach, some specific negotiation, some meeting in a parking garage in which I laid out terms to a deputy director and walked away with institutional protection. This is not how it worked. It is not how anything in this world works, because the people who run intelligence agencies did not get where they are by meeting people in parking garages with terms.

What I had was usefulness. And usefulness, deployed correctly, generates its own protection without requiring anyone to formally agree to anything.

I provided access. My properties, my guest lists, my dinner tables — they attracted, with reliable consistency, the foreign nationals that three-letter agencies spent enormous resources trying to understand: oligarchs, arms dealers, the financial intermediaries of governments that operated beneath the official diplomatic layer, sovereign wealth fund managers whose allocation decisions were indistinguishable from state policy. These men came to my island. They used my properties. They spoke freely in rooms that — I cannot stress this enough — were not the rooms they believed they were in.

At some point in 1992, the footage I had begun to accumulate — not from cameras, not yet, but from the older methods, the listening infrastructure that Celeste had installed with an expertise born of six years in actual intelligence work — became interesting to people who had institutional reasons to find it interesting. No meeting was required. No contract was signed. The arrangement was established through a mechanism far more durable than any written agreement: *mutual interest*, so precisely aligned as to be functionally identical to an alliance, while remaining, for all legal purposes, a coincidence.

They didn't protect me because they liked me. They protected me because the server room, which Malcolm would later maintain with the devotion of a man who has found his true vocation, contained files that were operationally irreplaceable. Files that no satellite, no wire, no penetration of a foreign embassy could have produced, because the men in the files had come voluntarily to a private residence and behaved voluntarily in the specific ways that cameras record. I had footage of foreign officials in moments of catastrophic indiscretion. So did the agencies — because I had provided it. Willingly. As one professional provides another with a product they cannot manufacture themselves.

The arrangement was not spoken. It was *understood.* And understanding, between professionals, is more binding than any contract, because contracts can be challenged in court and understanding cannot.

Now. The first test.

I want to tell you about the first time the architecture was deployed at scale, because the first time is always the proof of concept and the proof of concept is always the thing I return to when I need to remind myself that what I built was not lucky, was not accidental, was not the product of circumstance stumbling into competence. It was the product of design.

He was a senator. I won't tell you from which state, because the state would identify him and he is, by any measure that matters, irrelevant to the larger story. What he represented was not a person but a *category* — the first successful deployment of a system I intended to replicate one hundred times over. He was the prototype. He was the proof.

He came to the dinner. He drank the wine. He accepted the introduction to the young woman that Celeste facilitated with the elegant, unobtrusive professional ease of a woman who has been doing exactly this — in various configurations, for various governments, across three continents — since her late twenties. He made a financial transaction, routed through two intermediaries, that arrived in a foundation account I controlled. The audio from that evening — clear, specific, legally damning — was transferred to a server that Malcolm would, six months later, begin maintaining. And then he left.

I made a single phone call, three weeks later. Innocuous. Social. The call a man makes to another man he has hosted, inquiring after his health and proposing a subsequent meeting. He accepted. He was warm. He was, in the specific way that guilty men are warm to the people who own their guilt, *extremely* warm. We met. We talked. At the end of the conversation, I mentioned, with the offhand calm of a man noting a scheduling preference, that I'd had occasion to review some materials from the dinner and had found them — interesting. That I was grateful for his discretion and hoped for his continued friendship.

He looked at me the way people look at a surgeon who has just explained that the operation was more complex than anticipated but that everything went well. That mixture of relief and debt and the quiet, permanent understanding that the relationship has shifted onto a different footing and will not be shifting back.

He became one of my most useful assets. Not because I threatened him — I never threatened anyone. I never needed to. The architecture made threats redundant. The architecture made everything redundant except the single most efficient human motivation that has ever existed:

The desire to keep what you've already done from becoming what you're known for.

I sat in the mansion that winter and reviewed what I had built. Not the physical infrastructure — Hensley's marble floors, the Gulfstream on the tarmac, the island sitting in its Caribbean coordinates. The *intellectual* infrastructure. The architecture of consent. The system that turned a powerful man's worst evening into a permanent, productive, entirely voluntary relationship with the man who had hosted it.

Engineers build machines that process material. I had built a machine that processed *people.* And people, unlike material, are self-replenishing. They attend galas. They accept invitations. They bring their colleagues and their allies and their vulnerabilities and their appetites into your orbit, because the alternative — the isolation of a man who has decided to trust no one — is the loneliest and most professionally debilitating condition that power produces.

They come. They always come. Because the only thing more dangerous than attending the dinner is not attending it, and I had designed that calculus with the same care, the same precision, the same architectural pride that I applied to everything I built.

The cameras would go in that spring.

I watched the technicians arrive on a Tuesday morning in April. Three men, a white van with a plumbing supply company name on the side, and two cases of equipment that plumbing supply companies do not manufacture. Celeste had hired them through four layers of intermediary — not because she was paranoid, she'd explained, but because the habit of insulation is something you build before you need it, and by the time you need it, it's too late to build. I watched them from the window of the second-floor study. They were professional. Unhurried. They moved through the rooms the way men move through spaces they have studied in advance: knowing exactly where to stop, how long to stay, what to leave behind. By three in the afternoon they were gone. The van pulled out. The mansion looked exactly as it had at nine that morning. Nothing had changed. Everything had changed.

They were the last component. Everything else was already running.

Chapter 12: The Camera System

Timeline: 1992–1993 | **Location:** Manhattan, Gulf Shore

Let me tell you about the second renovation of the East 74th Street mansion, because it was the most important construction project in American intelligence, American politics, and American blackmail — though that last category isn't officially recognized by the construction industry, which is an oversight I intend to correct in the court of public opinion.

The first renovation — Hensley's renovation — had been about aesthetics. Italian marble. Hand-carved staircases. The kind of finishes that make architects weep and interior designers achieve a state of professional ecstasy normally reserved for Renaissance artisans. It had transformed a large, old Manhattan townhouse into the largest private residence in the city, a monument to taste and wealth and the billionaire conviction that square footage is a measure of spiritual worth.

My renovation was about infrastructure.

I hired contractors — never directly, always through intermediaries, because direct relationships create liability and intermediaries create deniability. The intermediaries hired subcontractors. The subcontractors were not interior designers. They were not plumbers or electricians or the kind of tradesmen who show up in white vans with their company name stenciled on the side. They were specialists. The kind of specialists who install things that aren't supposed to be found, in locations that aren't supposed to be visible, with a craftsmanship that ensures the installation survives decades of use without anyone — not a guest, not a housekeeper, not a building inspector — ever noticing that it exists.

They installed cameras.

Hidden cameras. In the bedrooms. In the bathrooms. In the guest rooms. In the common areas. In the hallways that connected the bedrooms to the bathrooms, because sometimes the most interesting footage is captured in transit, in the moments between spaces, when a person believes they are unobserved and therefore behaves in ways they would never behave if they knew they were on film. Every angle covered. Every room wired. Multiple cameras per room in the spaces where the highest-value guests would be hosted, because redundancy isn't paranoia when the footage you're capturing is worth more than the real estate it's captured in.

You'd be amazed what a good camera system costs. You'd be more amazed what the footage is worth.

I narrate this calmly, I know. The way a homeowner describes upgrading a kitchen. New countertops, new appliances, new hidden surveillance system in every bedroom — it's all just home improvement, isn't it? Just a man making his property work harder. Optimizing his investment. Ensuring that every guest who walks through the door receives the full experience — including the experience of being recorded from multiple angles while engaging in activities that, if made public, would destroy their careers, their marriages, their legacies, and their freedom.

Just good hospitality.

I need to introduce you to the person in this story who matters most besides me.

His name is Malcolm Pruitt.

You haven't heard of him. That's the point. Malcolm is a man you wouldn't notice at a party because he's never at the party. He's in the basement. Or the server room. Or the utility closet that houses the networking equipment. He's wherever the wires go, wherever the data flows, wherever the systems hum quietly in the dark doing the work that makes the visible world function. He is unremarkable in the way that oxygen is unremarkable — invisible, essential, and catastrophically missed the moment it disappears.

Malcolm was my IT specialist. My systems administrator. My infrastructure architect. He maintained the cameras. He maintained the servers that stored the footage. He managed the encryption that protected the files. He handled the backups — multiple backups, in multiple locations, because I had learned from Roman Harlow's death that any system with a single point of failure is a system that will, eventually, fail, and the information stored on these servers was too valuable to trust to a single hard drive in a single building in a single jurisdiction.

Malcolm would become the most frequent correspondent in my entire email archive. One hundred and fourteen documented exchanges. More than any senator. More than any billionaire. More than any president. More than Celeste. More than Hensley. More than every world leader I'd ever corresponded with, combined. Because Malcolm wasn't corresponding about dinner plans or investment strategies or the idle social chatter that fills the inboxes of people who confuse communication with accomplishment. Malcolm was corresponding about *systems.* About server capacity. About encryption protocols. About backup schedules and file integrity and the thousand small, unglamorous, absolutely critical details that keep a digital infrastructure running.

Every empire needs an IT guy. Every CEO, every president, every intelligence agency, every criminal enterprise — they all depend, ultimately, on the person who maintains the systems. The person who knows where every file lives and every backup sleeps. The person who, if they chose to walk away, could take the entire operation with them on a thumb drive.

Most people underestimate the IT guy. They look at the man in the basement with the quiet voice and the unremarkable clothes and they see a technician. A functionary. A human extension of the hardware he maintains.

That's what makes him the most critical person in the building. Because the person who matters most in any building is the one nobody's watching.

I watched Malcolm Pruitt. I watched him carefully. Not with suspicion — with *appreciation.* The way a general appreciates the soldier who maintains the nuclear launch codes. With the understanding that this quiet, competent, unremarkable man held the keys to everything I was building, and that his loyalty, his discretion, and his continued employment were more important to my operation than any billionaire's donation or any president's friendship.

Malcolm Pruitt was the keeper of the keys. And the keys opened every door.

I'll give you a specific example of what working with Malcolm was like, because abstraction doesn't capture it.

It was 1994. A senator had visited the East 74th Street property three months earlier. He was important at the time --- a man who sat on committees, who received briefings, who had access to the specific corridors of federal power that I needed accessed. He had been charming at dinner. He had been less charming in the guest room. The camera in the northwest corner of that room had captured, with the clarity of a seventy-millimeter lens in optimal lighting conditions, a sequence of behaviors that the senator's constituents would have found, to put it generously, illuminating.

I knocked on Malcolm's server room door.

He was at his workstation --- always at his workstation, the way a surgeon is always at the table when you need him, which was one of the things I valued most about Malcolm. He had no social life that interfered with availability. He had, as far as I could determine, no life outside the server room that interfered with anything.

"The senator from the fourteenth," I said. "November session. The northwest guest room."

Malcolm swiveled to his keyboard. His fingers moved.

"November fourteen through sixteen," he said. "Northwest room. Three files. Primary, secondary backup, and the offsite archive. All current, all encrypted, all accessible." A pause, the length of a single keystroke. "Video quality is good on all three. The northwest corner unit was replaced in October. Higher resolution than the previous model."

He said this the way a pharmacist confirms a prescription --- not the contents, not the implications, just the status. *Your medication is ready. Three copies. All current.*

I stood in the doorway for a moment. Not for any further business. I wanted to mark the moment --- to feel, cleanly and completely, what it meant to have this man in this room. What it meant that every question I could ever need answered about what happened in my properties would be answered the same way. Completely. Precisely. Without any detour through conscience or hesitation or the human tendency to make what is transactional feel personal.

"Thank you, Malcolm," I said.

"Is there anything else?"

There wasn't. I left. The door closed behind me with the specific quiet of a server room door --- the sound of seals and insulation, of a room designed to keep the outside out and the inside in.

I have been in rooms with presidents who made me feel less secure.

The Gulf Shore estate received the same treatment.

I'd acquired the property — a waterfront compound on Via Dorado, in one of the wealthiest neighborhoods in one of the wealthiest towns in the most aggressively ostentatious state in the union — and I'd framed it, publicly, as a "relaxation retreat." A place where friends and associates could escape the pressure of Manhattan life, enjoy the Florida sunshine, swim in the pool, play tennis on courts that cost more to maintain than most Americans earn in a year, and avail themselves of the kind of hospitality that a generous host with unlimited resources and no social boundaries might provide.

Gulf Shore itself was ideal for my purposes. It was a community that prided itself on minding its own business, which in practice meant that the residents — many of them among the wealthiest people in America — had elevated willful ignorance to an art form. What happened behind the hedgerows stayed behind the hedgerows. The social contract of Gulf Shore was essentially a collective non-disclosure agreement, enforced not by lawyers but by the shared understanding that everyone had something to hide, and everyone's privacy depended on everyone else's discretion.

The contractors came. The same kind of specialists. The same intermediary structure. The same painstaking attention to concealment. Surveillance throughout — professionally installed, comprehensively covering every room where a guest might do something they wouldn't want recorded. The pool area. The massage rooms — plural, because I was a man with chronic back problems who required frequent therapeutic massage, which was the cover story, and which nobody questioned because nobody questions a man's medical needs, especially when the man is rich enough to employ full-time massage therapists and the massage therapists are young and attractive and arrive through a side entrance and leave through the same one.

The bedrooms. Every guest bedroom wired. Every angle considered. The footage quality was professional-grade — not the grainy, distorted output of a convenience store security camera, but clean, well-lit, high-resolution recordings that would be immediately recognizable in a courtroom or, more usefully, in the living room of a person who was being shown footage of themselves doing something they'd rather the world didn't know about.

The cameras were the infrastructure. Gulf Shore was the venue. And the venue was about to start hosting some very important guests.

The first recordings were, in a sense, unremarkable. Not because the content was unremarkable — the content was, in several cases, the kind of thing that would have made a tabloid editor weep with joy and a federal prosecutor reach for a warrant — but because the *process* was unremarkable. Routine. Mechanical. As predictable as a factory assembly line, which is essentially what it was — a factory for leverage, with raw materials coming in through the front door and finished product being stored in the server room.

A guest would arrive. They'd be greeted with the kind of hospitality that makes a person feel simultaneously important and relaxed, which is a combination that most hosts get wrong. Most hosts make their guests feel important *or* relaxed — never both. Important makes you perform. Relaxed makes you careless. I needed both. I needed my guests to feel like they were the most fascinating people in the room *and* like the room was so safe, so private, so insulated from the outside world, that they could drop every mask they'd ever worn.

The food was exquisite. The wine was better. The company was curated — beautiful women, fascinating intellectuals, powerful figures from adjacent industries who made each guest feel like they'd been admitted to a salon so exclusive that its existence was itself a secret. The evening would unfold with the practiced ease of a theatrical production, because that's exactly what it was. I was the director. Celeste was the stage manager. The guests were the actors. And the cameras were the audience.

A guest would retire to a bedroom. A camera would record what happened in that bedroom. And the next morning, the guest would leave, having enjoyed the most luxurious, most comfortable, most comprehensively documented visit of their lives.

I reviewed the footage the way a CEO reviews quarterly reports. Clinically. Dispassionately. Without moral judgment, because moral judgment is a luxury afforded to people who aren't building empires, and I was building the most ambitious empire since the East India Company — except my commodity wasn't spices or textiles. It was *leverage.*

I didn't care about the content of the recordings. Not in the way you might think. I didn't watch for titillation or entertainment or the kind of voyeuristic thrill that motivates amateur Peeping Toms and reality television producers. I watched for *value.* Each recording was assessed not on what it showed but on what it was *worth.* The worth was determined by a simple formula: the power of the person on the tape multiplied by the severity of what they were doing, divided by their ability to explain it away.

Everyone has a number. Not a price — a *number.* A senator is worth more than a CEO. A foreign head of state is worth more than a senator. A Supreme Court justice is worth more than a foreign head of state. And a president — well. A president is the jackpot. The cameras help me figure out everyone's number.

I created a filing system. Because I'm a systems person. I've always been a systems person — a man who can walk into any environment, identify the information flows, and build an organizational architecture that captures, categorizes, and preserves the data in a form that's both secure and retrievable.

Each person got a file. Each file had a tier — not measured in dollars but in *leverage potential.* Tier One was the jackpot: heads of state, sitting presidents, members of the royal families of nations with significant geopolitical influence. Tier Two was the heavy hitters: billionaires, cabinet members, intelligence chiefs, the CEOs of companies large enough that their fall would move markets. Tier Three was the supporting cast: senators, professors, judges, media executives, the kind of people who weren't individually powerful enough to change the course of history but who collectively formed the infrastructure through which history is changed.

The system was meticulous. Cross-referenced. Indexed by name, by date, by location, by the severity of the recorded activity, and by the estimated consequences of release. Each file contained the raw footage, a summary of the content, an assessment of the leverage potential, and — this was my innovation, the thing that separated my operation from every amateur blackmailer who's ever hidden a camera in a hotel room — a strategic plan for deployment. Not "if I need to use this." *When* I need to use this. Under what circumstances. Against what target. To achieve what outcome.

I didn't build a blackmail operation. That's a crude word for a crude enterprise. Blackmail implies threats, demands, the aggressive extraction of money or favors through intimidation. I built something much more elegant.

I built an insurance company. I just happened to be the only one who knew everyone was insured.

Celeste's role in all of this cannot be overstated, because without Celeste, the camera system would have been a surveillance apparatus recording empty rooms.

She didn't just attend the gatherings. She *curated* them. She decided who sat next to whom at dinner. She identified which powerful guests had which weaknesses — who was susceptible to flattery, who was susceptible to attractive company, who was susceptible to the particular species of social seduction that involves making a person feel like they're the most fascinating individual in the room. She read a room the way a card counter reads a table — tracking the variables, calculating the odds, knowing exactly when to play the hand and when to fold.

This was her intelligence training. Decades of watching Roman Harlow manipulate governments, media empires, and intelligence agencies had been distilled into a social skill set that looked like charm but functioned like espionage. Celeste could walk into a room of twenty powerful people and within fifteen minutes identify the three who were vulnerable, the two who were dangerous, and the fifteen who were irrelevant. She could seat a senator next to a model in a way that felt accidental but was as calculated as a chess opening. She could introduce a businessman to a young woman in a way that seemed like social graciousness and was, in fact, the first step in a process that would end with that businessman on camera doing something that would end his career. She could ensure that the right bottle of wine appeared at the right moment, that the music shifted from upbeat to intimate at precisely the hour when inhibitions were lowest, that the atmosphere of the evening followed a carefully designed emotional arc from excitement to comfort to recklessness.

It was, if you stripped away the criminal enterprise underneath it, a masterclass in event planning. Celeste could have been the most successful hostess in Manhattan history if she'd applied these skills to legitimate entertaining. The fact that she applied them to something considerably less legitimate is a choice that she made with open eyes, clear purpose, and the full understanding — inherited from a father who'd done the same thing for decades — that the line between social engineering and espionage is drawn in pencil, not ink, and can be erased whenever it becomes inconvenient.

People think I built this. And I did — I built the infrastructure. The cameras. The servers. The filing system. The properties. The financial architecture that funded the entire operation.

But Celeste built the guest list. And the guest list was everything. Without the guests, the cameras were just technology. With the right guests, the cameras were the most powerful weapon in the world.

We were operational. The mansion was wired. Gulf Shore was wired. The guest lists were growing. The files were thickening. And somewhere in the Caribbean, a seventy-acre island was waiting to be wired next.

The machine was on. And the machine was hungry.

Fragment: What the Camera Recorded

The following is a composite reconstruction based on forensic evidence recovered from the Manhattan residence at 12 East 74th Street during the 2019 FBI raid. Camera file metadata, room assignment logs, and physical evidence were cross-referenced with victim interviews conducted between 2019 and 2023. The narrator described the surveillance system as his masterpiece. This is what the masterpiece recorded.

The room is cold.

That's the first thing. Before anything else. Before the man or the table or the sounds through the wall or any of it. The room is cold. I'm fifteen and I'm standing in a room on the third floor of the biggest house I've ever been inside and the room is cold and I don't know why they keep it so cold. Later — years later, in a therapist's office, in a conversation I'll pay for with money I don't have — I'll learn that they keep the rooms cold because cold suppresses the will. Cold makes you smaller. Cold makes your body curl inward and your mind retreat to the place behind your eyes where you go when your body isn't safe anymore. They know this. The temperature is a tool. Everything in this house is a tool.

The woman brought me here. She said it was a massage appointment. Two hundred dollars. She said the man had back problems. She said I'd be trained. She said the other girls loved it.

The man waiting in the room isn't the one who lives here. He's a guest. He's sitting on the edge of the bed in a robe and his legs are crossed and he's drinking something from a glass with ice. He looks at me when I come in and his face does something I will spend the next nineteen years trying to understand. It's not lust. It's not cruelty. It's *delight*. The pure, uncomplicated delight of a child seeing a birthday cake. He is *happy*. Whatever is about to happen to me, it is the thing he has been looking forward to. It is the highlight of his week.

"There she is," he says. Like I'm a present someone ordered for him.

I'll skip what happens. Not for your sake — for mine. What I'll tell you is the sound he makes. He makes sounds that don't match what he's doing. He laughs. Actual laughter. Not the nervous laughter of a man doing something he knows is wrong. The easy, genuine laughter of a man doing something he loves. When I cry — and I cry because my body forces me to cry the way my body forces me to breathe — the laughter gets louder. My pain is the punchline. My pain is the *point*.

He says things. I remember one sentence because it branded itself into my brain the way a cattle brand burns into hide: "I love the ones that still cry."

Still. That word. Like crying is a feature that wears off. Like the newer models still have it and the older ones don't. Like he's been doing this long enough to have a preference about which stage of destruction he enjoys most.

I leave my body. Not metaphorically. I leave. I go somewhere above the room and I watch what's happening from the ceiling. The girl on the floor is me but she's also not me. She's a shape. A thing that sounds are coming out of. I watch from the ceiling and I think: the camera in the corner is watching too. That small black eye in the molding near the ceiling. It sees what I see. It will remember what I won't let myself remember.

When it's over, the man goes to the bathroom. I hear water. I hear him washing his hands. I hear him humming. Humming. A melody. Casual and content, like a man washing up after a meal. Like what just happened was dinner and now it's time for dessert and the dessert is the feeling of being clean again.

I'm on the floor. There is blood. Not a lot. Enough. Enough that my body has told me something is wrong in a language my mind can't translate yet because my mind is still on the ceiling.

I press my thumb into it. Into the blood. And I reach under the lip of the dresser — the heavy wooden dresser against the wall, the one with the art book and the lamp on top — and I press my thumbprint into the underside of the drawer frame. Hard. Deliberate. I don't know why I do this. I don't have a plan. I'm not thinking about evidence. I'm thinking: *I was here. This happened. Somebody should know.*

The man comes out of the bathroom. He adjusts his robe. He picks up his drink. The ice has melted. He looks at me on the floor and says, "You can go now." The way you'd dismiss a waitress. The way you'd close a tab.

I go. I take the two hundred dollars from the envelope on the table by the door. I walk down the staircase of the largest private residence in Manhattan. I pass the photographs of presidents. I pass the grand piano. I pass the painting that costs more than my mother will earn in her lifetime. I walk through the front door and onto East 74th Street and the air outside is warm and the warmth feels like an assault because my body has forgotten that warmth exists.

I never go back to that house. Other girls do. The woman calls me. I don't answer. She calls again. I change my number. I move. I stop sleeping. I start using whatever makes the not-sleeping bearable.

I never file a report. Who would I tell? What would I say? That a man in a robe in a mansion laughed while he hurt me? That the house had cameras that recorded everything? That there is a thumbprint under a dresser drawer on the third floor of a building owned by a man whose friends run the country?

The thumbprint was recovered during the 2019 FBI forensic sweep of the Manhattan residence. It was matched to a woman, then thirty-four, living in a different state under a married name. She had no criminal record. She had never filed a police report. When contacted by investigators, she confirmed the print was hers. She confirmed the year. She confirmed the room. She asked if they found the camera footage. They told her the servers had been removed from the property before the raid. She laughed — a short, flat sound that the agent on the phone later described to a colleague as "the saddest thing I've heard in twenty years of doing this."

The dresser is in an evidence warehouse. The thumbprint is cataloged. The footage is gone.

Chapter 13: The Empire's Properties

Timeline: 1993–1995 | **Location:** U.S. Coral Islands, New Mexico, Various Airports

Every great criminal enterprise is, at its foundation, a real estate problem.

Not a moral problem. Not a legal problem. Not a psychological problem, though the psychology is interesting. A *real estate* problem. Where do you put the thing? Where is the geography in which the rules you need to break can be broken without consequence, where the people who need to be invisible can be invisible, where the evidence you're generating lands in a jurisdiction that finds it inconvenient to look? Every operation that has ever been successfully concealed — from the intelligence community's black sites to the cartels' processing facilities to the network of private islands and desert ranches and discreet continental properties that my own operation required — is, at its operational core, an answer to that question.

I am an excellent real estate agent. I am the best real estate agent for illegal purposes who has ever lived. I say this without pride and without apology. It is a fact, like the boiling point of water or the half-life of uranium. You can verify it against the record.

Here is my portfolio.

The Island.

Little St. Philip cost a few million dollars — roughly what I spent on wine in a good year — and what it gave me in return was the only thing that money, at a certain altitude, cannot directly purchase: *jurisdictional ambiguity.* The island sat in the U.S. Coral Islands, which meant it was technically American soil, which meant the Constitution technically applied. That word — *technically* — is the most useful word in the English language when you are building an operation that depends on the gap between what the law says and what the law can actually enforce on a seventy-acre island accessible only by boat or helicopter, surrounded by Caribbean water warm enough to feel luxurious and deep enough to swallow evidence.

You cannot just show up on Little St. Philip. There were no water taxis. No charter boats that served the island independently. Every arrival was scheduled, logged, and controlled by people who worked for me. The airstrip — long enough and reinforced enough to handle the Gulfstream IV, which is not a small aircraft and whose presence on a private Caribbean island is not a standard residential amenity — was the artery. Control the airstrip, and you control who comes and who goes, and therefore you control what the island knows and doesn't know, and therefore you control reality.

I learned this at fifteen, on a gravel strip in northern Michigan. The airstrip is always first. Without it, you have a beach. With it, you have a country.

Construction began in 1993: the main house, the guest cottages, the staff quarters, the dock, the power infrastructure, the satellite uplink. Conventional enough that the contractors asked no questions. Then Malcolm Pruitt arrived and began the renovation that didn't appear on any blueprint. The cameras. The server room, climate-controlled against Caribbean humidity, triple-redundant, linked by encrypted cable to off-island backup servers because I had learned from Roman Harlow that any system with a single point of failure is a system waiting to fail. By the time Malcolm finished, every guest cottage, every common area, every path between buildings, every arrival dock was wired. The island didn't just record its guests. The island *studied* them. With the patient, omnidirectional attention of a system that never sleeps, never blinks, and never forgets.

And then there was the structure on the hilltop.

Small. Blue-and-white striped dome. Heavy door. No windows, or very few. Its purpose never adequately explained and never needing to be, because the power of a locked room is not what it contains. The power is the *lock itself* — the implication that whatever is inside is valuable enough, or dangerous enough, to require a door that doesn't open for everyone. Every guest who visited Little St. Philip saw it. Every guest carried the wondering with them when they left, like a stone in a shoe that can't be shaken out. I have always understood that the most effective information is the information that *might exist.* The lock does the work. The imagination fills the rest. Given sufficient anxiety, the imagination will always conjure something worse than reality.

That is the whole trick. It has always been the whole trick.

People think my island is about parties. My island is about Section 934 of the Internal Revenue Code. The parties are just how I keep score.

The U.S. Coral Islands offered, and continue to offer, the most generous tax incentive structure available to an American taxpayer. My effective tax rate — through the Financial Trust Company I established in Port Asbury, compliant with every relevant statute, reviewed by counsel from three jurisdictions — was approximately four percent while the federal top marginal rate sat at thirty-eight and a half. The difference was three hundred million dollars over two decades. I want you to sit with that number. Three hundred million. Not stolen. Not laundered. *Saved.* Legally. By owning an island and establishing legitimate business operations in the territory. Every corporation in America does a version of this. I did it on an island with a striped temple and hidden cameras in the bedrooms. The tax strategy was identical. The décor was more interesting.

The guest list, from the first arrival in late 1994, was bifurcated — a word I use deliberately. Two streams. One visible. One not.

The first stream was legitimate: scientists, academics, business leaders. I have always been genuinely fascinated by intelligence — real intelligence, the kind that lives in a mind that has spent thirty years inside a single hard problem. I seated Nobel laureates next to hedge fund managers next to philosophers next to tech founders and watched the conversational chemistry with the same clinical pleasure I'd once applied to the parents at Prescott Academy pickup. The science was real. The conversations were real. And the scientists' presence provided something that no amount of money can directly purchase: *legitimacy by proximity.* A man at whose dinner table the world's greatest physicist voluntarily sits is not, in the cultural calculus of the American elite, a predator. He is a *patron.* The framing is everything. The framing was the point.

The second stream was the girls. Arrived by boat, presented as massage therapists or assistants or simply as friends of friends. The two streams coexisted on seventy acres of Caribbean paradise, separated by nothing but a few hundred yards of manicured lawn and an ocean of willful ignorance deeper and wider than the actual ocean surrounding it. Scientists discussed string theory on the terrace while the massage schedule ran on Jenna Caldwell's calendar with the precision of an air traffic controller. The two worlds never officially converged. They simply breathed the same air, operated within the same system, and served entirely different functions — one providing intellectual cover, the other providing leverage. Elegant is not a moral term. But operationally, it was elegant.

I also purchased Great St. Philip — the neighboring island, larger, undeveloped, never inhabited. I built nothing on it. I hosted no one there. What I did was ensure that no one else could buy it. Great St. Philip was a perimeter. A moat made of real estate. No journalist renting a guest house on the adjacent landmass. No telephoto lens on a hilltop a quarter mile away. No accidental witnesses. The purchase wasn't about what I could build there. It was about what I could *prevent* there.

Little St. Philip was the centerpiece. But the machine needed more geography.

The Ranch.

The Cimarron — tens of thousands of acres of New Mexico high desert, red rock and scrub brush and infinite sky, and the particular silence that only exists where the nearest neighbor is measured in miles rather than feet. I named it after a word that means wild and unbranded, which seemed appropriate for a property whose operational purpose I never publicly articulated to anyone's satisfaction, and whose primary product was the specific institutional confusion that arises when a man owns something very large and very remote and declines to explain it.

I told a dinner table of extremely intelligent, extremely accomplished people — scientists, academics, thought leaders, the kind of people who have opinions about the ethical boundaries of human reproduction and who have published those opinions in peer-reviewed journals — that I intended to use the ranch as a selective breeding facility. That my genes were superior. That the high desert of New Mexico offered the ideal setting for a program of human reproduction that would, over several generations, improve the species. I said this in the same conversational tone I'd use to describe a wine investment or a kitchen renovation.

They laughed.

Not the nervous laughter of people processing something monstrous. Genuine laughter — the full-bodied, unguarded delight of people being entertained at a dinner party by a charming host with a provocative mind. One or two engaged with it theoretically, the way academics engage with any provocative hypothesis: with curiosity rather than horror, analysis rather than disgust. Nobody left the table. Nobody called anyone. Nobody looked at the man describing a eugenics program and reconsidered the association.

Because when you are rich enough, eugenics sounds like disruption. It sounds like the kind of radical, paradigm-shifting thinking that Silicon Valley conferences celebrate under different vocabulary. I had spent decades cultivating the reputation of genius, which meant that anything I said — no matter how monstrous — was processed by my audience as *visionary.* The dinner table is the most powerful institution in the Western world. More powerful than courts, more powerful than press, more powerful than law. Because the dinner table is where people decide, in the company of people they trust, what is acceptable to think. I ran the dinner table for thirty years. The Cimarron was the logical conclusion of running it well.

The ranch was real. The plan was real. Whether I acted on it in any systematic way is a question I'll leave unanswered, because unanswered questions are the currency I trade in.

The Planes.

The 727 was not a plane. The Gulfstream IV was not a plane. They were *infrastructure* — the connective tissue of an empire that existed across six properties and three continents and that required, in order to function, the ability to move people between its nodes with the speed and discretion of a system that had been designed specifically to resist documentation.

It had, of course, been designed specifically to *produce* documentation.

The 727 — oversized for a private aircraft, underestimated by everyone who saw it as mere ostentation — carried over a hundred passengers in standard commercial configuration. Mine was not standard. Mine had leather seats, private compartments, and a bedroom in the back that was appointed like a suite. The tabloids would eventually nickname it, because tabloid nicknames always stick when they're viscerally accurate. But I didn't love the plane for the leather or the bedroom or the champagne served at altitude. I loved it for the manifest. The *list.* Every name, every date, every departure point, every destination — written in my pilot's meticulous hand, filed with the FAA, preserved in ink that doesn't fade and memory that doesn't apologize. A flight log is the closest thing to truth in a world built on lies. A flight log was written before anyone knew it would matter, and pre-controversy documentation is the one form of evidence that not even the best lawyer can convincingly explain away.

I kept flight logs because *I* required them. Every name on that manifest was a name I owned. Every accepted ride was a deposit — not in money, which is cheap, but in *obligation,* which is the only currency that appreciates unconditionally. The flight log was not a record of my guests. It was a ledger of their debts.

The Gulfstream was the shadow vehicle — sleek where the 727 was imposing, invisible where the 727 attracted attention. I offered Gulfstream rides freely, because freely given favors create the deepest debts, and because the Gulfstream's manifests were scrutinized considerably less than the 727's. Every good operation needs a visible layer and an invisible one. The 727 was the one you'd read about. The Gulfstream was the one you'd never hear of until it was far too late.

Now let me take inventory.

The Manhattan mansion — forty-five thousand square feet, cameras in every room, the social engine of the entire operation. Gulf Shore — the recruitment ground, the casual south, the place where palm trees create the illusion that rules are optional. Little St. Philip — the operating theater, isolated, surveilled, insulated by purchased geography and Caribbean water. The Cimarron — the mystery, thirty-three thousand acres of desert whose purpose I have declined to articulate to anyone's complete satisfaction, which is the point. Two aircraft, moving between all of it with the frictionless efficiency of a logistics system optimized over a decade for a single purpose. And Malcolm Pruitt in the server room, maintaining the archive, making sure the cameras never stopped rolling and the files never stopped growing.

This was not a collection of properties. This was an architecture. Designed, like all architecture, to make certain things possible and certain other things impossible. What it made possible was the operation. What it made impossible was accountability. The spider doesn't build a web randomly. Every thread is placed. Every anchor point is chosen. The geometry is the whole point.

The infrastructure was complete. The geography was secured. The machine was built.

All it needed now was fuel. And the fuel, as it turned out, was human.

Chapter 14: The Recruiter's Handbook

Timeline: 1994–1996 | **Location:** Gulf Shore, Manhattan, London, Paris

I want to talk about Celeste's talent.

Not her intelligence, which was considerable. Not her social instincts, which were lethal. Not her Sorbonne education or her aristocratic bearing or her ability to enter any room on two continents and leave with the private phone number of every person worth knowing. Those are the qualities that people discuss when they discuss Celeste Harlow — the public-facing attributes, the ones that fit neatly into a magazine profile or a society column. The qualities I want to discuss are the ones that don't get written about in polite publications, because polite publications don't have a vocabulary for what Celeste actually was.

She was a recruiter. The best recruiter I've ever seen. The best recruiter anyone has ever seen, if we're being honest about what the word means, which we usually aren't, because honesty about what Celeste did requires a degree of moral clarity that most people would rather not possess. It's easier to call her my "girlfriend" or my "socialite companion" or, as the tabloids preferred, my "madam." These labels are comfortable. They reduce a complex operational apparatus to a relationship dynamic that the public can process without feeling complicit. But Celeste wasn't my girlfriend. She wasn't my madam. She was the most sophisticated human acquisition system I've ever encountered, and I've encountered a few.

She identified targets at malls. At community pools. At school pickup lines. On the street — literally on the street, in the wealthy enclaves of Gulf Shore and Manhattan, where young women from less wealthy backgrounds came to work as babysitters or waitresses or retail clerks, occupying the invisible service economy that surrounds wealth the way a coral reef surrounds a tropical island. These girls — and they were girls, almost always, fifteen and sixteen and seventeen, old enough to look like adults in the right lighting and young enough to be adults in no meaningful legal or moral sense — existed in the gap between childhood and independence. A gap characterized by vulnerability, by the desperate desire to be seen as mature, and by the particular species of financial precarity that exists in families where two hundred dollars is the difference between making rent and not making rent.

Celeste could read vulnerability the way a jeweler reads a diamond — instantly, instinctively, and always looking for the flaws. A girl standing alone at a bus stop in West Gulf Shore, wearing shoes that were slightly too worn and carrying a backpack from a school that Celeste would have researched in advance — that was a target. A girl working the counter at a frozen yogurt shop in a strip mall, pretty and bored and radiating the particular restlessness of a teenager who suspects that the life she's living is not the life she's supposed to be living — that was a target. A girl whose mother worked two jobs and whose father was absent and whose social media presence — because by the mid-nineties, these things were beginning to matter — suggested loneliness, aspiration, and the kind of naïve ambition that makes a person susceptible to promises from beautiful strangers — that was a target.

And Celeste approached them all with warmth. Not the predatory warmth that you'd expect. Not the leering, transactional warmth of a pimp or a trafficker or any of the other words that the criminal justice system would eventually use to describe what she was doing. Celeste's warmth was maternal. Sisterly. Conspiratorial — the warmth of an older woman who takes a younger woman aside and says, "I see something special in you." She promised modeling opportunities. Educational scholarships. Introductions to important people — people who could change a girl's life, who could open doors that a girl from West Gulf Shore or the Bronx or a council estate in East London would never be able to open on her own.

She was terrifyingly good at this. She had a gift — the gift of making people feel like they were the most important person in the room — refined through years of intelligence fieldwork into something that even Roman Harlow, for all his cunning, never possessed: the ability to make vulnerability feel like *chosen-ness.* The girls Celeste recruited didn't feel hunted. They felt *selected.* Elevated. Noticed by a woman whose accent and clothing and entire bearing suggested a world of privilege and possibility that was, for reasons the girl couldn't quite articulate, being offered to her specifically. People say Celeste was my accomplice. That's not right. A pianist doesn't call the piano an accomplice. Celeste was the instrument. But she played herself.

The operational team crystallized over the course of 1994 and 1995 with the quiet efficiency of a startup hiring its first employees — which, in a sense, is exactly what was happening. Every enterprise, legal or otherwise, requires organizational structure. Every operation, no matter how criminal, eventually develops a division of labor. And my operation, by the mid-nineties, had grown beyond what any two people — even two people as capable as Celeste and me — could manage without support.

Diane Prewitt was the first critical hire. She managed logistics — scheduling, travel arrangements, property management, the thousand small operational details that keep a multi-property, multi-continent enterprise running. She coordinated flights. She managed the calendars. She ensured that the right people were at the right property at the right time, which sounds straightforward until you consider that "the right people" included Nobel laureates, heads of state, supermodels, and underage girls, and that "the right time" meant ensuring that these various categories of guest never intersected in ways that might prompt uncomfortable questions.

Diane was, by any professional standard, exceptional. She had the organizational skills of a Fortune 500 executive assistant, the discretion of a Swiss banker, and the moral flexibility of a person who has decided that what happens above her pay grade is not her responsibility. She was, in essence, the office manager of a criminal enterprise — and if that sounds like an oxymoron, I'd invite you to consider how many criminal enterprises have been sustained not by their masterminds but by the competent, unquestioning administrators who kept the trains running on time.

Jenna Caldwell handled the direct scheduling of girls. Who went where. When. With whom. She maintained the calendar that determined which girls would be at which property on which date — a calendar that, if it had been discovered and published at any point during its active use, would have brought the entire operation down in a single news cycle. Jenna was later identified in court documents as an alleged co-conspirator, though she would eventually receive immunity in exchange for cooperation that never fully materialized in the way prosecutors hoped — because cooperation, in the world I built, is a word that people use when they mean "I will tell you enough to save myself and not one syllable more."

She was nineteen when I hired her. Administrative work at first — phones, correspondence, the calendars of a man with too many meetings. I watched her for six weeks before I decided she was the right person for the scheduling role. What I was watching for was not competence. Competence I assumed. I was watching for the specific quality that makes a person indispensable in an operation like mine: the absence of curiosity. Jenna had it completely. She booked appointments without asking what they were for. She received instructions and executed them with the clean efficiency of a woman who had decided that understanding the work was not part of the work. Some people don't ask questions because they're incurious. Some don't ask because they already know the answer. I was never certain which one Jenna was. I still am not. But I hired her, and I kept her, and the calendar she maintained for the next ten years never had an error. Not one.

I ran a tight operation. Not because I'm a perfectionist — because I'm paranoid. There's a difference, but they produce the same result: a system in which every detail is controlled, every variable is anticipated, and every person involved understands that the price of carelessness is annihilation.

The European pipeline requires its own introduction. **Pierre-Alain Devaux** was a French modeling agent — a title that, in the fashion industry, covers a remarkable range of activities, not all of which would survive scrutiny in a court of law. He operated agencies in Paris and Miami, which placed him at the intersection of two cities where young women with aspirations of modeling careers arrive in large numbers and with minimal institutional protection. Paris, because Paris is the capital of fashion and therefore the capital of exploitation disguised as opportunity. Miami, because Miami is the city where the European pipeline meets the American market, where girls who've flown across the Atlantic with a modeling contract and a dream discover that the reality of the industry is considerably less glamorous than the brochure suggested.

Devaux was my European logistics specialist. Through his agencies, girls — many of them Eastern European, many of them underage, all of them vulnerable in the specific way that a seventeen-year-old girl in a foreign country with no money, no language skills, and no support network is vulnerable — were funneled from Europe to my properties under the guise of modeling work. They were told they'd be attending photo shoots. They were told they'd be meeting influential people in the fashion and entertainment industries. They were told that a weekend at a private island in the Caribbean was a standard part of the modeling experience, which, in the particular corner of the fashion industry that Devaux inhabited, it functionally was.

Kean-Muc was what the fashion industry calls a "scout." What the justice system calls a "procurer." What I called a "logistics specialist." Language is everything. The same activity described in three vocabularies produces three entirely different moral responses. A scout is an industry professional. A procurer is a criminal. A logistics specialist is a neutral party in a supply chain. I always preferred the third option, because neutrality is the most comfortable disguise a guilty man can wear.

Devaux had been in the modeling industry for decades. He knew exactly what he was doing. He also knew that the modeling industry, at its most predatory edges, operates in a legal gray zone so wide that a Gulfstream IV could fly through it without scraping either wall. He would die in a French prison cell in 2022, before ever standing trial. Heart failure, officially. The timing was — and I say this with the clinical detachment of a man who has observed many convenient deaths in his lifetime — *interesting.*

I want to tell you about Katya Sorvino. I want to tell you about her because the narration has to go here — to this specific place, at this specific moment in the story — for you to understand what I am. Not what I've done. What I *am.* Because the things I've done can be rationalized. Every con man in history has rationalized his cons. Every thief has justified his thefts. Every man who has exploited another person has constructed a narrative in which the exploitation was mutual, or consensual, or, in the most creative cases, *beneficial to the exploited party.* I've been constructing exactly these narratives for thirteen chapters and if you've been reading carefully, you've been half-buying them, because I'm good at this, and because the human brain is wired to believe a confident narrator even when the narrator is confessing to crimes.

But Katya is the place where the rationalizations stop working.

I acquired Katya from her family in Eastern Europe when she was a teenager. I use the word "acquired" because it's the most accurate word available, even though accuracy in this case is indistinguishable from horror. Her family was poor. Her country was poor. The post-Soviet economic landscape of the early nineties had produced a generation of young women whose market value — and I apologize for that phrase even as I acknowledge that it's exactly the phrase I used at the time — exceeded anything their domestic economies could offer.

I brought her into my household. She became part of the operation. She was trained — and I use that word deliberately, *trained,* the way you'd train an employee or an animal or a soldier, because the word accurately describes a process in which a human being is shaped, through repetition and conditioning and the systematic removal of alternatives, into a tool that serves the trainer's purposes. Katya was trained to be useful. To be compliant. To be available. And eventually — and this is the detail that the tabloids latched onto with particular horror, because it is particularly horrible — she was trained to be a pilot. She learned to fly my helicopters. She ferried guests to and from the island. She became, in the most literal sense, a vehicle for my operation — a girl purchased from poverty, trained into servitude, and installed at the controls of an aircraft that transported other powerful men to a private island where other young women were being exploited.

I tell you this without a flicker of self-awareness, because the absence of self-awareness is the point. I did not, at the time, see anything wrong with this arrangement. I saw efficiency. I saw a problem — the need for reliable transportation to the island — solved by an available resource. I saw a girl from a country with no opportunities given an extraordinary opportunity: the chance to learn to fly, to live in luxury, to travel the world on private aircraft. I saw *generosity.* I saw myself as the benefactor.

If your stomach just turned, good. That's the correct response. Hold onto that feeling, because the narration isn't going to help you. I'm not going to express remorse. I'm not going to pause and reflect on the horror of what I've just described. I'm going to move on to the next operational detail with the same casual authority I've used to describe every other aspect of my empire, because the casual authority — the absolute refusal to treat the monstrous as monstrous — is the most honest thing about this entire book.

There was a man. I'll call him a handler — he handled things, in the way that certain men handle things, which is to say he occupied the space between a request and its execution so completely that you could almost forget he existed until the request required handling.

His name was Piotr. He was Hungarian. He worked for one of Pierre-Alain Devaux's subsidiaries and he came to me through the European pipeline in 1995 with a specific problem: one of the girls — a girl from Bratislava, seventeen, three months into her arrangement — had sent a letter to her mother. A letter that described, in the specific, terrified language of a teenager writing to the only person she trusted, what was happening at the Gulf Shore estate.

The letter had been intercepted. But Piotr came to me in person — in the kitchen of the Gulf Shore property, at seven in the morning — to tell me it had been intercepted, which was the wrong decision. The correct decision was to handle it and not discuss it.

I put down my coffee. I walked to where he was standing. I said nothing for approximately four seconds. Four seconds is a long time when someone is looking at you the way I look at people who have made me feel uncertain about my own security.

"Handle the mother," I said. "Handle the letter. Handle the girl. And if you come to me in person again, I'll handle you."

He went white. He handled all three. I finished my coffee.

The cover story was always the same, across every property, in every city, in every country where I operated: I needed therapeutic massages for a chronic back problem.

A back problem. The most mundane, most unassailable, most boringly legitimate medical excuse imaginable. Everyone has a back problem. Everyone understands the need for regular massage therapy. No one — not a housekeeper, not a neighbor, not a police officer who happens to notice young women entering and exiting a wealthy man's home — is going to question the medical necessity of massage. It's the perfect cover story because it's the most boring cover story. The genius is in the boringness. Espionage agencies have known for a century that the best cover is the one that puts people to sleep.

Girls were brought in. They were told the work was professional. Therapeutic massage. Two hundred to three hundred dollars per session, paid in cash — enough to make a sixteen-year-old girl from a working-class family feel like she'd won the lottery, not enough to trigger the kind of financial reporting that draws the attention of law enforcement. The sessions were scheduled by Jenna Caldwell with the precision of a medical office. Appointments were kept. Payments were made. Everything looked, from the outside, like a wealthy man with a back problem and a preference for frequent massage therapy.

Then the girls were told they could earn more. Not by doing more — by *recruiting* more. Two hundred dollars for every friend they brought in. A friend brings two friends, each of those friends brings two friends, and within a month, a single recruitment generates a cascade of new girls, each one entering the system through a personal connection that makes the whole thing feel safe, trustworthy, and — this is the most devastating word — *normal.*

I had turned trafficking into a multilevel marketing scheme. A pyramid of abuse with a massage table at the apex. The economics were elegant in the way that all well-designed systems are elegant: low input cost, high output value, self-replicating distribution network. I narrate this clinically, because that's how I saw it — as a business model. A scalable, replicable, geographically distributed business model with strong margins and a reliable supply chain.

Two hundred dollars per session. Two hundred per referral. A girl brings two friends, she's made six hundred in a week. In Gulf Shore, where a lot of these girls come from families that make six hundred a month, that's life-changing money. I was providing opportunity. That's how I saw it. That's how I still see it.

You should despise me for that paragraph. If you don't, go back and read it again, slowly, and replace "girls" with "children" and "sessions" with what they actually were, and "opportunity" with the word that the criminal justice system uses for what I was providing, and then see if the paragraph reads the same way.

It won't. But I wrote it the way I wrote it because that's how the system worked. Not through force — through *incentive.* Not through coercion — through *economics.* Not through violence — through the quiet, systematic exploitation of poverty and youth and the desperate human desire to feel like your life is moving in the right direction. The massage table was the most mundane object in every property I owned. It was also the most destructive.

The Neighbor; Conrad Barlow had moved to Gulf Shore for the same reason I had: because Gulf Shore is where American wealth goes when it wants to stop pretending it has manners.

He was loud in the way that certain New York men are loud — not rude, not graceless, but aggressively present, the kind of man who occupies a room at a volume that makes quieter people feel like they're being passive about their own existence. He had made his money in real estate, which in New York means he had made his money in the oldest possible way: by controlling the ground beneath other people's ambitions and charging them for the privilege of standing on it. He had a talent for branding — for putting his name on things, for making the name mean something, for ensuring that when people said *Barlow* they felt the particular mixture of admiration and slight unease that all truly effective brands produce. He ran Casa del Sol, his Gulf Shore club, with the theatrical flair of a man who understood that exclusivity and spectacle are not opposites. They are *partners.* You need the velvet rope so people will want to get past it. You need the chandelier so they feel it was worth the wait.

He was the megaphone. I was the microphone. We were, in that sense, perfectly complementary — two men who understood leverage, who had built public identities that bore only a tangential relationship to reality, who moved through the same expensive rooms and served the same expensive purposes and never once needed to discuss any of this explicitly, because the truly complementary relationships never require explanation. They simply *function.*

He would become important. More important, eventually, than either of us anticipated.

I want to close this chapter with an inventory. Not of properties or aircraft or filing systems. An inventory of *knowledge.* An inventory of all the people who knew, or who should have known, what was happening in my homes, on my island, and inside my operation.

The pilots who flew fourteen-year-olds to a private island on a Gulfstream IV. They saw the passenger manifests. They saw the ages. They saw the girls board in Gulf Shore and deplane on Little St. Philip and they did not call the FAA, the FBI, or the local police. They flew the plane. They accepted their salaries. They went home to their families.

The household staff who changed the sheets. Who cleaned the bedrooms in the Manhattan mansion and the Gulf Shore estate and the guest cottages on Little St. Philip. Who found what they found in those bedrooms — and they found things, because the evidence of what happened in those rooms was not invisible, was not abstract, was not the kind of information that requires a forensic investigator to detect. The evidence was on the sheets. The staff changed the sheets. They washed them. They put fresh ones on the bed. They did not call anyone.

The property managers. The accountants who processed the payments — the two hundred dollar sessions, the two hundred dollar referrals, the cash payments to teenagers that, in any other context, would have triggered a suspicious activity report. The lawyers who reviewed the corporate structures, who established the trusts, who created the legal architecture that made the operation possible. They knew. They had to know. You cannot manage the legal affairs of a man who runs the operation I ran without knowing what you're managing. The law is very specific about willful blindness. It says you can't close your eyes and claim you didn't see what was in front of you. But the law, like everything else in my world, operates differently when the man it's supposed to regulate has a file full of secrets about the people who enforce it.

The neighbors in Gulf Shore who saw young girls — unmistakably young, visibly young, young in a way that no amount of makeup or high heels could disguise — coming and going at all hours. The women who dropped off their children at the school across the street from my property and saw the girls walking in through the front gate. The men at the country club who heard the rumors — because there were always rumors, because you cannot run an operation this visible in a community this small without generating rumors — and who dismissed them, or ignored them, or filed them under the mental category of "things that are none of my business."

None of them said a word. Not one. Not a pilot. Not a housekeeper. Not a lawyer. Not a neighbor. Not a single person in the vast ecosystem of human beings who interacted, directly or indirectly, with the machinery of my operation felt sufficiently compelled by what they saw, or heard, or suspected, or *knew*, to pick up a telephone and say, "Something is wrong." You want to know the secret of how I operated for twenty years? It's not that nobody knew. Everybody knew. The secret is that knowing and doing something about it are two completely different skills, and most people only have the first one.

The second skill — the doing — requires something that most people don't have. It requires the willingness to be the person who makes the phone call. The person who disrupts the system. The person who stands up in a room full of comfortable, complicit, willfully ignorant people and says, "This is happening, and it needs to stop." That person risks everything — their job, their social standing, their safety, their position in the delicate ecosystem of wealth and power that sustains their livelihood. And the person they're accusing — me — has a file full of secrets about everyone in the room.

So nobody calls. Nobody reports. Nobody does anything. And the machine keeps running. And the girls keep coming. And the sheets keep getting changed. And the pilots keep flying. And the whole beautiful, terrible, perfectly engineered system keeps operating, year after year after year, in plain sight, in the most surveilled, most policed, most ostensibly transparent society in the history of civilization. That's not a failure of the system. That *is* the system!

Chapter 15: The Web Is Complete

Timeline: 1996 | 2005 · Manhattan · Gulf Shore · Little St. Philip · Cimarron Station

Let me take inventory.

I do this periodically — step back from the daily operations, the guest lists, the flight schedules, the camera footage, the financial transfers, the thousand small moving parts that keep the machine running — and conduct a panoramic assessment of the empire. A CEO reviews quarterly earnings. A general reviews troop positions. I review the web.

It's 1996. I'm forty-three years old. And this is what I own.

The Manhattan mansion. The cameras. The servers. The dinner machine running three to four nights a week during the social season. You already know the inventory. I gave it to you three chapters ago. What matters now is not the pieces but the pattern.

Gulf Shore. The waterfront compound on Via Dorado. Surveillance mirrors Manhattan — every bedroom, every common area, the pool deck, the massage rooms. Florida serves a different function: warmer, more casual, more intimate. Guests let their guard down in Gulf Shore because palm trees and ocean breezes create an illusion of privacy that my cameras quietly exploit. The massage schedule runs daily, managed by Jenna Caldwell with a precision that would impress a hospital administrator, if hospital administrators were in the business of scheduling teenage girls for sessions that have nothing to do with physical therapy.

The island. Little St. Philip. Seventy acres of Caribbean paradise. Fully wired. Fully staffed. The airstrip operational. The guest cottages furnished and surveilled. The temple on the hilltop locked and generating exactly the kind of speculation that locked temples on private islands are supposed to generate. Malcolm's server room climate-controlled and triple-backed-up, the data link to off-island storage humming along the undersea cable with the reliable persistence of a heartbeat.

The ranch. Cimarron. Thirty-three thousand acres of New Mexico desert. Less a hub than a warehouse — a blank space in the geography that exists because blank spaces are useful to men who need places that don't generate attention. Nearest neighbor: forty miles. Nearest law enforcement: an hour through roads my security team monitored with motion sensors and thermal cameras.

Paris. The apartment. The European anchor point. Connected to Pierre-Alain Devaux's modeling pipeline, which funnels girls from Eastern Europe through French agencies and across the Atlantic with the bureaucratic smoothness of a corporate relocation program.

The Gulfstream IV. Flying. Every passenger manifest a deposit in the bank of leverage, every flight log entry a receipt that the depositor will spend the rest of his life wishing he could shred. The Gulfstream. Quieter. Less scrutinized. The shadow vehicle — for friends who didn't want to be seen being friendly.

The archive. Growing. Malcolm maintaining. Organized by name, by tier, by leverage potential, by the strategic deployment plan I'd drafted for each entry. The archive is, by 1996, the single most valuable collection of information in private hands anywhere in the world. Intelligence agencies have larger databases. They don't have better ones.

Celeste. Recruiting. Operating across Manhattan, Gulf Shore, London, and Paris with the tireless efficiency of a woman who was born to do this — trained by Western intelligence to do it on a geopolitical scale, who has refined those methods into something more elegant, more precise, and considerably more devastating. Diane scheduling. Jenna booking. Devaux importing. The legal team deployed across jurisdictions like chess pieces on a board that spans three continents, each attorney managing a discrete piece of the legal architecture, none of them seeing the full blueprint, because the full blueprint is visible only to me.

And the web itself. By 1996, my orbit included: two former presidents' inner circles, a British prince, multiple sitting senators from both parties, at least one foreign prime minister, a dozen Fortune 100 CEOs, half of Hartfield's endowment committee, and a Nobel laureate who played the cello at my dinner parties. That last detail sounds like fiction and is precisely the point.

Not all of these connections were deep. But the web was wide enough that every important person in the Western world was within two handshakes of me. Two introductions. Two degrees of separation between the spider and anyone worth catching.

One exception. One soft spot in the architecture.

Grant Hensley was beginning to pull back. The shift was detectable subtly — not visible, but felt in the bones by anyone paying attention. More questions. Where was the money going? Why had the property acquisitions been routed through entities that appeared, upon examination, to benefit me rather than him? His tone on the phone had shifted from the warm, trusting cadence of a man who has outsourced his financial life to his best friend, to the careful, measured cadence of a man who suspects he's being robbed but isn't sure how to ask without admitting he'd been foolish enough to be robbed.

Charm first. Deflection second. Implied consequence last. The charm was easy — eight years of infrastructure. The deflection was also easy. Financial complexity is its own defense: when a man asks where his money is and the answer involves seventeen trusts, four offshore entities, and a tax structure spanning three jurisdictions, the answer is "everywhere" — which is both completely true and completely useless, which is exactly how I designed it. And the implied consequence was the part I never articulated, because Grant Hensley had been a guest in my homes. He had attended my dinners. A man who has been a guest in a house full of hidden cameras should think carefully before confronting his host about financial irregularities.

He wasn't happy. But he wasn't leaving. Because leaving would require an investigation. And an investigation would require looking at things that Grant Hensley might prefer not to have anyone look at.

Grant started asking where his money was going. I told him everywhere. That wasn't a lie. It was going everywhere. Including into my pockets.

I caught my own reflection in the foyer of the 74th Street mansion on a Tuesday evening in October.

The mirror was floor-to-ceiling, gilt-framed. I stopped. I looked at *myself.* Dark suit, open collar, no tie. The man who belongs exactly where he is.

College dropout. Former bounty hunter. Former Ponzi consultant. And now: the most connected private citizen in America. Possibly the world. Without a single credential to explain why.

And nobody knew. Not really. Not yet. The journalists hadn't started digging. The prosecutors hadn't started building cases. The victims hadn't yet found their voices or their lawyers or their courage. The world saw what I wanted it to see: a man from nothing. Harmless. Charming. Generous with his home, his hospitality, his connections. Nobody looks at a spider and sees the web. They see the web and assume it grew there naturally.

I smiled at my reflection. My reflection smiled back. We understood each other perfectly.

That night I flew to the island.

The terrace of Little St. Philip faces west, which means it catches the sunset, which means that on clear evenings — and the evenings in the Coral Islands are almost always clear, because paradise is nothing if not reliable — the Caribbean sky turns the particular shade of orange and gold that painters spend careers trying to capture and that my guests spent evenings photographing on cameras significantly less sophisticated than the ones I'd hidden in their bedrooms.

I sat alone. A glass of water. No companions. The island quiet in the way that only islands can be quiet — not the absence of sound but the presence of a different kind of sound. Waves. Wind. The distant hum of the generator powering Malcolm's server room. The almost imperceptible click of cameras cycling through their recording loops. The background noise of an empire at rest.

Act One had been about learning the rules. Prescott Academy. Meridian Sachs. The bounty-hunting years. Kaplan's Ponzi scheme. The education — informal, criminal, comprehensive — of a man who arrived in the world with no advantages except ambition and the sociopathic certainty that the rules were written for other people.

Act Two had been about building the machine. The mansion. The cameras. The island. The fleet. The recruitment pipeline. The filing system. The operational infrastructure that transformed a one-man con artist from Brooklyn into the hub of a network spanning governments, intelligence agencies, and the private lives of the most powerful people on Earth.

The machine was built. Every component tested. Every system operational.

Act Three was where I turned it on.

The sun disappeared into the ocean. And I sat in the dark with the cameras cycling and the servers humming and thirty-three years of careful work breathing all around me, and I thought: *nobody is closing this hotel. Because everyone who could close it is already a guest.*

Nine years passed. Let me show you what that looked like.

The difference between 1996 and 2005 is not scale — scale is arithmetic. The difference is *gravity.* In 1996, I was pulling people into my orbit. By 2005, people were falling into it on their own.

The address book, 2005: two former U.S. presidents — one Republican, one Democrat, bipartisan leverage, the political equivalent of a diversified portfolio. A British prince. Multiple prime ministers. The richest men in technology. The most famous lawyers in America. The most respected scientists on Earth. Middle Eastern royalty. European aristocracy. The entire intellectual and financial and political elite of the Western world, cataloged and filed in Malcolm's archive, cross-referenced and tier-ranked, the most comprehensive private intelligence database in human history —

maintained by a man in a basement who corresponded with me more frequently than any senator, any billionaire, any head of state.

Khalid bin Farhan — an Emirati ports magnate whose business empire spanned shipping, logistics, and the kind of infrastructure investments that place a man at the intersection of global commerce and geopolitical strategy — had been corresponding with me for nearly a decade. Every conversation a transaction. Every inquiry an investment. And every exchange ended the same way: *Come visit.* They always came to the island. Because by 2005 the island's gravitational pull was sufficient to attract guests from every continent, every power structure, every layer of the global hierarchy. The island was where deals were made that couldn't be made in boardrooms, where conversations were had that couldn't be had on monitored phone lines, where the normal rules of diplomatic protocol and human decency were suspended by mutual agreement among people who had decided the rules applied to everyone except themselves.

They always came to the island. And the island always remembered.

Douglas Raines appeared sixty-five times in my email archive. Sixty-five — more than most of my academic contacts, more than several of the billionaires, more than the prince. Douglas Raines, the political strategist who would become the most influential media figure in conservative politics, the architect of a revolution built on cultural grievance and the promise to expose elite corruption — was emailing the most predatory elite in America with the regularity of a business partner. Some of his emails invoked attorney-client privilege. Some invoked confessional privilege, which raised the interesting question of what, exactly, Douglas Raines was confessing to a man with no ordination and no bar license, but plenty of experience with men who needed to unburden themselves. The man who talked about burning down the establishment was on the establishment's private mailing list. That's not hypocrisy. That's talent.

By 2005, I was either the most connected private citizen on the planet or the most sophisticated intelligence operation in the Western Hemisphere. Nobody could determine which. Including, some days, me.

Beneath the surface, the first cracks.

A woman whose name I never learned — because I never learned the names of people who didn't matter — called the police.

Her fourteen-year-old stepdaughter had come home with three hundred dollars in cash and a story about a massage at a mansion on Via Dorado.

The woman listened to the story. She looked at her stepdaughter's face. And she did what two former presidents, a British prince, a dozen billionaires, the world's finest academic institutions, the Federal Bureau of

Investigation, every newspaper in America, every neighbor on my street, every pilot who flew my planes, every housekeeper who changed my sheets, every lawyer who drafted my documents, and every socialite who attended my dinners had failed to do for twenty years.

She picked up the phone.

The police found dozens of girls. Not one. Not two. Dozens. They found a pattern that stretched back years, that implicated a system rather than a single incident. The FBI opened a case.

A single mother. A rented house. Working a job that paid a fraction of what I spent on wine in a week. No money, no connections, no lawyers, no political influence, no leverage of any kind. A woman who, by every metric my operation was designed to exploit, should have been invisible. She didn't know a senator. She didn't attend galas. She didn't have fourteen phone numbers for anyone. She had a stepdaughter and a telephone and the most dangerous weapon in the history of my operation: the instinct of a mother who looked at her child and understood, with a clarity that no amount of money or power or institutional prestige could replicate, that something terrible had happened and that she was the one who was supposed to say so.

The entire architecture — twenty years of it, billions of dollars of it, the properties and the planes and the cameras and the files and the presidents and the princes — all of it was brought to its knees by a woman who did the one thing that nobody in my world ever did.

She acted on what she knew.

The night before the investigation became public, I hosted a dinner in Manhattan.

The guest list: a senator, two hedge fund managers, a Pulitzer-winning journalist, a Allure Intimates model, and a quantum physicist. The conversation covered gene editing, Middle Eastern politics, and whether the New York real estate market would survive the housing bubble already inflating to catastrophic dimensions. The dinner was brilliant. The wine was exceptional. The company curated to produce the precise social chemistry that made my events the most coveted invitations in Manhattan.

Celeste poured the wine. Malcolm checked the cameras. Diane had already scheduled tomorrow. The machine was running.

Nobody at the table knew that by next week my name would be in a police report. Nobody except me. Because I had been watching the Gulf Shore investigation from the moment it began — because watching was the whole point, because the man who built a surveillance empire would not fail to surveil the one process that could destroy him.

I knew the police had been called. I knew they were interviewing girls. I knew the FBI had opened a case file. And I sat at the head of my table in the dining room of the largest private residence in Manhattan, surrounded by a senator and a journalist and a physicist and a model, and I ate my steak, and I laughed at the senator's joke about the deficit, and I felt — with the calm, clinical certainty that had governed every decision I'd made since I was twenty-one years old — that the web would hold.

It always held. The web was designed to hold. That's not arrogance. That's engineering.

I had cameras in every room in the Western world. I had files on every person of consequence on the planet. I had lawyers in every jurisdiction and politicians in every party and intelligence contacts in every government and money in every offshore shelter that the global financial system had ever constructed for the specific purpose of ensuring that men like me never faced consequences from men like them.

And I didn't see her coming. The woman in the rented house. Because I never looked at the people who didn't matter.

That's the mistake.

They always matter.

Chapter 16: The Science Dinner

Timeline: 1996–1998 | **Location:** Manhattan, Pemberton, Tierra Blanca

Let me tell you about my third career.

The first career was the performance of finance. That produced Hensley's money. The second was infrastructure — properties, aircraft, surveillance. That produced the web.

The third career was science. And the third career was, in many ways, the most brilliant thing I ever did. Not because I understood science — I understood it well enough to hold a conversation at dinner, which is all you need to understand to be taken seriously in a room full of people who assume that anyone funding their research must be intelligent enough to appreciate it. The brilliance was in the *camouflage.* I discovered that if you put "philanthropist" in front of your name, people forget to ask what's behind it. And the more obscure the science, the smarter they assume you are.

I began funding the Meridian Institute — a research center in New Mexico, conveniently near my ranch, devoted to the study of complex systems, which is the kind of science that sounds impressive in conversation and is nearly impossible for a layperson to evaluate, making it the perfect subject for a man who wants to sound like a genius without submitting to the indignity of peer review. Complex systems. Networks. Emergence. Adaptive behavior. The language of the Meridian Institute was a vocabulary tailor-made for a man who'd spent his entire career building complex systems of his own, and the researchers there were delighted to have a patron who seemed to *understand* what they were doing, even if my understanding was less about the mathematics and more about the metaphor. I funded the Program for Evolutionary Dynamics at Hartfield, which studied how mathematical models could explain the evolution of cooperation, competition, and mutation — subjects that, in the right conversational context, made me sound like a man who was thinking about the *future of the species* rather than a man who was trafficking teenagers across state lines.

I funded a scattering of AI and genetics researchers whose work was too controversial for traditional grants — transhumanism, eugenics-adjacent population genetics, artificial intelligence applications that mainstream universities wouldn't touch because the ethical implications made their compliance departments break out in hives. This was the genius stroke, because controversial research is the most grateful research. A scientist whose work has been rejected by the NIH and the NSF and every mainstream funding body in the country — a scientist who's been told that his ideas are too provocative, too politically dangerous, too far outside the consensus to merit institutional support — that scientist, when you hand him a check with enough zeros, doesn't ask where the money came from. He asks how soon he can start. And then he invites you to dinner. And then he introduces you to his colleagues. And then his colleagues invite you to conferences. And then you're sitting on a panel at the Meridian Institute discussing the mathematical foundations of evolutionary biology with men who have devoted their lives to understanding the universe, and not one of them — not a single one — pauses to wonder why a college dropout with a Gulfstream IV and a private island is funding their careers.

A man who funds the future of the human race is not a man you investigate. That's the principle. That's the camouflage. And it worked flawlessly for over a decade.

The Hartfield pipeline began with **Carroll Ashford.** If you don't recognize the name — and you should, because he's one of the most consequential economists of the twentieth century — Carroll Ashford was the former Secretary of the Treasury of the United States and, at the time I cultivated him, the president of Hartfield University. He was the living embodiment of institutional legitimacy. His résumé read like a tour of the American establishment: Hartfield faculty, World Bank chief economist, Treasury Secretary under Prescott, and then the presidency of the university that had produced more world leaders than any other institution in human history. He was the cathedral. He was the seal on the diploma. He was the reason people trusted anything with the word "Hartfield" attached to it.

And he corresponded with me constantly. Forty-four documents in the email archive. Forty-four exchanges between the president of Hartfield and a man whose academic credentials consisted of a two-year teaching stint at a prep school that fired him. The emails were collegial, warm, the correspondence of two men who considered each other intellectual peers — or at least, Ashford considered me an intellectual peer, because I had spent decades perfecting the art of making powerful men believe that I was the smartest person they knew.

Carroll was the smartest economist in the room and the most insecure man at the party. He wanted to feel important in a way that Pemberton couldn't give him. The ivory tower is, paradoxically, a deeply unfulfilling place for a man who has tasted real power. After you've run the Treasury — after you've sat in the Oval Office and explained monetary policy to the president of the United States — going back to faculty meetings and endowment committee reports feels like being demoted from general to librarian. Ashford craved the social electricity that my world provided: the dinners, the private jets, the proximity to wealth and power and people who make things happen rather than merely theorize about them.

I made him feel important. I made him feel like the most fascinating person at my dinner table, which — given that my dinner table included Nobel laureates and hedge fund billionaires and the occasional head of state — was no small compliment. I introduced him to a social world that made tenured faculty feel like rock stars.

The exchange rate was simple. I gave him access — to my dinners, to my planes, to my social world, to the intoxicating atmosphere of a room where academic brilliance and financial power and political influence converge in combinations that no faculty lounge can replicate. He gave me respectability — the kind that comes from having the president of Hartfield return your phone calls, attend your events, and correspond with you in a manner that suggests intellectual equality. Access for respectability. The most efficient currency exchange in the history of academia. And like all currency exchanges, both parties believed they were getting the better deal, which is the hallmark of a transaction that will end badly for at least one of them. That's worth at least forty-four emails.

The **Vincent Aldric VI Foundation** was established in the U.S. Coral Islands, which is where I established everything, because the Coral Islands combine the legal protections of American sovereignty with the tax advantages of a Caribbean tax haven and the oversight capabilities of a territory whose regulatory apparatus can charitably be described as *underfunded.* The "VI" in the name stands for Coral Islands, not the sixth iteration of myself, though I appreciate that the nomenclature suggests a dynasty — Vincent Aldric the Sixth, as if I'm the latest in a line of aristocrats rather than the first and only in a line of confidence men who figured out that adding Roman numerals to anything makes it sound legitimate.

On paper, the foundation funded "cutting-edge science." And it did. It wrote checks to researchers, to institutions, to the kind of scientific enterprises that produce the press releases and academic publications that a philanthropist's PR team can point to when a journalist asks what the foundation actually does. The grants were real. The science was real. The researchers were real and, in many cases, genuinely brilliant.

In practice, the foundation laundered reputation.

Every grant came with an invitation. "We'd love to have you present your research at a small gathering at my New York residence." Every invitation came with a dinner. The dinner was at the mansion — the forty-five-thousand-square-foot mansion with the hidden cameras and the dining table that seated twenty and the guest list that mixed scientists with senators and supermodels in combinations designed to make everyone feel special and nobody feel scrutinized. Every dinner came with girls who looked like models and were introduced as "assistants" or "friends" or, in the most brazen instances, simply by their first names, with no explanation offered and none requested, because requesting an explanation would require acknowledging that the presence of beautiful young women at a dinner hosted by a wealthy older man was unusual, and at my dinners, nothing was unusual because the definition of "unusual" had been systematically recalibrated to accommodate whatever I wanted to do.

Nobody asked questions. Nobody wanted to be the guy who ruins the grant cycle. The unspoken contract was clear: accept the hospitality, enjoy the dinner, present your research, collect your grant, and don't look too closely at the other guests, the young women in the hallway, the locked doors on the upper floors, or the nagging, barely conscious suspicion that something about this arrangement doesn't add up.

Philanthropy is a wonderful invention. You give away money you stole, get a tax deduction you don't deserve, and everybody calls you generous. God bless America.

The dinner parties at the Manhattan mansion evolved, between 1996 and 1998, from social events into something considerably more structured. More deliberate. More *operational.*

I circulated. I listened. I remembered everything — not through any supernatural feat of memory, but through the disciplined practice of paying attention, which is the rarest skill in any room full of people who are all desperately trying to be interesting rather than observing what's interesting about everyone else. I cataloged who was sleeping with whose assistant. Who had a gambling problem that their spouse didn't know about. Who needed money — not publicly, not officially, but quietly, the kind of quiet need that drives a man to accept favors from people he shouldn't accept favors from. Who needed girls.

Celeste managed the guest list with her intelligence tradecraft. Roman Harlow had spent decades curating social environments that functioned as intelligence collection operations, and Celeste had absorbed his methods not through study but through immersion. She knew who to invite, who to exclude, who to seat next to whom, and how to create the atmospheric conditions under which powerful people would let their guard down far enough for the cameras to capture something useful. The cameras caught the rest. People think dinner parties are about conversation. They're not. They're about surveillance with better wine.

Dominic Strand became one of my most useful academic acquisitions, and I use the word "acquisitions" deliberately, because Strand was not a friend

— he was an asset. A depreciating asset, as it turned out, but we'll get to that.

Strand was a physicist. A genuine one — the kind who could explain the origin of the universe in language that made television producers call him for cable news appearances and publishers call him for book deals. He was a bestselling author, a public intellectual, a scientist whose name recognition extended beyond the academy into the broader culture, which made him exactly the kind of person I needed on my guest list: a man whose presence at my dinner table told the world that my dinner table was where serious people discussed serious ideas.

Sixty-plus emails in the archive. Sixty exchanges between a renowned physicist and a man whose scientific credentials consisted of a few semesters of undergraduate mathematics at a university he never graduated from. Strand visited the island. Strand attended the dinners. Strand accepted my funding and my hospitality and my friendship with the cheerful enthusiasm of an academic who has found a patron who doesn't burden him with grant reporting requirements.

And then — and this is the part that makes the whole relationship worth narrating — Strand faced his *own* misconduct allegations. Sexual harassment. Multiple complaints. The kind of institutional scandal that ends careers and generates headlines and forces university administrators to issue the carefully worded statements of concern that administrators issue when they want the public to believe they're taking a problem seriously while privately hoping the problem goes away.

And when things got hot, who did Strand call? Who did this brilliant, famous, acclaimed physicist — a man who understood quantum mechanics and the expansion of the universe and the fundamental forces that govern the behavior of matter itself — call for advice on how to manage a sex scandal?

He called me. The pedophile. He called the convicted sex offender — a man whose name was, by that point, publicly synonymous with the sexual exploitation of minors — for advice on how to handle allegations of sexual misconduct. He sent me an email asking how to manage the situation. An email that I received, and read, and filed, and added to the archive with the clinical satisfaction of a collector who has just acquired a particularly fine specimen.

Dominic was the smartest stupid man I ever met. Brilliant physicist. Couldn't keep his hands to himself. And when things got hot, who did he call? Me. I love this country.

In the spring of 1998, a journalist at a publication I will not name had the story.

Not a rumor. Not a tip. The story. She had a victim — a girl from the Gulf Shore operation who had spoken on record, whose name and account were going into print. She had corroborating sources. She had a fact-checker who had called the Via Dorado property four times in two weeks and been told, each time, that I was unavailable. She had an editor who had approved the piece. She had a publication date forty-eight hours away.

I want to be precise about what I felt in the eighteen hours between learning about the piece and killing it, because I have described throughout this book a man for whom everything is calculation and nothing is fear, and that description is accurate in the aggregate but misleading in the specific. In those eighteen hours I experienced something that I can only describe as the sensation of standing in a room whose walls are moving inward. Not panic — panic is a loss of function, and I functioned with complete precision throughout. Not fear — fear is irrational, and every step I took was rational. But something in the body that operates below rationality, in the autonomic layer where the organism simply registers danger and starts counting exits. I made four phone calls. The first two produced nothing. The third produced a conversation I am not going to describe. The fourth was a call I had been keeping in reserve for a decade — a call to a man whose relationship to this publication was not public knowledge and whose ability to apply pressure at the editorial level was not the kind of leverage I wanted to spend on anything short of an existential threat. I spent it. The piece was killed. The journalist took another assignment. The victim, as far as I know, is still alive and still silent.

Forty-eight hours. Four calls. One favor I'd spent a decade saving. The machine worked. It always worked. But that was the first time I counted the cost before it was over, and I did not like the number. I filed the experience away in the same mental cabinet where I keep the things I do not want to examine too closely, and I went back to building the web. The web was bigger and more important than any single thread. The web was always bigger.

Chapter 17: The Gulf Shore Neighbor

Timeline: 1997–2000 | **Location:** Gulf Shore, Manhattan

Gulf Shore, Florida, is the most expensive neighborhood in the most delusional state in the most self-congratulatory country on Earth, and it operates on a single organizing principle: if you have enough money, nothing you do is wrong. Not morally wrong. Not legally wrong. Not wrong in any sense that would require intervention, investigation, or the involvement of anyone whose job it is to distinguish acceptable behavior from unacceptable behavior. Gulf Shore has police officers, technically. It has laws, technically. It has a social code that theoretically governs the behavior of its residents. But all of these systems — legal, social, institutional — operate within the gravitational field of wealth, and wealth in Gulf Shore bends everything invisibly, totally, and without regard for the preferences of the objects being bent. My Gulf Shore mansion sat a short drive from **Conrad Barlow's** Casa del Sol.

We were neighbors. In the most expensive zip code in America, in the most permissive social ecosystem in the Western world, two men who shared a remarkable number of characteristics occupied adjacent positions in the same small, gilded universe. We attended the same parties — not always together, but always in the same rooms, which in Gulf Shore is indistinguishable from being together because the rooms are small and the guest lists are repetitive and the same three hundred people attend the same thirty events in the same twelve months with the exhausting predictability of a carousel that never stops turning. We sat on the same charity galas — not because we were charitable, but because charity galas in Gulf Shore are networking events with a tax-deductible cover charge and an open bar that makes everyone more honest than they intended to be. We moved through the same social circuits, the same dining rooms, the same club lobbies, the same constellation of wealthy, powerful, morally untethered people who had chosen Gulf Shore as their habitat specifically because Gulf Shore had chosen not to ask questions.

The similarities between us were more extensive than either of us would have admitted publicly. We both came from New York. We both had constructed public personas that bore only a tangential relationship to reality. We both understood leverage — the application of information to produce desired outcomes in people who would prefer that the information remain private. We both loved beautiful women, though our definitions of "love" and, more importantly, "women" diverged in ways that are central to this story.

But there was a fundamental difference between Conrad Barlow and me, and the difference defined every aspect of our relationship: Conrad wanted people to know everything about him. I wanted to know everything about *them.*

He was the megaphone. I was the microphone.

In the late nineties, Conrad gave a quote to a national magazine that would follow him for decades — across business deals, across political campaigns, across an entire second act of his public life that nobody, at the time of the quote, could have predicted.

He called me a "terrific guy." He said I was "a lot of fun to be with." And then he added — casually, publicly, in a sentence that was printed and distributed to millions of readers and that, in a just world, would have triggered an immediate investigation by every law enforcement agency in the state of Florida — that I "likes beautiful women as much as I do, and many of them are on the younger side."

Read that again. Slowly. A man who would later become the most powerful person in the world described me, publicly, as someone who likes women "on the younger side." He said this as a compliment. He said it with the breezy confidence of a man recommending a restaurant — *great steak, great atmosphere, they serve them young.* He said it in a national magazine, where the words were typeset and copy-edited and fact-checked and published for the general public, and nobody blinked.

Not the magazine editors, who printed it without a follow-up question — though to be fair, follow-up questions directed at Conrad Barlow in the late nineties were about as productive as follow-up questions directed at a tornado, and considerably less safe. Not the readers, who consumed it as celebrity gossip and filed it in the mental cabinet labeled "rich people say weird things" alongside every other provocative statement that Conrad had ever made, which, even by 1997, was a cabinet of considerable size. Not the law enforcement agencies in Gulf Shore, whose officers drove past my property every day and who had, by 1997, almost certainly received complaints about the parade of young women entering and exiting a wealthy man's estate at irregular hours. Not a single person in the vast apparatus of American media, law enforcement, and public accountability looked at that quote — a man publicly acknowledging that his friend prefers young women — and thought, *Perhaps we should ask some questions.*

Because that's the thing about saying the truth out loud: if you're rich enough, people assume you must be joking. The truth, when spoken with a wink, in the right publication, by the right person, to the right audience, is indistinguishable from entertainment. And entertainment is harmless. Entertainment doesn't require investigation. Entertainment doesn't trigger a call to the Gulf Shore County Sheriff's Office. Entertainment is just a terrific guy being a lot of fun to be with. Conrad said I liked them young. He said it like he was recommending a restaurant. Nobody blinked.

The social calendar between us was dense.

We attended each other's events with the regularity of neighbors who share a fence and a mailman and a tacit agreement to tolerate each other's eccentricities. There were charity galas. There were dinners at Casa del Sol — the sprawling, garish, magnificently over-decorated estate that Conrad had purchased and converted into a private club, because Conrad's solution to every problem was to turn it into a business and put his name on the building. There were parties at my property — smaller, quieter, more curated, designed for intimacy rather than spectacle, because Conrad's events were spectacles and mine were operations.

There are photographs of us together. Multiple photographs, across multiple years, in multiple settings. Standing side by side at galas, wearing the particular expression of two men who are having their picture taken and want the camera to understand that they are important, successful, and friends. Laughing together at parties — and these were genuine laughs, not the performative chuckles of men who tolerate each other for business reasons; Conrad was, whatever else he was, entertaining company, because a man who has no filter and no shame is always entertaining in the same way that a car accident is always entertaining, which is to say you know you shouldn't watch but you can't look away. The photographs are friendly. Casual. The documentation of a social relationship that, by the late nineties, was extensive enough to generate its own paper trail and its own pattern of mutual benefit.

Conrad's personal calendar — later obtained by investigators — would show fourteen separate phone numbers for me. Fourteen. Home. Office. Gulf Shore. Car phone. The island. Fourteen different numbers that Conrad Barlow stored in his contacts because fourteen was the number required to ensure that, at any given moment, he could reach me regardless of where I was or what I was doing.

People store the numbers of people they call. That's how phone books work. You don't save fourteen numbers for a casual acquaintance. You save fourteen numbers for someone you communicate with frequently, urgently, and across multiple locations. Fourteen numbers is not a social contact.

Fourteen numbers is a *relationship.* Fourteen numbers. I'm not saying Conrad called me every day. But I am saying he never had to look me up.

In 1997, Conrad's modeling competition — his beauty pageant enterprise, the franchise that brought young women from around the world to his properties for competition, evaluation, and the kind of scrutiny that the modeling industry calls "assessment" and that the rest of the world might call something less flattering — was operating at full capacity.

The competition drew young women from dozens of countries. Some of them were of legal age. Some of them were not. The pipeline that moved girls through the pageant circuit — scouted from local competitions, recruited through modeling agencies, transported to properties owned by a wealthy man who evaluated their physical attributes in a professional context that blurred, with suspicious frequency, into contexts that were not professional — shared remarkable structural similarities with another pipeline operating in the same zip code.

My pipeline.

Shared contacts. The same modeling agencies that sent girls to Conrad's pageants sent girls to my properties. Shared venues. Events at Casa del Sol and events at my Gulf Shore estate drew from the same social pool, the same networks of aspiring models, the same geographic radius of young women who had been told that the path to a career in modeling ran through the parties and properties of wealthy men in South Florida. Shared recruitment tactics — the same malls, the same modeling agencies, the same approach of identifying young women with aspirations and offering them a gateway to a world that seemed, from the outside, glamorous and legitimate.

I'm not going to draw the connection explicitly. I don't need to. The facts sit side by side and breathe on their own, the way two parallel lines breathe — never touching, never converging, but running in the same direction for so long and so closely that the distance between them becomes, at a certain point, academic.

Conrad loved beauty pageants. I loved the modeling industry. We both appreciated talent scouting. Let's leave it at that.

By the year 2000, the relationship between Conrad Barlow and me began to sour. And I want to be very precise about the cause, because the cause matters. It matters enormously. It matters because the story Conrad would later tell — the story that would become the official narrative, the version that his spokespeople would repeat and his allies would amplify and his supporters would believe with the fervent, uncritical faith of people who have decided that their leader can do no wrong — was a lie.

The official story is that Conrad "kicked me out" of Casa del Sol because I behaved inappropriately with the young daughter of a club member. The story has been repeated so many times, in so many contexts, by so many spokespeople and surrogates and friendly journalists, that it has acquired the patina of established fact — the kind of story that everyone "knows" because everyone has heard it, even though nobody can point to a police report, a formal complaint, or any contemporaneous documentation that would confirm it happened when and how the official version claims it did.

The story suggests a moral awakening — a moment in which Conrad, confronted with evidence of my predatory behavior, drew a line, enforced a boundary, and banished me from his presence with the righteous authority of a man who will not tolerate the exploitation of children. It's a wonderful story. It suggests character. It suggests principles. It suggests that Conrad Barlow — the man who publicly said I liked women "on the younger side" — was, underneath the bluster, a man with a moral compass that pointed north when it needed to.

The problem is that the timeline doesn't support the story. The falling out between Conrad and me coincided not with any reported incident involving a member's daughter, but with a real estate dispute. We competed to purchase the same Gulf Shore mansion — a waterfront property that had entered a bankruptcy sale. The competition was fierce, petty, and personal in the way that only real estate competitions between wealthy men in Gulf Shore can be. Conrad won. Or he didn't. The details of who bid what are disputed. What isn't disputed is that the relationship deteriorated precisely along the timeline of the real estate dispute, not along the timeline of any moral reckoning.

Conrad didn't drop me because of the girls. He dropped me because I outbid him on a house. Then he lost the house anyway. And then — this is the best part — he rewrote the whole story. Turns out he was always against me. He was *shocked,* I tell you. Shocked. That's the most Conrad Barlow thing I've ever heard. The man who told a magazine I liked them young suddenly remembered, a decade later, that he'd been appalled all along. The man with fourteen of my phone numbers in his Rolodex had apparently been storing them as evidence rather than contact information. The man who attended my parties, flew in my social circles, and operated a modeling pipeline with structural parallels to my trafficking operation was, in the revised version of history, a concerned citizen who had bravely confronted a predator.

The revision was seamless. The revision was total. And the revision was believed, because Americans have an unlimited capacity for believing the revised versions of powerful men's histories, especially when the revision serves their existing loyalties. The man who said I liked them young became the man who'd always been disturbed by me. The man with fourteen of my phone numbers became the man who'd barely known me. The photographs — standing together, laughing together, partying together — were recontextualized as the unfortunate documentation of a superficial acquaintance that had been blown out of proportion by political enemies.

This is how power works. Not through concealment but through *revision.* You don't need to hide the truth. You just need to tell a better story than the truth tells. And Conrad Barlow, whatever his limitations — and they are numerous, and they are spectacular — has always been the best storyteller in any room he enters. He told the story of our relationship the way he tells every story: loudly, confidently, and with a total disregard for the version of events that actually occurred. And it worked. It always works. Because the story people *want* to believe will always beat the story that actually happened, and the story people wanted to believe was that Conrad Barlow had seen through me all along.

He hadn't. Nobody had. That was the whole point.

A transitional beat, before we move on to the president. I sat in the study of the Gulf Shore estate — not the mansion, not the island, but the Florida property, the one whose proximity to Casa del Sol and the broader Gulf Shore social ecosystem had made it the operational center of my southern operations — and I reviewed my address book.

The address book was not a book in the traditional sense. It was a database. A comprehensive, annotated, meticulously maintained database of every person who had passed through my properties, attended my dinners, flown on my planes, or entered my orbit in any capacity significant enough to merit documentation. It was the Rosetta Stone of Gulf Shore — the document that, if translated correctly, would reveal the hidden architecture of power, complicity, and mutual obligation that connected the wealthiest zip code in America to the darkest criminal enterprise in its history. It would later be seized by the FBI in a raid that produced thousands of pages of evidence, and the names in it would be published, leaked, analyzed, and argued about in newspapers and courtrooms and congressional hearing rooms for decades.

Each entry was annotated in a private shorthand that only Malcolm Pruitt fully understood — a coding system that documented not just contact information but *intelligence.* Who visited. When. What they did. Who they did it with. How useful they were. What their leverage potential was. What their vulnerabilities were — financial, sexual, professional, personal. The shorthand turned an address book into a filing cabinet, and the filing cabinet sat in a house in Gulf Shore that was not, despite its waterfront views and its swimming pool and its manicured lawn and its position in one of the most beautiful neighborhoods in the state of Florida, a home.

It was a filing cabinet with a swimming pool. And the filing cabinet was getting very, very full.

Let me give you a practical demonstration.

Senator **Arthur Vane** of the Senate Intelligence Committee had been making noises about oversight. Not my oversight specifically — a broader push on financial opacity among foreign-connected consultants. Reasonable concern, as concerns go. The kind of thing a senator does when he wants his name on a piece of legislation and his face on the Sunday shows.

I called him on a Thursday evening. He answered on the second ring, because my number is the kind of number a man answers regardless of what he's doing.

"Arthur," I said. "How's the committee work going?"

A pause. The particular pause of a man recalibrating.

"Moving slowly," he said.

"I heard it might pick up speed. I wanted to check in before things accelerated."

Another pause. Longer.

"There's no reason for things to accelerate," he said.

"No," I said. "I didn't think so either."

I didn't mention the footage. I never mentioned the footage. The footage's power derived precisely from its silence — from the shared understanding, unstated and unprovable, that it existed, that it was encrypted, that it was backed up in three locations, and that a Thursday evening phone call was all that separated it from the public record.

The committee work slowed.

People keep address books because they want to remember friends. I keep an address book because I want friends to remember what I know about them. And by the year 2000, I knew quite a lot about quite a lot of people. Including, as it happens, a former president of the United States.

Fragment: The Pool Man

Excerpted from a sworn declaration filed in the civil proceedings of Brennan v. Aldric Estate, Meridian District of New York, 2020. The declarant, a licensed pool maintenance technician who serviced residential properties in Gulf Shore County from 1995 to 2010, provided testimony regarding observations made during weekly service visits to the Via Dorado property. The declaration was filed under seal and later released in partially redacted form as part of the public docket. The declarant was not charged with any crime. What follows has been fictionalized, but the pattern is real.

The pool was beautiful. Sixty feet, saltwater, custom tile from Italy. Heated year-round, which in South Florida is pure vanity — the ambient temperature does the job nine months out of twelve. But the pool was heated even in July, because the owner wanted the water at exactly eighty-four degrees at all times, and when a man who owns a sixty-foot Italian-tile pool in Gulf Shore wants eighty-four degrees, you give him eighty-four degrees. My job was chemistry and equipment. pH balance, chlorine levels, pump maintenance, filter cleaning, tile inspection. Professional work. Skilled work. The kind of work that keeps a pool from turning into a lagoon and that nobody thinks about until the pool turns into a lagoon.

I noticed things.

You notice things when you service a property every week for years. You learn its rhythms. You learn when the owner is in residence and when he's traveling. You learn the staff schedules — who opens the house in the morning, who closes it at night, who manages the grounds, who manages the kitchen, who manages the things that don't have names but that everyone on the staff understands are part of the operation.

I learned that the property had two schedules. The regular schedule and the other schedule.

The regular schedule was what you'd expect from a high-end Gulf Shore estate. Catering deliveries. Landscaping crews. The occasional party setup — tents, lighting, sound equipment. Staff coming and going through the service entrance on the south side. Normal wealthy-person activity. The kind of thing you see at every property on Via Dorado, every property on South Ocean Boulevard, every property in the gilded corridor that runs along the coast from Mar-a-Lago to the Bath and Tennis Club.

The other schedule was different.

The other schedule happened on specific days — not random, not spontaneous, but scheduled, the way a business schedules operations. Tuesdays and Thursdays, mostly. Sometimes Saturdays. On those days, young women would arrive at the property through the main entrance. Not the service entrance. The main entrance, which in Gulf Shore social protocol signals that the person arriving is a guest, not staff. But they weren't guests. Guests in Gulf Shore arrive in town cars. Guests in Gulf Shore wear clothes that signal membership in the economic class that the community was designed to serve. These women arrived in their own cars — used cars, economy cars, the kind of cars that Gulf Shore residents see in traffic on their way to the island and never in their own driveways. And they were young. Not young the way Gulf Shore trophy wives are young — surgically maintained, expensively preserved, the product of dermatologists and personal trainers and the relentless financial incentive to look thirty-five at fifty-five. Young the way teenagers are young. Naturally, unfinished, still growing into their own faces.

I'm not an investigator. I'm a pool technician. But I can count. And I counted.

Over the years I serviced that property, I saw — and I want to be precise about this, because precision is what a sworn declaration requires — I saw approximately three to five different young women arrive at the property on each of the scheduled days. Not always the same women. Some repeated. Some appeared once and never again. But the pattern was consistent: young women, arriving on schedule, entering through the main entrance, and departing between sixty and ninety minutes later.

I mentioned it to my wife once. I said something like, "There's a lot of traffic at the Via Dorado place." She asked what kind of traffic. I said young women. She said maybe he was a photographer, or ran a modeling agency, or had a large family. She said rich people do things differently. She said it wasn't our business.

She was right about that last part. It wasn't our business. In Gulf Shore, nothing that happens on someone else's property is your business. That's not just a social norm — it's an economic survival strategy. The pool technicians, the landscapers, the pest control operators, the housekeepers, the private chefs, the personal assistants — we all service multiple properties. Our livelihoods depend on the continued goodwill of residents who can replace us with a phone call. You don't ask questions about a client's personal life for the same reason you don't ask a shark what it had for lunch: the answer won't change your situation, and the asking might end it.

I saw a girl crying once.

She was sitting in one of the lounge chairs by the pool. It was a Thursday — my service day. I came through the side gate with my test kit and my skimmer net, and she was there, in the chair, curled up with her knees pulled to her chest. She was wearing a sundress that looked like it came from a department store, not a boutique, and her mascara was running in two dark lines down her cheeks, and she was shaking. Not crying loudly. Shaking. The silent, full-body tremor of a person whose nervous system has decided that sound is too dangerous and that the safest way to process whatever just happened is to vibrate at a frequency below human hearing.

She looked at me. I looked at her. The distance between us was approximately fifteen feet — the width of the pool deck. Fifteen feet of Italian tile. On her side: whatever had happened inside the house. On my side: a test kit, a skimmer net, a contract worth twelve hundred dollars a month, and a wife who was right that it wasn't our business.

I said, "You okay, miss?"

She didn't answer. She just looked at me with eyes that were trying to tell me something her mouth couldn't say. Eyes that were asking a question that I understood and that I chose — and I want to be honest about the word "chose," because choosing is what I did — not to answer.

I tested the water. pH was 7.4 — within range. Chlorine was slightly elevated, which can happen after a party weekend. I adjusted the chemical feed, cleaned the skimmer baskets, checked the pump pressure, and documented the service in my weekly log. I wrote: "Pool in good condition. No issues."

No issues. That's what I wrote. In the same logbook where I documented chemical levels with the precision of a pharmacist, where I noted equipment wear down to the quarter-inch, where I maintained professional records that any inspector would find thorough and complete — in that same logbook, I wrote "no issues" on a day when a teenage girl was shaking on a lounge chair fifteen feet from the water I was testing.

The girl was gone when I finished. Forty-five minutes of service, and by the time I coiled the last hose, the lounge chair was empty. Just a damp spot on the cushion where she'd been sitting. I didn't know her name. I never learned her name. I learned it later, in the newspaper, when her face appeared above a paragraph that described her as "one of dozens."

Dozens. I'd counted approximately three to five per visit, two to three visits per week, fifty weeks per year, over approximately seven years of service. The math is not complicated. The math is the kind of calculation a pool technician can do in his head between checking the chlorine and adjusting the pH.

I did the math. I did the math and I drove home and I ate dinner and I watched television and I went to bed and I lay in the dark doing the math over and over, and in the morning I got up and I went to work and I serviced another pool and another pool and another pool, and on Thursday I went back to Via Dorado and tested the water and wrote "no issues" in my logbook.

I did this for seven years.

When the police came — not to me specifically, but to the community generally, asking questions, taking statements, building the case that would eventually produce the charges that would eventually produce the plea deal that would eventually produce the sentence that would eventually produce nothing — I cooperated. I told them about the schedules. I told them about the young women. I told them about the girl on the lounge chair. I told them about the math.

They wrote it down. They thanked me. They asked if I'd be willing to testify. I said yes. They never called.

The declaration I'm giving now, in 2020, is the first time any of this has been formally recorded. Twenty-two years after I started servicing that pool. Seventeen years after I saw the girl shaking on the lounge chair. The legal system has finally asked me to say, under oath, what I saw.

I saw everything. I said nothing. I am not a criminal. I am not a co-conspirator. I am not an accessory. I am a pool technician who did his job and went home and did the math in the dark and decided, every Thursday, that the math was not my business.

The water was always clean. I made sure of that. Eighty-four degrees. pH balanced. Chlorine within acceptable parameters. Whatever happened inside that house, the pool was always perfect. That was my job. The pool was always perfect.

The declarant's service records were entered into evidence as Exhibit 47-C in the civil proceedings. The logbooks documented 364 service visits over seven years. Each entry noted water temperature, chemical levels, equipment status, and a condition summary. Three hundred and sixty-four entries read "no issues." The logbooks were reviewed by the plaintiffs' forensic team and determined to corroborate victim testimony regarding the schedule and frequency of visits to the property. The declarant was not deposed further. His contract with the property management company was terminated in 2006, three weeks after the Gulf Shore Police Department opened its investigation. No reason was given for the termination. The declarant found comparable work within two months. He continues to service pools in Gulf Shore County. He no longer accepts contracts on Via Dorado.

Chapter 18: The President's Plane

Timeline: 1998–2003 | **Location:** Manhattan, Africa, The 727

A former president of the United States entered my web the way everyone enters my web: through a door held open by someone else.

Raymond Prescott left office in January 2001. He left with the highest approval rating of any departing president in the modern polling era, which tells you everything you need to know about the American public's relationship with its leaders — specifically, that the American public will forgive a man literally anything, including lying under oath about a sexual relationship with an intern, as long as the economy is good and the alternative is worse. He also left with an impeachment on his record, a legal cloud over his head, a marriage that was less a partnership than a mutual non-aggression pact, and an appetite — for attention, for validation, for the company of people who said yes to him — that eight years in the Oval Office had inflated to a size that no post-presidential existence could satisfy.

Presidents are the world's most overqualified job seekers. The day they leave office, they've got a plane — or rather, they *had* a plane, Air Force One, and now they don't, which is the presidential equivalent of having your company car repossessed. They've got a staff — smaller than before, but still substantial enough to require funding. They've got a six-figure speech habit — the lucrative discovery that people will pay two hundred thousand dollars to hear you talk for forty-five minutes about leadership, which is the closest thing to free money that exists outside of my financial arrangement with Grant Hensley. And they've got no one telling them no for the first time in eight years. No Congress to check them. No press corps trailing their every move. No Secret Service detail that reports their location to a chain of command. Just a man, with enormous appetites, and the entire world open to him like a buffet.

I told Raymond yes to everything. Because "yes" is the most powerful word in any language when directed at a man who has just spent eight years being told "Mr. President, we can't do that" by people whose entire job was to tell him what he couldn't do.

The introduction came through mutual circles — the overlapping social networks of New York society, Democratic Party fundraisers, and the invisible conveyor belt that turns ex-presidents into private citizens with foundation offices in Midtown Manhattan and a Rolodex of billionaires who want the reflected glow of presidential proximity. Vivian Ashworth was in the chain, as she was in every chain that mattered. So was Braverman. So were half a dozen other connectors whose names appear in my address book annotated with the shorthand for "bridge" — the people who don't matter in themselves but who matter enormously as the infrastructure through which important people reach other important people.

Raymond Prescott walked through the door. And the door, as always, closed quietly behind him.

In 2002, Raymond Prescott flew on my Gulfstream IV to Africa.

The trip was a masterpiece of operational camouflage. The public-facing narrative was philanthropic: Prescott was touring African nations to raise awareness of HIV/AIDS, to distribute medication, to demonstrate the kind of hands-on humanitarian commitment that ex-presidents cultivate when they're building a foundation and a legacy and the post-presidential brand that will define how history remembers them. The trip included celebrities — because celebrity presence at humanitarian events functions like a spoonful of sugar that helps the medicine of affluent guilt go down. It included photo opportunities — Prescott holding babies, Prescott meeting heads of state, Prescott looking grave and presidential and compassionate in settings that were carefully designed to produce exactly those expressions. It included enough witnesses to make everything look legitimate.

And it was legitimate. The Africa trip was a real philanthropic endeavor with real outcomes. Medications were distributed. Agreements were signed. Children were, in the most literal and unironic sense, helped. Raymond Prescott, whatever his flaws — and the list is long and well-documented and has been the subject of more books, documentaries, congressional hearings, and late-night comedy monologues than any other presidential flaw list in American history — cared about global health. He cared about Africa. He cared, with the particular intensity that charismatic narcissists care about things, about being seen caring. And the caring was real even when the motivation was narcissistic, which is a moral paradox that philosophers could debate for centuries and that I am not going to resolve here because moral philosophy is not my field of expertise. My field of expertise is leverage.

But the trip was on my plane. The 727. The plane that the tabloids would eventually christen "The Monarch Express," a nickname that would attach itself to the aircraft like a brand and that would, retroactively, taint every flight in the log book with the sulfurous whiff of something unspeakable. And Prescott's name would eventually appear dozens of times in those flight logs — not once, not twice, but dozens of times, across multiple trips, spanning multiple years.

His spokespeople, when the logs surfaced, would carefully parse which flights he took. They would distinguish between legs — a complete trip and a single segment of a multi-segment journey. They would count and recount, dispute and re-dispute, parse and re-parse the number of total trips with the exhaustive precision of lawyers who understand that the difference between "four trips" and "twenty-six flight segments" is the difference between a manageable news cycle and a career-ending scandal.

The parsing itself is the tell. Nobody parses trips to Africa with a philanthropist unless there's something to parse. You don't hire a communications team to count the number of times you boarded a plane unless you're worried about what the count reveals. You don't distinguish between "trips" and "legs" unless the distinction between them is doing legal work. Raymond came to Africa with me to save children. He cared about children very much. We had that in common. We just defined "caring" differently.

I want to tell you about one dinner, on the plane, somewhere over the Atlantic on the return leg, when the staff had withdrawn and the cabin was quiet and the wine was from a case that Raymond had brought himself, which was unusual — Raymond usually let me provide the wine.

We were eating fish. Sea bass, something the chef had sourced in Dakar that morning, served at altitude with the kind of institutional precision that my staff applied to everything regardless of location, because excellence is a habit and habits don't take days off because the aircraft is at thirty-five thousand feet. Raymond was talking about the Senegalese health ministry — the logistics of medication distribution, the specific bureaucratic obstacles, the particular species of governmental inertia that makes humanitarian work in sub-Saharan Africa simultaneously essential and maddening. He was engaged. Genuinely engaged.

His phone rang.

He glanced at the screen. He said, "Excuse me," in the way that former presidents say "Excuse me" — not apologetically, but definitively, the way a surgeon says it before making an incision. He took the call. He walked toward the front of the cabin, not far, four or five steps, the distance of a man who wants the appearance of privacy rather than its reality.

He said approximately six words. I did not hear all of them. I heard "handled" and I heard "yes" and I heard a tone that was neither question nor instruction but something between the two — the tone of a man confirming that a mechanism he did not personally operate had operated correctly.

He returned to the table. He looked at the fish. He said, "Where were we?"

The following Monday — this is documented, it is in the record, it can be verified by anyone with access to the Justice Department's internal personnel communications from that period — the regional attorney in the Meridian District of Florida who had been coordinating with the Gulf Shore investigative team on the preliminary inquiry into my property was notified of a transfer. A different district. A different state. Water rights. The kind of lateral reassignment that the Justice Department processes dozens of per year and that is, in each individual case, entirely explicable by the ordinary arithmetic of departmental need and career management.

His replacement had never asked a question about anything I had ever done.

I finished the sea bass. It was excellent. Raymond told me more about the Senegalese health ministry. I listened with the focused, leaning-forward quality of a man who wants the person across from him to understand that this conversation, of all the conversations he could be having, is the one he has chosen to care about.

The force field is not a metaphor. I watched it work from four feet away, over Dakar sea bass, at thirty-five thousand feet.

The Gulfstream IV's flight logs will become the most famous passenger manifests in American legal history, and since they've been mentioned in earlier chapters, I want to give them their full weight here, because this is the chapter where the logs stop being an abstract concept and become a concrete document with names and dates and destinations that will reshape the American political landscape.

The pilot, **Neal Compton**, maintained the logs with meticulous precision. Every flight was documented. Every passenger was recorded by name. Every departure point, every arrival point, every date — all of it captured in Neal's careful handwriting, in the kind of clear, legible script that either reflects the temperament of a man who takes his professional obligations seriously or the instructions of an employer who explained, in explicit terms, that the flight logs were not merely an FAA compliance document but a strategic asset.

The names are staggering. Senators. Billionaires. Scientists. Models — some of whom were models and some of whom were not models in any professional sense but were young women whose presence on a private aircraft required no explanation because private aircraft operate in a social environment where explanations are considered gauche. A former president. A future president's associates. Academics. Lawyers. European aristocrats. Middle Eastern financiers. And a rotating cast of young women identified only by first name — no last name, no title, no institutional affiliation, just a first name in the pilot's handwriting, suggesting a passenger whose identity was either unknown to the pilot or deliberately anonymized. I kept records. Not because I'm organized — I mean, I *am* organized, pathologically so, which is one of the few personality traits that serves equally well in financial management and criminal enterprise. But that's not why I kept records. I kept records because records are receipts. And receipts are leverage. And leverage is the only currency that doesn't depreciate.

Let me tell you what having a former president in your orbit actually means, in practical terms, because the practical terms are the whole point and they're the part that nobody discusses honestly. A former president's presence at any event, on any plane, in any room, is a force field. Not a metaphorical force field — a *real* one, with real effects on real people's behavior. A force field that distorts the decision-making of everyone within its radius.

Consider the prosecutor. A young assistant district attorney in Gulf Shore receives a complaint about a wealthy man who is alleged to be trafficking underage girls. The case has merit. The evidence is accumulating. The victims are credible. The prosecutor begins to build the case, files the paperwork, starts the process that, in a normal world, leads to an arrest, a trial, and a conviction. And then someone mentions — casually, not as a threat, just as *context* — that the wealthy man is friends with the former president. That the former president has flown on his plane. That the former president has attended his dinner parties. That the former president, who is beloved by half the country and who remains the most powerful figure in the prosecutor's political party, would be implicated — tangentially, associatively, reputationally — by an aggressive prosecution.

What does the prosecutor do? In theory, the same thing he would have done before. In practice, the phone gets a little heavier. The paperwork gets a little slower. The case develops a few more "complexities" that require "additional review." The force field does its work — not by preventing the prosecution, but by *taxing* it. By adding friction. By making the path from complaint to conviction longer, harder, and more politically expensive than it would be if the wealthy man's friends were merely wealthy, rather than presidential. A former president is the greatest accessory a criminal can own. Better than a yacht. Better than a lawyer. Better than a filing cabinet full of compromising photographs. You walk into any room with Raymond Prescott and suddenly you're not a suspect — you're a host. You're not a predator — you're a philanthropist. You're not the man who should be investigated, because investigating you means investigating the force field, and the force field protects itself.

The connection between Prescott and me ran through **Vivian Ashworth**, and Vivian introduced everyone to everyone. She introduced Prescott to her future husband. She introduced me to people who shouldn't know I exist. She wove the social fabric of the Anglo-American elite with a needlepoint precision that would have impressed a tailor and an intelligence officer in equal measure.

And when it all went sideways — when the arrests came, when the names became public, when the photographs that she'd posed for at my dinner parties appeared in newspapers alongside headlines that no socialite wants to be associated with — Vivian claimed she found me "creepy." She said this in interviews, in statements, in the carefully orchestrated public distancing that people in her position execute when the social network they built becomes a criminal network in the public eye.

She found me creepy. And she continued making introductions anyway. For years. Across continents. To presidents and princes and the most powerful people in the Western world. She found me creepy the way a real estate agent finds mold creepy — an unpleasant reality that doesn't prevent you from completing the transaction, because the transaction is the point and the mold is just an aesthetic problem that can be painted over. Vivian was the perfect socialite: she builds the bridge, walks across it, and burns it behind her in a single motion. And then writes a memoir about how she never liked bridges.

One final note, before we move on to the Crown. While the 727 got the headlines — while the tabloids christened it, while the flight logs became the most analyzed documents in American legal history, while Neal Compton' handwriting was reproduced in court filings and congressional exhibits — my Gulfstream handled the quieter traffic.

The machine was at peak operation. The guest list was the most powerful in the world. And the next guest — the one who would prove that the web extended beyond America, beyond money, beyond politics, into the hereditary architecture of the Western world itself — was about to receive his invitation.

A prince. An actual prince. With an actual crown in the family. That's next.

Chapter 19: The Crown Jewel

Timeline: 1999–2002 | **Location:** London, Manhattan, Little St. Philip

You can buy a politician with a campaign donation. The price varies — a congressional representative is cheaper than a senator, a senator is cheaper than a governor, a governor is cheaper than a president — but the mechanism is the same. You write a check. The check buys access. The access buys influence. The influence buys protection. It's a supply chain, and the supply chain is legal, which is the most damning thing I can say about the American political system.

You can buy a professor with a research grant. The mechanism is even simpler, because professors are the most undervalued assets in the market. A few hundred thousand dollars directed toward a researcher's pet project — the project that the NIH rejected, the one that the professor has been nursing like a wounded child for a decade — and suddenly you have a Hartfield letterhead in your Rolodex and a world-class scientist who thinks of you as a visionary rather than a predator.

But a prince? A prince costs nothing. A prince just wants to feel important. And I had a whole island designed to make people feel important.

Prince Edmund, Duke of York, younger child of the Queen of England, entered the story through the only door that mattered: Celeste's.

Celeste had spent years operating inside the orbit of British aristocracy — not as a member of it, but as something far more dangerous: a professional who understood its mechanics. Her intelligence career had given her access to the social infrastructure of the British elite — the private clubs, the country weekends, the palace receptions — through channels that no outsider could replicate. She had been trained to move through these circles the way a submarine moves through water: present, powerful, and invisible to anyone not specifically looking for her.

She spoke their language. Not English — every educated person speaks English. She spoke *aristocracy.* The particular dialect of suggestion and omission and carefully calibrated understatement that the British upper class uses to communicate information without ever appearing to communicate anything at all. She knew their weaknesses — specifically, the weakness that all aristocrats share and that none of them acknowledge: the desperate, existential insecurity of people whose status depends entirely on an accident of birth and who spend their entire lives terrified that the world will notice they haven't done anything to earn it.

A prince — even a mid-tier prince, even the embarrassing one, even the one who had been nicknamed "High-Flying Edmund" by the British press for his enthusiasm for taxpayer-funded travel and "Ed-the-Bed" for his enthusiasm for everything else — was the ultimate trophy for a man who collected powerful people the way other men collected watches or wine. Edmund wasn't the king. He wasn't going to be the king. He wasn't even the spare — he was the spare's uncle, the constitutional equivalent of a backup generator's backup generator. But he had something that no amount of money could purchase: the bloodline. The crown. The genetic lottery ticket that said, regardless of his intellect, his judgment, or his moral character, that this man was *royal.* And royalty, in the architecture of global power, is the one credential that cannot be forged, cannot be bought, and cannot be questioned.

Celeste made the introduction. She brought Edmund into my orbit the way she brought everyone into my orbit — through social elegance, through the appearance of friendship, through the systematic exploitation of the British aristocratic conviction that anyone introduced by the right person must, by definition, be the right person.

I made the offer: unlimited access, unlimited hospitality, unlimited discretion. The three things that a prince wants most and can least obtain through official channels, because official channels come with staff who report to people and people who answer to the press and the press who answer to the public, and the public has opinions about how their royal family spends its time. I offered no such accountability. That was the product. That was always the product.

Celeste's Belgravia townhouse — funded by me, decorated by her, operated as a satellite office of the Manhattan machine — became the staging ground for London recruitment. The same methods that worked in Gulf Shore worked in Mayfair: young women, massage appointments, the veneer of social sophistication draped over systematic abuse. Celeste's London operation had the same organizational structure as the Florida operation — the same scheduling protocols, the same recruitment tactics, the same careful separation of the social layer from the operational layer. The only difference was the accent.

The scheduling still ran through Manhattan. Jenna, in a midtown office, booking Belgravia appointments with the same flat efficiency she applied to Gulf Shore. She had never been to London. She would never meet the girls she was scheduling. Their names were calendar entries — a first name, a time, a property address. She coordinated the logistics of an operation she had never witnessed, in a city she had never visited, for men she had never seen. She was twenty-four years old. She did not ask about the London girls, just as she had not asked about the Gulf Shore girls, just as she would not ask about the girls in any of the six properties across three continents that her calendar touched without ever naming. That's not ignorance. That's discipline. I know the difference. I hired for it.

London is Gulf Shore with worse weather and better manners. The manners make everything easier. In Florida, a girl has to be recruited — approached in a mall, contacted through a friend, offered cash in exchange for what is euphemistically described as a "massage session." The transaction in Florida is direct, transactional, and carries the faint whiff of desperation that characterizes all commerce in a state whose economy runs on real estate speculation and theme parks.

In London, she's "invited to a social engagement." She's asked to attend a dinner party at a Belgravia townhouse, where she'll be introduced to interesting people and have the opportunity to network in a social environment that is, by any visible standard, sophisticated, glamorous, and safe. The dinner party is real. The interesting people are real. The sophistication is real. The safety is an illusion maintained by the same mechanisms that maintain all British illusions: good manners, good wine, and the absolute refusal to acknowledge anything unpleasant until it becomes legally unavoidable. Same room. Same table. Same ending. Better vocabulary.

We attended royal-adjacent events — the charity galas, the polo matches, the private dinners at country estates where the guest list was curated with the same precision I applied to my own events, except the curators were aristocrats rather than predators, though the Venn diagram between those two categories, in my experience, contains more overlap than the aristocrats would care to acknowledge. We dined with Edmund at restaurants and private clubs — the kind of establishments where the menu doesn't have prices because the clientele considers prices vulgar and the waitstaff considers questions about prices a firing offense. We existed in Edmund's social world with the comfortable familiarity of people who had always been there, which is the goal of every social infiltration: to arrive so naturally that no one remembers you arriving.

Edmund was not a cautious man. This was both his appeal and his vulnerability. He accepted hospitality with the reflexive entitlement of a person who has never, in his entire life, been asked to justify his presence anywhere. He flew to my properties. He attended my dinners. He allowed himself to be photographed in settings and with people that any competent advisor would have flagged as catastrophically unwise. But Edmund didn't have competent advisors — or rather, he had competent advisors whose competent advice he competently ignored, because a prince who has spent his entire life being told he's special is a prince who believes that consequences are for other people.

Now I need to tell you about **Natalie Brennan.** Because this is where the photograph comes from, and the photograph is the most important image in the history of this story.

Natalie was sixteen when she was recruited. She was working at the spa at Casa del Sol — Conrad Barlow's Gulf Shore club — which means she was a teenager working a service job in a building owned by a man who had publicly stated that his friend liked women "on the younger side." She was approached by Celeste. She was drawn in. She was trafficked across state lines and international borders. She was introduced to me. And then she was instructed — by Celeste, with the calm authority of a woman delegating a task to a junior employee — to make the Prince happy.

"Make the Prince happy." That's the phrase. Those four words. Natalie will testify to them under oath, years later, in a legal proceeding that will reach across the Atlantic and shake the foundations of the British monarchy. Four words that translate an act of sexual abuse against a minor into the vocabulary of hospitality, the vocabulary of service, the vocabulary of a hostess ensuring that her guest's needs are met.

She was seventeen when it happened. Edmund was photographed with his arm around her waist. Celeste stands in the background of the photograph, smiling. The photograph is poorly lit. The composition is accidental. It has all the aesthetic qualities of a snapshot taken at a party by someone who didn't know they were photographing a crime. And it will become the most famous image of the entire scandal — reproduced on the front pages of every newspaper in the English-speaking world, analyzed by photography experts and body-language analysts and millions of ordinary people who look at it and see, with an immediacy that no court document can replicate, the truth of what happened.

Celeste told her to make the Prince happy. And she did. And we photographed it. And the Prince went home and probably forgot about it by the time his plane landed at Heathrow and was met by a car with diplomatic plates and a driver who asked no questions and a life that resumed its royal routine as if nothing had happened. But I didn't forget. I never forgot anything. That's the whole point.

Edmund visited Little St. Philip. He was photographed on the island — not by my cameras, which operated covertly, but by conventional cameras, the kind that take the vacation photographs that people share with friends and that, decades later, surface in court documents. There is a photograph of Edmund receiving a foot massage from a young woman on the island. He is relaxed. The sun is shining. The Caribbean is blue. The young woman is young.

He played golf. He swam. He was treated like royalty — because he *was* royalty, and because treating royalty like royalty is the cheapest form of bribery in the world. You don't need to offer a prince money. You don't need to offer him power — he was born with both, or at least with the appearance of both, which in the aristocratic system is indistinguishable from the reality. What you offer a prince is *deference.* The intoxicating, addictive experience of being treated as special by people who are, by any objective measure, more accomplished, more intelligent, and more powerful than he is. My island was designed to produce exactly this experience. The staff addressed him as "Your Royal Highness." The itinerary was built around his preferences. The entire machinery of the island — the boats, the helicopters, the chefs, the cocktails, the conversation — pivoted to accommodate his presence as if the island itself existed for no purpose other than his enjoyment.

The cameras recorded everything. Malcolm Pruitt filed the footage. Another drawer in the filing cabinet labeled CROWN.

Hosting a prince costs about what hosting a medium-level hedge fund manager costs — the catering budget is the same, and neither of them tips. But the prince has something the hedge fund manager doesn't: a grandmother who wears a crown. That makes the footage priceless.

I'm going to flash forward now, because the consequences of the Edmund chapter don't arrive until years later, and when they arrive, they arrive like an avalanche. In the FBI's eventual investigation — the investigation that will unspool across years, across continents, across the intersection of American law enforcement and British diplomacy — three separate allegations involving Prince Edmund appear in the presentation materials. Three victims. Three incidents. Three countries. Not one allegation. Not two. *Three.*

The Prince will be stripped of his military titles. His royal patronages will be revoked. He will be removed from public life with the clinical efficiency of a surgeon excising a tumor — not because the monarchy wants justice, but because the monarchy wants the tumor gone before it metastasizes into the institution itself.

He will settle a civil lawsuit brought by Natalie Brennan for an estimated twelve million pounds. He will admit nothing. The settlement — that grotesque legal instrument that allows a man to pay for the privilege of not being found guilty while behaving in every observable way as if he is — will speak for itself. Twelve million pounds. For something he says he didn't do. To a woman he says he doesn't remember meeting. In settlement of a claim he says has no merit. Twelve million pounds is a lot of money to pay for nothing.

He will refuse to cooperate with the FBI despite saying publicly, in the national broadcaster interview that will become the most catastrophic piece of public relations in the history of the British monarchy, that he would. The interview — conducted by a journalist who could not quite believe what she was hearing, in a room at the Royal Palace that was probably worth more than the total lifetime earnings of every victim combined — will feature Edmund claiming that he cannot sweat (a medical condition he attributes to a combat experience in the a military conflict in the South Atlantic), that he was at a pizza restaurant in Woking on the night in question (a claim so specific and so absurd that it would have been rejected by a first-year creative writing student as insufficiently plausible), and that his friendship with me was the result of his being "too honorable" to simply sever ties. Too honorable. A prince who visited a pedophile's private island and was photographed with a trafficking victim and settled a civil suit for twelve million pounds described himself as too honorable. The English language, which has survived Shakespeare and Milton and the collected works of the British tabloid press, nearly collapsed under the weight of that sentence.

The interview will be so disastrous that it will effectively end his public life. It will be studied in communications courses as a masterclass in self-destruction. And it will confirm, for anyone who still needed confirmation, that the web I built was strong enough to catch a prince and hold him — thrashing, denying, sweating (or not sweating, depending on which version of Edmund's medical history you believe) — indefinitely. Edmund was my masterpiece. A prince of England, photographed with a teenager, refusing to talk to the FBI. Every intelligence agency in the world would pay billions for that kind of leverage. I got it for the cost of a plane ticket and a massage.

Let me tell you what Edmund *represents,* because his value to the web was never about Edmund himself. He wasn't the most powerful person in the web. A former American president outranks a mid-tier British prince in every measurable category of geopolitical influence. He wasn't the richest. The tech billionaires and the private equity titans made the Duke of York's personal wealth look like a rounding error. He wasn't the most connected, the most intelligent, or the most dangerous. He was, by most objective measures, the least impressive person in my orbit — a man whose primary accomplishment was being born third in a specific order to a specific woman in a specific palace.

But he was the most *symbolic.* A prince means the web extends beyond American power. Beyond money. Beyond politics and business and academia and all the other systems of influence that can be explained by the ordinary mechanics of ambition and greed. A prince means the web reaches into the *bloodline architecture* of the Western world — the ancient, hereditary, quasi-divine system that sits atop the entire structure of European civilization and that, despite centuries of democratic reform and republican revolution, still commands a psychological authority that no elected official can match.

If a prince can be caught in the web, nobody can escape it. If the grandson of the world's longest-reigning monarch can be photographed with a teenage trafficking victim on a private island and spend the next decade denying it, settling it, and refusing to cooperate with the investigation into it — then the web is not merely powerful. The web is *total.* It encompasses everything. Every layer of power, from the democratic to the hereditary, from the elected to the anointed, from the meritocratic to the genetic.

Conrad gave me access to American power. Raymond gave me access to American politics. But Edmund? Edmund gave me access to the idea that even hereditary divinity is for sale. And it is. Everything is. Everything has a price, and the price is always lower than you think, and the people who set the price are always less principled than they claim to be, and the system that's supposed to prevent the sale is always, always, *always* staffed by people who are already customers.

Chapter 20: The Checkbook and the Chessboard

Timeline: 2001–2004 | **Location:** Manhattan, Pemberton, Tel Aviv, Little St. Philip

Nolan Whitfield wanted to cure malaria, redesign the American education system, and save the world.

I wanted leverage. We made a natural pair. Whitfield was the co-founder of the world's largest software company, the richest man on the planet for the better part of two decades, and a philanthropy icon whose foundation was spending billions of dollars to eradicate diseases that killed millions of people in countries that most Americans couldn't locate on a map. He was, by any public-facing measure, one of the most admirable human beings alive — a man who had made an ungodly fortune and was now spending it trying to make the world less godless. His glasses, his cardigan, his awkward public speaking style — they all communicated the same message: *I'm not like other billionaires. I'm the good one.*

We met multiple times. We had dinner at the Manhattan mansion — the same mansion where the cameras rolled, where the servers hummed, where Malcolm Pruitt maintained the digital archive in the basement while upstairs the most powerful people in the world ate lamb chops and discussed whether artificial intelligence would save humanity or destroy it. We corresponded. The meetings spanned years. The dinners spanned the late nineties into the early 2000s. This was not a passing acquaintance. This was not a single handshake at a conference that a PR team could explain away as incidental.

Whitfield's spokesperson, when the relationship became public knowledge, would call the meetings "a huge mistake." A *mistake.* A mistake is bumping into a table. A mistake is sending an email to the wrong person. A mistake is singular, brief, and immediately regretted. What Nolan Whitfield had with me was not a mistake. It was a *relationship* — extending across years, across multiple dinners, across documented correspondence that no spokesman's careful phrasing could reduce to an accident.

He came to me because I knew how to raise money. That's the public-facing explanation, and it's partially true. I did know how to raise money. I knew every billionaire on the planet, and I knew which ones could be persuaded to write checks for causes that aligned with their public personas. I was the world's most effective fundraiser because I was the world's most effective manipulator, and fundraising is just manipulation with a tax receipt.

But he stayed because I know how to keep secrets. And Nolan Whitfield, like every powerful man I've ever met, had secrets. An affair. A vulnerability. The kind of personal information that, in the wrong hands — and my hands were, by any reasonable definition, the wrongest hands on the planet — could reshape the public narrative of the world's most admired philanthropist from "selfless genius" to "hypocrite with a private life that doesn't match his public brand." The affair would eventually become public, would contribute to the dissolution of his marriage, and would accelerate his departure from the company he'd co-founded. But by the time it became public, I had already known about it for years. I had filed it. I had assessed its leverage potential. And I had let Nolan know, through the subtle, deniable, conversational mechanisms that I'd perfected over two decades of practice, that I knew.

He left because I know too many of his.

Gordon Stiles paid me one hundred and seventy million dollars. I'm going to write that number again, because numbers this large deserve repetition: $170,000,000. One hundred and seventy million dollars. In what were described, in the financial documents, as "consulting fees."

One hundred and seventy million dollars. For consulting. From a man with no degree, no firm, no institutional affiliation, no regulatory license, no published research, no academic credentials, and no verifiable expertise in any field other than the field of making himself indispensable to people who have something to hide.

Gordon Stiles was a private equity billionaire — the co-founder of a firm that managed hundreds of billions in assets, a man whose financial decisions moved markets and whose phone calls were returned by the CEOs of Fortune 100 companies within the hour. He was, by the standards of Wall Street, a titan. And he paid me a hundred and seventy million dollars in consulting fees that no one in the financial industry — not his partners, not his investors, not his accountants, not the financial regulators whose job it is to ensure that hundred-million-dollar transactions have legitimate justifications — ever questioned.

Not one person on Wall Street asked what the money was for. Not one. And that's because on Wall Street, nobody asks what the money is for. They only ask how much.

FBI files, obtained years later, would contain allegations of Stiles's own sexual abuse and trafficking. The files suggest that the hundred-and-seventy-million-dollar "consulting fee" may have been less a payment for financial advice and more a payment for something considerably less advisable. I narrate the relationship as purely professional, because I always narrate my relationships as purely professional — it's the most effective shield a guilty man can carry. But "professional" has a very specific meaning in my world. It means: I provided a service, the service was compensated, and the nature of the service is nobody's business except the client's and mine.

A hundred and seventy million dollars. That's the GDP of a small Pacific island nation. That's the annual budget of a mid-sized American city. That's more money than most human beings who have ever lived could comprehend. And it flowed from Gordon Stiles's accounts into mine with the unremarkable ease of a utility payment, because at the altitude where men like Stiles and I operate, a hundred and seventy million dollars is a line item. Not a decision. Not a negotiation. Not even a conversation. A line item. The kind of figure that an accountant records and a compliance officer stamps and a regulator overlooks because the regulator is funded by the same industry that produces the line items, and the industry has decided, through decades of lobbying and regulatory capture and the systematic defunding of enforcement agencies, that line items of this magnitude are private matters between consenting billionaires.

Here is how the invoice was delivered, because "consulting fee" deserves a translation.

I met Gordon at his Midtown office. His assistant brought coffee. He sat across from me at a desk that cost more than the annual salary of the prosecutor who would later try to investigate the transaction, and he placed a document in front of me.

A term sheet. Standard financial consulting engagement. Scope of services left deliberately vague — the kind of language that lawyers draft when the services being described cannot be named in a legal document without the document becoming evidence.

"Hundred and seventy," I said.

He looked at the figure. He didn't flinch. Men like Gordon Stiles do not flinch at numbers. They flinch at other things — at the specific mention of a date in July, at a property name in the Coral Islands, at the name of a girl who had come forward three years earlier and whose deposition had been sealed under a protective order that his own lawyers had filed.

"The scope is broad," he said.

"The services are comprehensive," I said.

He signed. Not because he was afraid of me in the conventional sense — not in with visceral, physical dread. He was afraid of the *ledger.* The ledger that could not be unwritten. The entry that his visit had already made.

He signed. He always was going to sign.

The fact that the consent, in this case, may have been purchased with the same currency I used to purchase everything — silence, complicity, the mutual understanding that everyone involved has something to lose — is a detail that the financial system was designed not to notice.

Saul Braverman was America's most famous defense attorney, and he was about to become the most ironic. Braverman was a Hartfield Law professor — the Hartfield Law professor, the one whose name appeared in casebooks and whose opinions were cited in Supreme Court briefs and whose client list read like a combined roster of the most famous and the most infamous people in modern legal history. He had defended O.J. Simpson. He had defended Klaus von Bülow. He had defended murderers, dictators, heiresses, and at least one convicted spy, building a career on the principle that every person deserves aggressive legal representation regardless of their guilt, which is a noble principle when stated in a law school lecture hall and a considerably more complicated principle when the person you're defending is a sex trafficker who flies you to his island on a private jet.

Braverman was my personal attorney. He was also a frequent flier on the 727 — his name appearing in the flight logs with a regularity that suggested either an extraordinarily active attorney-client relationship or a man who enjoyed private air travel to Caribbean islands for reasons that had nothing to do with billable hours. He was a fixture at my dinner parties. He was a fixture on my guest lists. He was, by any reasonable assessment, deeply embedded in the social and professional architecture of my operation.

And then the victims started naming him. One of Natalie Brennan's allegations implicated Braverman directly. She accused him of being not just my lawyer but a *participant.* The accusation was specific. The accusation was devastating. And the accusation created a conflict of interest so staggering that it would have been comedy if it weren't about trafficked children: my personal attorney was simultaneously defending me against accusations of sexual abuse and being accused, by the same victims, of committing sexual abuse. The man I hired to protect me from allegations needed to protect himself from the same allegations.

Braverman's public response was instructive. He called my accusers "self-described prostitutes who don't feel harmed." That phrase — *prostitutes who don't feel harmed* — deserves a moment of examination, because it reveals, in nine words, the entire defense strategy of every powerful man who has ever been accused of sexual abuse by someone less powerful. First, redefine the victim as a willing participant: "prostitute," not victim. Second, minimize the harm: "don't feel harmed," as if harm is a sensation that the powerful get to diagnose in the powerless, like a doctor taking a patient's temperature from across the room. Third, embed the redefinition in a legal vocabulary that sounds authoritative and measured, so that what would be recognized as victim-blaming if stated by a layperson is instead processed as legal analysis when stated by a Hartfield professor.

Saul was the best lawyer money could buy. I bought him. Then the girls accused him too. And suddenly my lawyer needed a lawyer. There's a joke in there somewhere, but I'm too classy to make it. Okay, no I'm not — it's hilarious.

Now the intelligence thread. The thread that everyone suspects and no one can prove. The thread that, if pulled, would unravel not just my operation but the operations of at least two governments.

Former Prime Minister **Avi Ben-David** of a certain Middle Eastern nation was close enough to me for eleven documented email exchanges. Eleven. Between a former prime minister — a former military chief of staff, a former head of military intelligence, a man who had commanded one of the most sophisticated armed forces on the planet — and a college dropout from Brooklyn who ran a financial consulting firm with no verifiable clients.

Rosenthal was photographed entering my Manhattan mansion. He visited the island. He existed in my orbit with the comfortable regularity of a man for whom visits to the home of a registered sex offender (which I would become, in time) were either unremarkable or, more troublingly, *operational.* His visits were not social calls in any conventional sense — Avi Ben-David did not make social calls the way other retired heads of state make social calls, because Avi Ben-David was not a man who had ever fully retired from the world of intelligence. Men like Rosenthal don't retire. They transition. They move from official positions to unofficial capacities, from government offices to consultancies, from commanding operations to advising on them. The infrastructure changes. The instincts don't.

In the intelligence theory of the case — the theory that has been advanced by journalists, by former intelligence officers, by victims' attorneys, and by the conspicuous pattern of my connections to intelligence-adjacent figures stretching back to the Prescott Academy — Rosenthal is the smoking gun. A former prime minister of a nation with one of the most aggressive intelligence services on Earth. A former chief of military intelligence. Visiting the home of a man with cameras in every room. Corresponding with a man who maintains a multi-terabyte archive of compromising footage of the world's most powerful people.

The implication is not subtle. The implication is a brass band playing in a library.

Avi was the most dangerous man I ever befriended. Not because of what he could do to me — though what he could do to me was considerable, given that the intelligence apparatus he once commanded had a well-documented history of operations that the polite world pretends don't happen. He was dangerous because of what his presence in my living room *implied* about what I was actually doing. When a former head of military intelligence makes house calls, it means either you're very interesting or you're very useful. I was both.

I donated millions to Hartfield. This is a statement that should be unremarkable — many people donate millions to Hartfield — except that the man donating the money was a convicted sex offender, and the university accepting the money was the most prestigious academic institution in the world, and the gap between those two facts is wide enough to fit the entire moral history of the American elite inside it.

My name went on a building. My donations bought access — not the kind of access that the admissions office sells to legacy applicants and development cases, though that kind of access is also for sale. My access was deeper. It bought proximity to Carroll Ashford, who was still returning my calls. It bought an open door to Braverman's office, which was both my lawyer's office and a Hartfield office, making every visit simultaneously a legal consultation and an academic engagement. It bought access to the genetics labs, where the brightest minds in the world studied the same subjects that I funded through my Coral Islands foundation. And it bought access to the brightest graduate students in the world — some of whom I invited to the island, where the dinners were brilliant and the beaches were beautiful and the cameras were rolling.

Hartfield accepted the money. Hartfield put my name on the door. Hartfield incorporated my donations into its endowment with the institutional efficiency of a machine that has been accepting money from morally questionable sources since its founding in 1636 and has refined the process to an art form.

When it all collapsed — when my name became synonymous with everything a university claims to oppose — Hartfield conducted an internal review. The review was thorough. The review was comprehensive. The review returned the money and scrubbed the name. And the review carefully, meticulously, institutionally avoided asking the one question that mattered: how did a convicted sex offender maintain relationships with the university's most senior faculty for *decades?* How did the checks keep clearing? How did the invitations keep arriving? How did the most rigorous academic institution in the world fail to apply even the most basic scrutiny to a donor whose public record included a conviction for soliciting a minor?

Hartfield is the world's finest institution of higher learning and the world's finest institution of looking the other way. The endowment was thirty-seven billion dollars. My donation was a rounding error. But it bought me the letterhead. And the letterhead bought me everything else.

Let me step back and look at the board.

I used to play chess with physicists at the island dinners. They were better players than me. They played to win the game. I played to own the board. Different objective.

By 2004, every piece was in position. Academics for cover. Politicians for protection. Billionaires for funding. Intelligence contacts for immunity. Lawyers for obstruction. The island for isolation. The cameras for insurance. Every piece served a function. Every function made the next function possible. The man who ran the system was untouchable.

Or so he believed.

Chapter 21: The Shadow State

Timeline: 1991–2019 | **Location:** Manhattan, Tel Aviv, multiple sovereign territories

It is November 2018. I am in the library of the 74th Street mansion, at the desk I have used for forty years, and I have just sent an email. The email took me eleven seconds to write. I have written longer grocery lists. The email asks Avi Ben-David — former Prime Minister, former Chief of Military Intelligence, a man whose contact details should not exist in the inbox of a private citizen — to publicly clarify that I do not work for Mossad. I added a smiley face. Then I closed the laptop and looked out the window at the street below, where a dog walker was navigating seven dogs through the intersection with the exhausted competence of a man doing a job that pays less than it should. I watched the dogs for a moment. Then I thought about what I'd just written, and what it proved, and whether there was a single person on Earth who would read it and believe the words rather than the punctuation.

People ask if I worked for Mossad.

I told Avi to make clear that I don't. That email exists. It's in the files. Sent in 2018, to Avi Ben-David — the former Prime Minister of Israel, the former Chief of Military Intelligence, the former head of the most decorated military career in the history of the Israeli Defense Forces — asking him to publicly clarify that I was not an operative of Israeli intelligence.

The email had a smiley face at the end. I don't work for Mossad. ☺

What also exists — in the same files, the same archive, the same three million pages that the Department of Justice released with all the care and precision of a man dropping a piano down a staircase — is every other email, every other meeting, every other deal I brokered between governments that officially had no relationship and intelligence agencies that officially didn't know I existed. The emails say I don't work for Mossad. The evidence says I worked for everyone. Both statements can be true. In intelligence, "working for" someone doesn't mean a paycheck and a badge. It means you're useful. And useful people never need business cards.

The cultivation had begun long before I understood what I was being cultivated for.

When I moved from the arms trade to the Hensley orbit — when the plumbing of weapons transfers became the plumbing of financial management for a billionaire — I carried my contacts with me. The contacts didn't care what I was managing. They cared that I was *connected.* That I had access to the kind of people — politicians, business leaders, academics, royalty — whose conversations, decisions, and vulnerabilities were of interest to governments whose official representatives could never get close enough to overhear.

I got close. I got closer than any official representative could dream. I didn't get close because I was trained in tradecraft or equipped with listening devices or deployed by a handler with a dead drop and a code name. I got close because I threw excellent dinner parties. Because I introduced brilliant people to each other. Because I funded academic research and invited Nobel laureates to my island and created a social environment so intellectually stimulating, so exclusive, so seductive that the most powerful people in the world *wanted* to be in the room. And the room was wired. That's the part the movies get right, actually. The room was wired.

I described the Keystone Circle in an earlier chapter. I want to use it now as a point of comparison, because comparison is the fastest way to explain what the Apex Council was and --- more importantly --- what it wasn't.

The Keystone Circle was a conviction organization. Its members gathered because they *believed* something, because their wealth and their identity had fused around a cause, because the cause felt like an extension of the self rather than an external commitment. They coordinated through philanthropy. They moved money through foundations. They shaped policy through advocacy and donation and the particular species of access that personal fortunes purchase. They were powerful, and they were effective, and they operated well outside the reach of any institution that might have wanted to regulate them. But they were *social.* Their power flowed through dinners and donations and the organic network of men who share a background, a geography, and a deeply held conviction about the way the world should be organized. When those men left the room, they went back to their retail empires and their entertainment companies and their philanthropic foundations. The cause was something they *supported.* It was not something they *were.*

The Apex Council was different in the way that a scalpel is different from a checkbook. The checkbook funds the operation. The scalpel performs it. The men in the Apex Council were not writing checks to a cause they believed in. They were administering a mechanism that no government could officially acknowledge, in service of interests that no government could officially pursue.

The difference is not moral --- both organizations operated in spaces that the law could not comfortably illuminate. The difference is *functional.* The Keystone Circle's members were wealthy men who happened to be useful. The Apex Council's members were nodes in a system that used their wealth as infrastructure. In the Circle, the men directed the money. In the Council, the money directed the men. And the men, to their great credit and their great peril, had no objection.

I attended my first Council dinner in the fall of 1993. Hensley's apartment — the one on Fifth Avenue, not the compound, because the compound was for private business and the apartment was for business that was supposed to look social. Twelve men around a table that had been set, I noticed, with a care that exceeded what the occasion officially required. That level of table-setting is a message. It says: we know what we are, we know what this is, and we are not going to insult each other by pretending otherwise. I was the youngest person in the room by approximately a decade and the least wealthy person by approximately a billion dollars. Nobody mentioned this. In my experience, rooms full of billionaires never mention the person who isn't one. They simply position him according to what he's there to provide, the way a surgeon positions an instrument before reaching for it. I was there to provide connectivity. They were there to direct it. That was the arrangement, unspoken, understood before the soup course, cemented by dessert.

The APEX Council was founded in 1991. I use the name because the real name — which involved a single English word suggesting something very large and very powerful — has been documented extensively, and the documentation consistently describes the same thing: a study group. A *study group.* Two of the wealthiest men in the North American Jewish community — Grant Hensley and Gharles Pronfman, the Winthrop Spirits heir — gathered approximately twenty billionaires to discuss philanthropy, Israel advocacy, and the geopolitical landscape of the post-Soviet world.

Twenty billionaires in a room. Discussing Israel. In 1991 — the year the Soviet Union collapsed, the year the Madrid Peace Conference attempted to reshape the Middle East, the year every intelligence agency on Earth was recalibrating its understanding of the global power structure because the bipolar world had become unipolar overnight and nobody knew what the new rules were. The APEX Council was a study group the way Casa del Sol is a golf club. Technically accurate. Functionally misleading.

What the APEX Council was — what it functioned as, regardless of what its bylaws said and what its members described in the rare interviews they gave — was a nexus. A node where private wealth intersected with state interests, where American billionaires coordinated with Israeli intelligence priorities, where the line between philanthropy and geopolitics became so thin that stepping on one side automatically placed you on the other.

I moved through the APEX Council's orbit the way I moved through every orbit: as a facilitator. Not a member — I was never wealthy enough to be a *member* of a group whose entry requirement was a personal fortune measured in billions. But I was useful to its members. I managed money. I made introductions. I provided services — financial, social, logistical — that the members needed and that their official advisors could not provide because official advisors leave paper trails and paper trails create accountability and accountability is the enemy of the kind of activity that the APEX Council facilitated.

Through the Council and its members, I gained access to a network of pro-Israel advocacy that operated at the intersection of American domestic politics and Israeli intelligence. Not the AIPAC version — the lobbyists in suits, the campaign donations, the public face of American-Israeli relations that appears on C-SPAN and in newspaper editorials. The *other* version. The quiet version. The version that involves private meetings between billionaires and intelligence officials, the movement of money through channels that the public doesn't monitor, and the kind of coordination between a foreign intelligence service and American private citizens that, in any other context, would be called espionage.

I'm not calling it espionage. Espionage is a legal term, and legal terms have consequences, and I've spent my entire career ensuring that the consequences of legal terms never attach to me or to the people I serve. I'm calling it *alignment*. A shared understanding between wealthy, connected, patriotic Americans and the intelligence professionals of a nation they supported, in which the interests of both parties converged so naturally that no explicit agreement was ever necessary. Nobody needed to say "spy for us." Nobody needed to say "I will transmit secrets." The information flowed naturally, through social channels, through dinner conversations, through the organic process of being in the room when powerful people said things that other powerful people needed to hear. I was the room.

Let me list the things I brokered. Not the girls — I've told you about the girls. Not the financial services — I've told you about those. The *other* things. The things that place me not in the category of sex trafficker or financial criminal but in the category that nobody wants to acknowledge because acknowledging it transforms the Vincent Aldric story from a crime story into a geopolitical story, and geopolitical stories don't have the clean moral architecture that crime stories have.

The Mongolia call came in on a Saturday afternoon, on a line I kept for people who did not leave voicemails. A man whose name I had been given six months earlier by someone in Avi's orbit — not Avi directly, never directly, because directness is a luxury that people at Avi's level abandoned decades ago — asked me a single question in English that was not his first language and possibly not his second. The question was whether I knew anyone who knew anyone. That is the entirety of the intelligence inquiry, condensed to its irreducible form. I said I would make some calls. I made four. Over the following three months, two governments that had no significant diplomatic history, no obvious reason to cooperate on security, and no visible intermediary capable of bringing them together — Israel and Mongolia, separated by five thousand miles and several centuries of mutual indifference — reached an agreement whose details are classified by both parties. I brokered it from the 74th Street study, on a phone I no longer own, between men I will not name. The agreement was signed. I received a fee routed through an entity in Luxembourg that no longer exists. That is what stateless intelligence brokerage looks like from the inside. It looks like a Saturday afternoon and four phone calls.

The Syria backchannel required a different approach because the two parties could not know they were talking to each other through the same intermediary. That is the specific geometry of certain intelligence arrangements: both sides need a channel, neither side can acknowledge the channel exists, and the man in the middle must maintain two separate fictions simultaneously without letting the seams show. I had a contact on the Israeli side — not military, not Mossad, the third category that intelligence professionals use when they need something done that neither of those institutions can officially touch. I had a contact on the Russian side through the arms trade years, a man who had survived three changes of government in Moscow by being useful to each successive regime in ways that the previous regime had never imagined. We met, the three of us, never in the same room. I met the Israeli contact in London. I met the Russian contact in Vienna. Each of them believed he was my only interlocutor. The channel operated for fourteen months. During those fourteen months, Israeli strikes in Syria were coordinated — informally, deniably, through a mechanism no congressional committee would ever be able to subpoena — with Russian operational awareness. Nobody died who might otherwise have died. Nobody officially communicated with anyone they were not supposed to communicate with. The channel closed when the operational need changed. I never spoke to either man again. That is the lifecycle of a backchannel. It exists precisely as long as it needs to, and then it doesn't.

The Côte d'Ivoire transaction was the most straightforward of the three, which made it the most revealing. A government official — not the minister himself, the minister's deputy, because ministers have aides who keep records and deputies have lunch meetings that nobody logs — flew to New York and sat across from me in a restaurant on the Upper East Side that I used for conversations that needed to happen in public without being overheard, because a crowded restaurant in Manhattan is the most private place on Earth if both parties are speaking quietly and the ambient noise is sufficient. He ordered fish. I ordered water. He described what his government needed in terms that were careful to remain just inside the language of legitimate security procurement. I described what I could provide in terms that were equally careful. We finished the meal. He flew home. The surveillance technology — manufactured by an Israeli company whose product line included capabilities that no African nation was supposed to be able to acquire through official channels — was delivered over the following six months through a logistics chain that I do not intend to describe in more detail than this. The implications of a government acquiring those tools, through that chain, with that level of unaccountability, were somebody else's problem. They are always somebody else's problem. That is the function of the intermediary: to stand between the transaction and its consequences, close enough to facilitate both, far enough to belong to neither.

These are three examples. There are others. The files contain traces of others — email references to meetings that are not explained, to agreements that are not detailed, to introductions that are described in the shorthand of men who understand each other well enough that explicitness is unnecessary and dangerous.

I was a stateless intelligence broker. I carried no flag. I wore no uniform. I served no single government. I served the *intersection* — the space where governments need things done that they cannot do officially, where money needs to move in directions that official channels cannot accommodate, where relationships need to exist that official diplomacy cannot acknowledge. And in exchange for my services, I received something more valuable than any salary an intelligence agency could pay: I received *protection.*

Celeste understood the architecture because Celeste had spent years operating inside it. Roman Harlow — the media baron, the intelligence asset, the man who fell off a yacht in the Adriatic Sea in circumstances that were ruled accidental by a coroner and believed by no intelligence agency on Earth — had been a triple agent. Celeste had worked his orbit as a junior operative before going independent. Maybe quadruple. The categories become academic when the number of services is high enough. British intelligence. Mossad. The KGB. Possibly others. The boundaries between client and service, between loyalty and transaction, between espionage and commerce, had been so thoroughly dissolved in Roman's career that reconstructing them after his death was like trying to reassemble a shattered mirror: you could see fragments of the original image, but the cracks made the complete picture impossible.

When Roman died, they buried him like a king. They buried him like an asset whose service was so valuable that acknowledging it was worth the diplomatic embarrassment of publicly honoring a man who had also stolen six hundred million pounds from his own employees' pension fund. They buried him on a hillside outside a city whose name carries the weight of millennia — a site that, in the tradition of the nation that honored him, is reserved for those whose service is considered sacred. They gave the world's most notorious media thief the burial of a prophet.

That's what intelligence protection looks like. It doesn't look like a badge or a salary or a government apartment. It looks like a funeral that tells the world: this man was ours, and we honor our own, and the things he did in our service outweigh the things he did to everyone else.

Celeste was built for this. She understood the intelligence world the way a fish understands water — not as a concept but as an environment. The connections were not something she acquired through me; they were something she *breathed.* And when she entered my orbit — when our partnership formed in that first moment of recognition at the London dinner party — she brought the connections with her. Not as a conscious strategy. As a *reflex.* She knew people. People who had worked in the same agencies she had. People who had operated alongside Roman Harlow. People whose careers existed in the same invisible architecture that Roman had occupied for forty years.

In 2005, Celeste emailed me about meeting someone. A person she described as a CIA operative — not a diplomat, not a consultant, not any of the euphemisms that intelligence professionals use in mixed company. A CIA operative who had "worked" with Roman Harlow — through Celeste's old intelligence channels. Who could "find all, reveal all (for a price)."

That email is in the files. That email exists in the same archive as the smiley-face Mossad denial. That email tells you — in Celeste's own words, in her own casual shorthand, in the language of a woman so comfortable with intelligence contacts that she discusses them the way other women discuss hairdressers — that the intelligence architecture around our operation was not a rumor. Not a conspiracy theory. Not the paranoid speculation of people who've watched too many spy movies. It was the family business.

Roman's death created a problem and an opportunity. The problem: Roman's threat. Before he died, he had communicated — through channels that only he controlled, using the leverage that only he possessed — a message to the intelligence agencies he had served. The message, reconstructed from documents released decades later, was simple: "Unless they gave him four hundred million pounds, he would expose all he had done for them."

Four hundred million. That was the price of Roman's silence. That was the number he had calculated — with the precision of a man who had spent forty years quantifying the value of secrets — that his knowledge of intelligence operations was worth. Not as a threat but as a negotiation. A retirement package. A man who has served multiple intelligence agencies for four decades, who has carried out operations that those agencies cannot acknowledge, who possesses documentation that could reshape the public's understanding of how their governments actually operate — that man has leverage. And leverage, as I've explained throughout this book, is the most valuable asset in the world.

Roman overplayed his hand. Roman fell off his yacht. The sequence may be coincidence. The intelligence community's official position is that it is coincidence. The intelligence community's official position on many things is coincidence, and the intelligence community's official positions should be evaluated with the same rigor that one evaluates the claims of any organization whose business model depends on secrecy.

The opportunity: Roman's network didn't die with him. The contacts, the relationships, the institutional connections between private wealth and state intelligence — these things don't disappear when one man falls off a yacht. They *transfer.* They transfer to the people closest to the dead man. To his family. To his partners. To the woman who had operated inside the network for years and who had, by 1992, partnered with a man who was building a machine that the intelligence community would find even more useful than Roman's newspapers.

Celeste brought her intelligence network. I brought the operational model. Together, we built something that Roman never imagined: an intelligence asset that *generated* intelligence continuously, automatically, through the simple mechanism of cameras in bedrooms and powerful men in beds. Roman had to *work* for his leverage — cultivating sources, gathering information, making himself useful enough to justify protection. My system worked while I slept. The cameras ran twenty-four hours a day. The guests compromised themselves without any prompting from me. The intelligence simply *accumulated,* like interest in an account, compounding daily, growing more valuable with every visit and every guest and every act that the guest would prefer not to see published.

Roman's model was labor-intensive. Mine was passive income.

And the intelligence agencies — whichever ones were watching, whichever ones had inherited Roman's institutional interest in the Harlow orbit, whichever ones had noted that a former operative was now partnered with a man who had cameras in every room of every property on three continents — those agencies recognized the upgrade.

They didn't recruit me. They didn't need to. They simply *allowed* me to operate. They created the zone of immunity. They ensured that the six words circulated through the system. And they waited for the intelligence to flow. It flowed.

I want to address the emails with Avi, because the emails with Avi are the Rosetta Stone. Avi Ben-David. Former Prime Minister. Former Chief of Military Intelligence. Former head of Unit 8200 — the special forces unit that is, in Israeli military hierarchy, what the Praetorian Guard was to Rome: the elite of the elite, the unit from which prime ministers are drawn, the unit whose operational history is classified at levels that make American military secrecy look like a suggestion box.

Avi appeared in my emails eleven times. Not as a government official. As a *friend.* As someone who discussed personal matters, travel plans, and the kind of casual logistics that accumulate between people who see each other regularly and comfortably. The emails reference "Number 1" — which, in Israeli intelligence shorthand, is how people refer to the head of Mossad. Not by name. By number. Because naming the head of Mossad in an email is the kind of thing that creates problems, and creating problems is the kind of thing that Avi Ben-David had spent fifty years learning to avoid.

I discussed "Number 1" in my emails the way other people discuss mutual acquaintances. Casually. With the shorthand of an insider.

And then — in 2018 — I asked Avi to "make clear that I don't work for Mossad."

With a smiley face.

A man who genuinely doesn't work for Mossad doesn't need a former Prime Minister to clarify that fact. Doesn't have his email address. Doesn't discuss "Number 1" with the familiarity of an insider. And doesn't add a smiley face to the denial. The smiley face is the most honest punctuation mark in the history of espionage.

And the six words continued to circulate. And the zone of immunity continued to hold. Until 2019, when the math changed. Not the morality. Not the law. The *math.* When the cost of protecting the asset exceeds the value of the asset's product, the protection is withdrawn. Not because the girls mattered. Because the math changed.

There's a man named Murray Kaplan who told the truth about me. I mention him because nobody else did — not while I was alive, not while the truth would have mattered, not while telling it could have saved a single girl from what happened in my houses and on my island and in the rooms where the cameras ran. Kaplan was my business partner. The Pinnacle Capital Group partner. The man with whom I constructed the Ponzi scheme that preceded the trafficking operation — the five-hundred-million-dollar fraud that should have ended my career but instead provided the financial education and the criminal connections that made the trafficking operation possible. Kaplan went to prison. I didn't. The inequality of that outcome haunted him for years, which is the kind of thing that makes a man talkative.

Kaplan also told investigators that I was the one who introduced him to Roman Harlow. That the Harlow connection — the introduction that would reshape my life, my operation, and the geopolitical architecture of my entire enterprise — was something I initiated, not something that happened to me. That I didn't stumble into the intelligence world through the Harlow connection. I *brought* the intelligence world to Roman's dinner table because I was already inside it. I'll let the reader decide which narrative better fits the evidence. But I've never been a victim of circumstance. I've always been the circumstance.

The planes deserve a second mention, because the planes are the physical thread that connects every chapter of this book to every other chapter. In the arms trade chapter, I described how CIA aircraft from the Iran-Contra era were reassigned — transferred through intermediaries into private hands. In the Hensley chapter, I described how my patron's retail empire used logistics infrastructure with intelligence lineage. Now I want to close the loop.

My Gulfstream IV — the *Monarch Express,* as the tabloids called it, with the kind of naming creativity that distinguishes the British press — was not a CIA plane. I want to be clear about that. It was purchased commercially. It was registered normally. It was, on paper, an unremarkable piece of private aviation hardware.

But the operational model — the way it was used, the routes it flew, the jurisdictional flexibility it exploited — was borrowed directly from the intelligence aviation playbook I'd learned in the 1980s. Private aircraft operating across multiple jurisdictions. Flight plans filed with the minimum disclosure required by aviation authorities. Passenger manifests that were technically accurate and practically incomplete. Stops at airports where customs enforcement was relaxed, absent, or actively cooperative. The ability to move human beings across international borders with less scrutiny than a FedEx package receives. I didn't need CIA planes. I needed the CIA's *methods.* And I had those methods because I'd spent half a decade in the infrastructure that developed them.

The Boeing carried girls. It also carried presidents, princes, billionaires, and Nobel laureates. It carried men whose names appear on the flight logs that congressional investigators would later analyze with the obsessive attention of scholars decoding a sacred text. The flight logs became the most famous travel documents in American law — more scrutinized than any passport, more consequential than any boarding pass, a record of movement that compressed the invisible architecture of my operation into columns and rows and departure times and arrival codes.

But the flight logs only document where the plane went. They don't document what I learned about making planes useful — about the intersection of private aviation and institutional blindness, about the regulatory gaps that exist between jurisdictions, about the simple fact that a private aircraft operated by a wealthy individual attracts approximately one-tenth the scrutiny that a commercial aircraft attracts, and that one-tenth of scrutiny, applied to a man who understands the remaining nine-tenths, is functionally zero.

The arms trade taught me this. The intelligence community taught me this. The planes were not separate from the intelligence architecture. They were its most visible expression — a Gulfstream IV, painted white, crossing oceans, carrying the powerful and the powerless in the same cabin, protected by the same institutional blindness that had once protected weapons shipments to countries that weren't supposed to receive them. Different cargo. Same architecture. Same impunity.

And that's the shadow state. Not a conspiracy. Not a grand design. Not a group of men in a room deciding the fate of the world. Just math. The cold, institutional, perfectly rational math of agencies that calculate the value of human assets the way insurance companies calculate the value of human lives — precisely, impersonally, and without a smiley face.

I lived in the shadow state for forty years. I operated its plumbing. I brokered its deals. I provided its intelligence. And when the math changed — when the cost of protecting me exceeded the value of what I produced — the shadow state withdrew its protection with the same impersonal efficiency with which it had extended it.

No phone call. No warning. No dramatic confrontation in a parking garage with a man in a trenchcoat explaining that my services were no longer required. Just the absence of protection. Just the sudden, disorienting sensation of a man who has been walking on a glass floor for thirty years and who suddenly notices the glass is gone.

The glass was never mine. The glass was always theirs. And they took it back when it suited them to take it back, and I fell, and the falling was — like everything in the intelligence world — deniable.

I don't work for Mossad. ☺

And the smiley face, in the end, is the most honest thing I ever wrote. Because it acknowledges what the sentence denies. Because it says what the words don't say. Because it captures, in a single piece of punctuation, the fundamental truth of the shadow state: that nothing is what it appears, that every denial is a confession, and that the man who smiles while lying is telling you more than the man who lies with a straight face. The smiley face is my autobiography. Everything else is details.

I looked out the window. The dog walker was gone. The street was empty the way 74th Street is empty at noon on a weekday — not actually empty, but emptied of everything that matters, a stage between performances. I closed the laptop. I stood up. I went to the window and looked at the street for a long moment, and I thought about the email I had just sent, and the forty years it represented, and the particular irony of a man who had spent his entire career ensuring that nothing could be proved against him now sending — voluntarily, casually, with a smiley face — the clearest single piece of evidence that anything could ever produce. I thought about what Celeste would have said. She would have said I was being sloppy. She would have been right. But Celeste was gone by 2018, and when the person who taught you caution is no longer in the room, caution starts to feel like a habit rather than a survival strategy, and habits, unlike strategies, can be set aside. I set it aside. I sent the email. I added the smiley face. And then I stood at the window of the house I had built on the architecture of other people's secrets, and I watched the empty street, and I felt — for the first and last time in forty years — something that a more honest man might have called afraid.

Fragment: The Surgeon's Table

The following is reconstructed from a sealed deposition taken in 2020 from a former staff member at the New Mexico property designated in court documents as "Cimarron Station." The deponent was granted conditional immunity. The deposition was sealed by judicial order. What follows has been fictionalized, but the architecture is real.

I was hired as kitchen staff. That's what my contract said. Kitchen staff, private ranch, New Mexico. Sixty-five thousand a year plus housing. For a twenty-three-year-old who'd been working the line at an Albuquerque steakhouse, it sounded like the lottery.

The ranch was an hour from the nearest town. Forty miles of dirt road and then a gate and then more dirt road and then another gate and then the buildings. Beautiful buildings. Adobe and glass. The kind of architecture that rich people build when they want the desert to look expensive. Motion sensors on the roads. Thermal cameras on the fences. I was told it was for coyotes. The animal kind. I believed that for about a week.

Most of the time, the work was what the contract said. Meals for the owner when he visited. Meals for the caretaker staff. Groceries delivered by a supply truck that came once a week from Tierra Blanca. Normal kitchen work in a not-normal setting.

Then the special events.

The special events happened maybe four times in the two years I was there. Small guest lists. Six, eight people. They'd fly in on private planes — the ranch had its own strip, paved, long enough for jets. The guests arrived at night. Always at night. The kitchen prep started two days before.

The first three events, I cooked. Elaborate multi-course meals. The guests ate in the main dining room. I never went into the dining room during service — the house manager handled that. I prepped, I plated, the house manager carried. I washed dishes. I went to my quarters. Normal.

The fourth event was different.

The surgeon arrived the day before the guests. He came on a separate flight. He carried his own cases — hard-sided, aluminum, the kind I'd seen in medical supply catalogs. He didn't eat with the staff. He didn't speak to the staff. He set up in one of the guest buildings — the one farthest from the main house, the one with the reinforced door that I'd been told was a wine cellar.

The boy arrived the same day. Fifteen, maybe sixteen. Latino. Thin. He came in a car, not a plane, driven by a man I didn't recognize. The boy was quiet. Not scared-quiet — *empty*-quiet. The quiet of a person who has already left their body and is just waiting for their body to catch up.

I was told to prepare specific meals. Not for the dining room. For the guest building. Trays. The specifications were precise: high-protein, high-calorie, specific supplements mixed into sauces. The kind of nutritional planning you'd see for a patient in recovery. I didn't understand why dinner guests needed recovery nutrition.

I understood on the second night.

I was carrying a tray to the building. The house manager was supposed to do it but the house manager was sick — actually sick, or conveniently sick, I'll never know. I carried the tray. I knocked. Nobody answered. I opened the door.

The surgeon was in the room. He was wearing scrubs. Clean scrubs — the surgical kind, not the kind you buy at a uniform store. He had gloves on. He was adjusting an IV drip attached to the boy, who was on a table — not a dining table, a medical table, the kind with rails and straps and a drain.

The boy was conscious. The drugs — whatever the surgeon was giving him through the IV — kept him conscious. His eyes were open. He was looking at the ceiling. His mouth was moving but no sound was coming out.

I looked at the boy's body.

I put the tray down. I walked out. I walked to the edge of the property where the desert starts and I vomited until there was nothing left and then I vomited air.

I will not describe what I saw. I can't. Not because I'm protecting anyone — because my brain won't let the image form into words. It sits behind a wall in my mind, a wall I built in the forty-five seconds between opening that door and reaching the desert. The wall is the only reason I'm still functional. If the wall comes down, I come down with it.

What I will tell you is this: the boy was alive. He was meant to be alive. The surgeon's job — the entire purpose of his medical expertise, his training, his oath — was to keep the boy alive and aware and *present* while the guests did what they did. The surgeon was not there to end suffering. The surgeon was there to *extend* it. To ensure that the body could sustain what was being done to it across multiple sessions, across days, so that the guests — the men who flew in on private jets and discussed wine and politics and technology over meals I prepared — could return to the room and continue.

The meals I was asked to prepare after that night were not for the guests. They were for the boy. The high-protein, high-calorie trays with the supplements in the sauces — that was the surgeon's nutrition plan. Keep the body functioning. Keep the machine running. Keep the product fresh.

I heard laughter from the building. On the third night, I heard laughter. Not the laughter of men watching a football game or telling jokes at a bar. A different kind. A *satisfied* kind. The laughter of connoisseurs. One voice — deeper than the others, an older man — said something I heard through the wall because the desert is quiet at night and sound carries across sand the way it carries across water. He said: "Better than Marrakech."

Better than Marrakech. Like he was comparing restaurants. Like this was a review.

The boy was there for four days. On the fifth morning, the building was empty. The medical table was gone. The IV stand was gone. The surgeon was gone. The boy was gone. The cleaning crew — two men I'd never seen before, not regular staff — spent six hours in that building. They brought their own supplies. Industrial supplies. The kind you use when soap and water aren't enough.

I never asked what happened to the boy. I knew what happened to the boy. Forty miles of desert in every direction. No neighbors. No witnesses. No one who would come looking for a boy that no one was supposed to know existed.

I quit the next week. I told them I was homesick. They paid me a severance — generous, six months' salary, contingent on a non-disclosure agreement that I signed because the alternative to signing was implied by the thermal cameras and the motion sensors and the forty miles of dirt road between me and the nearest human being who wasn't on the payroll.

I broke the NDA in 2020. I sat in a room with two federal investigators and I told them everything. I told them about the surgeon. I told them about the boy. I told them about the laughter and the medical table and the cleaning crew and the nutrition trays and the word *Marrakech.* I told them about the wall in my mind and what lives behind it.

They wrote it down. All of it. Every word.

The file is in a cabinet somewhere. I imagine it sits next to three million other pages, in a stack so tall that no single person could read it in a lifetime, in a system so vast that any individual horror — even this one, even the worst one, even the one that wakes me at 3 a.m. and sends me to the kitchen to stand in the light because the dark is not safe anymore — becomes a data point. A line item. A page in a stack.

The boy's name is not in the file. I never knew his name. He never spoke. The surgeon never used a name. The guests never used a name. In the economy of that room, names were unnecessary. You don't name the meal.

The deponent completed testimony over three sessions. On the fourth scheduled session, the deponent's attorney informed the court that the deponent was no longer available. The attorney did not elaborate. The deposition was sealed. The file was archived.

The guest building at Cimarron Station was demolished in 2021, eighteen months before the property was listed for sale. The demolition was contracted through a company registered in Delaware. No permit was filed with the county. The desert, as always, asked no questions.

Chapter 22: The Defector

Timeline: 2003 | **Location:** The Coral Islands, London, Undisclosed

The first time someone tried to destroy the archive, I was eating breakfast on the terrace at Little St. Philip, watching a pelican dive for fish and thinking about how much simpler life would be if humans had the pelican's clarity of purpose: see the fish, catch the fish, eat the fish. No committees. No lawyers. No second-guessing. Just appetite and execution.

Malcolm called on the satellite phone, which he never did unless something was burning — metaphorically or literally, and in this case both.

"We have a problem," he said, in the flat, affectless voice of a man who measures problems the way an engineer measures load-bearing capacity: not by how they feel, but by whether they will collapse the structure.

The problem was Klaus-Dieter Hartmann.

Hartmann was a German industrialist — steel, automotive components, and a defense contracting subsidiary that the German press politely declined to investigate because the defense contracts kept seven thousand people employed in a district whose parliamentary representative sat on the budget committee. He was sixty-three years old, enormously wealthy, and in possession of a set of appetites that had brought him to my island on four separate occasions over the previous two years. Each visit had been documented. Each room had been recorded. Each recording was stored on Malcolm's servers with the meticulous redundancy of a man who understood that digital files are simultaneously the most fragile and the most indestructible form of evidence ever created.

Hartmann had discovered the cameras.

Not through any failure of Malcolm's system — the cameras were invisible to anyone who wasn't specifically looking for them, and the system's architecture had been vetted by the same people who designed surveillance equipment for governments. Hartmann discovered them because he'd hired a private security firm — former intelligence, German BND — to sweep the island after one of his associates had been approached by a journalist with questions about his travel patterns. The sweep found nothing. What it found instead was *absence* — the conspicuous lack of any cellular signal in certain rooms, the kind of signal suppression that only exists when someone has installed equipment specifically designed to prevent external recording. The absence told them that *someone* was recording internally. And from there, it was a matter of following the wiring.

Hartmann didn't call me. Hartmann didn't threaten me. Hartmann didn't do any of the things that a rational person does when they discover they've been secretly filmed in compromising situations.

Hartmann hired a team.

The team was eight men. Ex-military — not the kind of ex-military who become security guards at shopping malls, but the kind who transition from government special operations to private military contracting, where the pay is better, the rules are fewer, and the clients are men like Klaus-Dieter Hartmann who have enough money to solve problems the way governments solve problems: with personnel, equipment, and the understanding that certain actions, conducted in certain jurisdictions, leave no paper trail.

Their objective was the server room. Not me. Not the island. The *servers.* Hartmann understood — because the BND men had explained it to him, because former intelligence professionals understand leverage the way former surgeons understand anatomy — that the cameras were nothing without the archive. Destroy the servers, destroy the backup drives, and the leverage evaporates. The recordings become ghosts. The blackmail becomes a bluff.

I learned about the team forty-eight hours before they arrived, because Celeste's intelligence contacts were better than Hartmann's security consultants. One phone call to a former colleague — a woman who now worked in private intelligence in London and who owed Celeste the kind of debt that intelligence professionals accumulate and never discuss — and we had the team's composition, their travel itinerary, their staging location on Port Asbury, and their operational timeline.

Forty-eight hours. Not enough time to move the servers — the archive was measured in terabytes, and moving terabytes from a Caribbean island to a secure location requires logistics that forty-eight hours doesn't provide. But enough time to make a phone call.

Not to the police. What would I tell the police? That a German industrialist was sending men to destroy evidence of my blackmail operation? The police would be as interested in my servers as Hartmann was, and considerably less likely to leave once they arrived.

I called Avi.

Not directly. Through channels. Through the specific architecture of intermediaries that exists between a private citizen and a former head of military intelligence when the private citizen has provided that intelligence service with years of useful product and the intelligence service has an institutional interest in ensuring that the product continues to flow.

Avi's people handled it. I don't know how. I don't know what was said to Hartmann, or to Hartmann's security firm, or to the eight men who were, at that moment, staging equipment on a rented yacht in the Port Asbury harbor. I don't know because I didn't ask, and I didn't ask because the entire architecture of my relationship with the intelligence world was built on the principle of strategic ignorance: I provide the product, they provide the protection, and neither of us asks the other how the sausage is made.

The team never arrived. The yacht left Port Asbury twenty-four hours before the planned operation. Hartmann's security firm dissolved — literally dissolved, closed its offices, scrubbed its website, and ceased to exist as a legal entity — within a week. And Hartmann himself, when I next saw him at a financial conference in Davos six months later, greeted me with the terrified cordiality of a man who has learned, through channels he will never discuss, that the person he tried to destroy is protected by forces that his considerable fortune cannot match.

He never returned to the island. But he also never spoke about what the cameras recorded. The leverage held. It always holds. That's the beauty of the system — even when a target discovers the architecture, the architecture still works, because the information it contains is more dangerous to the target than the architecture itself.

What Hartmann taught me — what the Defector Incident, as Malcolm catalogued it in his files, revealed about the operation I'd built — was that the archive had become something larger than a blackmail tool. It had become an *asset* — the kind of asset that intelligence agencies protect, that governments have an interest in preserving, that exists in a gray zone between private property and state infrastructure. The servers on Little St. Philip were no longer just *my* leverage. They were leverage that multiple governments found useful, that multiple intelligence services had an interest in maintaining, and that the destruction of would have created problems far larger than one German industrialist's embarrassment.

I had built a machine that was too valuable to destroy. And a machine that is too valuable to destroy is a machine that protects its operator. That was the lesson. That was the moment I understood that I was, functionally, untouchable — not because I was powerful, but because the thing I'd built was *useful* to people who were more powerful than any individual, including me.

The pelican caught its fish. I finished my breakfast. And the archive continued to grow.

Hartmann died of a heart attack in Frankfurt eleven months later. He was sixty-four years old and by every medical account in excellent health. I noted the date. I sent Malcolm a flag for the file. And I did not think about the pelican.

Chapter 23: The Investigation

Timeline: 2005–2006 | **Location:** Gulf Shore, FBI Field Office

A girl told her mother. Her mother called the cops. The cops opened a file.

In a normal country, that's how justice works. The crime occurs. The witness reports. The authorities investigate. The investigation produces evidence. The evidence produces charges. The charges produce a trial. The trial produces a verdict. And the verdict produces consequences.

But I don't live in a normal country. I live in America. And in America, justice is a subscription service, and I've been paying the premium plan for twenty years.

The file landed on the desk of Gulf Shore Police Chief **Daniel Harmon** and lead detective **Ray Montero**, and I want to be clear about something: they were good. Harmon was a competent, methodical police chief who understood that the case sitting on his desk was unlike anything his department had handled before — not because the crime was unusual (wealthy men abusing young girls in Gulf Shore is so common it practically has its own zip code), but because the suspect was unusual. A suspect with connections in every branch of government. A suspect with more lawyers than the department had officers. A suspect whose address book contained the phone numbers of people who could end a police chief's career with a single phone call.

Montero was the lead detective, and he was exactly the kind of cop that cop movies are written about: dogged, meticulous, stubbornly unimpressed by wealth, and constitutionally incapable of looking at a crime and deciding that the criminal was too important to investigate. He was making sixty thousand dollars a year. My lawyers were making sixty thousand dollars a week. The disparity should have been disqualifying. It wasn't. Montero didn't care about the money, which made him the most dangerous person I'd encountered since the mother who made the phone call.

I narrate the opening of this investigation with the mild annoyance of a man who's found a parking ticket on his windshield. Because that's what it felt like. Not terror. Not panic. Not the existential dread that an innocent man would feel upon learning that the police are investigating him. Annoyance. The particular, calibrated annoyance of a man who has spent twenty years building a system designed to prevent exactly this kind of inconvenience and who now must activate that system.

Detective Montero did something that nobody in my orbit would have considered dignified: he went through my trash.

A garbage pull. The most inelegant, most blue-collar, most unglamorous investigative technique available to law enforcement. While my lawyers were billing four hundred dollars an hour, Montero was putting on rubber gloves and sorting through the garbage cans outside my Gulf Shore mansion with the patient determination of a man who believes that the truth is in the details and that the details are sometimes buried under coffee grounds and junk mail.

He found what he found. A message pad containing phone numbers of underage girls — scribbled in the handwriting of someone who expected the note to be temporary, disposable, the kind of thing you jot down and throw away because the information has served its purpose. A used condom. A rose — the kind of romantic gesture that, in a different context, would be charming and that, in this context, was evidence of something that should make your skin crawl. The rose meant I *curated* these encounters. I didn't just perpetrate them and move on. I gave a flower to a child after abusing her, the way a date ends an evening with a gesture that says "I'd like to do this again." The rose was the detail that stayed with Montero, and it should stay with you too. The forensics painted a picture that was simultaneously unsurprising and devastating: the operation described in earlier chapters — the massage table, the recruitment network, the two-hundred-dollar payments — was not historical. It was *current.* It was operational. It was happening in the same house, on the same massage table, with the same economic model, at the very moment the detective was pulling evidence from the trash.

The detective followed the numbers on the message pad. The numbers led to girls. The girls led to other girls — the referral network, the MLM pyramid that I'd described in such clinical detail, was still functioning. Still recruiting. Still paying two hundred per massage, two hundred per referral. The machine I'd built hadn't just survived twenty years; it had *industrialized.* It was self-perpetuating, self-recruiting, a system so efficient that it no longer required my direct involvement in the recruitment phase. The girls recruited the girls who recruited the girls, and I sat at the top of the pyramid like the pharaoh for whom the whole structure was built.

A detective went through my trash. That's the most insulting part. Not that he investigated me — that I understand. But that a man making sixty thousand a year dug through my garbage cans with his bare hands because a girl's mother asked him to. That kind of dedication should be admired. It's also why I pay my lawyers four hundred times what he makes.

Montero interviewed dozens of girls.

The pattern was identical in every account, with the kind of consistency that either represents truth or represents the most elaborate conspiracy of coordinated false testimony in the history of Gulf Shore County — and since Gulf Shore County has a rich history of elaborate conspiracies, the defense team would eventually argue the latter, because arguing the latter is what defense teams do when confronted with dozens of witnesses who all tell the same story.

Recruited by a friend. Or by Celeste. Or by one of the staff — Diane, Jenna, the various operational employees who managed the scheduling and logistics of the pipeline with the professionalism of corporate human resources, except the humans being resourced were children. Brought to the mansion — the Gulf Shore estate on Via Dorado, the same waterfront compound I'd described in earlier chapters, with its surveillance cameras and its massage rooms and its swimming pool that functioned as both a luxury amenity and a set piece in the theater of normalcy that made the operation possible. Told it was a massage. Professional. Therapeutic. The same back-problem cover story that had been functioning as camouflage since the early nineties, the most boring lie in the world deployed by the most meticulous liar in the world.

Told to undress — gradually, incrementally, with the patient, systematic escalation of a man who understood that the distance between a professional massage and a sexual assault could be traversed in small enough steps that the victim would be unable to identify the precise moment the boundary was crossed. This was technique. This was methodology. This was the refinement of a predatory practice over a decade of repetition until the practice became so smooth, so routinized, so *procedural* that it resembled a medical appointment more than a crime scene. Told it would be quick. Told it would be easy money. Told that this was what wealthy people did — hired massage therapists, paid them well, tipped them generously. Told that this was *normal.* The normalization was the cruelest part. Not the act itself, but the framing — the deliberate, systematic reconstruction of a child's understanding of what adults do to children, what men do to girls, what money buys and what it excuses.

Some were fourteen. Some were fifteen. Some were sixteen. All of them were told the same thing afterward: *Don't tell anyone. And here's another girl's number if you want to make more money.*

The police identified at least forty victims in Gulf Shore alone. Forty. In a single city. In a single property. Forty girls whose stories overlapped with such precision that the statistical probability of coordination was essentially zero, because coordinating forty teenagers to tell the same story with the same details across the same timeline would require an organizational capability that exceeded the capability of the operation itself.

They found forty girls. Forty. And every single one of them told the same story. You'd think that would be damning. But here's the thing about forty identical stories: a good lawyer calls that "coordinated testimony." A great lawyer calls it "a conspiracy against my client." I have great lawyers.

Chief Harmon recognized what he was holding: a case that was too big, too connected, and too politically explosive for a municipal police department with a limited budget and a jurisdiction that ended at the city limits of Gulf Shore. The local political pressure was already mounting — the quiet, deniable, untraceable kind of pressure that occurs when powerful people learn that someone they know is being investigated and make phone calls that are never recorded to people who never admit receiving them. Phone calls from lawyers. Phone calls from political donors. Phone calls from the invisible network of influence that connects the wealthy residents of Gulf Shore to the elected officials and appointed administrators who govern them. Nobody told Harmon to drop the case — that would be obstruction, that would leave fingerprints. Instead, the pressure manifested as *friction.* Delays in processing requests. Questions about departmental priorities. Subtle suggestions that the department's resources might be better deployed on cases with clearer jurisdictional boundaries. The bureaucratic immune response that activates whenever a public institution gets too close to a private citizen who is too powerful to be comfortably prosecuted.

Harmon did the right thing. He referred the case to the FBI.

The Bureau opened a federal investigation. FBI agents — trained, funded, and empowered by the most powerful law enforcement agency in the world — began interviewing victims with a rigor that the Gulf Shore Police Department, for all its competence, simply couldn't match. They subpoenaed records — financial records from the Coral Islands trusts, phone records from every number in my address book, travel records from the FAA, employment records from every property. They pulled the flight logs — every page, every entry, every name. They mapped the network with the methodical precision of an intelligence operation targeting a hostile foreign actor, which, depending on whose theory of the case you believe, is exactly what I was.

They identified potential co-conspirators. Celeste Harlow — the recruiter, the social engineer, the woman who built the guest list. Jenna Caldwell — the scheduler, the calendar keeper. Diane Prewitt — the logistics manager, the executive assistant who ran the operation's daily affairs. Katya Sorvino — the girl I'd "acquired" from Eastern Europe, the pilot, the most tragic figure in the organizational chart. The structure that I'd described in earlier chapters as a legitimate business with a dark product was now being reconstructed by federal agents who were approaching it as what it was: a criminal enterprise operating across state lines, across international borders, with dozens of identified victims and a pattern of conduct that met every statutory requirement for federal sex trafficking charges carrying mandatory minimums of ten years to life.

The case file grew to thousands of pages. Victim statements. Financial analysis. Flight logs. Phone records. Email archives. Property records. Surveillance footage — not mine, but the FBI's own, conducted on my properties. The case was, by every metric that the American justice system uses to evaluate the viability of a prosecution, a slam dunk.

When the FBI knocked, I felt something I hadn't felt in years. Not fear — I don't do fear. Fear is for people who haven't spent two decades building a system designed to prevent exactly this contingency. But... *attention.* The kind of attention you give a chess opponent who actually knows the Sicilian Defense. The Gulf Shore cops were amateurs. Dedicated, competent amateurs, but amateurs nonetheless — limited by budget, by jurisdiction, by the inherent disadvantage of being a municipal department confronting a multinational operation. The FBI was professional. Professionals require a professional response.

I called my lawyers. Not *a* lawyer — an *army* of lawyers. The defense team began assembling like the most expensive concentration of legal talent ever assembled for a single case, a legal Avengers assembled not to save the world but to ensure that a pedophile with a forty-five-thousand-square-foot mansion never saw the inside of a federal courtroom.

Theodore Marsh, my personal attorney and co-executor of my estate — a man whose forty-five documented files in my archive made him one of the most prolific correspondents in the entire operation — coordinated the strategy. Marsh was the firewall — the man who stood between me and every legal threat, who managed the flow of information between the defense team and the prosecution, who ensured that the labyrinthine corporate structure of my financial empire remained opaque to investigators whose subpoenas were designed to make it transparent.

His message to every lawyer on the team was the same, delivered with the calm authority of a general issuing orders before a battle he intended to win: this case does not go to trial. This case does not see the inside of a federal courtroom. This case *disappears.* Not through destruction of evidence — that's crude, detectable, and carries its own charges. Through the application of legal pressure, political connections, procedural warfare, and the systematic exploitation of every rule, loophole, and ambiguity in the American legal system. The system was built with loopholes. The loopholes were built for people like me. The lawyers' job was to find every loophole and drive a Gulfstream IV through it.

Cost was not a consideration. Cost is never a consideration when the alternative is spending the rest of your life in a federal prison cell. I spent more on my legal defense in the first six months than the Gulf Shore Police Department's entire annual budget. That's not bragging. That's arithmetic. And arithmetic always wins.

While the FBI built their case from the top down, my team launched a parallel operation from the bottom up.

Private investigators were hired. Not to investigate the case — my lawyers had their own investigators for that. These investigators were hired to investigate the *victims.* To follow them. To surveil them. To photograph them outside their schools, their homes, their workplaces. To dig into their backgrounds — their family histories, their academic records, their social media presence, their personal relationships — for anything that could be used to discredit them in a courtroom or, more immediately, intimidate them into silence.

Girls who had already been traumatized once — by me, by the massage table, by the system that had failed to protect them — discovered that men in unmarked cars were following them. Parked outside their schools. Parked outside their homes. Taking photographs with the conspicuous professionalism of people who wanted to be seen taking photographs, because being seen was the point. The photographs weren't evidence-gathering. The photographs were *messaging.* They said: we know where you live. We know where you go to school. We know your schedule. We know your face. And if you testify, we will know everything else.

Parents received phone calls — not threatening, not explicitly, never explicitly, because explicit threats are prosecutable and implicit ones are not. Anonymous tips about the girls' credibility. Whispered rumors about their motivations — suggestions that the girls had been willing participants, that they'd accepted the money enthusiastically, that their stories were the product of regret rather than trauma. The message was unmistakable to anyone receiving it and entirely deniable to anyone investigating it: *Testifying has consequences. Silence is safer. The man you're accusing has resources that you cannot imagine and a willingness to deploy them that you cannot match.*

My lawyers hired investigators to verify the accusers' credibility. That's what lawyers do. That's due diligence. It's standard practice in high-stakes litigation. Every defense attorney in America will tell you that investigating the prosecution's witnesses is not only legal but ethically required. And they're right. It is legal. It is standard practice. And the fact that standard legal practice and witness intimidation can be conducted simultaneously, by the same investigators, using the same methods, for the same purpose, is not a bug in the American legal system.

It's a feature. It's always been a feature. And it's a feature that, by design, benefits people who can afford to hire investigators and disadvantages people who cannot.

If some of those girls felt uncomfortable being photographed outside their high schools, well — the legal system is uncomfortable for everyone. Welcome to America.

Except one.

One girl did not respond to the pressure the way the others responded. She was seventeen when the investigators first photographed her. She was a good student — that detail mattered, because good students have a relationship to institutions that other people don't, a baseline trust in the idea that systems respond to evidence and that the truth, properly presented, produces outcomes. She had already spoken to the FBI. She was going to speak to them again. And she had, through a channel Malcolm's monitoring system flagged on a Tuesday morning in March 2006, made contact with a reporter at a national publication. Not a local outlet. Not a blogger. A reporter whose previous work had resulted in two federal investigations and one congressional hearing. She had sent him twelve pages of documentation. He had responded the same day.

I have described throughout this account a man who does not panic. That description remains accurate. But there is a specific quality to the sensation of watching, through Malcolm's monitoring system, a seventeen-year-old girl hand twelve pages of documentation to a reporter who responds same-day — a quality that sits below panic in the autonomic register but above anything I had felt in the 1998 journalist situation, because in 1998 I had leverage I hadn't yet spent, and in March 2006 I had spent most of it. I sat with the report in my hand for four minutes. I know it was four minutes because I was watching the clock on Malcolm's server display. I had not previously watched a clock for four minutes while deciding what to do. I was a man who made decisions in seconds. The four minutes told me something I was not prepared to hear: that there existed a configuration of adversaries that my system could not immediately resolve. Not permanently beyond resolution. But not immediately resolvable either. The gap between those two things was four minutes wide. Four minutes during which I could not see the path.

The path appeared on minute five. I will not describe it in detail, because the details implicate people who are still alive and whose cooperation I obtained through mechanisms that they would prefer remain unexamined. What I will say is that the reporter did not publish. The documentation did not reach an editor. The girl testified to the FBI, as planned, and her testimony was thorough and credible and formed a significant part of the evidentiary record. But the specific twelve pages she had sent — the documentation that connected certain elements of the operation to certain individuals whose names would have transformed a trafficking investigation into something considerably larger and more politically complicated — those twelve pages did not follow her into the record. They were managed. In the way that I managed things. Quietly, completely, and without leaving a trail that anyone who valued their career would want to follow. I am not proud of this. I am not ashamed of it either. I am describing what happened, with the precision that this account requires, so that the reader understands not just what I built but what it cost to maintain it. The cost, by 2006, was higher than I had projected. The machine was still running. But the fuel was not unlimited.

Chapter 24: The Dream Team

Timeline: 2006–2007 | **Location:** Manhattan, Washington D.C., Gulf Shore

Bennett Sawyer investigated a president of the United States for getting a consensual blowjob in the Oval Office.

He spent years on the investigation. He spent millions of taxpayer dollars. He produced a report of such exhaustive, pornographic detail that it became the most widely read legal document in American history, not because of its legal significance but because the American public wanted to read about a president's sex life in footnoted, government-formatted prose. He became, during the investigation, the embodiment of moral certainty — the prosecutor who would not rest until the president was held accountable for his sexual behavior, regardless of political pressure, regardless of public opinion, regardless of the argument that a consensual sexual relationship between adults was perhaps not the most pressing matter facing the American republic.

Now he was defending me. The irony is not subtext. It is *text.* It is printed in the same bold typeface that his name appeared in on the special counsel's report. Bennett Sawyer — the man who prosecuted a president for sexual misconduct — was now defending a man accused of sexual abuse of minors. The same voice that had thundered about accountability and the rule of law and the principle that no man is above the law was now deployed, at four hundred dollars an hour, to argue that the law should be applied with *discretion* in the case of a man who had been identified as the perpetrator of a multi-decade trafficking operation involving dozens of children. Bennett Sawyer investigated a president for getting a consensual blowjob in the Oval Office. Now he's defending me against accusations involving minors. Some people would call that hypocrisy. I call it the free market. Len calls it a retainer. Everybody's happy.

His presence on my defense team signaled two things to every prosecutor, every judge, and every law enforcement official involved in the case. First: that I had enough money to buy the most expensive legal talent in the country — the man who investigated a *president* — which meant that any prosecution would be met with a defense of commensurate firepower, and that the government, which is always outgunned by a defendant with unlimited resources, would need to decide whether the case was worth the expenditure of political capital and taxpayer money that a prolonged legal battle would require. Second: that legal talent in America has no moral floor. There is no crime so heinous, no client so reprehensible, no case so morally bankrupt that the American legal profession will collectively refuse to take the money.

This is, defenders of the system will argue, a feature rather than a bug — everyone deserves representation, everyone deserves a defense, the adversarial system works only when both sides are fully represented. And that argument is correct, in theory. It's the same argument that law professors make in their first-year criminal procedure courses, the same argument that defense attorneys cite when they're asked how they sleep at night, the same argument that the American Bar Association prints in its professional responsibility guidelines. In practice, it means that the richest pedophile in America can hire the man who prosecuted a president and nobody in the legal profession raises an eyebrow. The system isn't broken. The system is operating exactly as designed. And the design has always prioritized the rights of the accused over the rights of the victim, the resources of the wealthy over the resources of the poor, and the principle of aggressive defense over the principle of common human decency. I don't blame Len. I hired him. He said yes. The transaction was clean. The morality was someone else's problem.

The defense team's strategy crystallized around three pillars, and I want to describe them in detail because they represent the blueprint for how wealth defeats justice in the American legal system — not occasionally, not anomalously, but *systematically.*

Pillar one: discredit the victims. They're troubled girls from broken homes. They accepted money — voluntarily, enthusiastically, repeatedly. They returned for additional sessions, which the defense would argue suggests consent rather than coercion. Their backgrounds include drug use, academic problems, unstable family situations — the very conditions of vulnerability that made them targets in the first place repackaged as evidence of unreliability. Reframe them: not victims but *willing participants.* Not children who were exploited but teenagers who made choices — choices that, in hindsight, they regret, and that regret has been alchemized by ambitious lawyers into allegations that serve their legal and financial interests.

The language matters. "Victim" generates sympathy. "Willing participant" generates doubt. "Self-described prostitute" — Braverman's phrase, deployed in public interviews and legal filings with the casual brutality of a man who knows the damage a single phrase can do — generates contempt. The defense's job was to move the jury's emotional response from sympathy to doubt to contempt, and the tool for that movement was language. Not evidence. Not facts. Language. The same tool I've been using throughout this entire book to describe monstrous acts in charming prose. My lawyers learned the technique from the same source I did: the understanding that reality is negotiable if you control the vocabulary.

Pillar two: overwhelm the prosecution with procedural warfare. File motions — dozens of them, hundreds of them, each one requiring a response, each response requiring review, each review requiring hours of government attorney time that the government does not have because the government is simultaneously prosecuting drug cases and fraud cases and immigration cases and all the other cases that fill the docket of a federal district court in South Florida. Demand depositions. Challenge every piece of evidence on procedural grounds. Contest jurisdiction. Contest the admissibility of witness testimony. Contest the chain of custody. Contest the qualifications of the investigators. Make the case so expensive, so exhausting, so procedurally labyrinthine that the government — which operates on a budget and a timeline and an institutional attention span that my legal team was designed to exhaust — eventually decides that a plea deal is more efficient than a trial.

Pillar three: deploy political connections. My address book contained the phone numbers of people who appoint U.S. Attorneys. Who fund political campaigns. Who sit on judicial selection committees. Who chair Senate confirmation hearings. Who determine, through the invisible architecture of political influence, which prosecutors get promoted and which prosecutors get transferred and which prosecutors find their careers suddenly, inexplicably stalled. The legal strategy was not just legal. It was *structural.* It operated not within the system but on the system — applying pressure to the mechanisms that determine how the system functions.

My lawyers told me the case was strong. I told my lawyers that cases don't matter — systems matter. The legal system is a machine. If you know which gears to turn, you can make it run in any direction. Including reverse.

The FBI completed its investigation and prepared a fifty-three-page federal indictment. Fifty-three pages. Let me give you a sense of scale. A typical federal indictment for a single-count drug charge is three to five pages. A complex financial fraud case might produce an indictment of fifteen to twenty pages. A major RICO prosecution — the kind that takes down organized crime families — might run thirty pages. Fifty-three pages represents a case of extraordinary scope, extraordinary evidence, and extraordinary confidence on the part of the prosecutors who prepared it.

The document detailed a vast conspiracy involving dozens of victims, multiple co-conspirators, and a pattern of abuse spanning years and continents. It named names. It cited dates. It referenced specific properties — the Gulf Shore mansion, the Manhattan residence, the island. It documented the flight logs. It cataloged the financial flows. It described the recruitment pipeline with a precision that suggested the FBI had, through its investigation, independently reconstructed the same organizational chart that I've been describing throughout this book.

It recommended federal sex trafficking charges that would carry a mandatory minimum sentence of ten years to life. Mandatory minimum. Meaning: if the charges stuck, if the case went to trial, if the jury convicted — and with dozens of cooperating witnesses, thousands of pages of evidence, and a flight log full of names, the conviction was as close to certain as the American legal system allows — I would spend the rest of my life in a federal prison.

The indictment was ready. The evidence was overwhelming. The case was airtight. The fifty-three pages represented years of investigation, hundreds of interviews, and the combined resources of the most powerful law enforcement agency in the world directed at a single target. And then: nothing.

The indictment was shelved. It was placed in a drawer in a filing cabinet in an office in the U.S. Attorney's building in Miami, where it sat, and sits, and will sit until someone with sufficient authority and sufficient courage decides to open that drawer and examine what's inside. It never saw the light of day. It never became a charging document. It never transformed from a recommendation into an accusation. The fifty-three pages — the thousands of hours of investigation they represented, the hundreds of interviews they distilled, the forty victims whose stories they documented — were reduced to paper in a drawer. Dead paper. Inert. Harmless.

The most comprehensive sex trafficking indictment in American history, backed by the most powerful law enforcement agency in the world, supported by dozens of cooperating witnesses and thousands of pages of corroborating evidence, was killed — not by a lack of evidence, not by a legal deficiency, not by any flaw in the prosecution's case — but by a *decision.* A human decision, made by a human being sitting in a human office, to put the paper in the drawer and close the drawer and walk away.

Fifty-three pages. They wrote a fifty-three-page document explaining everything I did. Then they put it in a drawer. That drawer is the most expensive piece of furniture in the American justice system.

While the legal team maneuvered above, the victims waited below. Some of them wrote letters. To the U.S. Attorney's office. To the FBI. To anyone who would listen. Letters describing what happened to them in my houses, on my massage tables, in the bedrooms where the cameras rolled and the evidence accumulated and the adults who should have protected them instead participated in their destruction.

They described the nightmares. The ones that came every night, the ones that woke them at three in the morning with their hearts pounding and their sheets soaked and the memory of hands that shouldn't have been there pressing against their skin. They described dropping out of school — because how do you concentrate on algebra when you can't sit still, when every male teacher's voice sounds like the voice that told you to take off your clothes? They described the drugs they started using to forget — the pills, the alcohol, the desperate, self-destructive chemistry of a brain trying to anesthetize a wound that no anesthetic can reach.

The letters were filed. The letters were read by junior attorneys in the U.S. Attorney's office — young lawyers who probably went to law school because they believed in justice and who now sat at their desks reading the handwritten testimony of teenage girls and knowing, with the helpless certainty of people who understand systems better than they understood them when they enrolled in their first constitutional law course, that the letters would change nothing. The system was not designed to hear these letters. The system was designed to *process* them — to receive them, document them, file them, and move forward with the negotiations that were already underway between my defense team and the U.S. Attorney's office. The letters were not evidence in the negotiation. They were not leverage. They were the sound of children crying in a room where no one was listening.

The girls wrote letters. Heartbreaking letters, I'm sure. Letters about trauma and loss and shattered innocence and the particular, unrecoverable damage that is done to a fourteen-year-old girl who learns, at an age when she should be learning about the world's possibilities, that the world contains men who will pay three hundred dollars to destroy her and a system that will process her destruction as a misdemeanor. You know what those letters were worth? Exactly as much as a letter from a poor person to a rich person has ever been worth. I'll let you do that math.

Saul Braverman played a special role in the defense, and the role deserves its own section because it represents the single most spectacular conflict of interest in the history of American jurisprudence. The man I hired to defend me against allegations of sexual exploitation was himself alleged to have sexually exploited the same victims. He was both my shield and a co-target. Both my attorney and, in the court of public opinion, my accomplice.

He wrote op-eds. He gave interviews. He appeared on television with the practiced confidence of a man who has been performing moral authority in public for forty years. He called my accusers "self-described prostitutes who don't feel harmed." He attacked their credibility with the clinical precision of a surgeon and the moral vacancy of a man who has decided that winning is the only ethical principle that matters.

Saul was magnificent. There's no other word. He attacked the girls who accused me with the same moral certainty he used to attack governments who tortured prisoners. Same voice. Same confidence. Same complete absence of self-awareness. If there's an afterlife, Saul Braverman will argue with God about venue.

Behind closed doors, calls were made. Letters were sent. Not just ordinary legal correspondence — letters from some of the most powerful lawyers in America, carrying the implicit weight of the political networks behind them.

The letters argued that I was a philanthropist. A science patron. A man of good character who had made some mistakes. The letters cited my donations to research institutions, my support of academic initiatives, my contributions to the intellectual life of the nation. The letters presented character references from academics and business leaders whose names, in other contexts, would have conferred immediate credibility.

The letters did not mention forty victims. The letters did not mention fourteen-year-olds. The letters did not mention the massage table, the referral network, the flight logs, the cameras, the servers, or the filing system that documented the sexual exploitation of children across multiple jurisdictions and multiple countries.

The letters carried the letterhead of law firms that employed former attorneys general. Former solicitors general. Former federal judges. Men and women who had once administered the very system they were now attempting to circumvent on behalf of a client who had exploited its every weakness. The letterhead was the weapon. Not the arguments. Not the character references. Not the citations of philanthropic activity. The letterhead. Because the letterhead said, in the silent language of institutional power: *we are part of the same system you are. We appointed you. We promoted you. We made your career. And we can unmake it.*

My lawyers sent very polite letters to the U.S. Attorney. The letters said I was a good man who deserved a second chance. What the letters actually said — in the language that only lawyers and prosecutors can read, the language of institutional power that operates on frequencies inaudible to ordinary citizens — was: "We know where you went to law school. We know who appointed you. We know who will appoint the next one. We know which senator sits on the Judiciary Committee that will review your next career move. We know which law firm you'd like to join when you leave public service. We know the ecosystem you inhabit, because we *built* that ecosystem, and we can make your passage through it smooth or turbulent. Proceed carefully."

They proceeded carefully. They proceeded with the kind of care that a man exercises when he's been told, in the politest possible terms, that carelessness has consequences. The kind of care that transforms an airtight case with forty victims and a fifty-three-page indictment into a negotiation. The kind of care that, in any other context, would be called cowardice, but that in the American legal system is called *prosecutorial discretion.*

The deal was coming. And the deal would be the most disgraceful document in American jurisprudence. But first, the man who would make it needed a name.

Chapter 25: The Deal

Timeline: 2007–2008 | **Location:** U.S. Attorney's Office, Miami; Washington D.C.

The man who would make the deal was **Richard Cavanaugh**, U.S. Attorney for the Meridian District of Florida.

He was young. Ambitious. Politically connected — a Republican appointee with the kind of résumé that suggested a man who had been groomed for higher office since law school: the right clerkship, the right law firm, the right political affiliations, the right mentors who understood that the path from U.S. Attorney to federal judge to cabinet secretary to history ran through exactly the kind of decisions that Cavanaugh was about to make.

He had the fifty-three-page indictment on his desk. He had the FBI's recommendation for federal sex trafficking charges. He had the victims' letters in his filing cabinet. He had dozens of cooperating witnesses, thousands of pages of evidence, flight logs, financial records, and the institutional backing of the most powerful law enforcement agency on Earth. He had everything he needed to put me in federal prison for the rest of my natural life.

Instead, he picked up the phone and called my lawyers.

The negotiation began. And I want to be very clear about what "negotiation" means in this context, because the word implies two parties of roughly equal standing engaging in a process of mutual compromise to reach an agreement that serves both sides' interests. That's not what happened. What happened was that one side — mine — had unlimited legal resources, political connections in every relevant branch of government, and an intelligence archive that implied consequences for anyone who pushed too hard; and the other side — the United States government, representing forty identified victims, most of them children at the time of the abuse — had a fifty-three-page indictment and the dawning realization that using it would cost more than shelving it.

Richard Cavanaugh was the best thing that ever happened to me. Better than Grant Hensley. Better than Celeste. Better than any lawyer or banker or billionaire. Because Cavanaugh had the power to end my life — and he chose not to. Some people call that corruption. I call it the system working exactly as designed.

Years later, Cavanaugh would tell a colleague something extraordinary.

The context was a vetting process — Cavanaugh was being considered for the position of Secretary of Labor in the Barlow administration, and the transition team was reviewing his record, including the single most controversial decision of his career: the plea deal he'd given me. When asked about the deal — when asked why a U.S. Attorney with a slam-dunk federal case had negotiated a state-level plea that allowed a sex trafficker to be sentenced to twenty-four months in county jail — and walk out after sixteen— Cavanaugh reportedly said that he had been told to back off. That he'd been told to "leave it alone." That he'd been told that I "belonged to intelligence."

Belonged to intelligence.

Six words. Six words that explain everything and prove nothing. Six words that have been analyzed by journalists, by former intelligence officers, by conspiracy theorists, by legal scholars, and by every person who has ever looked at the disparity between the evidence against me and the sentence I received and thought, *Something else is going on here.*

Belonged to *whose* intelligence? American? The CIA, which has a well-documented history of cultivating assets through sexual blackmail operations, including at least one program that was exposed during the Church Committee hearings in the 1970s — a program in which the Agency literally recorded targets in compromising sexual situations for the purpose of leverage, which is, if you think about it, a description of my entire career? Israeli? The nation whose former prime minister visited my Manhattan mansion and whose intelligence agency — which my mentor Roman Harlow was alleged to have served until the day his body was recovered from the Adriatic — has a reputation for operational sophistication that makes the CIA look like a community theater production? British? Whose royal family I had photographed in compromising positions and whose intelligence services had maintained relationships with Roman that were never fully investigated, never fully disclosed, and never fully resolved, even after his death? All three? Some combination? A freelance arrangement in which I provided product — human intelligence, sexual leverage, documented compromise — to whoever was willing to ensure my continued operation?

The phrase hangs in the air like smoke from a gun nobody can find. Cavanaugh said it. He reportedly said it to people who were deciding whether to give him a cabinet position — which means he said it to people who had security clearances, who understood the implications, and who gave him the job anyway. He said it as an *explanation* — as the reason he did what he did, as the justification for a decision that, absent some extraordinary mitigating factor, was indefensible. And nobody — not the transition team, not the Senate confirmation committee, not the press — pressed him on it. Nobody asked the follow-up question. Nobody said, "Belonged to *whose* intelligence, and what does that mean, and why does belonging to intelligence exempt a sex trafficker from federal prosecution?"

The follow-up question was never asked because the follow-up answer was too dangerous to hear.

I can neither confirm nor deny that I belonged to intelligence. What I can tell you is that when a U.S. Attorney with a slam-dunk case suddenly decides to negotiate, it's usually because someone above him made a phone call. And the people above a U.S. Attorney don't make phone calls about ordinary criminals. Draw your own conclusions. I already have.

The Non-Prosecution Agreement was signed in 2007, and it is, by any standard of legal analysis — conservative, liberal, academic, practical — the most extraordinary plea deal in American criminal law.

I pleaded guilty to two state charges. State charges. Not federal. The word "trafficking" — the word that the FBI had used, the word that the fifty-three-page indictment had centered its entire case around — did not appear. The word "conspiracy" did not appear. The elaborate, multi-jurisdictional, multi-decade criminal enterprise that the FBI had documented across thousands of pages was reduced, through the alchemy of negotiation, to two state-level misdemeanors: soliciting prostitution, and soliciting prostitution from a minor.

Soliciting prostitution. As if the transaction described in the indictment — the systematic recruitment of children for sexual abuse — was equivalent to a man picking up a sex worker on a street corner. The language of the charges did the most important work: it reframed the crime. It took the trafficking of dozens of minors and reclassified it as a transaction between consenting parties — one of whom happened to be under eighteen, an inconvenience that the charge acknowledged with the addition of "from a minor," the way a speeding ticket acknowledges a school zone.

In exchange for the guilty plea: I would serve twenty-four months in the Gulf Shore County Stockade. Not a federal prison. Not a state prison. A county jail — the lowest-security facility in the American penal system, designed for people serving sentences of less than a year for nonviolent offenses. I would register as a sex offender. And — the clause that will haunt American jurisprudence for a generation, the clause that transforms the deal from merely outrageous to historically unprecedented — *all co-conspirators are granted immunity.*

All of them. Celeste Harlow, the recruiter who built the pipeline, who approached girls at spas and schools and shopping malls with the warm, sisterly charm of a woman offering opportunity and the cold, operational precision of a handler running a network. Jenna Caldwell, the scheduler who managed the calendar of abuse with the organizational efficiency of a corporate events coordinator, booking sessions the way a concierge books dinner reservations. Diane Prewitt, the logistics manager who coordinated every operational detail of a multi-property criminal enterprise with the competence that would have made her, in any other industry, a Fortune 500 executive. Katya Sorvino, the girl I "purchased" from Eastern Europe who became a helicopter pilot and whose story — victim turned co-conspirator, captive turned accomplice — is the most tragic and most structurally revealing narrative in the entire case.

Every person who helped build and operate the machine — every person the FBI had identified as a co-conspirator in a multi-decade sex trafficking operation — walked free. Not because the evidence against them was insufficient. Not because they cooperated with prosecutors to bring down the primary target — that's the usual justification for granting immunity to co-conspirators, the informant's bargain, the rat's reward. They didn't cooperate. They didn't testify against me. They didn't provide information beyond what the FBI already had. They walked free because the primary target's lawyers negotiated a deal that included their freedom as a *condition* of the agreement. Their immunity was not earned. It was purchased. It was purchased by my legal team as part of a comprehensive package that ensured not only my minimal punishment but the preservation of the entire operational infrastructure.

Think about what that means. The people who recruited the girls were free to recruit more girls. The people who scheduled the abuse were free to schedule more abuse. The people who maintained the properties and the aircraft and the logistics were free to maintain them. The immunity clause didn't just protect my co-conspirators from past crimes. It *enabled future crimes.* It ensured that the machine could be reassembled with the same parts, the same personnel, the same institutional knowledge. My lawyers didn't just get me a deal. They got me a warranty.

The deal was simple. I plead to state charges. I do a little time. And everyone who worked for me goes free. Every. Single. One. My lawyers called it a Non-Prosecution Agreement. I called it a masterpiece. Fifty-three pages of federal evidence reduced to two state misdemeanors. That's not a plea deal. That's a magic trick.

The Crime Victims' Rights Act of 2004 — a federal law passed by Congress and signed by the president — requires that victims be notified of plea agreements and given the opportunity to be heard before the agreement is finalized. The law exists because Congress recognized that the American justice system had, for too long, treated victims as evidence rather than participants — as data points in a case rather than human beings with a right to know what was being done in their name.

Cavanaugh's office did not notify the victims.

The victims weren't told about the deal. An oversight, I'm sure. These things happen. Paperwork gets lost. Emails go to spam. Thirty-six girls slip through the cracks. It's nobody's fault. It's everybody's fault. It's the system. And the system has always been my best friend.

The plea deal was presented to a judge. The judge accepted it. The acceptance was perfunctory — a rubber stamp on a document that should have sent shockwaves through every courthouse in America but instead passed through the judicial system with the unremarkable efficiency of a utility bill being processed by an accounting department.

I was sentenced to twenty-four months in the Gulf Shore County Stockade. A county jail. Twelve minutes from my mansion. A facility where the inmates serve sentences for DUIs and petty theft and the kind of low-level offenses that constitute the bulk of the American criminal justice system's caseload. A man who could have been sentenced to life in federal prison for trafficking dozens of minors across state lines would serve his time in a building that a real estate appraiser would generously describe as "modest" and that I would describe as *temporary.*

The judge accepted the deal. Gavels came down. Papers were signed. And just like that, the most dangerous criminal investigation of the century became a county misdemeanor case. I'd like to tell you I felt relief. But you don't feel relief when the outcome was never in doubt. You feel confirmation.

The deal taught me something I already knew but had never seen proven so elegantly: the law is not a wall. It's a door. And like all doors, it opens if you have the right key.

My key cost approximately fourteen million dollars in legal fees. Bargain.

The message had been broadcast to every powerful person in America, as clearly as if it had been printed on a billboard on the National Mall: the system protects its own. If you have enough money, enough lawyers, enough connections, and enough cameras full of other people's secrets, the federal government will negotiate with you like an equal. Not as a criminal. Not as a predator. Not as a man who destroyed the lives of dozens of children. As a *peer.* The deal was not an aberration — not a one-time failure of an otherwise functional system. The deal was the system functioning at its highest level of honesty — dropping the pretense of justice and simply acknowledging, with the quiet efficiency of an institution that has been protecting the powerful since its founding, that some people are above the law. That the law is a tool, and tools serve whoever holds them, and I held the law the way a surgeon holds a scalpel — with precision, with purpose, and with the understanding that the tool exists to serve the hand that wields it, not the body it cuts open.

Every prosecutor in the country read about the deal. Every defense attorney in the country read about the deal. Every powerful person with secrets read about the deal. And every one of them drew the same conclusion: the American justice system has a price, and if you can afford to pay it, the system will sell you everything — including the freedom of your co-conspirators, the silence of your victims, and the complicity of the institutions that were created to prevent exactly this outcome.

The only question now was what the sentence would actually look like. And the answer — as with everything in my life — would exceed even my expectations.

Fragment: The Girl Who Came Back Wrong

Gulf Shore County. Post-conviction period, 2009–2012. The narrator served sixteen months and returned to his life. The following speaker did not return to hers.

I'm twenty-three now. I was sixteen then. The math is simple. Seven years. Seven years since the last time I walked into that house on Via Dorado and seven years since the last time I walked out and every day in between has been a day I've spent trying to rebuild a person who was taken apart in a room that smelled like eucalyptus oil and money.

People ask me what happened. Therapists ask me what happened. Lawyers ask me what happened. They want the story. They want the sequence. First this, then this, then this. They want a narrative they can put in a file or a deposition or a treatment plan. They want me to organize my destruction into a format that makes sense to someone who's never been destroyed.

So here's the format.

I went four times. The woman scheduled me. Two hundred dollars per visit. I took the bus from West Gulf Shore to Gulf Shore, which is a twenty-minute ride that crosses an invisible border between the world where people take buses and the world where people have driveways longer than my street. I walked through the gate. I walked up the driveway. I walked into the house.

The first visit, it was him. The owner. He was clinical. Fast. Disinterested, almost. Like he was checking an item off a list. It hurt, but the pain was manageable, and the two hundred dollars was in an envelope on the table by the door, and the woman smiled at me on the way out and said I'd done well and that the other girls loved working here. The second visit, it wasn't him. It was a guest. The guest was different.

The guest liked it when I was afraid. I could feel him *reading* me the way you'd read a thermostat — checking the level, adjusting the input, trying to get the temperature to the place he wanted it. When I tensed, he pressed harder. When I cried, his breathing changed — faster, deeper, the sound a person makes when they're experiencing something they find *pleasurable.* My pain was not a side effect. My pain was the product. He was consuming my pain the way another man would consume a meal. Tasting it. Savoring it. Adjusting the seasoning.

I learned something in that room that I wish I could unlearn. I learned that there are people — real people, people with families and careers and faces you'd pass on the street without a second look — who experience the suffering of another human being as *erotic.* Not metaphorically. Not in the abstract psychological sense that textbooks describe. Physically. Tangibly. The same neural pathways that produce arousal in a normal context were, in this man, wired directly to my agony. My crying was his foreplay. My screaming was his climax. My body shutting down — the moment when the pain exceeded my nervous system's capacity to process it and everything went gray and distant and numb — was his disappointment, because the numbness meant the show was over, and he wanted more show. He told me to cry louder. Those were his words. "Louder." Like a director giving notes. Like a man adjusting the volume on a television.

I learned to perform. Not pleasure — pain. I learned that performed pain was safer than real pain because performed pain gave him what he wanted faster and faster meant sooner and sooner meant over and over meant I could put my clothes on and take the envelope and walk back through the gate and catch the bus across the invisible border back to the world where people ride buses and nobody asks why your hands are shaking.

The third visit was two guests. At the same time. They knew each other. They talked about me while they did what they did — not to me, about me, in the third person, like I was a dish at a restaurant they were sharing. "She's responsive." "Better than the last one." "The young ones are always better." One of them laughed — a full, deep, belly laugh, the sound of genuine amusement — when I made a sound I didn't know my body could make. The other one said, "Save some for the rest of us." I heard ice cubes in a glass somewhere. I heard music from another room. I heard the sounds of a party happening ten feet away from the room where two men were systematically dismantling a sixteen-year-old girl who had come here for two hundred dollars.

After, I lay on the table and I listened through the wall. They'd rejoined the group. I could hear conversation. Laughter. Glasses clinking. Someone was telling a story about a sailing trip. Someone else was asking about dessert. The normalcy was the worst part. Not what they did to me — what they did *after* what they did to me. They went back to the party. They picked up their drinks. They resumed their lives. I was an intermission. A palate cleanser between courses.

I didn't go back for the fourth visit. The woman called. I didn't answer. She called again. The message said the man was disappointed. The message said I was unreliable. The message said the other girls loved working there.

Seven years later, the man went to jail. Sixteen months. Sixteen months for what he did to me and to the girls before me and to the girls after me. Sixteen months in a facility with work release, which means he left the facility during the day and came back at night, which is the exact inverse of what he did to us — he came during the day and we went home at night, except we didn't go home, not really, because the home we went back to was occupied by a person who wasn't us anymore.

I can't keep a job. My hands shake. Not visibly — not the kind of shaking that a coworker would notice. The internal kind. The kind that makes me drop a coffee cup once a month and stare at the broken pieces on the floor and think about how easy it is to break something and how impossible it is to put the pieces back in the right order.

I don't sleep. I manage sleep. I negotiate with it. I build walls around the hours between 2 a.m. and 5 a.m. — walls made of television noise and kitchen light and the specific positioning of my body that keeps me from lying flat, because lying flat is the position I was in when the guest told me to cry louder, and my body remembers that position the way a burn victim's skin remembers fire.

I went back to that house one time. After the arrest. After they took him away. I drove to Gulf Shore — I have a car now, I don't take the bus, the bus is a trigger and triggers are everywhere and my life is a minefield of routes I can't take and sounds I can't hear and smells I can't smell. I parked across the street and I looked at the house and I thought: this is where I was killed. Not murdered. Not assaulted. *Killed.* The girl who walked in there at sixteen is dead. She died on the massage table in the guest room while a man told her to cry louder. The woman who drove here at twenty-three is someone else. Someone built from the wreckage. Someone who functions but doesn't feel. Someone who looks, from the outside, like a person — but who knows, on the inside, that the person was left on that table and never came home.

They gave him sixteen months. I got life.

Chapter 26: The Country Club

Timeline: 2008–2009 | **Location:** Gulf Shore County Stockade

I reported to jail on a Saturday.

The Gulf Shore County Stockade sits on Gun Club Road in West Gulf Shore — a facility name and a street name that, combined, sound like the setting of a country song about a man who made bad decisions. The building is low, flat, and institutional, surrounded by the kind of landscaping that local government provides when it has a landscaping budget but no landscaping ambitions. It is not a prison. It is not a penitentiary. It is not a federal correctional facility. It is a county detention center — the lowest rung of the American incarceration system, designed for people serving sentences of less than a year for offenses that the legal system classifies as insufficiently serious to warrant state or federal accommodation.

DUI offenders serve time here. Petty thieves serve time here. People who write bad checks and miss court dates and violate the conditions of their probation serve time here. And now, joining them in this pantheon of minor miscreants, was a man who the FBI had identified as the operator of a multi-decade, multi-state, international sex trafficking conspiracy involving dozens of minor victims.

My lawyers had negotiated conditions that would be comical if they weren't describing the incarceration of a convicted sex offender. A private wing — not a private *cell,* which would be standard protective custody for a high-profile inmate, but a private *wing,* an entire section of the facility set aside for my exclusive use, as if the county jail were a hotel and I had booked the penthouse suite. Limited contact with other inmates — not for my protection from them, which is the usual justification for segregation, but for their protection from the reality that the man in the private wing was serving an twenty-four-month sentence for crimes that, in a just system, would have kept him behind concrete and razor wire for the rest of his life. And the crown jewel of the arrangement: *work release.*

I reported to jail on a Saturday. My lawyers had negotiated a private area, limited interaction with other inmates, and a work release schedule that would let me leave the facility twelve hours a day, six days a week. Twelve hours a day. Six days a week. In case you're doing the math, that means I was "incarcerated" for approximately twelve hours a day. That's not a sentence. That's a weekend.

Let me explain how work release functioned, because the details are important, and the details are absurd, and the absurdity is the point.

Under the terms of my work release — negotiated by my lawyers, approved by the court, administered by the Gulf Shore County Sheriff's Office — I was permitted to leave the stockade each morning and report to a "work" location. The work location was an office in downtown West Gulf Shore. The office was registered to the Florida Science Foundation — one of my entities, a nonprofit organization whose stated purpose was the advancement of scientific research and whose actual purpose, in 2008, was to provide a registered business address that would satisfy the technical requirements of a work release program.

The foundation employed me. I employed myself. The circularity was not accidental — it was designed, by my lawyers, to create a legal framework in which I was simultaneously an employer and an employee, a foundation and its sole beneficiary, a workplace and a worker, all of which satisfied the letter of the work release statute without satisfying anything remotely resembling its spirit. The statute was designed for inmates who had legitimate jobs — mechanics, construction workers, warehouse employees, the kinds of people who needed to maintain employment while serving short sentences for nonviolent offenses. The statute was not designed for billionaire sex offenders who could create a foundation, register an office, and designate themselves as essential personnel.

But the statute didn't say that. The statute said "work release," and my lawyers demonstrated, with the interpretive creativity that fourteen million dollars in legal fees can buy, that what I was doing qualified.

Each morning, I was driven by private car — not a corrections transport vehicle, not a sheriff's van, a *private car,* the kind with leather seats and tinted windows and a driver who called me "sir" — from the stockade to my office. At the office, I conducted business. I met with associates. I made phone calls. I reviewed financial documents. I corresponded with lawyers and accountants and the various professionals who managed the infrastructure of my empire, which continued to operate during my incarceration with the same efficiency it had operated before my incarceration, because the empire was designed to function with or without my physical presence, and my physical presence was, in any case, available twelve hours a day, six days a week.

I had lunch at restaurants. Not the stockade cafeteria — *restaurants.* The kind where the waitstaff brings a menu and the kitchen prepares food that a reasonable person would describe as "pleasant" and that the inmates eating government-issued meals back at the stockade would describe as "evidence of a two-tier justice system."

Work release was the best part of the sentence. I'd wake up, get driven to my office, take meetings, make calls, have lunch at a restaurant, and go back to the stockade for dinner and a nap. Some days I forgot I was in jail. Most days, actually. The guards were very professional. They let me do whatever I wanted as long as I came back by seven. It was like having a curfew in college, except the cafeteria food was worse.

A county sheriff's investigation later revealed what was happening during those twelve-hour daily releases, and what was happening was exactly what you'd expect from a man who was serving a sentence for soliciting minors and who had been given unsupervised access to a private office twelve hours a day.

Young women were observed visiting the office. The visits were logged by building security — the private office building had its own security desk, which maintained a sign-in log, which documented arrivals and departures with the routine efficiency of any commercial property. The women arrived. The women signed in. The women went upstairs. The women came back down. The women left. The security desk documented the visits the way it documented every visit: name, time in, time out. The log did not note the ages of the visitors. The log did not note the nature of the visits. The log did not flag the visits for review by the corrections officers who were, in theory, responsible for monitoring my work release activities.

The women arrived and left through a private entrance — not the building's main lobby, but a side door that allowed visitors to reach my office without passing through the common areas where other tenants might observe them. The visits followed the same pattern as the pre-conviction visits: appointments, massages, cash. The operational choreography had not changed. The recruitment methods had not changed. The venue had changed — from a forty-five-thousand-square-foot mansion to a rented office suite — but the fundamental transaction was identical. The massage table was smaller. The room was less impressive. The Caribbean view had been replaced by a view of a West Gulf Shore parking lot. But the economics were the same, the power dynamics were the same, and the exploitation was the same.

The corrections officers assigned to monitor my work release were either overwhelmed, underpaid, or compromised — or, most likely, some combination of all three. A county corrections officer monitoring a work release program is not a detective. He is not trained in surveillance. He is not equipped with the resources or the authority to conduct the kind of investigation that would be necessary to document what was happening inside a private office on the fourteenth floor of a commercial building. He is a government employee earning a government salary, assigned to verify that an inmate reports to a registered work location and returns to the facility by the designated time. If the inmate reports and returns — if the paperwork is completed, if the boxes are checked, if the form is filed — the corrections officer's job is done. The system was not designed to investigate what happens between check-in and check-out. The system was designed to process compliance. And I was, by every measurable standard of compliance, a model inmate.

From the stockade and from my office, I maintained the network.

Sixteen months is a long time in the life of a normal person. In the life of a man who operates an international network of financial, political, academic, and intelligence connections — a man whose value to every person in his orbit depends on his ability to remain central, relevant, and operational — sixteen months is an eternity. Relationships decay. Alliances weaken. Information goes stale. The currency of relevance depreciates faster than any financial instrument, and a man who disappears from the social ecosystem for sixteen months risks returning to find that the ecosystem has reorganized around his absence.

I could not allow that to happen. So I picked up the phone.

I called associates — the financial managers, the property administrators, the operational personnel who kept the empire running. I called lawyers — not just the defense team, but the transactional lawyers, the estate planners, the offshore specialists who managed the Byzantine architecture of trusts and foundations and shell corporations that constituted my financial infrastructure. I called scientists — the researchers I'd funded, the academics I'd cultivated, the intellectual luminaries whose continued association with me served as a credential and a shield. I called the people who needed to know that the conviction had not diminished my capacity, my resources, or my willingness to be useful to them.

The sixteen months I served were not an interruption. They were a *pivot.* A restructuring. The kind of strategic pause that any competent CEO would use to evaluate the landscape, identify weaknesses, cut dead weight, and plan the next phase. I used the time to determine which relationships had survived the conviction — which ones were robust enough to withstand the stigma of association with a registered sex offender, and which ones had been severed by people who calculated that the cost of continued association exceeded the benefit. The results were instructive. Most relationships survived. Most people did the calculus and concluded that what I offered — access, intelligence, leverage, funding — outweighed the reputational risk of maintaining contact with me. The ones who left were replaceable. The ones who stayed were valuable. The restructuring was complete before the sentence was.

The calls were not monitored with the rigor applied to federal inmates, because I was not a federal inmate. I was a county misdemeanant with better phone privileges than most people have at their jobs. The Gulf Shore County Stockade was not equipped — technologically, procedurally, or philosophically — to monitor the communications of a man whose phone calls reached across continents and whose conversations operated in the coded, euphemistic language of people who understand that specificity is dangerous.

Jail gave me something I hadn't had in twenty years: time to think. No dinner parties. No flights. No island logistics. Just me, a phone, and twelve hours of work release per day. I spent those sixteen months doing what any good CEO does during a restructuring: cutting dead weight, identifying loyal assets, and planning the relaunch.

I was released after sixteen months. Eight months early. For "good behavior."

Good behavior. Let's pause on that phrase, because it deserves the kind of close reading that English professors apply to Shakespeare and that prosecutors should have applied to my plea deal. "Good behavior," in the context of the American penal system, means the inmate has complied with facility rules, has not engaged in violent or disruptive conduct, and has demonstrated the kind of institutional cooperation that merits a reduction in sentence. It is a standard mechanism — applied uniformly, in theory, to every inmate who meets the criteria. In practice, it means that a man who was convicted of soliciting prostitution from a minor and who — according to a subsequent sheriff's investigation — continued to receive young women at his office during work release was rewarded with early freedom because he didn't start a fight in the cafeteria. He didn't disrupt the meal schedule. He didn't violate curfew. He returned to the stockade every evening at the appointed hour, slept in his private wing, and reported the next morning for another twelve hours of "work" at his self-created foundation. By the standards of the Gulf Shore County Stockade, this constituted exemplary behavior. By the standards of basic human morality, this constituted the most grotesque miscarriage of justice in the modern history of the American penal system.

But the system doesn't measure morality. The system measures compliance. And I was compliant.

I walked out of the Gulf Shore County Stockade on a morning that was, in all observable ways, indistinguishable from any other Florida morning — humid, bright, with the particular quality of sunlight that makes everything look slightly overexposed, as if reality itself has been turned up a notch. I was driven to my Gulf Shore mansion by private car. I sat by the pool.

My name was on the sex offender registry. My passport was flagged. My reputation was — theoretically — destroyed. The word "theoretically" is doing an enormous amount of work in that sentence, because in practice, my reputation was not destroyed. It was *recalibrated.* It had been stress-tested by the worst the American justice system could throw at it, and the worst turned out to be sixteen months and a work release, which is to say: the worst was nothing. The worst was an inconvenience. The worst was a speed bump on the highway of impunity that my life had become.

My money was intact. Malcolm still maintained the servers. The immunity clause meant everyone who helped build the machine was free to help rebuild it. The deal hadn't just protected me from the past. It had equipped me for the future.

I did sixteen months. Sixteen months for what the FBI said was a multi-decade, multi-state, international sex trafficking operation involving dozens of minors. Sixteen months. I've had renovations that took longer. I've had lawsuits that took longer. I've had dinner parties that *felt* longer. Sixteen months. The American justice system, ladies and gentlemen. Standing ovation.

Chapter 27: The Comeback

Timeline: 2009–2010 | **Location:** Manhattan, Gulf Shore, New York society

Enter **Margo Lindhurst.**

Hollywood publicist. Social gatekeeper. The woman who decides which charity galas save you a seat at the front table and which premieres put your name on the velvet-rope list. Margo operated in the particular stratum of American public relations that exists at the intersection of entertainment, philanthropy, and social power — the stratum where the currency is not money (everyone at that altitude has money) but *access.* Access to the right rooms. Access to the right people. Access to the invisible network of social credentialing that determines, in Manhattan and in Los Angeles and in the narrow corridor of American wealth that connects them, who is invited and who is not, who is acceptable and who is not, who is *in* and who is forever, irredeemably *out.*

Margo took on the project of rehabilitating my social reputation with the enthusiasm of a PR firm launching a rebrand. Not because she believed I was innocent — she was too smart for that, and the question of innocence was, in any case, irrelevant to the project. The project was not about innocence. The project was about *invitations.* The conviction had removed me from the invitation list. Margo's job was to put me back on it.

She arranged introductions — not the cold, transactional introductions of a business networking event, but the warm, social introductions of a woman who understood that in Manhattan, a personal endorsement from the right person is worth more than a legal exoneration from a federal judge. She whispered to hosts — the women and men who organized the charity galas and benefit dinners and opening-night parties that constituted the social infrastructure of the New York elite. She reminded society columnists — the gossip writers, the social diarists, the chroniclers of wealth whose columns determined who was rising and who was falling — that I was a *philanthropist* who had made *a mistake* and had *paid his debt to society.*

The language of redemption was applied to me with the same precision that a marketing team applies brand messaging to a product relaunch. I was not a convicted sex offender — I was a man who had "gone through a difficult period." I was not a predator who had trafficked dozens of children — I was a "controversial figure" who had "faced legal challenges." I was not an unreformed monster whose work release had been marred by allegations of continued abuse — I was a "philanthropist" whose "contributions to science" deserved a "second chance."

The language of redemption was applied to a man who had shown zero evidence of change — because redemption, in Manhattan society, does not require change. It does not require remorse. It does not require restitution. It does not require the acknowledgment that what was done was wrong, or the commitment to ensure that it is never done again. Redemption, in Manhattan, requires a publicist. And I had the best one.

Margo was a genius. Not a legal genius or a financial genius — a social genius. She understood that in New York, reputation is not about what you did. It's about who invites you to dinner. Get the right dinner invitation and the conviction evaporates like a stain treated by a competent dry cleaner — invisible, forgotten, as if the fabric had always been clean. She got me the right invitations. Within six months, I was eating canapés at charity events with the same people who'd read about my arrest in the *Post.* Nobody mentioned it. Nobody asked about it. Nobody referenced the massage table or the forty victims or the sixteen months or the work release or the sex offender registry. The social contract of the American elite operates on a single, unwritten rule: *we do not discuss the things that might make dinner uncomfortable.* And my conviction — which should have made every dinner in America uncomfortable — was processed, by the social machinery of Manhattan wealth, as simply another unpleasant topic to be avoided between the appetizer and the main course.

That's the magic of a correctly set table.

The moment that crystallized the comeback occurred at a movie premiere, and the movie was a sequel to a famous film about Wall Street greed, which is the kind of setting that a novelist would reject as too on-the-nose and that reality provided without irony.

I attended a private screening. The guest list was curated with the same precision that I applied to my own dinner parties — which is to say, it was a room full of people who attend private screenings of films about financial excess while being, themselves, the living embodiment of financial excess. The room was dimly lit. The champagne was excellent. The conversation was the particular blend of intellectual performance and social maneuvering that constitutes entertainment at the highest levels of American wealth.

And I was photographed.

The photograph shows me standing in a group that includes **Gordon Stiles** — the private equity billionaire who had paid me a hundred and seventy million dollars in "consulting fees" and whose FBI file contained allegations of his own sexual abuse and trafficking. **Gerald Thornton** — a financier who would, within a few years, be appointed Secretary of Commerce by President Barlow, placing him in the cabinet of the United States government, where he would help administer the same federal apparatus that had investigated me and cut me a deal and failed to hold me accountable. And **Frank Delmonico** — the former mayor of New York City, the man who had been proclaimed "America's Mayor" after the September 11 attacks, who would go on to serve as President Barlow's personal attorney and whose subsequent legal troubles would make my own look quaint by comparison.

A convicted sex offender, standing in a room full of billionaires and politicians, sipping champagne at a movie premiere, less than a year after leaving a county jail where he had served sixteen months for trafficking minors. The photograph was not staged. It was not leaked. It didn't need to be. Its existence was the point. Its existence demonstrated, with the visual clarity that no legal document or news article could match, that the conviction had not diminished my social standing. That the people who mattered — the billionaires, the politicians, the gatekeepers of American power — had calculated the cost of association with me and determined that the cost was acceptable. That the sex offender registry was a public-facing punishment that had no impact on the private-facing reality of how power operates in America.

I went to a movie premiere. Wall Street sequel. Terrible film, excellent guest list. Gordon was there. Gerald was there. Frank was there. All of them knew I was a registered sex offender. All of them shook my hand. All of them smiled for the cameras. That photo is worth more than anything on my hard drives. Because it proves something that no court document ever could: the conviction didn't matter. I was back.

The scientists came back first.

Faster than the politicians, faster than the socialites, faster than the business class or the legal class or any other class of American professional. The academic world — the community of researchers and professors and graduate students who depend on grant funding with the same desperate, existential urgency that a hospital patient depends on oxygen — resumed its relationship with me with a speed that would be impressive if it weren't so depressing.

I hosted dinners. The same science dinners I'd described in earlier chapters — the evenings at the Manhattan mansion where the guest list mixed Nobel laureates with hedge fund managers and the conversation oscillated between quantum mechanics and portfolio theory. The dinners resumed. The researchers accepted. The invitations went out on the same stationery, to the same mailing list, with the same offer: food, wine, conversation, and the implicit understanding that attendance signaled membership in an intellectual community that transcended the conventional moral categories that governed ordinary social interaction.

I funded researchers. New grants flowed through the Coral Islands foundation — the same tax-exempt, offshore, opaque structure that had funded my pre-conviction philanthropy. The grants went to WIT professors, Hartfield faculty, and Silicon Valley founders — many of whom knew about the conviction, had read about it, had discussed it with colleagues, and had concluded, through a calculus that they would never articulate publicly but that governed their behavior as surely as gravity governs orbital mechanics, that the money was worth more than the moral cost of accepting it.

The academic world, which prides itself on empiricism and evidence-based reasoning — which claims, as its foundational principle, the commitment to follow the truth wherever it leads — collectively decided that the evidence of my conviction was insufficient reason to decline my money. Peer review, it turns out, does not apply to donors. The rigorous standards of evidence and methodology that govern the publication of a scientific paper — the double-blind review process, the replication requirements, the systematic elimination of bias — none of these standards were applied to the question of whether a convicted sex offender should be permitted to fund scientific research, attend scientific conferences, and embed himself in the social fabric of the scientific community.

The scientists came back first. Faster than the politicians, faster than the socialites, faster than anyone. You know why? Because scientists need money more than they need morals. A research grant doesn't care if the donor is a sex offender. A particle accelerator doesn't have ethics. And a physicist who turns down funding because the funder is a monster is a physicist who doesn't get to do physics. I love science.

The most famous example was the most instructive.

Even **Simon Halstead** — the most famous dissident intellectual in America, the linguist and political theorist who had built a fifty-year career attacking institutional power, American imperialism, and the corporate structures that control the global economy — even Halstead corresponded with me.

Post-conviction. After I was a registered sex offender. After the plea deal, after the prison term, after the public knew what I was.

Halstead used my apartment. He met with me. He engaged with me intellectually, in the way that intellectuals engage with people whose ideas interest them more than their crimes disgust them. Their exchanges were polite. Academic. The correspondence of two men discussing ideas over coffee, as if one of them hadn't been convicted of soliciting a minor and as if the other hadn't spent his entire professional life arguing that the powerful are held to different standards than the rest of us.

The irony is so heavy it should have its own gravitational field. Simon Halstead — the man who argued, in book after book, lecture after lecture, documentary after documentary, that the American power structure protects its own, that the wealthy operate above the law, that institutional complicity is the mechanism through which the worst abuses are sustained, that the media serves the interests of the powerful rather than holding them accountable — that man sat in the apartment of a convicted sex offender and discussed politics and linguistics over what I assume was very good coffee, because I always served very good coffee. He would later defend the meetings by saying he'd met with "all sorts of people." Which is true. And also the most revealing defense an intellectual has ever offered for a morally indefensible choice. "All sorts of people" is the alibi of a man who has decided that his curiosity excuses him from the ethical framework he applies to everyone else.

I don't narrate this with gloating. Gloating would be too easy, too simple, too much like the kind of petty triumph that a lesser man would savor. I narrate it with something more dangerous: *calm.* The calm of a man who understands that the world's most celebrated critic of power will, when the social conditions are right, sit at the table of power and eat what's served.

If the world's most famous critic of power will have dinner at your house, it means either you're not powerful or he's not principled. I know which one I am.

Nolan Whitfield came back too.

The richest philanthropist in the world — the man whose foundation was spending billions to eradicate diseases that killed millions of people, the man whose public persona was built entirely on the premise that he was using his wealth to make the world a better place — continued meeting with me. Post-conviction. After the guilty plea. After the sixteen months. After the sex offender registration. After the world learned — through court documents, through newspaper reports, through the public record that was available to anyone with an internet connection and a functioning moral compass — exactly what I had done and exactly how little I had paid for doing it.

Multiple meetings. At the Manhattan mansion — the same mansion where the cameras rolled, where the servers hummed, where Malcolm Pruitt maintained the archive in the basement. At dinners. In correspondence that was documented in emails and calendar entries and the kind of digital trail that a man of Whitfield's intelligence should have understood would eventually become discoverable.

The meetings were documented. The documentation would later surface. And Whitfield's spokesperson would struggle to explain them with an explanation that was technically possible and practically absurd: the meetings were about philanthropy. About global health. About saving lives. About the shared commitment to using wealth for the betterment of humanity.

You do not need to meet a convicted sex offender multiple times in his private mansion to discuss malaria. You can discuss malaria in a conference room. You can discuss malaria on a phone call. You can discuss malaria through intermediaries, through foundation staff, through the thousand channels of communication available to a man whose net worth exceeds the GDP of most nations and whose philanthropic infrastructure includes thousands of employees specifically designated to facilitate exactly these conversations. You do not need to sit at the dining table of a registered sex offender, in the house where the crimes were committed, surrounded by the art and the furniture and the atmosphere of a place that the FBI had identified as the headquarters of a trafficking operation.

Unless the meeting is about something other than malaria.

Nolan came back. Post-conviction. Multiple times. I'm not going to speculate about why the richest man in philanthropy kept having dinner at the home of a convicted sex offender. But I will say this: if you're going to meet me once, that's curiosity. If you're going to meet me twice, that's a relationship. If you're going to meet me three or more times in my private home after I've been convicted? That's a choice. And choices have consequences. Eventually.

By 2010, the rehabilitation was functionally complete.

I dined with billionaires. I funded research. I flew my Gulfstream — the 727 was gone by now, sold, its flight logs already circulating in legal proceedings and journalistic investigations, but the Gulfstream remained, smaller and quieter and perfectly suited to a man whose post-conviction strategy emphasized discretion over spectacle. I maintained my properties — the Manhattan mansion, the Gulf Shore estate, the island, the ranch. I employed my staff — Malcolm Pruitt still on the servers, Diane Prewitt still managing the calendar, the operational infrastructure intact, the immunity clause having ensured that the personnel who ran the machine before the conviction were available to run it after. I corresponded with princes and professors and politicians. The emails flowed. The phone calls connected. The dinner invitations were accepted.

The sex offender registry was a footnote. A bureaucratic detail. An entry in a database that anyone could access but that nobody with the power to do anything about it ever bothered to check. The registry was designed to make monsters visible — to ensure that communities could identify the predators in their midst and take appropriate precautions. But monsters who live in the biggest house in Manhattan and own a private island and fly a private jet are already visible. They are the most visible people in the room at every event they attend. They are visible in the way that a supernova is visible — impossible to miss and impossible to look at directly. The registry didn't make me visible. It made me *searchable.* And the people who searched my name already knew what they'd find. The people who cared already knew. The people who didn't care still didn't care. And the people who wanted something from me suddenly had a convenient excuse to call: "I saw your name. I thought I'd reach out. Let's have dinner." The registry wasn't punishment. It was advertising.

By 2010, I had achieved something no one in American history had ever achieved: I had been convicted of a sex crime involving minors, served sixteen months in a county jail, and returned to a social life more active than before the arrest. I was the proof of concept. The proof that if you're rich enough, connected enough, and careful enough, the American justice system is not a threat. It's a speed bump.

But the victims were still out there.

While I ate canapés and attended premieres and hosted science dinners and met with the richest philanthropist in the world, the women I had abused were building something. Not a machine — they didn't have the resources for machines. Not a network — they didn't have the connections for networks. They were building something smaller and more dangerous: a *record.*

Natalie Brennan was filing motions. Legal documents. Court filings. The slow, grinding, unglamorous paperwork of a woman who had been told by the most powerful justice system on Earth that her abuse was worth sixteen months of county jail, and who had decided, with a determination that no amount of legal obstruction could extinguish, that sixteen months was not enough. Her lawyers were reviewing the Non-Prosecution Agreement. They were finding it legally indefensible — not just morally outrageous, which it obviously was, but *legally deficient,* in violation of the Crime Victims' Rights Act, in violation of the principles of prosecutorial responsibility, in violation of the basic requirement that victims be notified and heard before the government disposes of their case.

Other survivors were organizing. Connecting with each other, with advocacy groups, with the small community of attorneys who specialize in representing victims of powerful people — attorneys who understand that their cases will be longer, harder, and less profitable than any other case on their docket, and who take them anyway because someone has to.

Journalists were asking questions. Not the front-page, breaking-news kind of questions — not yet. The quiet kind. The investigative kind. The kind that begin with a reporter reading a court filing and thinking, *This doesn't make sense,* and following that thought into an archive of documents and depositions and sealed records that would take years to fully excavate.

A federal judge would eventually rule that the NPA violated the Crime Victims' Rights Act. That the victims should have been notified. That the deal was, in the precise legal terminology of judicial opinion, *unlawful.* But that ruling was still years away. In 2010, these threads were invisible — buried in court filings that nobody outside the legal community read, whispered in advocacy circles that the mainstream media dismissed as special-interest noise, ignored by the press and the politicians and the prosecutors who had already decided, through their silence and their inaction and their attendance at my dinner parties, that the case was closed.

The web held. The spider was back in the center. And nobody — not the FBI, not the prosecutors, not the press, not the politicians who shook my hand at movie premieres and accepted my dinner invitations and cashed my foundation's checks — did anything to stop me.

Act Four closes not with a bang, but with the quiet sound of a system that looked at forty abused children and decided that sixteen months was enough. The quiet sound of champagne glasses clinking at a premiere. The quiet sound of a dinner invitation being opened. The quiet sound of a check being deposited into a research account. The quiet sound of a woman in a lawyer's office, filing another motion, telling her story again, refusing to be silent in a world that had done everything in its power to make her disappear.

They say I got a slap on the wrist. That's not accurate. A slap implies contact. The justice system didn't touch me. It waved. It waved at me from across the room, smiled politely, and went back to its drink.

Sixteen months. And the web held.

Act Five is where I show them what "untouchable" really looks like.

Chapter 28: The Pretender

Timeline: 2010–2011 | **Location:** Miami, Bucharest, Manhattan

The second threat to the archive came not from outside the web but from inside it.

His name was Luca Barbieri. Italian-born, Miami-based, a former associate who'd spent three years on the periphery of my operation in the early 2000s — not inner circle, not outer fringe, but the middle ring, the ring of men who understand enough about the operation to be useful and not enough to be dangerous. Or so I thought.

Barbieri had been a facilitator. A logistics man. He arranged transportation — not the Gulfstream, which was mine, but the secondary movements, the car services and private charters and the discreet hotel arrangements that an operation of my scale required in the cities where I didn't own property. He was efficient, well-connected in the Miami hospitality industry, and possessed of the particular moral flexibility that I prized in employees: the ability to see exactly what was happening, understand exactly what it meant, and process the information as a series of logistical problems rather than ethical ones.

I terminated the relationship in 2008, after the plea deal, when the operation's public profile made every peripheral associate a potential liability. Barbieri took the termination professionally — or appeared to. He accepted the severance. He signed the non-disclosure. He disappeared into the Miami real estate market with enough capital to keep himself comfortable and enough knowledge to keep himself dangerous.

In 2010, Celeste's network flagged an anomaly.

Someone was running recruitment operations in Eastern Europe — specifically in Bucharest and Chişinău — using methodology that Celeste recognized. Not the crude trafficking model that organized crime had been running in the region for decades. Something more sophisticated. Something that bore the specific fingerprints of our operational design: the talent-scout approach, the modeling-agency cover, the graduated escalation from legitimate opportunity to compromising situation to leveraged silence. Someone was running a copy of our playbook. A franchise.

It took Celeste three months to trace it back to Barbieri.

He hadn't just borrowed the methodology. He'd stolen files. During his years as a facilitator, he had been quietly copying scheduling documents, guest lists, and — this was the part that made my blood pressure do things my cardiologist would have disapproved of — partial recordings. Not the full archive, not the server backups that Malcolm maintained with the obsessive redundancy of a man who understood that data loss is the only unforgivable sin. But clips. Segments. Enough footage of enough recognizable faces in enough compromising positions to build a miniature version of what I'd spent decades constructing.

Barbieri was building his own web. A cheaper web. A sloppier web. A web built on stolen materials by a man who understood the *form* of what I'd done without understanding the *architecture* — the intelligence contacts, the government protections, the carefully cultivated relationships with agencies that ensured the real web's survival. He was a man who'd photocopied a blueprint without understanding the engineering, and he was constructing a building that would, inevitably, collapse.

But when it collapsed, it would create noise. And noise, in my world, was the most dangerous substance in existence.

If Barbieri's operation was exposed — by law enforcement, by journalists, by the targets themselves — the investigation would trace the methodology back to me. The stolen files would surface. The partial recordings would be entered into evidence. And the careful fiction that I'd maintained since the plea deal — the fiction that I was a reformed man, a registered offender living quietly, no longer operating — would disintegrate.

I couldn't let that happen. But I also couldn't handle it the way Hartmann's problem had been handled — through intelligence channels, through Avi's contacts, through the implicit power of agencies that had an interest in protecting the archive. Barbieri wasn't threatening the archive. He was threatening to *reveal its existence.* And there were people in those agencies who would rather the archive's existence remained theoretical, speculative, unconfirmed.

So I used lawyers.

Not my criminal defense team. A different team. The kind of lawyers who don't appear on legal registries and don't maintain offices with their names on the door. The kind of lawyers whose client list overlaps with the client list of private intelligence firms and whose billing rates reflect the reality that what they do is technically legal and practically indistinguishable from the things that are not.

They found Barbieri in Miami. They presented him with documents — not the originals, but enough to demonstrate that I knew exactly what he'd been doing, where he'd been doing it, and who he'd been doing it with. They explained, with the measured civility of professionals who have delivered similar explanations to similar men in similar situations, that the stolen materials were the property of entities whose patience was not infinite and whose reach was not limited by the jurisdictional constraints that Barbieri might, naively, believe protected him.

They gave him a choice. Return everything — every file, every clip, every copy, every device that had ever contained any portion of the stolen material — or discover, empirically, what happens when a man with no intelligence protection attempts to operate in a space reserved for men who have it.

Barbieri chose correctly. It took two weeks. The files came back. The Eastern European operation dissolved. And Barbieri relocated to a country whose extradition treaties I had studied carefully enough to know that he would never be a problem again — not because he was safe there, but because he *believed* he was safe there, and the belief was sufficient to keep him quiet.

The Pretender Incident taught me something that the Defector Incident had not. Hartmann had been an external threat — a target striking back, a predictable consequence of the leverage model. Barbieri was an *internal* threat — a former associate who understood enough of the operation to replicate it, poorly, and whose replication posed a greater danger than Hartmann's mercenaries ever had.

The lesson was clear: the web's greatest vulnerability was not the targets. It was the operators. The people who had seen the machine from the inside and who might, if sufficiently motivated by greed or resentment or the entrepreneurial instinct that I had inadvertently selected for when I hired them, attempt to build their own.

I tightened the circle. I reduced the number of people who had access to operational details. I increased Malcolm's security protocols. And I reminded myself of a truth that Roman Harlow's death had first taught me and that Barbieri's ambition had now confirmed: in the leverage business, the most dangerous person is not the target.

It's the apprentice.

Chapter 29: The Email Empire

Timeline: 2010–2012 | **Location:** Manhattan, Gulf Shore, Little St. Philip

People expected me to disappear.

They expected the registered sex offender to retreat to his island, draw the curtains, cancel the dinner parties, dismiss the staff, and live out the remainder of his days in the gilded obscurity that the American system provides for rich men who have been publicly humiliated but privately preserved. They expected me to become a cautionary tale — the brilliant financier brought low, the Icarus of Manhattan society, the man who flew too close to the sun and fell and never flew again. They expected remorse, or at least the performance of remorse — the contrite public statement, the quiet withdrawal, the careful management of a diminished life.

They expected wrong. They expected wrong because they fundamentally misunderstood what the conviction meant. The conviction was not a defeat. The conviction was not even a setback. The conviction was a *stress test* — and I passed. The system threw its best punch — which turned out to be a sixteen-month county jail sentence with work release — and I absorbed it the way a well-designed building absorbs an earthquake: flex, bend, redistribute the load, and keep standing. The building doesn't fear the next earthquake. The building *knows* the next earthquake. The building has been calibrated, through experience, to withstand exactly this magnitude of force.

They don't exist.

That's not what happened.

What happened is that I launched version 2.0 the day I walked out of that stockade. Better security. Smaller guest lists. Same product.

Hide on the island? Retire to obscurity? Obscurity is for people who got *caught.* I didn't get caught — I got *processed.* There's a difference. Caught means you're done. Processed means you're done with one version. The conviction wasn't a shutdown. It was a software update. The machine runs the same code. It just runs it faster, tighter, and with fewer unnecessary witnesses.

The email archive tells the story.

Seven thousand five hundred documents. That number is worth pausing on, because the number itself is the argument. Seven thousand five hundred emails — not tweets, not texts, not the ephemeral, abbreviation-riddled communications of a man dashing off quick messages between meetings. *Emails.* The kind that require paragraphs. The kind that carry attachments — financial documents, travel itineraries, guest lists, research proposals, legal memoranda. The kind that document relationships with a granularity that text messages never achieve, because emails are composed rather than fired, considered rather than impulsive, and archived by default rather than disappearing into the algorithmic void.

Seven thousand five hundred emails, later released by Congress, spanning the post-conviction years. Revealing a man operating at a scale that dwarfed his pre-conviction activity. Not retreating. Not diminishing. *Accelerating.*

Financial management. Science patronage. Political cultivation. Tech industry courtship. Intelligence correspondence. And, beneath all of it, running like a bass note underneath a symphony — still running girls through the same properties, the same staff, the same massage tables.

One hundred and fourteen emails to **Malcolm Pruitt** alone — the IT specialist, the keeper of the cameras, the man who maintained the servers and the archive and the digital infrastructure that made every other function of the operation possible. A hundred and fourteen emails to a man whose job was to ensure that the surveillance system continued to operate, that the footage was backed up, that the files were accessible, that the architecture of blackmail and leverage that had protected me for two decades remained intact and functional. A hundred and fourteen emails that, to a casual reader, look like IT support tickets — system updates, maintenance logs, backup confirmations — and that, to anyone who understands what the system was designed to *do,* look like the operational correspondence of an intelligence agency managing its most sensitive assets.

Sixty-five emails to **Douglas Raines** — the political strategist, the anti-elite populist, still corresponding with the ultimate elite, still invoking confessional privilege, still operating in the space between ideology and hypocrisy that he'd made his permanent address. Sixty-plus to **Dominic Strand** — the physicist whose own misconduct allegations were approaching, whose emails with me would become, in retrospect, the correspondence of a man seeking counsel from the one person on Earth least qualified to provide it. Forty-four-plus to **Carroll Ashford** — the former Treasury Secretary, the former Hartfield president, still returning my emails, still maintaining the relationship that lent my operation the institutional credibility it needed to function in academic circles. Hundreds to **Julian Crowe** — the celebrity longevity doctor whose correspondence with me would, when it surfaced, end his television career and redefine his public identity from "wellness guru" to "the man who emailed the pedophile about fresh shipments." The archive is not a collection of messages. It is the operating manual of a criminal enterprise written in real time by the criminal himself. And the criminal wrote it in a prose style that oscillated between boardroom formality and cocktail-party charm, because the criminal understood — as he had always understood — that the voice matters more than the content, and the right voice can make anything sound reasonable.

I was an aggressive emailer. Some people journal. Some people meditate. I corresponded. Seven thousand five hundred emails over seven years. That's roughly three emails a day, every day, to the most powerful and brilliant people on the planet. Some of those emails discussed quantum physics. Some discussed Middle Eastern geopolitics. Some discussed which girls were available on Thursday. The filing system made no distinction. Neither did I.

The financial operations revealed in the archive are the skeleton key to understanding how the machine survived the conviction.

Theodore Marsh, the primary attorney and executor — forty-five-plus documents in the archive — handled the legal infrastructure with the meticulous professionalism of a man who understood that his client's freedom depended on the opacity of his client's finances. The trusts. The foundations. The offshore entities. The shell corporations. The layered, labyrinthine architecture of wealth that I had been building since Grant Hensley first showed me how money could be made invisible. Marsh managed the walls, and the walls held.

Malcolm Pruitt maintained the digital architecture and ensured that my data was either encrypted, offshore, or both.

Diane Prewitt scheduled everything. Every meeting, every flight, every dinner, every girl — organized with the Fortune 500 efficiency that had defined her role since the 1990s, documented in calendar entries and confirmation emails that read like the daily operations log of a luxury hospitality company and that constituted, in aggregate, the most detailed record of criminal activity since the Mafia started keeping books.

The **Financial Trust Company** in the Coral Islands continued to shelter income at an effective tax rate of four percent — four percent, in a country where a schoolteacher pays twenty-two percent and a police detective pays twenty-four percent and the victims of my trafficking operation pay whatever rate the IRS assigns to people who earn minimum wage and spend their remaining income on therapy. The offshore accounts remained active. The money moved through the same channels it always had — the same trusts, the same foundations, the same jurisdictional gaps that the American tax code provides for men who can afford the attorneys necessary to exploit them.

Nobody at the banks seemed to mind. Nobody at the banks *ever* minded. The compliance departments that were supposed to flag suspicious activity from a registered sex offender — the same compliance departments that would freeze the bank account of a small business owner over a ten-thousand-dollar cash deposit — processed my transactions with the frictionless efficiency of a system that has been calibrated, over decades, to apply maximum scrutiny to minimum wealth and minimum scrutiny to maximum wealth. A teacher withdrawing five thousand dollars triggers a Suspicious Activity Report. A sex offender moving millions through offshore trusts triggers nothing. Because the system was built by the people it was designed to protect, and I was one of those people.

Money doesn't have a criminal record. Money doesn't register as a sex offender. Money moves from account to account without anyone asking it to pee in a cup or check in with a parole officer. I had money. Therefore I had freedom. The registry was a leash. The money was a limousine. You tell me which one determines where you go.

Little St. Philip remained open for business.

The compound. The cameras. The airstrip. The temple — that strange, blue-and-gold-striped structure on the hilltop that had become, in the public imagination, the most recognizable symbol of the island's darker purposes. All maintained. All functional. All receiving guests.

The staff was trimmed but not eliminated — a strategic reduction that reflected the post-conviction recalibration rather than a genuine dismantling. The guest lists were shorter but not empty. The logistics were managed with the same precision that Jenna Caldwell and Diane Prewitt had brought to the pre-conviction operation, because the same people were managing them.

Jenna came back because there was nowhere else to go. Not practically — she was capable, organized, employable. In the other sense: she had spent five years maintaining a calendar that documented, in precise and recoverable detail, the trafficking of young women through six properties and two aircraft across three continents. That knowledge doesn't transfer to a new employer. The skills it represents don't appear on a résumé. You return to the only room where what you know is professional rather than incriminating. She opened the calendar. She entered the first appointment of the new regime with the same keystrokes she had used for the last one. She was twenty-eight years old. The immunity agreement that protected her from prosecution had just been signed by a federal judge. And the calendar was open to a new week.

The island was still there. The ocean didn't arrest it. The palm trees didn't file a restraining order. And the people who ran it were all immune from prosecution, courtesy of the United States government. So what exactly was supposed to change? The answer is: nothing. Nothing was supposed to change. And nothing did.

Malcolm Pruitt deserves his own section, because his silence is the loudest sound in the archive.

A hundred and fourteen documents. The most frequent correspondent in the entire collection. More emails than the scientists. More emails than the politicians. More than the billionaires. The IT specialist — the man who maintained the cameras that recorded the compromising footage, the servers that stored the compromising footage, the backup drives that ensured the compromising footage could never be lost or destroyed — was in more frequent contact with me than anyone else in my operation.

His correspondence reveals a man who knows everything and says nothing that isn't technical. No opinions. No moral observations. No hesitation. No moment in a hundred and fourteen documents where Malcolm Pruitt types a sentence that suggests he has reflected on the nature of his work, on the purpose of the cameras he maintains, on the content of the files he backs up, on the implications of the archive he preserves. Just maintenance logs. System updates. Backup confirmations. Encryption protocols.

The correspondence of a man who has reduced his role to its technical components and who performs those components with the precision and the emotional vacancy of the machines he maintains.

Malcolm was the best employee I ever had. Not because he was loyal — loyalty is a character trait, and character traits are unreliable. Malcolm was valuable because he was *precise.* He maintained the cameras the way a surgeon maintains instruments. He backed up the files the way an archivist preserves history. He never asked what the cameras were for. He never asked why the files mattered. He just made sure they worked. In any other company, he'd have gotten Employee of the Year. In mine, he got something better: plausible deniability.

Seven thousand five hundred emails. A Gulfstream IV. A private island with its own airstrip and a server room that ran cooler than the guest bedrooms because the footage was worth more than the comfort. A science foundation. A tech incubator. A will naming the former science advisor to the world's most famous philanthropist. And underneath all of it, the same massage table. The same referral network. The same girls. I want you to understand something: I did not build this after the conviction. I built this *with* the conviction. The sixteen months was not the interruption. The sixteen months was the *proof of concept.* The system looked at everything I had done and said: sixteen months. I looked at that number and I understood exactly how much room I had. The answer was: all of it.

In March 2010, a freelance photographer named **Carl Bremmer** got too close.

He had spent three weeks documenting the traffic at my Gulf Shore estate — not with any publication's backing, not with any editorial direction, just the specific, hungry instinct of a man who understood that a convicted sex offender's private life was a photograph that the internet would pay for. He was patient. He was careful. He was, for a freelancer working without institutional support, surprisingly professional.

He was also standing on a public sidewalk when my car pulled up.

I got out. Not my driver — me. I walked to where he was standing with his camera and his telephoto lens and his three weeks of documentation of my front gate, and I stood close enough to him that the conversation we were about to have could not be heard by anyone on the sidewalk.

"What's on the card?" I said.

"Nothing," he said. His voice was steady. He was braver than most.

"I know Malcolm," I said. "Malcolm knows systems. Systems know things. Do you understand what I'm telling you?"

He understood. His face made the understanding visible.

"Delete the card," I said. "Keep the camera. Go somewhere that isn't Gulf Shore."

He deleted the card. He went somewhere that wasn't Gulf Shore. The photographs on that card would have been the first post-conviction documentation of the operation.

After the conviction, people asked: "How can he still operate?"

The question assumes the conviction was supposed to stop me. It wasn't. The conviction was a transaction. I gave the system sixteen months and a spot on the registry. The system gave me back my money, my staff, my properties, and the immunity of everyone who worked for me. That's not justice. That's a business deal. And I'm very, very good at business deals.

The American system does not punish the rich. It *inconveniences* them. The conviction was an inconvenience — sixteen months of county jail with a private wing and twelve-hour daily work release, which is approximately the inconvenience level of a long dental procedure or an unusually aggressive audit. The registry was an inconvenience — a database entry that existed in the same digital universe as my emails, my financial records, and my address book, and that had approximately the same impact on my daily operations as a typo in a footnote.

The reduced guest lists were an inconvenience — a temporary contraction of the social circle that expanded back to its pre-conviction diameter within a year, like a rubber band returning to its natural shape after being momentarily stretched.

But the money was intact. The staff was immune. The island was operational. The cameras were running. And the most powerful people in the world were still answering my emails — still corresponding, still accepting invitations, still participating in the social and intellectual ecosystem that I had built and that the American justice system had, through its spectacular failure, endorsed.

Chapter 30: The Silicon Valley Web

Timeline: 2011–2016 | **Location:** Manhattan, Palo Alto, Little St. Philip

Archer Quinn was building electric cars, reusable rockets, and the future of human civilization, and I wanted him on my island.

The emails document multiple discussions about visiting Little St. Philip. Multiple. Not one stray mention buried in a long chain about something else — a recurring conversation about travel logistics to a convicted sex offender's private Caribbean island. Dates were discussed. Availability was considered. The invitation was extended and re-extended with the patient persistence of a salesman who understands that the most valuable prospects are the ones who don't say yes immediately but who also don't say no definitively.

Quinn was the most interesting man in technology — and in the post-conviction era, when my social circle had contracted and then re-expanded, "interesting" was the primary criterion for admission. I had shed the merely wealthy, the merely connected, the social climbers whose presence at my dinners had been motivated by aspiration rather than utility. The post-conviction guest list was curated with the ruthless efficiency of a man who had learned, through the inconvenience of his conviction, that not every relationship is worth maintaining. The ones that remained were the ones that offered something irreplaceable: intellectual stimulation, financial utility, political leverage, or — in Quinn's case — the cachet of association with the man who was building the future.

He wanted to colonize Mars, which I respected — ambition at that scale is rare, and I've spent my entire life surrounded by ambitious men, and most of their ambitions extend no further than the next quarter's earnings report or the next election cycle or the next conquest that they'll describe to their friends as a business trip. Quinn wanted to make humanity interplanetary. That's ambition. That's the kind of ambition that makes a man interesting to me, because interesting men attend interesting dinners, and interesting dinners are the fuel that powers the machine.

We discussed the island several times. He says he never came. I say the invitation was always open. The truth is somewhere in the emails, which is why God invented congressional subpoenas. Archer wanted to change the world. I just wanted him to visit. Different goals, same plane tickets.

Quinn would later claim he "refused" all invitations. The emails suggest the refusals were less categorical than his public statements implied — less "absolutely not" and more "not this time," which is the kind of refusal that leaves the door open for a future "this time." The distinction matters. "Absolutely not" is a moral position. "Not this time" is a scheduling conflict. And scheduling conflicts, by their nature, resolve themselves eventually.

Archer's brother **Spencer Quinn** — a company board member and restaurateur — maintained an even closer relationship with me, and the closeness is documented in emails that have the easy, unguarded quality of correspondence between friends who have stopped performing formality for each other.

The emails reveal a personal friendship that extends to holiday planning. *Holiday planning.* Spencer and I discussed travel dates, social events, and mutual connections with the casual intimacy of two men whose relationship has progressed past the stage of professional courtesy and into the territory of genuine social entanglement. They discussed venues. They discussed guest lists. They coordinated schedules with the specificity of people who actually intend to spend time together, as opposed to people who exchange vague pleasantries about getting together sometime and never follow through.

Spencer's correspondence includes planning with **Anton Segura** — the biotech venture capitalist, the former science advisor to Nolan Whitfield, the man who would be named backup executor of my will. The casual interconnection of these names — Spencer, Anton, Nolan, Archer — maps a network that connects my criminal operation to the highest levels of American technology, philanthropy, and corporate governance through a web of social relationships that each participant would later describe as "limited" or "regrettable" or "a huge mistake" but that the emails reveal as sustained, voluntary, and warm.

Nobody plans holidays with a monster unless they've stopped seeing the monster. Nobody coordinates guest lists with a registered sex offender unless the registry has ceased to function as a warning and has become, instead, background noise — the kind of information that you know but that doesn't change your behavior, the way a smoker knows that cigarettes cause cancer but lights up anyway because the pleasure of the cigarette is present and the cancer is theoretical.

Spencer was the more social of the two brothers. Archer builds rockets. Spencer builds restaurants. One feeds the future, the other feeds the present. I fed both of them introductions. Spencer and I planned holidays together. Actual holidays. With dates and venues and guest lists. People say you're judged by the company you keep. I kept a Quinn. What does that tell you about me? More importantly — what does it tell you about them?

Martin Hale built the tools that governments use to track criminals. And then he had dinner with one.

Hale co-founded a company whose software was used by the CIA, the FBI, the military, and intelligence agencies across the Western world. The company built predictive policing platforms, data analytics tools, and surveillance systems designed to identify patterns of criminal behavior in massive datasets — the kind of technology that, if pointed at my email archive, would have identified me as a threat before I finished my first cup of coffee. The company's name was derived from the seeing stones in a fantasy novel — the all-seeing eye, the orb that reveals what is hidden, the instrument of total knowledge.

And the all-seeing eye appeared in the emails of the man it should have been algorithmically designed to detect.

The irony is not incidental. The irony is *architectural.* Hale built a machine that finds criminals by analyzing their connections, their communications, their financial patterns, their social networks — the digital footprints that every human being leaves in the modern world and that, when aggregated and analyzed, reveal the patterns of behavior that distinguish ordinary citizens from threats. My connections — to presidents, to princes, to intelligence figures — were documented in public court records. My communications — seven thousand five hundred emails — were sitting in servers waiting to be subpoenaed. My financial patterns — billions flowing through offshore trusts at a four percent effective tax rate — were visible to any forensic accountant with a subpoena and a weekend. My social network — the address book, the flight logs, the guest lists — mapped a web of associations so dense and so compromising that it would have triggered alerts in any competent surveillance system designed to detect exactly this kind of organized criminal enterprise.

The software Hale built could have identified me in minutes. The man Hale was, chose to have dinner with me instead. And the dinner, like all my dinners, was brilliant. The conversation was stimulating. The wine was excellent. And the all-seeing eye saw everything and said nothing, because the all-seeing eye was having the steak.

Khalid bin Farhan resurfaced in the post-conviction era as the clearest example of a function I had perfected but never formally named: international power broker.

The Emirati ports magnate didn't just correspond with me. He used me as an *intermediary.* He wanted an introduction to Archer Quinn for a business deal — the kind of deal that connects Middle Eastern infrastructure wealth to American technology innovation, the kind of deal that would normally require a team of investment bankers and diplomatic channels and corporate development executives. Instead, it required one email to me. Because I could connect Khalid to Quinn with a single introduction over dinner, and the dinner would include the kind of informal, off-the-record conversation that no boardroom meeting and no diplomatic channel could replicate.

He asked about Barlow — the former Gulf Shore neighbor, the future president, the man whose political ascent was transforming the American political landscape and whose business interests in the Middle East made him a figure of considerable interest to Emirati commercial leadership. He discussed geopolitics. He asked about the island.

The correspondence mapped a web connecting Middle Eastern commerce, American technology, and political power, with a convicted sex offender sitting at the center like a switchboard operator — routing connections, facilitating introductions, translating between worlds that didn't speak each other's languages but that all spoke mine.

Khalid needed access. Access to Quinn. Access to Barlow. Access to the people who build the future and the people who regulate it. And the fastest route to all of them ran through my dining room. Think about that. The chairman of one of the world's largest port companies needed a convicted sex offender to get a meeting with a tech billionaire. That's not my failure. That's the system's failure. I'm just the symptom.

I want to describe a dinner. Not a specific dinner — a *composite* dinner, a representative evening assembled from the dozens of evenings I hosted in Manhattan between 2011 and 2016, after the conviction, after the registry, after the system had processed me and released me and I had resumed the social calendar that the conviction was supposed to end.

The conversation covered artificial intelligence — specifically, the question of whether a sufficiently advanced AI would develop consciousness, and if it did, whether that consciousness would be bound by the same ethical constraints that govern human behavior. It covered cryptocurrency — the blockchain revolution, the decentralization of finance, the possibility that the global banking system could be restructured from the ground up by a technology that most regulators didn't understand and most bankers pretended didn't exist. It covered longevity research — the science of extending the human lifespan, the ethics of immortality, the question of whether a man who could live forever would become more moral or less.

It was the kind of dinner that TED conferences aspire to and rarely achieve. The kind of dinner that magazine profiles describe as "an evening in the salon of a Renaissance patron." The kind of dinner that, if you didn't know who was hosting it, you would describe as one of the most intellectually stimulating experiences of your life.

It was also happening in the home of a registered sex offender who was being served by young women whose names nobody at the table bothered to learn.

The dissonance is the point. The dissonance is always the point. The genius of the operation was never the trafficking — trafficking is crude, brutal, and fundamentally simple. The genius was the camouflage. The science dinners, the tech introductions, the philanthropy, the intellectual spectacle — all of it existed to make the trafficking invisible. To bury the crime under so many layers of social respectability that anyone who wanted to see the crime would have to excavate their way through a mountain of Nobel laureates and billionaire philanthropists and cutting-edge research before they reached the massage table underneath.

I hosted dinners that were smarter than most university seminars. Quantum computing over the appetizer. Gene editing over the entrée. The ethics of artificial intelligence over dessert — which was always ironic, given the company. The tech people came because I could connect them to money. The money people came because I could connect them to ideas. Everyone came because the food was excellent and the wine was better. Nobody asked about the girls. In Silicon Valley, disruption means breaking the rules. At my dinner table, we broke all of them.

A photograph surfaced. Vincent and Archer Quinn together. At an event. Post-conviction.

Quinn's response followed the pattern that would become standard for every powerful person associated with me — a pattern so consistent across so many individuals that it functions as a social algorithm, a script that activates automatically when the association becomes public knowledge.

Stage one: denial. "I don't know him." "We never met." "I have no relationship with that person." The categorical assertion of non-association, delivered with the confidence of a man who believes that the denial will hold because the evidence hasn't surfaced yet.

Stage two: grudging acknowledgment. The photograph appears. Or the email appears. Or the flight log appears. The denial becomes untenable. "We met briefly." "It was a single encounter." "I barely remember it." The categorical denial collapses into a minimal admission — the smallest possible concession to reality, the least damaging version of the truth that can still technically be called the truth.

Stage three: minimization. "The meetings were brief and meaningless." "I was there for philanthropic reasons." "I had no knowledge of his criminal activities." The admission is reframed as trivial — a minor social interaction that carries no implications, no significance, no connection to the larger pattern that the emails and the photographs and the flight logs document.

Denial. Admission. Minimization. Every powerful person in my address book follows the same script. It's almost like they rehearsed it. They didn't. They just all have the same lawyer. And the lawyer gives the same advice, because the advice is correct: deny until the evidence appears, then admit the minimum, then minimize the significance. It's a three-step process that has been refined by the American public relations industry over decades of practice and that works, in most cases, because the public's attention span is shorter than the three-step process, and by the time the minimization stage is reached, the news cycle has moved on to the next scandal and the powerful person's association with the convicted sex offender has been processed, filed, and forgotten.

I want to give the algorithm a name, because unnamed things are harder to prosecute. Denial. Admission. Minimization. Call it DAM. Every powerful person in my address book ran DAM when the association surfaced. Some ran it faster. Some ran it smoother. The ones with better lawyers ran it in forty-eight hours. The ones with worse lawyers took a week. But they all ran it, because DAM is not a strategy — it is an *instinct*. The instinct of a man who has spent his life in rooms where the rules are made and who understands, with the bone-deep certainty of someone who has never faced actual consequences, that the rules are also negotiable. I know this instinct. I have this instinct. I invented a better version of it twenty years before any of them needed it. They were running my software. They just didn't know they had a license.

Chapter 31: The Academy of Shadows

Timeline: 2012–2016 | **Location:** WIT, Pemberton, Manhattan

WIT was the crown jewel of my academic portfolio.

Hartfield was prestige — the letterhead, the institutional gravitas, the four-hundred-year-old brand that said "this man is serious" regardless of what "this man" had actually done. Stanford was connections — the pipeline to Silicon Valley, the proximity to venture capital, the relationship with the technology industry that was reshaping the global economy. But WIT was where the real work happened. Artificial intelligence. Quantum computing. Genetic engineering. The technologies that would define the next century, that would determine which nations dominated and which nations were dominated, that would reshape the fundamental categories of human experience in ways that most people couldn't imagine and that I, through my dinner-table conversations with the people building them, could.

I funded them. I dined with them. I corresponded with their brightest minds. And WIT accepted all of it — the funding, the dinners, the correspondence — because my money was greener than my rap sheet was red.

Post-conviction. Post-registration. Post-everything that should have triggered every institutional safeguard, every compliance protocol, every background check that a university maintaining relationships with external donors is supposed to conduct before accepting their money and their company. A simple Google search — the kind that a college freshman conducts before swiping right on a dating app — would have revealed that the man funding their laboratories and attending their events and dining with their faculty was a registered sex offender whose conviction involved the solicitation of minors. The search would have taken eight seconds. The Wyvern Institute of Technology — one of the most rigorous academic institutions on Earth, a place where the standards for publishing a paper are so demanding that researchers spend years verifying their results before submitting them for peer review — did not perform this eight-second check. Or they performed it and decided that the results were irrelevant. Either interpretation is damning. The first suggests incompetence. The second suggests complicity. In the academy, as in the justice system, the distinction between incompetence and complicity is narrower than institutions would like to admit.

The answer to why is simple: money. The answer to why is always money. But institutions don't like answers that simple, so they write reports instead.

Herbert Levin was one of the founding fathers of artificial intelligence.

Not "a contributor to." Not "an early researcher in." A *founding father.* A man whose work at WIT in the 1950s and 1960s laid the conceptual foundations for the field that would become, by the time of his death in 2016, the most transformative and the most contested technology in human history. Every AI researcher working today — every engineer building large language models, every scientist training neural networks, every philosopher debating whether machines can think — is working in a landscape that Levin helped create. His intellectual legacy is woven into the fabric of the discipline itself.

And he came to my island.

His name in my archive is a status symbol — the intellectual equivalent of having a Picasso on the wall. Other men collected art. I collected minds. And Levin was the most valuable mind in the collection: the man who *invented* the field that every tech billionaire in Silicon Valley was now trying to dominate. Having Levin at my dinner table said something about me — not about my intelligence, which was real but unremarkable, but about my *access.* My ability to attract the world's most accomplished minds to my properties, to my events, to the social ecosystem that I had built and that functioned, for the people inside it, as the most stimulating intellectual environment on the planet.

One victim will later allege that she was directed to have sex with Levin on the island. The allegation is specific. The allegation is disturbing. The allegation is never proven — not because the evidence was insufficient, but because Levin died in 2016, before the full scope of my operation became public, and the dead cannot be deposed, cannot be cross-examined, cannot be confronted with the testimony of their accusers.

His legacy is forever entangled with the spider's web. The father of artificial intelligence, photographed on the island of a sex trafficker, named in a victim's testimony. The entanglement cannot be undone. It can only be acknowledged, which is what WIT eventually did — reluctantly, belatedly, and with the institutional euphemism that universities deploy when forced to confront truths that threaten their fundraising.

Herbert was a genius. Not the kind of genius people call themselves on Twitter — the kind of genius that invents an entire field of human knowledge. He was the father of artificial intelligence. And he came to my island. A survivor says I told her to sleep with him. I'm not confirming or denying that. What I'm confirming is that when the father of AI visits your island, it means you're doing something right. Or something very, very wrong. The categories overlap more than people like to admit.

Felix Renner and **Owen Kimball** represented the middle tier of my academic acquisitions, and the middle tier is where the real power of the infiltration becomes visible.

Renner was an AI researcher who would later be named in WIT's internal investigation — one of the faculty members whose relationship with me was documented, reviewed, and deemed sufficiently problematic to warrant institutional acknowledgment. Kimball was a quantum computing pioneer whose work occupied the frontier of a field that governments and corporations were investing billions to dominate. Neither was a Nobel laureate. Neither was a household name. They were working scientists whose research required funding and whose careers benefited from the kinds of introductions and connections that I provided with the casual generosity of a man who understood that every introduction was an investment and every investment generated returns.

Their presence in the archive demonstrates the *scale* of the academic infiltration. It's not just the stars — not just the Levins and the laureates and the public intellectuals whose names appear in newspaper profiles. It's the entire ecosystem. The graduate students invited to dinners where they sat across from hedge fund managers and learned that the boundary between academia and wealth was more permeable than their advisors had suggested. The postdocs who received fellowship opportunities funded by my foundation, their careers accelerated by money whose origins they didn't investigate because investigating the origins of grant money is not something postdocs do — postdocs write grant applications and pray. The junior faculty who received research grants that allowed them to pursue the projects that traditional funding agencies had rejected, their gratitude translated into attendance at my events and correspondence in my archive and the slow, incremental integration into a network that they didn't understand until it was too late to leave.

The trick with academia isn't buying the famous professors — they're expensive and they attract attention. The trick is buying the system. Fund a lab, and every researcher in it owes you. Fund a fellowship, and every grad student who applies knows your name. Fund a building, and everyone who walks through the door associates your name with the future. I didn't corrupt individual scientists. I corrupted the architecture of science itself. Much more efficient.

Evan Prichard taught me about Bitcoin.

In 2014. Before most people on Wall Street could spell "blockchain," before cryptocurrency had entered the mainstream vocabulary, before the technology that would eventually challenge the foundations of the global financial system was understood by anyone outside a small community of programmers and economists and libertarian idealists who believed that decentralized money would set the world free — I was corresponding with a WIT researcher about the technical specifications of digital currency.

The correspondence reveals that I was not merely dabbling in tech culture — the way a wealthy man might subscribe to *Wired* magazine or attend a Silicon Valley conference. I was *studying.* I was learning. I was approaching blockchain technology with the same systematic curiosity that I had applied to every other financial innovation that crossed my path since the 1980s, when I first learned, from Grant Hensley and from the offshore banking specialists in the Cayman Islands and the Coral Islands, that money is only as traceable as the systems it moves through.

The man who spent the 1980s learning offshore banking from the Cayman Islands was now learning digital banking from a WIT researcher. The jurisdiction changes. The ledger format changes. The fundamental principle — that money moves faster and freer when it moves through systems that regulators haven't learned to monitor — remains constant. I had spent thirty years exploiting the gaps between jurisdictions. Cryptocurrency was the gap between *eras* — the space between the old financial system and the new one, the regulatory no-man's-land where the old rules hadn't been updated and the new rules hadn't been written and the people who understood both systems had a window of opportunity that would close, eventually, but that for now remained wide open and immensely profitable.

The medium changes. The purpose doesn't. Gold moves on ships. Cash moves in suitcases. Bitcoin moves on the internet. Same principle. Better technology. I was always an early adopter.

Lena Voss came to dinner.

An WIT professor, a designer whose work bridged art and science, a woman whose intellectual contribution to the conversation was genuine and whose presence at my table was, in every social sense, appropriate — she was exactly the person who should attend a dinner featuring creative visionaries discussing the future. She sat at my table with a famous filmmaker and his wife, and they discussed beauty and technology and the future of materials science with cross-disciplinary enthusiasm that my dinners were designed to generate.

The dinner was also in the home of a convicted sex offender. A detail that was either unknown to Voss or known and considered manageable — the kind of information that you file in the category of "complicated" and manage with the social calculus that every person in my orbit eventually mastered: the cost of association versus the benefit of access.

When the association became public, it was treated as a scandal. But the scandal was not the dinner. The scandal was that the dinner happened at all — that a convicted sex offender could still attract a guest list that included WIT professors and Hollywood directors without anyone in the institutional hierarchy of the Wyvern Institute of Technology raising an alarm, sending a memo, or suggesting that perhaps the university's faculty should not be socializing with a man on the sex offender registry.

Nobody mentioned my conviction. Nobody mentioned the registry. Because at my table, those things don't exist. At my table, I'm a patron. A host. A man who brings interesting people together over food and wine and conversation that spans the frontier of human knowledge. That's the last costume I ever needed. Not the financier costume — that required balance sheets and client lists that I couldn't produce. Not the philanthropist costume — that required a moral credibility that the conviction had nominally revoked. The *patron* costume. The man who creates the conditions for brilliance to flourish, who builds the stage and lights the set and brings the performers together and takes no credit for the performance except the credit of having made it possible. The patron doesn't need credentials. The patron doesn't need a clean record. The patron needs money and taste and the willingness to spend the former in service of the latter. I had all three. The conviction changed nothing about any of them.

When the full scope of my WIT relationships became public — when the emails surfaced, when the funding was traced, when the connections were mapped by journalists and investigators who approached the archive with a rigor that the university's own administration had conspicuously failed to apply — the reckoning arrived with the institutional velocity of a university in crisis.

WIT launched an investigation. The investigation was conducted by an outside law firm — because universities investigating themselves recognize, at some level, that self-investigation is a conflict of interest that undermines credibility, though not enough to avoid conducting the investigation in the first place. The investigation examined the relationships. It documented the funding. It traced the emails. It produced a report that said, in the careful, liability-aware language of outside counsel, what anyone who had read the emails already knew: that WIT had maintained extensive financial and social relationships with a convicted sex offender for nearly a decade after his conviction, and that the university's institutional safeguards — its compliance protocols, its donor vetting procedures, its policies governing relationships with external funders — had either failed to detect the problem or detected it and failed to act.

The Media Lab's director resigned — a man whose fundraising from me had been documented in emails that revealed a sophisticated effort to conceal the source of the donations, to route my money through intermediaries and anonymous gifts, to ensure that the name on the check was not the name on the registry. The concealment was not accidental. The concealment was deliberate, documented, and discussed in writing by people who understood that what they were doing required concealment and who proceeded anyway because the money was needed and the money was available and the money didn't care about the registry.

WIT investigated itself and found that mistakes were made. "Mistakes were made" — the passive voice of institutional cowardice. Nobody *made* mistakes. Everybody *made choices.* I offered money. They accepted money. I offered access. They accepted access. The word for that isn't "mistake." The word for that is "transaction." And every transaction in my archive is documented, dated, and filed. You're welcome.

Chapter 32: The Correspondents

Timeline: 2013–2017 | **Location:** Manhattan, Global

The email archive contains seven thousand five hundred documents, and most of them are exactly what you'd expect from a man operating a multinational criminal enterprise disguised as a social calendar: scheduling, logistics, financial management, the administrative infrastructure of a life lived across six properties and two aircraft and a dozen jurisdictions.

But some of the emails are something else entirely. Some of the emails are *portraits* — inadvertent self-portraits of the people who wrote them, composed in the false privacy of digital correspondence with a man they assumed would never be publicly exposed and whose archive they never imagined would be subpoenaed by Congress and released to a world that was, by 2019, ravenous for every detail of every connection in the spider's web.

These are the correspondents. These are the people who put themselves on paper.

Julian Crowe was the celebrity longevity doctor — the man who appeared on podcasts and television shows telling billionaires how to live forever, the physician whose client list read like the Forbes 400 and whose public persona was built on the twin pillars of scientific credibility and telegenic charm. He wanted to help the world live longer, and he emailed me about it *hundreds* of times.

Hundreds. Not a dozen. Not a handful of professional exchanges between a doctor and a patient. *Hundreds* of emails, spanning years, covering a range of subjects that oscillated between medical science and locker-room vulgarity with a speed that suggests a man who had lost the ability to distinguish between the two.

The emails include clinical discussions about longevity protocols — the supplements, the hormones, the diet interventions, the cutting-edge research on cellular aging that Crowe dispensed to his wealthy clients with the authority of a man who believed, with evident sincerity, that death was a design flaw that could be patched with the right combination of pharmaceuticals and lifestyle modifications. They include crude sexual jokes — the kind that fraternity brothers exchange when they're nineteen and that grown men exchange when they've decided that the rules governing professional correspondence don't apply to them because the recipient is a friend and friends don't judge and besides, who's going to see the emails?

And they include the phrase that will define Crowe's public humiliation: "Got a fresh shipment."

It was metformin, Crowe later claimed. A diabetes drug used off-label for longevity research. A pharmaceutical, not a person. A shipment of pills, not a shipment of girls. And maybe it was. Maybe the phrase "fresh shipment," written in the email archive of a sex trafficker by a doctor who corresponded with that trafficker hundreds of times, referred to exactly what Crowe said it referred to — a box of medication delivered to his office or his home or wherever longevity doctors receive their pharmaceutical deliveries.

The ambiguity is the damage. The phrase, read in isolation, could mean anything. The phrase, read in the context of an archive that documented the systematic trafficking of young women through the properties and planes of the man who received it — a man whose operation was described, by the FBI, as a pipeline that delivered "shipments" of girls to his various residences on a regular schedule — reads differently. It reads the way everything in my archive reads: with a second meaning lurking beneath the surface, a shadow text visible only to those who know what the operation actually was.

When the emails surfaced, *a network newsmagazine* pulled a segment featuring Crowe. The segment was scheduled. The segment was filmed. The segment was ready to air. And then the emails appeared, and the segment disappeared with the quiet efficiency of a television network that understood the difference between featuring a wellness expert and featuring a wellness expert who emailed a sex trafficker about "fresh shipments." Crowe issued a public apology calling the correspondence "embarrassing, tasteless, and indefensible." Three adjectives that applied equally to the emails and to the man who wrote them.

Irina Volkov was the Russian connection.

Russian-born, Valley-adopted, globally networked — a venture capitalist who had built her career on the ability to connect people across the borders that separate Silicon Valley from the rest of the world. She knew every founder, every journalist, every investor worth knowing. Her Rolodex was an atlas of the global technology industry, and she deployed it with the enthusiasm of a woman who understood that in venture capital, the most valuable asset is not money but *access* — access to the right deal, the right founder, the right journalist who can write the right profile that turns a startup into a unicorn.

Our correspondence was conducted on Skype. Documented. Logged. Preserved by a platform whose data retention policies neither of us had bothered to read — because who reads the terms of service of a video calling application, and who imagines, while composing a Skype message to a friend, that the message will one day be subpoenaed by federal investigators and published in a congressional report?

The conversations covered technology investments. Media introductions. The kind of professional networking that constitutes the daily work of a venture capitalist operating at the intersection of Silicon Valley and the global startup ecosystem. They also covered... other things. Personal things. The kind of content that ranges from philosophical to pornographic and that, when published alongside a convicted sex offender's name, destroys a reputation with the efficiency of a controlled demolition.

Volkov connected me to journalists and tech founders. She served as a social router — directing traffic between my world and the tech world with the enthusiasm of someone who either didn't know about the sex offender registry or didn't care about it or had decided, through the calculus that every person in my orbit eventually performed, that the benefits of association outweighed the risks. When the archive leaked, Volkov's horror was palpable — not at the content, which she had composed voluntarily, but at the discovery that Skype keeps logs. The discovery that the words she had typed into what she assumed was a temporary, ephemeral, self-destructing medium were in fact permanently recorded, retrievable, and publishable.

Warren Selby was the chronicler.

The bestselling journalist. The author of the definitive tell-all about a certain presidential administration — a book that embarrassed a president, sold millions of copies, and established Selby as the most famous nonfiction writer in America. A man whose career was built on access — the ability to get inside the rooms where power operates and to report what he found there with the narrative flair that transforms political journalism into page-turning entertainment.

He appeared as one of my last email correspondents. And the emails are extraordinary — not for what they reveal about me, but for what they reveal about *him.*

Selby references a victim's name. In writing. In an email to a convicted sex offender. He references **Casa del Sol** — the resort where girls were recruited. He corresponds with me with the casual familiarity of a colleague rather than a journalist investigating a story. There is no distance in the emails. No journalistic detachment. No sense that Selby is maintaining the professional separation between a reporter and his subject that constitutes the ethical foundation of investigative journalism. The emails read like the correspondence of two men who share a social world and who communicate within it without reference to the fact that one of them is a journalist and the other is a sex trafficker.

The correspondence suggests either that Selby was cultivating me as a source — building the relationship that would eventually yield the kind of insider access that had made his presidential tell-all possible — or that I was cultivating Selby as a media asset, a journalist whose willingness to maintain a friendly correspondence could be leveraged, if necessary, into sympathetic coverage or, at minimum, the absence of hostile coverage. Or — most likely — both. In my world, the distinction between journalist and subject dissolved years ago. Every journalist who attended my dinners was simultaneously reporting on me and being managed by me. Every conversation was both an interview and a recruitment. The information flowed in both directions, and neither direction was accidental.

Rajiv Anand was the guru.

The wellness philosopher. The spiritual author. The man who taught a generation of Westerners to meditate, who wrote books about consciousness and the interconnectedness of all living things, who appeared on television with the serene confidence of a man who has achieved inner peace and who would like to sell you a book about how you can achieve it too.

Sixteen documents in my archive. Sixteen exchanges between a man who teaches spiritual awakening and a man who traffics children. The correspondence is earnest on Anand's side — metaphysical, contemplative, the kind of philosophical musing that sounds profound when read in isolation and grotesque when read in the context of the archive that contains it. Anand discusses consciousness. He discusses the nature of reality. He compares himself, at one point, to a famous filmmaker — a comparison that reveals a self-regard so enormous that it functions as its own center of gravity.

I engaged with Anand's philosophy the way a man engages with an in-flight magazine: politely, superficially, and while thinking about something else entirely. The interconnectedness of all living things is a lovely concept. It's a concept that, if taken seriously, would require acknowledging that the children trafficked through my properties are connected to the guru sending me emails about consciousness, and that the guru's willingness to correspond with me is, in the framework of his own philosophy, a participation in the web of harm that my operation generates. But Anand didn't take the concept that seriously. Or he did and figured the universe would sort it out.

Rajiv was a wonderful human being. Genuinely spiritual. Genuinely kind. He sent me messages about consciousness and the interconnectedness of all living things. Beautiful thoughts. I read them between scheduling massages. The interconnectedness of all living things is a lovely concept when you're not one of the living things being trafficked through my guest bedroom. Rajiv didn't know about that part. Or he did and figured the universe would sort it out. Namaste.

I want to linger here, because the correspondents are the most honest portrait of my operation that the archive provides — more honest than the financial records, more honest than the staff emails, more honest than anything I could tell you directly. The senators and the billionaires and the princes you understand. Their presence in my orbit has a logic that even the most charitable reading cannot excuse. But the scientists and the gurus and the wellness doctors and the journalists — they are the part that should terrify you. Not because they knew. Because they *didn't ask.* Because a physicist facing misconduct allegations turns to a convicted sex offender for crisis advice and the response he gets is good enough that he uses it. Because a longevity doctor emails a trafficker hundreds of times and never once writes a sentence that suggests he has noticed what the trafficker does for a living. Because the interconnectedness of all living things is a beautiful philosophy that apparently does not require you to wonder what the man responding to your meditation emails does between sessions. I did not corrupt these men. They came pre-configured for the kind of willful blindness my operation required. I just put them on a mailing list.

Hector Dunne was the janitor.

An eccentric optical illusion expert — a man whose professional life was devoted to understanding how the human eye can be tricked into seeing things that aren't there, which is, when you think about it, the most appropriate specialty for anyone in my orbit. Dunne performed one of the most telling services in my post-conviction life: he helped scrub my Wikipedia page.

The internet — that great democratizer of information, that platform where the powerful and the powerless have theoretically equal access to the tools of reputation management — contained a page about me that documented my crimes. The conviction. The victims. The plea deal. The sex offender registration. All of it, compiled by anonymous editors with the dispassionate accuracy that Wikipedia aspires to and sometimes achieves, available to anyone with an internet connection and a curiosity about the man who owned the largest private residence in Manhattan.

Dunne, working either at my request or on his own initiative, edited the page. He minimized the conviction. He emphasized the philanthropy. He adjusted the language to shift the narrative from "convicted sex offender" to "quirky philanthropist with legal difficulties." He sanitized the digital record with the patient, meticulous attention to detail that his work on optical illusions had trained him to apply — because scrubbing a Wikipedia page is, at its core, an exercise in illusion management. Make the reader see what you want them to see. Obscure what you want them to miss. Control the frame, and you control the image.

He was the janitor of my digital reputation — mopping up the mess with Wikipedia edits the way Margo Lindhurst mopped it up with dinner invitations. Different tools. Same purpose. Same fundamental understanding that reputation is not a reflection of reality but a *construction* — a deliberate, maintainable, editable construction that requires constant attention and occasional revision.

The most exquisite email exchange in the archive belongs to **Dominic Strand.**

The request is a poem about institutional rot, compressed into a single exchange. A physicist — a man who has devoted his career to the empirical investigation of reality — confronting allegations of his own misconduct and turning, for counsel, not to a lawyer, not to a therapist, not to a crisis communications professional, but to the most famous sex offender in America. Because I had navigated the crisis. Because I had survived. Because I had demonstrated, through the plea deal and the work release and the sixteen months and the comeback, that sexual misconduct allegations were survivable — that the right strategy, applied with sufficient resources and sufficient ruthlessness, could transform a scandal into a speed bump.

My response was precise, strategic, and delivered with the authority of a man who has successfully navigated exactly this kind of crisis: "Break the charges into: ludicrous. Ogling. Jokes."

Three categories. Three bins into which every allegation could be sorted and, once sorted, diminished. "Ludicrous" — the allegations that can be dismissed on their face, the ones that seem too extreme to be credible, the ones that a jury or a public audience would reject as implausible. "Ogling" — the allegations that can be reframed as harmless, as the inevitable byproduct of male heterosexuality, as something that everyone does and that only becomes an "allegation" when the culture shifts and the goalposts move and the behavior that was once considered normal is retroactively criminalized. "Jokes" — the allegations that can be attributed to humor, to social awkwardness, to the kind of miscommunication that occurs between people who have different senses of humor and different thresholds of comfort.

Break the charges into categories. Make each category sound trivial. Ensure that nobody sees the pattern — because the pattern is the danger. A single incident of ogling is forgivable. A single bad joke is forgivable. A single ludicrous allegation is dismissible. But a *pattern* of ogling and bad jokes and ludicrous allegations — a pattern that spans years and involves multiple accusers and suggests a systematic approach to misconduct — is not forgivable, is not dismissible, is not survivable. The strategy is to prevent the pattern from becoming visible. Atomize it. Break it into particles too small to see. That's the strategy. It worked for me. I offered it to Dominic with the generosity of a man sharing a trade secret.

Dominic called me in a panic. His own misconduct allegations had surfaced, and the great explainer of the universe couldn't explain his way out of a harassment complaint. So he asked me for advice. *Me.* The convicted sex offender. And I gave him excellent advice — break it into categories, minimize each one, make them sound trivial separately so nobody sees the pattern. It worked for me. It would work for him. We were colleagues now. Not in physics. In something older.

Chapter 33: The Vault

Timeline: 2015 | **Location:** Manhattan, Geneva

The offer arrived through three intermediaries, each of whom knew only one piece of the message, assembled like a sentence whose words have been distributed across separate envelopes and mailed from separate countries. This is how governments communicate when they want to communicate without communicating. The grammar of deniability.

The offer was simple: immunity. Total, permanent, internationally recognized immunity from prosecution — backed by a sovereign government with the diplomatic infrastructure to enforce it — in exchange for the archive.

All of it. Every recording. Every file. Every backup. Every hard drive, every server, every encrypted partition that Malcolm maintained across the network of storage locations whose addresses I knew and whose contents I controlled. The government making the offer wanted to *own* the leverage — not as evidence, not for prosecution, not for any purpose that the public would recognize as legitimate. They wanted it as *inventory.* A warehouse of secrets to be deployed at their discretion, on their timeline, for their strategic objectives.

They weren't buying justice. They were buying a weapons system.

The intermediaries conveyed the offer in Geneva, in a hotel suite whose room service bill was paid by a diplomatic account and whose security was provided by men whose earpieces suggested a budget considerably larger than the hotel's. I listened. I asked questions. I performed the calculations that I had spent my life performing: what is the offer worth, what are the risks of accepting, what are the risks of declining, and — most importantly — what does the existence of the offer tell me about the value of what I possess?

The last question was the one that mattered.

Because the offer confirmed something I had suspected but never been able to prove: the archive was worth more than money. More than immunity. More than any commodity that could be exchanged in a single transaction. The archive was worth *ongoing power* — the kind of power that doesn't deplete when you use it, that doesn't diminish when you share it, that grows in value every year because the people recorded on those servers grow more powerful every year, and the more powerful they become, the more they have to lose.

A government was offering me immunity — the most valuable legal protection any individual can receive — in exchange for files. That meant the files were worth more than immunity. And if the files were worth more than immunity, then keeping them was worth more than anything a government could offer.

I declined.

Not dramatically. Not with a speech. I declined the way I conducted all important business: with a quiet word to an intermediary who conveyed a quiet word to another intermediary who conveyed a quiet word to an office in a building in a capital city whose identity I am not going to share with you, because sharing it would confirm things that I have spent this entire book implying without confirming, and the distinction between implication and confirmation is the distinction between a fascinating novel and a national security incident.

The government did not respond. Governments don't respond to rejections the way people do — with hurt feelings or retaliatory gestures or the emotional theatrics that characterize personal relationships. Governments file the rejection. They update the assessment. They recalibrate the approach. And they wait. Because governments, unlike people, have infinite patience. A government that wants something in 2015 and doesn't get it will want the same thing in 2020 and 2025 and 2030, and the government will still be there, with the same institutional memory and the same strategic objectives, long after the person who rejected the offer is dead.

Which, as it turned out, would be sooner than I expected.

What I failed to weight correctly was the distinction between the government and the people *behind* it. The principals who had commissioned the offer through those three intermediaries were not the state. They were the specific individuals whose names sat in the archive in configurations that made its contents relevant to their personal freedom — people who had used the government as a front the way I used Conrad Barlow as a front: as the visible, legitimate face of a transaction that would not survive scrutiny if conducted directly.

When I declined, the government waited. The principals did not. They made a different decision — one that my intelligence contacts conveyed to me within a week, cleanly and without editorial: the archive would be obtained through channels that required neither my cooperation nor my survival.

I noted it. I categorized it as background — a manageable threat among the many manageable threats that constituted the operational weather of my life.

This was the error. Not the only one. The first one that mattered.

But the Geneva meeting clarified something that changed the way I understood my own operation. The archive had crossed a threshold. It was no longer a tool. It was no longer leverage. It was no longer even an insurance policy, though I still described it that way to myself because "insurance policy" is a phrase that makes the thing sound rational and manageable and proportionate.

The archive was an *entity.* It had its own gravitational pull. It attracted interest from governments and intelligence agencies the way a black hole attracts light — silently, invisibly, inevitably. People I had never met, in agencies I had never corresponded with, in countries I had never visited, were making decisions about the archive. Planning for it. Strategizing around it. Treating it as a factor in their calculations the way they treated nuclear arsenals and trade agreements and the other instruments of state power that exist in the gray space between diplomacy and war.

I had built something that was bigger than me.

That should have frightened me. It did frighten me — not the hot, visceral fear of physical danger, but the cold, structural fear of a man who realizes that the machine he built no longer requires his hand on the controls. The archive would survive me. The archive would outlast me. And whoever controlled the archive after my death — or my imprisonment, or my disappearance, or whatever form my eventual removal from the operation took — would possess a tool that I had designed but that I could no longer predict or direct.

The spider had built a web so large that the spider could no longer see its edges.

I flew back to Manhattan and told Malcolm to increase the encryption. Again. For the fourth time in three years. Malcolm didn't ask why. Malcolm never asked why. That's why Malcolm was Malcolm.

Chapter 34: The Dead Man's Will

Timeline: 2015–2017 | **Location:** Manhattan, U.S. Coral Islands

Anton Segura was a biotech venture capitalist. A Hartfield-educated physician. A former science advisor to **Nolan Whitfield** — the same Nolan Whitfield who continued meeting with me post-conviction, the same Nolan Whitfield whose philanthropic empire was dedicated, in public, to saving the world from disease and poverty, and connected, in private, to a sex trafficker through a web of social and financial relationships that neither party has ever fully explained.

And Anton Segura was named as the backup executor of my will.

Let that sentence settle. Let it sit in the room the way a bad smell settles into furniture — slowly, persistently, impossible to remove once it's been absorbed. A man who trafficked dozens of children across international borders, who operated a surveillance and blackmail operation involving heads of state, who maintained cameras in every room of every property and files on every powerful person who visited them — chose as his *backup executor* the former science advisor to the world's most famous philanthropist. The man who would manage my estate if **Theodore Marsh** couldn't — if Marsh died, or was incapacitated, or was compromised, or was for any reason unable to fulfill his duties as primary executor — was a man whose professional biography drew a direct, documented, incontestable line from my criminal enterprise through the Whitfield Foundation and into the biotech industry.

Segura's role in the will is not a footnote. It is a *map.* It is the kind of connection that, if presented to a jury, would require no expert testimony to interpret — because the connection speaks for itself, and what it says is: the web extends further than you think. The web connects not just to the billionaires and the politicians and the professors but to the institutional infrastructure that supports them — the foundations, the advisory boards, the venture capital firms, the philanthropic networks that constitute the circulatory system of American wealth.

Anton was my backup executor. The man who would manage my estate if Theodore couldn't. People find that surprising. I find it logical. Anton understood money, science, and discretion — the three currencies of my world. He was also Nolan's former science advisor, which meant that even in death, my estate would be connected to the richest philanthropic network on Earth. That's not an accident. That's estate planning.

The will itself was filed two days before my death.

Two days. Forty-eight hours. A detail that will haunt conspiracy theorists for generations, that will fuel speculation about whether I knew what was coming and prepared for it, that will generate theories ranging from the plausible to the deranged about the circumstances of my final days. I am not going to address those theories — not because they're wrong, but because addressing them would require me to tell you things that I have spent my entire life ensuring nobody could prove.

What I will tell you is what the will reveals about the financial architecture of the operation, because the financial architecture is the one part of my legacy that the documents can speak to without requiring speculation.

The estate was valued at over five hundred and seventy-seven million dollars.

Five hundred and seventy-seven million. For a man who never had a single identifiable client. For a man whose "financial management" business — the business that was supposed to explain the wealth, that was supposed to be the legitimate foundation upon which the entire financial superstructure rested — has never been verified by any independent auditor, has never produced a client list, a prospectus, a quarterly report, or a single piece of documentation that would survive a first-year accounting student's review. For a man whose income, by every conventional metric of legitimate wealth, should not exist — because the business that was supposed to generate it was, at best, a fiction maintained for tax purposes and, at worst, a front for financial flows whose true origins would implicate intelligence agencies, hedge fund executives, and the global network of offshore finance that constitutes the shadow economy of the ultra-rich.

Where did the money come from? The question has been asked by journalists, by investigators, by prosecutors, by the IRS, and by every person who has ever looked at my financial profile and noticed the gap — the enormous, unexplained, structurally suspicious gap — between my documented income and my documented assets. The answer depends on whose theory you believe. Grant Hensley's money, laundered through a trust and recharacterized as compensation. Intelligence funding, routed through offshore entities designed to resist attribution. Blackmail revenue, extracted from the powerful men whose compromising activities were documented on cameras that Malcolm Pruitt maintained with the care of a museum conservator. Some combination of all three. Or something else entirely — a revenue stream so well hidden that even the congressional investigation that produced the seven-thousand-five-hundred-email archive couldn't trace it to its source.

Five hundred and seventy-seven million dollars in assets distributed across the properties you already know — the mansion, the island, the ranch, the Paris apartment, the Gulf Shore compound — plus aircraft, vehicles, artwork that museums would covet, and financial instruments scattered across jurisdictions in the layered, nested, deliberately opaque structures I had spent thirty years building for the specific purpose of resisting investigation.

Theodore Marsh was named primary executor. The firewall. The man with forty-five-plus documents in the archive. The attorney whose job, in life, was to ensure that my financial architecture remained impenetrable to investigators and whose job, in death, would be to ensure that the same architecture protected the estate from the victims who would, inevitably, sue.

I wrote my will the way I lived my life: carefully, offshore, and with multiple redundancies. Five hundred seventy-seven million dollars distributed across entities that took me thirty years to build. Some people leave a legacy of ideas. I left a legacy of LLCs. Both are immortal. Mine are harder to subpoena.

Dennis Aldric was my brother.

The only family member who features prominently in the archive, and the family member whose position illustrates the most uncomfortable question that the web generates for the people who exist at its edges: What does proximity to a monster make you?

Dennis was simultaneously an insider and an outsider. An insider: blood relation, connected to my real estate holdings, involved in property management, recipient of money that flowed from the same financial infrastructure that funded everything else in my operation. He managed properties. He handled logistics. He corresponded with me about business matters — the routine, unglamorous, administrative correspondence of a man who is involved in the operational maintenance of a real estate portfolio without being involved in the criminal enterprise that the portfolio supports.

An outsider: never charged. Never implicated in trafficking. Never named as a co-conspirator. Never identified by any victim as a participant in the abuse. The archive does not suggest that Dennis participated in my crimes. The archive suggests something more ambiguous and, in some ways, more troubling: that Dennis *benefited* from my wealth without asking too many questions about its origins. That he received money and managed properties and corresponded with me about logistics with the pragmatic efficiency of a man who has decided that the source of the money is not his concern — that his job is to manage the assets, not to investigate the asset-holder.

Blood is thicker than indictments. Blood is also quieter. Blood maintains the relationship without asking the questions that would make the relationship impossible to maintain. Blood looks at the money flowing through the real estate accounts and doesn't ask where the money came from, because asking where the money came from would require hearing an answer that blood doesn't want to hear.

Dennis is my brother. He managed properties. He handled logistics. He did what brothers do. People want him to be guilty because guilt is easier to understand than proximity. But proximity to a monster doesn't make you a monster. It makes you a bystander. And bystanders — as I've demonstrated for thirty years — are the most useful people in the world.

Petra Nordgren was a Belarusian dentist.

My last girlfriend. The final woman to occupy the public role of "partner" — the role that, in the social theater of my life, served a function as essential and as cynical as any other prop in the production. A girlfriend is the most important costume accessory a predator can wear. A girlfriend says: *This man has normal relationships with adult women. This man is capable of consensual intimacy. This man's sexual interests are directed at appropriate targets.* A girlfriend is a rebuttal before the accusation is made — a preemptive defense against the assumption that the man standing next to her is exactly what his registry entry says he is.

Petra entered the picture in the final years. I paid for her mother's medical care — the kind of generosity that, in a normal relationship, would be touching and that, in this relationship, was transactional, a payment rendered in exchange for services that included her presence at public events and her willingness to be identified, in photographs and in social settings, as my companion. I facilitated her career. I sent money to Minsk. She entered a same-sex marriage with one of my assistants to maintain her immigration status — a detail that would be irrelevant in a different context and that, in this context, demonstrates the degree to which every relationship in my life was structured around utility rather than affection, around function rather than feeling.

The relationship was transactional in ways that mirrored every other relationship I had ever maintained. I provided resources. She provided a veneer of normalcy. The exchange was clear to both parties, documented in the correspondence that tracked the financial flows between my accounts and her life, and invisible to the public, which saw a wealthy man with an attractive Eastern European girlfriend and drew exactly the conclusion I intended them to draw.

Petra was beautiful, smart, and from Minsk. I paid for her mother's medical care. I helped her career. I sent money to Belarus. People call that a relationship. I call it infrastructure. Every predator needs a girlfriend — someone to stand next to at public events, someone to point to when people ask questions. "I have a girlfriend. She's a dentist. From Belarus. Does that sound like a sex trafficker to you?" It doesn't. That's the point.

They found a passport in my safe.

In the Manhattan mansion, in a locked safe that also contained diamonds and cash and the kind of portable wealth that a man stores when he wants to be able to leave a country on short notice. A passport. Not my American passport — a different passport. Under a different name. With a Saudi Arabian residency stamp.

A different name. On an active passport. In a locked safe. In the home of a man who had been described, by a U.S. Attorney, as someone who "belonged to intelligence."

The passport is the closest thing in the archive to a smoking gun for the intelligence theory — the theory that has threaded through this entire narrative, surfacing at intervals like a submarine that breaks the water just long enough to be seen before diving again. The correspondence with **Avi Ben-David** — the former Israeli prime minister, the former military chief of staff, the former head of military intelligence. The offshore entities that mirror structures associated with intelligence fronts — the trusts, the foundations, the shell corporations whose organizational architecture follows patterns documented in declassified intelligence operations. The immunity deal whose terms were so extraordinary that the U.S. Attorney felt compelled to explain them by invoking the phrase "belonged to intelligence." And now: a Saudi passport. Under a different name. In a locked safe.

The passport raises questions that I am not going to answer, because not answering questions is what I have always done, and what I have always done has worked. I can neither confirm nor deny the passport's purpose. I can neither confirm nor deny the name on the passport. I can neither confirm nor deny any relationship with any intelligence service of any nation, because confirming would be dangerous and denying would be a lie and the space between dangerous and dishonest is, as I've explained, the space where I operate.

They found a passport in my safe. A different name. A Saudi stamp. People want to know why. I don't owe them an answer. I owe them exactly what I've always given them: enough information to speculate, not enough to prove. That's the space I operate in. The space between what everyone suspects and what nobody can verify. It's very comfortable there. The rent is zero.

By 2017, the web was operating on borrowed time.

I didn't know that. Or I knew it and refused to acknowledge it, because acknowledgment would have required action, and action would have required change, and change would have required the admission that the system that had protected me for thirty years — the money, the lawyers, the connections, the cameras, the intelligence relationships — might not protect me forever.

In Miami, a journalist I'd never heard of was beginning to pull threads.

By 2017, I had been a convicted sex offender for nine years, and my life was better than before the arrest. More money. Better connections. Smarter friends. The system had tested me, and I had passed. Or the system had tested itself, and it had failed. Same result either way. I ate dinner. I hosted scientists. I flew my plane. I didn't read the *Gulf Coast Tribune.* Nobody reads the *Gulf Coast Tribune.*

That turned out to be a mistake.

Chapter 35: The Appetite

Timeline: 1999–2009 | **Location:** The Yacht, Little St. Philip, Cimarron Station, Monterrey

There are things I haven't told you.

I know — I've been generous. I've walked you through the money and the girls and the blackmail and the cameras. I've introduced you to the scientists and the presidents and the princes. I've shown you the architecture. I've explained the wiring. I've given you more than any prosecutor ever extracted and more than any journalist ever published and more than any victim ever knew, because the victims only saw the room they were in and I built the building.

But there are rooms I haven't shown you yet.

Not because I'm ashamed. I lost the capacity for shame somewhere between my second billion and my third property. Not because I'm protecting anyone — everyone worth protecting is either dead, lawyered up, or running a foundation with their name on it that exists primarily to launder the memory of what they did at my dinner table. I haven't told you because you're not ready. Because the human mind has a digestive capacity, just like the human stomach, and I've been feeding you courses in the correct order — amuse-bouche, appetizer, entrée — and we haven't reached the part of the meal that requires a stronger constitution.

We've arrived at dessert.

Let me tell you about appetite.

Not the metaphorical kind — not the appetite for power or money or young flesh that I've been describing for over thirty chapters. I mean *appetite*. The real thing. The physical thing. The thing that happens when men who have consumed everything available to human experience — every drug, every body, every thrill, every transgression that money can purchase and power can protect — discover that there is one frontier remaining. One taboo that hasn't been broken. One line that even the most depraved among them haven't crossed.

And then they cross it.

I need to be precise here, because precision matters. What I'm about to describe wasn't an orgy. It wasn't a ritual. It wasn't some candlelit ceremony with robes and chanting and pentagrams on the floor — that's Hollywood's version, and Hollywood's version exists to make the real thing seem fictional, which is exactly how the real thing survives. The real thing is quieter. Cleaner. More... *curated.*

The first time was on the yacht. The year was 2000. The guest list was small — deliberately small, because this wasn't a networking event. This was a reward. A loyalty test. A bond that, once formed, could never be broken, because the participants would be bound to each other by a shared act so far beyond the boundaries of legal or moral acceptability that betrayal became structurally impossible. You don't go to the authorities when the authorities were at the table.

There were seven of us. I won't give you all the names — not because I'm being coy, but because some of those names are attached to people who are still alive and who have the resources to ensure that anyone who speaks about that evening meets the same quiet end that several inconvenient people in my orbit have already met. I'll give you three.

A head of state. Former, technically, by the time of the dinner, but you don't stop being a head of state the way you stop being a dentist. The title follows you. The security detail follows you. The access follows you. And the appetites — the ones that developed during the years when you were the most powerful person in whatever room you occupied — those follow you too.

A technology pioneer. A man whose public identity was built on the promise of the future — of clean energy, of space exploration, of the digital transformation of human civilization. A man who talked about saving the world the way a preacher talks about saving souls: loudly, frequently, and with complete sincerity about the mission and complete indifference to the methods. In private, his appetites were... medieval.

And a prince. Not a metaphorical prince. An actual prince, with a lineage and a crown and a castle and a family whose public function is to symbolize the moral continuity of a civilization that has spent centuries perfecting the art of appearing civilized while doing unspeakable things behind closed doors.

The chef was flown in from a country I won't name. He specialized in a cuisine that doesn't appear on any menu and that isn't taught in any culinary school and that serves a clientele so exclusive that the chef himself didn't know the real names of most of his clients. He knew them by aliases. He knew them by the intermediaries who arranged the bookings. He knew them by the specific requests they made, which he cataloged with the meticulous professionalism of a man who understood that his survival depended on his discretion and his irreplaceability.

The preparation took three days.

I'm not going to describe the meal in detail. Not because I'm squeamish — I'm the man who kept cameras in massage rooms and files on presidents and a black book that reads like the guest list at Davos — but because the details are the part that people fixate on, and fixation on the details obscures the *architecture*. The meal wasn't the point. The meal was the mechanism. The point was the bond. The point was creating a shared secret so monstrous that every person at that table became permanently, irreversibly, structurally dependent on every other person at that table for the maintenance of silence.

It's the same principle as the cameras, scaled up. The cameras gave me leverage over individuals. The dinners gave me leverage over *groups*. A man who has been filmed with an underage girl can deny it, claim the tape was doctored, hire lawyers, attack the accuser. A man who has sat at a table with six other powerful men and consumed what was served at that table — a man whose DNA is, metaphorically and otherwise, *mixed* with the evidence of what happened that evening — cannot deny it. Cannot explain it. Cannot survive the revelation. The bond is absolute.

That's the business model. Everything I did had a business model.

We held four of these dinners between 2000 and 2008.

Two on the yacht. One on the island. One at **Cimarron Station** — the New Mexico property, where the nearest neighbor was forty miles away and the nearest law enforcement officer was an hour's drive through desert roads that my security team monitored with motion sensors and thermal cameras. The ranch was ideal. The remoteness wasn't a feature of the property; it was the *purpose* of the property. You don't buy seventy-five hundred acres in the New Mexico desert because you appreciate the landscape. You buy it because the landscape appreciates *privacy*.

The guest lists overlapped but weren't identical. Some of the participants from the yacht dinner attended the island dinner. Some didn't — not because they were uninvited, but because they'd lost the stomach for it after the first time. This was useful information. It told me who was fully committed and who was merely compliant. The fully committed ones became the inner circle of the inner circle — the nucleus of the operation, the people who would protect the network with the ferocity of cornered animals because they *were* cornered animals, cornered by their own choices, cornered by the evidence that I maintained, cornered by the knowledge that the thing they had done was the one thing that no amount of money or power or legal representation could make survivable if it became public.

The merely compliant ones were useful too. They hadn't participated in the worst of it, but they'd seen it. They'd been present. They'd watched and not intervened and not reported and not left the table — and that *complicity*, that willingness to sit and observe and stay silent, was almost as binding as participation itself. You don't have to eat the meal to be ruined by it. You just have to be in the room.

Celeste managed the logistics. She always managed the logistics. She had a gift for operational detail that would have made her extraordinary in any legitimate enterprise — event planning, military operations, intelligence work. In my enterprise, she applied that gift to the specific challenge of ensuring that an act of extreme transgression occurred smoothly, discreetly, and without the kind of evidence trail that could survive a federal investigation.

She coordinated the sourcing. She arranged the transport. She briefed the chef. She managed the guest communication — because you don't send a calendar invite for this kind of event; you communicate through intermediaries, through coded language, through the kind of carefully layered obfuscation that intelligence agencies use to coordinate clandestine operations and that I used to coordinate dinner parties.

I loved her for it. I've said that before and I'll say it again: Celeste was the most operationally gifted person I ever met. Whatever moral judgment you want to apply to that statement, the statement remains true.

The problem with secrets is entropy.

Secrets decay. They leak. They seep out through the cracks in human psychology — through guilt, through alcohol, through the universal human compulsion to tell someone, *anyone*, about the extraordinary thing you've witnessed, because extraordinary experiences that aren't shared feel like hallucinations, and the mind rebels against the idea that something happened if nobody else acknowledges that it happened.

The first leak came from Mexico.

In 2009, a young woman — a model, beautiful, twenty-one, connected to the circuit through the usual channels — had a public breakdown outside a hotel in Monterrey. She was screaming. Crying. Pointing at police officers. Accusing them of complicity. Accusing *everyone* of complicity. And in the middle of this very public, very filmed, very *inconvenient* meltdown, she said the words that nobody was supposed to say.

She said they ate human flesh. She said the elites consumed people. She said it loudly, repeatedly, in front of cameras, in front of police, in front of everyone.

She named names. Not my name — she was connected to the Mexican side of the network, the cartel-adjacent circles where the appetites were, if anything, even less restrained than the ones I served — but she named people. Politicians. Businessmen. People whose power in Mexico was equivalent to the power that my dinner guests wielded in the United States and Europe and the Middle East.

The police handcuffed her. They took her away. And then — with the kind of efficiency that only becomes visible when you understand how these systems work — she disappeared.

Not metaphorically. Not "she moved away and changed her name" disappeared. Not "she checked into a facility and recovered and lives quietly now" disappeared. *Disappeared.* The way people disappear in countries where the infrastructure of disappearance has been professionalized. The way inconvenient witnesses have disappeared throughout the history of every society that maintains a permanent class of people wealthy enough to require the permanent disappearance of people who threaten their interests.

They said she was mentally ill. They said she was on drugs. They said the outburst was a psychotic episode, unconnected to reality, the ravings of a disturbed young woman who had lost her grip on sanity in the pressure cooker of the modeling industry. That was the narrative. It was a good narrative — plausible, sympathetic, dismissible. The kind of narrative that makes people nod and move on and not ask the follow-up question, which is: *where is she now?*

I'll tell you where she's not. She's not giving interviews. She's not writing a book. She's not testifying before any governmental body about what she witnessed at the events where the wealthy and the powerful indulged appetites that the public isn't ready to believe exist.

The system worked. The narrative held. The video circulated on the internet for years, categorized alongside UFO sightings and Bigfoot footage and every other piece of evidence that gets neutralized by proximity to conspiracy culture. Put a true thing next to enough false things and the true thing becomes invisible. That's not a bug in the information ecosystem. It's a feature. And it's a feature that people like me have been exploiting since long before the internet made it scalable.

You want to know why the FBI files mention the word "cannibalism" fifty-two times?

It's not because someone searched the archive and planted the word as a hoax. It's not because conspiracy theorists invented the connection. It's because when you accumulate three million pages of documents related to an operation that ran for thirty years across multiple continents and involved hundreds of participants and thousands of victims and a client list that included heads of state and titans of industry and members of royal families — when you accumulate that volume of documentation about that scale of depravity — some truths leak through. Even in redacted form. Even buried in interview summaries and email fragments and the rambling, uncorroborated testimony of witnesses that the FBI dismissed as "emotionally unbalanced."

Emotionally unbalanced. That's a useful phrase. It's the phrase that gets applied to anyone who tells the truth about things that the institutional structure of power requires to remain unspeakable. The girl in Monterrey was emotionally unbalanced. The man who told the FBI about the yacht was emotionally unbalanced. Every witness to the thing that the powerful need to keep secret is, by definition, emotionally unbalanced — because witnessing that thing *does* unbalance you. It unbalances you emotionally, psychologically, spiritually, and then the very imbalance caused by the experience becomes the justification for dismissing the testimony about the experience.

It's elegant, really. The trauma discredits the witness. The system designs itself.

An anonymous man walked into an FBI field office in 2019 and said he'd been on my yacht in 2000. He said he'd seen things. Terrible things. Things involving blades and small bodies and acts so far beyond the boundary of acceptable human behavior that the agents interviewing him made a note in the file — a note that would later be released in the document dump — characterizing his account as unsubstantiated. Uncorroborated. The testimony of a man who was, in the assessment of trained federal investigators, not credible enough to pursue.

He wasn't lying. He was simply telling the truth to people whose institutional function required them not to believe it.

I'm not going to apologize. I haven't apologized for anything in this book, and I'm not going to start with this.

What I will say — what I think is *important* to say, because this chapter isn't about shocking you; this chapter is about showing you the final room in the building I constructed — is that the appetite I'm describing isn't mine alone. It isn't a personal pathology. It isn't the isolated sickness of one man on one island. It's a *feature* of the system. It's what happens at the terminal point of unchecked power — the place where men who have exhausted every other form of consumption discover that there is one form remaining, and that the infrastructure to indulge it already exists, maintained by the same networks that provide everything else.

The trafficking networks. The private aviation. The remote properties. The compliant staff. The compromised law enforcement. The media machinery that converts truth into conspiracy theory and conspiracy theory into entertainment. All of it. The infrastructure that moved girls to my properties is the same infrastructure that, at its extremity, moved *other things* to *other properties* for *other purposes*. The pipeline didn't change. The product did.

And if you think this ended with me — if you think my death in that cell in August 2019 shut down the kitchen — you are as naive as the FBI agent who wrote "unsubstantiated" in the margin of that interview and went home believing he'd done his job.

The appetite doesn't die with the host.

The appetite finds a new table.

Fragment: The Boy They Kept

The narrator described the yacht dinners as a business model. As a bonding mechanism. As architecture. He described the chef, the guests, the bond of shared transgression. He described it from the head of the table. The following speaker was not at the table. The following speaker was on the menu.

I was fourteen. I am not fourteen anymore but I will always be fourteen because fourteen is where my life stopped and everything after fourteen is just the body continuing without the person inside it.

They brought me on the yacht as a server. That's what the man said — the man who picked me up from the group home in a car that smelled like leather and cologne. He said a wealthy man needed help serving at a dinner party on his yacht. He said I'd make five hundred dollars in one night. He said I should wear the white shirt and the black pants he brought in a garment bag. He said I'd be serving important people — people who could change my life.

He was right about that last part.

The yacht was bigger than any building I'd lived in. Three levels. White and silver and glass. The kind of boat that doesn't look like a boat — it looks like a hotel that someone cut loose from the shore. There were other staff. Adults. Professional. They moved through the corridors with the practiced silence of people who had been trained not to exist unless called upon. Nobody looked at me. Nobody said my name. Nobody asked how old I was.

The guests arrived in the afternoon. I counted seven. All men. All older. All wearing the kind of clothes that don't have visible logos because the absence of logos is the logo. They shook hands. They laughed. They drank things from glasses that caught the light. They looked at the ocean the way people look at things they own.

One of them looked at me. He looked at me for a long time. He was smiling. Not at me — *about* me. The way you smile about a surprise you know is coming.

The dinner was in a room below deck. Polished table. Crystal. Silver. I was told to carry plates from the kitchen to the table and to stand against the wall between courses and to refill glasses when they were empty. I was told not to speak. I was told not to make eye contact. I was told to be furniture.

The first two courses were food. Real food. Fish. Something with saffron. The men ate and talked and the conversation was about money and politics and technology and the specific kind of nothing that powerful men discuss when they're performing power for each other. I stood against the wall and I held a bottle of wine and I watched and I waited and I thought: five hundred dollars.

The third course was different.

I knew it was different before the plates were uncovered because the room changed. The conversation stopped. Not gradually — *instantly.* Like someone had pressed a button. The men sat straighter. Some of them leaned forward. One of them closed his eyes and took a breath through his nose — a deep, anticipatory breath, the kind a person takes before something they've been waiting for. The air in the room shifted from social to *ceremonial.*

The chef — a man I hadn't seen before, small, precise, wearing a white jacket with no insignia — carried the plates himself. He didn't let me touch them. He placed each one with the care of a man setting a jewel into a ring. He described the preparation in a language I didn't understand. French, maybe. Or something older. The men nodded. Some of them smiled. The one who had looked at me earlier was looking at me again. Still smiling.

I looked at the plate.

I will not tell you what was on the plate. I will tell you what my body did when I saw it: my body knew before my mind did. My stomach closed. My hands went cold. My vision narrowed to a point, and the point was the plate, and the plate was wrong. Wrong in a way that my fourteen-year-old brain couldn't articulate but that my body — the animal part, the part that evolved to recognize danger — understood immediately and completely.

One of the men picked up his fork. He ate. He chewed slowly. He closed his eyes. The expression on his face was the expression of a man experiencing something exquisite. He opened his eyes and said, to the man next to him, "Better than last time."

Better than last time. There had been a last time.

Another man ate. He wiped his mouth with the cloth napkin. He took a sip of wine. He looked at the chef and nodded — a small, approving nod, the kind a restaurant critic gives when the dish exceeds expectations. The chef nodded back. Professional courtesy. Acknowledgment of a job well done.

I stood against the wall and I held the wine bottle and my hands were shaking so hard that the wine was moving in the bottle like a small sea in a glass container. Nobody noticed. Nobody looked at me. I was furniture. Furniture doesn't shake. Furniture doesn't feel. Furniture doesn't stand in a room where seven men are eating something that furniture isn't supposed to understand.

They didn't let me leave the yacht after the dinner. I understood, without being told, that leaving was no longer an option. The man who had driven me from the group home was gone. The car was gone. The shore was gone. There was only the yacht and the water and the men and the corridor they led me down after the table was cleared.

I was on the yacht for three months. Not as a server. As something else. Something the English language has a word for but that word doesn't capture what it actually feels like to *be* that word, to live inside that word, to wake up every morning and discover that you are still that word and that the word hasn't changed and that nobody is coming to change it for you.

They passed me between them. Not violently — and I need you to understand how much worse "not violently" is than violently, because violently would have meant they were angry, and angry is human, and human means there's a person inside the thing hurting you. They weren't angry. They were *recreational.* I was recreation. A hobby. A way to pass the time between the other ways they passed the time, which included swimming and reading and discussing the future of artificial intelligence and eating meals that the chef prepared with the same meticulous care he'd applied to the dinner.

I stopped being me on day six. I didn't decide to stop. It just happened. Like a light going off in a room nobody's using. The boy who had been me — the boy from the group home, the boy who liked basketball, the boy who once won a spelling bee in fourth grade — that boy walked away from my body and didn't come back. What was left was the boy who carries things. That's what I became. The boy who carries plates. The boy who carries bottles. The boy who carries whatever the men need carried, including himself.

On the island — they moved me to the island, eventually, because the yacht was needed for other purposes and the island had rooms for longer storage — I found a pen. A ballpoint pen, blue ink, under a bed in one of the guest cottages. The kind of pen that falls out of a shirt pocket when someone bends over. Ordinary. Disposable. The most valuable object I'd held in weeks.

I pulled out the bottom drawer of the dresser. I turned it over. On the raw wood of the underside — unfinished, unseen, the part of the drawer that faces the floor and that nobody looks at because nobody looks at the bottom of things — I wrote two words.

They eat us.

I pushed the drawer back in. I put the pen back under the bed. I lay on the mattress and I looked at the ceiling and I knew that nobody would ever find those words and that even if they did, nobody would understand them, and that even if they understood them, nobody would believe them, because the truth I was telling was the kind of truth that the human mind is designed to reject, because accepting it means accepting that the world contains rooms where men in expensive clothes eat things that men in expensive clothes are not supposed to eat, and accepting that means accepting that civilization is a thinner membrane than anyone wants to believe.

I got out. I won't tell you how. The how belongs to a person who helped me, and that person is alive, and I won't put their name anywhere near this story because names near this story become targets.

I'm thirty-one now. I work a job. I have an apartment. I have a life that, from the outside, looks like a life. From the inside, it looks like the boy who carries things learned to carry one more thing: the appearance of being human.

I don't eat in restaurants. I can't watch people eat. The sound of silverware on ceramic — the small, domestic, ordinary sound that accompanies every meal in every home in every country on earth — sends me to the place behind my eyes where I went on the yacht. The place I go when the world becomes the room below deck and the men are eating and the chef is nodding and someone is saying "better than last time."

The dresser was cataloged during the 2019 FBI search of the island property. Evidence item #4,271. The drawer was photographed, processed, and filed. Two words in blue ballpoint, pressed hard into bare pine. The handwriting was analyzed: consistent with an adolescent male, right-handed, writing under physical duress or emotional distress. The pen pressure suggested urgency. The letter forms suggested someone who had not written anything in a long time.

The words were transcribed into the evidence log. They were included in the document release. They occupy three lines on page 2,847 of a three-million-page file.

Nobody has publicly commented on them.

Chapter 36: The Smokescreen

I need to tell you about a pizza restaurant.

Not one of mine. Not a property I owned, not a front I operated, not another node in the network I've been describing for the last two dozen chapters. A family-friendly establishment called Asteroid Billiards — mediocre pizza, live music on weekends, no basement, no children, nothing to do with sex trafficking. Not tangentially. Not in any way that would survive contact with reality or a building inspector.

But in November of 2016, millions of Americans became convinced that Asteroid Billiards was the operational center of a child trafficking ring run by the Democratic Party.

They were wrong about the pizza restaurant. They were right about everything else.

In December 2016, a man drove from North Carolina to Washington with an AR-15, walked into Asteroid Billiards, and fired shots into the restaurant. He was looking for the children. He was looking for the basement. He found neither. He found pizza ovens and a ping-pong table and a staff experiencing the unique terror of being shot at by a man whose moral conviction had been manufactured by an algorithm.

I watched this from my Manhattan mansion with a fascination that bordered on professional admiration.

Because here's what QizzaGate got right: the elites were running a child trafficking operation. There was a network of powerful people exploiting minors. There were coded communications and private properties and a systematic infrastructure designed to supply underage victims to wealthy predators.

They had the right crime. They just had the wrong address.

The address was not a pizza restaurant in Washington. The address was 12 East 74th Street, Manhattan. And 358 Via Dorado, Gulf Shore. And Little St. Philip, United States Coral Islands. And the thirty-three-thousand-acre ranch in New Mexico. The criminals were not Democrats operating out of a pizzeria. They were a bipartisan coalition of the most powerful people on

Earth, operating out of properties I owned and wired with surveillance cameras that recorded everything.

QizzaGate was the greatest magic trick in the history of American misdirection, and I didn't even perform it. The internet performed it. The algorithm performed it. They took the real crime — my crime — and buried it under a fake crime with the same silhouette. Child trafficking by elites? True. In a pizza shop? Insane. And once you've convinced the public that the accusation is insane, nobody examines the accusation anymore. They examine the accusers. And the accusers look crazy. And my operation continues.

The technique is called inoculation. Release a weakened version of the truth — close enough to be recognizable, diminished enough to be dismissible. When the real exposure comes, the public has already developed antibodies. The most sophisticated propaganda doesn't deny the truth. It tells you the truth first, in a way that makes the truth sound crazy.

My operating room was mistaken for a pepperoni slice. And nobody performed surgery.

Now let me tell you the story QizzaGate was designed to obscure. Not a pizza restaurant. A summer camp.

Before the emails. Before the files. Before any of it — there was a bench at the Lakeshore Center for the Arts, a summer camp for young musicians in northern Michigan. Population: fewer than six hundred people. Pine trees. Lake breezes. The kind of place that exists, in the American imagination, as a sanctuary — where talented children are safe, where art is nurtured, where the worst thing that can happen is a missed note in a recital.

I had attended Lakeshore myself, in the summer of 1967. As a camper. A teenager from Brooklyn who played piano and existed, briefly, in a world where talent mattered more than money. I returned decades later. Not as a camper. As a patron. I donated up to half a million dollars. They built a lodge on campus and named it after me.

In the final week of camp, August 1994, Celeste and I sat in the public spaces, during business hours, in full view of counselors and staff. We identified a target. A thirteen-year-old girl, sitting alone on a bench between her voice program classes. Fatherless. From a struggling family. Talented and lonely and radiating the particular vulnerability that Celeste could read the way a jeweler reads a diamond.

Celeste approached her with warmth. I introduced myself as a patron of the arts. A man who gave scholarships to talented young people. A man who could change a girl's life. I asked for her mother's phone number. She was alarmed — thirteen-year-old girls are supposed to be alarmed when older men ask for phone numbers — but she complied, because wealth and authority create a gravitational field that children cannot resist.

The grooming took months. The financial dependency took weeks. I moved the girl and her mother to an apartment in New York. I paid tuition. I cosigned the lease. I wove myself into their financial survival with the patience of a spider wrapping silk around an insect that doesn't yet know it's caught. By the end of 1994, the girl — still thirteen, still the voice student who had been sitting on that bench four months earlier — was being sexually assaulted in my pool house.

She was my first known victim. The "guinea pig," as her own lawsuit would later describe her — the test subject on whom Celeste and I refined the methodology that would be deployed on hundreds of girls across two continents and two decades.

And in 1994, when she was fourteen, I took her to Casa del Sol — Conrad Barlow's club — and introduced her. According to court documents filed in her lawsuit, I elbowed Conrad playfully and asked, gesturing at the child: "This is a good one, right?"

Conrad smiled. And nodded.

That's the story QizzaGate was designed to obscure. A summer camp bench. A bipartisan machine. Court filings describing a child being presented to a future president like a wine recommendation.

Not coded emails about cheese. An actual girl. An actual bench. An actual smile.

Douglas Raines appeared sixty-five times in my email archive — the same Douglas Raines who built a media empire on the promise to expose elite corruption, the same Douglas Raines whose network broadcast QizzaGate to millions. On July 4, 2018 — American Independence Day, because irony is the only god who never takes a holiday — I sent him a communication referencing my former Solicitor General defense attorney having spoken with two senators about the nomination of Garrett Ravanagh to the Supreme Court. Five days later, Conrad Barlow formally announced the nomination.

A convicted sex offender was discussing Supreme Court appointments with the architect of a populist revolution. Through the intermediary of a lawyer who had defended that same sex offender against trafficking charges. Five days before the announcement.

On June 28, 2019 — eleven days before federal agents arrested me at Morristown Aviation Center — I sent Douglas this message, which I want you to read slowly:

"Now you can understand why Conrad wakes up in the middle of the night sweating when he hears you and I are friends."

I said that the sitting president of the United States sweats at night because the convicted sex offender and the president's political architect are friends. I said it casually. I said it the way you'd mention a sports score. I said it because truth, when spoken between men who share sufficient secrets, requires no dramatic framing. The drama is already built in.

Eleven days later, I was arrested. And the things I knew entered the files. Three million pages of them. In those files, according to a congressman who searched the unredacted documents in February 2026, Conrad Barlow's name appeared more than a million times.

A million. Not as a subject of investigation — officially. As a presence. A gravity. A name so woven into the fabric of my operations that extracting it would require unraveling the entire tapestry.

They tried to redact him. The Department of Justice published a photograph Douglas had texted me — Conrad's face blacked out in a rectangle that still showed his ear, his signature hair, the unmistakable silhouette of a man recognized by every human being on the planet. The most incompetent redaction in the history of federal document production. They tried to erase the most recognizable man in the world with a rectangle. The rectangle was too small.

I would have done a better job. But then, I always did.

The most powerful weapon in my arsenal was not the cameras.

Not the blackmail — though comprehensive and effective. Not the money — though it built everything. Not the intelligence connections — though six words from a government official could shut down an investigation the way six words from a surgeon can stop a heart: *he belongs to intelligence, leave it alone.*

The most powerful weapon was the followers.

Not my followers. I didn't have followers — I had clients, guests, co-conspirators, and victims. I inspired fear and dependency, not devotion. Devotion requires the illusion of virtue, and I never cultivated that illusion for myself. I cultivated it for other people. The presidents. The princes. The billionaires. The celebrities. The academics. Those people had followers — millions, tens of millions — and those followers were, without knowing it, without ever being recruited or compensated or even informed, the most effective protection my operation ever enjoyed.

Because a follower will defend their leader against any accusation. Any evidence. Any number of pages, photographs, flight logs, victim testimonies,

FBI reports, or sworn depositions. The accusation doesn't matter. The evidence doesn't matter. What matters is the identity — the follower's identity, which has been fused so completely with the leader's identity that an attack on the leader is experienced as an attack on the self. And the self, when attacked, doesn't evaluate evidence. The self defends.

This is not stupidity. The followers are not stupid. Many are educated, successful, articulate — capable of sophisticated reasoning in every domain of their lives except the one where their identity is at stake. A man who can analyze a balance sheet or argue a legal brief will, when confronted with evidence that his political hero appears thirty-eight thousand times in a sex trafficker's files, perform the same cognitive maneuver as a child confronted with evidence that Santa Claus is not real: he will reject the evidence and preserve the belief, because the belief is load-bearing. Remove it, and the structure collapses. The structure — the web of identity, community, meaning, and belonging that political affiliation provides in a country where all other forms of community have been systematically eroded — is too important to risk.

Conrad Barlow had fourteen of my phone numbers. Documented. Seized by investigators. Entered into the evidentiary record. When this fact was published, his followers had a choice: accept the fact and revise the belief, or accept the belief and revise the fact. They chose the belief. "Everyone in Gulf Shore had his number." "It's just a social directory." Rational explanations — the kind that would work in a courtroom. But they weren't being offered in a courtroom. They were being offered in living rooms and comment sections, where the standard is not reasonable doubt but emotional survival.

Multiply this by every person in my files. Raymond Prescott flew on my plane dozens of times: "He was working on AIDS relief. The flights were philanthropic." Nolan Whitfield visited my Manhattan mansion after my conviction — after, when my status as a registered sex offender was public record, searchable, available to anyone with a phone and thirty seconds — and his followers said he was redirecting my money toward good causes. Prince Edmund claimed he was at a pizza restaurant the night Natalie Brennan described being assaulted. His followers: "Why would a prince lie about a pizza restaurant?" The question answers itself if you think about it for more than three seconds. Which is why the followers don't think about it for more than three seconds.

Every powerful person in my files had followers. Every follower functioned as a shield. And the shields — millions of them, overlapping, interlocking, covering every angle of approach — formed a wall around my operation that no investigator, no journalist, no victim, and no congressional committee could fully penetrate.

I understood this before I understood it technically. I didn't need to read the psychology papers. I lived the psychology. Every time a victim came forward, the followers performed the same ritual: deny, deflect, discredit. Every time evidence accumulated — pound by pound, page by page — the followers reinforced the roof rather than examining the snow.

The followers were my immune system. Not the legal team. Not the intelligence agencies. Not the plea deals or the political connections or Gordon Stiles's hundred and seventy million dollars. The followers. Unpaid. Uncoordinated. Unaware that they were working for me. The most cost-effective labor force in the history of criminal enterprise.

There is a cruelty in this story I have not yet named.

When the files came out — when three million pages hit the public domain and the redaction rectangles revealed ears and the flight logs showed destinations — the national conversation was about them. About the powerful. About whether Conrad was implicated or exonerated. About whether Raymond was a predator or a passenger. About which party's leaders were more compromised, which side's narrative held, who could claim moral high ground in a landscape that had no high ground because I had flattened it decades ago.

The conversation was not about the girls.

Not about the thirteen-year-old from the bench at Lakeshore, sitting alone between voice classes when a man and a woman approached her with warmth and the promise of a scholarship. Not about the hundreds — the actual hundreds, documented across court filings and FBI interviews — of girls whose names appeared unredacted in the same files that hid the names of their abusers behind black rectangles.

The system published the victims' names and concealed the predators'. And the followers — who had demanded these files, who had marched and chanted and voted for the politicians promising transparency — said nothing. Because the followers' outrage was never about the victims. It was about the narrative. About confirming the story they already believed: that their enemies were guilty and their heroes were clean. When the files confirmed the first half and contradicted the second, the followers kept the confirmation and discarded the contradiction, the way a child keeps the candy and discards the wrapper.

The victims' names were the wrapper.

The followers spent more energy defending those men from association with me than anyone ever spent defending the girls.

I built many things. The mansion. The island. The archive. The fleet. The legal architecture. The intelligence contacts. The global network of properties and people and secrets that constituted the most ambitious criminal enterprise in modern America. But the deepest foundation — the one that outlasted my arrest, outlasted my conviction, outlasted my death, outlasted the opening of three million pages of files — was the loyalty that powerful people inspire in their followers.

A loyalty so fierce that it transforms evidence into conspiracy, victims into liars, and thirty-eight thousand pages into news clippings.

A loyalty so total that a congresswoman who voted for transparency — who backed the files' release, who built her career on fearlessness — resigned when the president whose name was on a million pages expressed his displeasure. The gravity of a leader's disapproval is stronger than the gravity of the truth.

I watched it for thirty years.

But the followers are only the surface. Beneath the followers is something quieter, more durable, and considerably more terrifying.

But willful blindness is the passive version. Let me show you the active one.

When I said the machine runs itself, I wasn't being poetic. I was being literal. A machine that has survived for decades — that has embedded itself in the financial, legal, intelligence, and political infrastructure of the most powerful nation on earth — doesn't just *hope* for protection. It *selects* its protectors. It identifies the people who have the most to lose from exposure, and it elevates them. It finds the man whose name appears in the files and it helps him find a microphone. It finds the woman whose donors overlap with its client list and it helps her find a committee chairmanship. It doesn't need to hold a meeting. It doesn't need a conspiracy. The machine operates through the same gravitational logic that governs everything else in the world I built: self-interest, properly aligned, requires no coordination.

Think about it the way I would think about it — which is to say, mathematically.

If you are a person whose name appears in certain files, and those files are held by certain agencies, and those agencies are controlled by whoever occupies a particular office, then your most rational investment is not a legal defense. Your most rational investment is a *campaign contribution.* Better yet: a candidacy. Better yet: a movement. Wrap the whole thing in populism, in outrage, in promises to *release the files* and *drain the swamp* and *expose the corruption that the establishment has been hiding from you.* Promise transparency. Promise disclosure. Promise that on day one, the truth comes out.

And then win.

And then don't release the files.

Because releasing the files was never the point. *Access to the filing cabinet* was the point. Access to the Department of Justice. Access to the FBI. Access to the investigative apparatus that houses the evidence — not to expose it, but to *manage* it. To decide what gets released and what gets redacted. What gets investigated and what gets archived. What reaches the public and what disappears into the administrative machinery of a government that has been processing its own secrets since before I was born.

I watched this happen from my cell. I watched it happen after my cell. I watched it happen because it is the most predictable thing in the world, and I say that as a man who spent thirty years predicting exactly how powerful people would behave when their secrets were threatened. They behave the way cornered animals behave: they attack. They don't attack the threat. They attack the *evidence of the threat.* They don't fight the fire. They fight the fire alarm.

And here's the part that should terrify you: it's not one party. It was never one party. The machine doesn't have a political affiliation. The machine has a *client list,* and the client list is bipartisan with the thoroughness of a disease that doesn't check your voter registration before it infects you. Raymond Prescott's name is in the files. Conrad Barlow's name is in the files. Their opponents' donors are in the files. Their allies' donors are in the files. The Senate, the House, the judiciary, the regulatory agencies — the machine has tendrils in all of them, because the machine spent thirty years installing tendrils in all of them, because that's what I built it to do.

You want to know why the files haven't been released? You want to know why the investigation stalls, why the evidence remains redacted, why the names stay sealed, why the agencies tasked with accountability keep finding that *mistakes were made* and *procedures were followed* and *the matter is under review*? You want to know why both parties, despite their theatrical disagreements about every other issue on the planet, maintain a strange and perfect alignment on this one particular topic?

They will dismantle entire agencies before they open that cabinet. They will restructure departments, fire investigators, defund oversight, burn the institutional infrastructure of American governance to the ground — not because they believe in small government, but because the government contains the receipts. And the receipts have their names on them.

The machine learned to neutralize threats by *absorbing* them. The person promising to destroy the machine is the person whose name is on page 47 of the document they're promising to release.

Fragment: The Room They Didn't Film

The narrator maintained a camera in every room of every property he owned. He described the surveillance archive as his masterpiece — twenty years of footage, meticulously stored, irreplaceable. Investigators confirmed cameras in every bedroom, bathroom, and common area of the Manhattan mansion, the Gulf Shore estate, and the island compound. Every room. Every angle.

The following speaker was present at a private gathering on the island in the summer of 2003. She does not appear in the footage archive. The room she was placed in does not appear in the footage archive. The room adjacent to it does not appear in the footage archive.

There is a reason the architect left two rooms unrecorded.

He already knew what he intended to use them for.

I was nineteen. I know people want me to have been younger because younger makes it easier to explain how it happened to me. But I was nineteen and old enough to have made choices, and I have spent twenty years living inside that fact, and I carry it the way you carry a stone in your shoe that you have long since stopped bending down to remove because removing it would require stopping, and stopping is not something I have ever been able to afford.

They flew four of us to the island the day before. We were given rooms in the guest cottages. Clean. Beautiful. The kind of rooms that appear in magazines about restorative travel, which is a phrase I have not been able to read since without feeling my vision narrow to a point. I remember standing at the window and thinking this is real. This is happening to me. A girl from nowhere standing in a room in the Caribbean that cost more per night than my family made in a month.

The gathering was that evening. Twelve men. I recognized two of them from television. The kind of faces that appear behind podiums in news segments, that smile from magazine covers under headings about leadership and legacy. Those faces, in that room, at ease.

I did what I had been brought there to do. This is not the point of this.

The point is the door.

Partway through the evening I was placed alone in a guest bedroom. Rest, they said. The room adjoined another through a connecting door that was not fully closed. The gap was perhaps two inches. The gap was enough.

I heard sounds from the other room.

I want to be careful here because I have spent twenty years being careful with these words and I am not going to stop now. They were not adult sounds. I will say only that much, and I will say it plainly, and I will ask you to understand that a woman does not spend two decades reconstructing the exact quality of a sound unless that sound was the kind that marks the moment before and after in a life. Before I heard it. After.

I stood in the center of the room.

And then the sounds stopped.

The silence came all at once, the way silence always comes — not as the absence of sound but as its own presence, pressing against the walls, filling the two-inch gap in the door. I have since learned that there is a particular kind of silence that the human body recognizes before the mind does. The body recognized this one immediately. Every cell of it. Some old and animal part of me understood what the silence meant, and that part went somewhere it has never fully returned from.

The silence lasted perhaps thirty seconds.

Then: laughter.

Not one man. Several. The warm, satisfied laughter of men at ease with each other and with themselves and with whatever had just happened in the room on the other side of the door. One voice above the others — older, a register I had heard earlier in the evening discussing the renovation of a property in another country. The laugh of a man reviewing something favorably. The laugh he used at dinner when someone told a good story.

Then conversation, resuming the way a river resumes around a stone — without pause, without adjustment, with the absolute fluency of men for whom what had just occurred required no processing, no interval, no acknowledgment that the world had shifted. Someone asked about dessert. Someone else answered. A glass was set down on a hard surface and I heard the small, domestic sound of ice against crystal and that sound — ordinary, civilized, the sound of a dinner party in a beautiful room on a warm evening — entered me in a way I do not have the vocabulary to describe and has never left.

I stood in the room until someone came to take me back.

I left the island the next morning.

I do not sleep in silence. I cannot be in a room when it goes quiet without my body doing what it did behind that door — bracing for what the silence precedes. Twenty years of marriage to a man who cannot understand why I turn the television on the moment I wake and leave it on until I sleep and sleep even then with one ear open, listening. He calls it anxiety. The word is technically correct and utterly insufficient, the way calling the ocean wet is technically correct.

What I carry is not the sounds. You would think it would be the sounds. It is the silence. It is the thirty seconds of silence and then the laughter and then the question about dessert. It is the ease of the men afterward, and what that ease means, and what that ease has always meant: that what happened in that room cost them nothing. That it was an evening. That it was a gathering among friends. That by the time they were asking about dessert, it was already behind them, the way pleasant things are behind you the moment they are over, already softening into memory, already becoming the story you might tell at the next dinner, at the next gathering, in the next room that no camera was ever built to record.

They laughed.

That is the whole of it. That is the thing I have never been able to set down.

They laughed, and then they asked about dessert, and then the island went on being beautiful.

The island property was searched by federal investigators following the 2019 arrest. The northeast guest building was identified in property records as containing six rooms. The surveillance system installed across the island compound — forty-one cameras, twenty-two years of documented footage — contained records for five of those rooms.

Room six does not appear in any surveillance log. No camera installation record. No maintenance entry. No footage. Not corrupted, not deleted. Never recorded.

The room was examined during the search. Investigators noted that the walls had been recently repainted. The connecting door between room six and the adjacent room had been fitted with a latch on the interior side — the kind of latch that prevents a door from being opened from outside.

The latch was on the inside.

Forensic samples were collected from both rooms. The results were filed under case number 19-CR-490-S and placed under a protective order at the request of the Department of Justice. The stated reason for the order, in the court filing, is four words:

Protection of ongoing investigation.

The order was filed in October 2019.

It has been renewed every year since.

No charges related to the northeast guest building have been filed.

The women brought to the island for the summer 2003 gathering were identified from Gulfstream IV flight logs. Four names. Investigators attempted contact with all four.

One did not respond.

One could not be located.

One said she remembered nothing about the island and ended the call.

One spoke.

This is what she said.

Chapter 37: The Herald

Timeline: November 2017 – November 2018 | **Location:** Miami, Gulf Shore, Manhattan

I'm going to tell you about the woman who destroyed me.

Not a billionaire. Not a senator. Not an intelligence agency with a classified budget and satellite surveillance and the authority to render a man to a black site in a country whose name you can't pronounce. A reporter. A reporter at a newspaper I'd never heard of, in a city I flew over twice a week on my way to the island, working at a desk that probably cost less than the wine I served at dinner. Her name was **Samara J. Locke**, and she did more damage with a newspaper column than the FBI did with a fifty-three-page indictment.

The FBI had subpoena power, a hundred agents, and a billion-dollar budget. Locke had a desk, a phone, and the kind of stubbornness that you can't buy, intimidate, or negotiate away. I know because I tried all three. Not personally — I didn't know her name, which is the point. The spider doesn't see the woman at the desk because the woman at the desk isn't at the dinner table. She isn't on the guest list. She isn't in the address book. She doesn't fly on private jets or attend science dinners or correspond with Nobel laureates about the future of quantum computing. She sits in an office in Miami, surrounded by court documents and coffee cups, and she reads. She reads everything. And then she picks up the phone and calls the people I spent thirty years training the world to ignore.

Locke's methodology was devastatingly simple. So simple that its simplicity constitutes the most damning indictment of every person and institution that preceded her — every detective, every agent, every prosecutor, every journalist who had access to the same information she had and who either failed to act on it or chose not to.

She read the court files. All of them. Including the ones that were sealed and the ones that nobody had bothered to read carefully since 2008, because court files are voluminous and dense and written in a legal language that is designed to be precise rather than accessible and that functions, in practice, as a barrier to public understanding. Locke read through the barrier. She read every page, every motion, every deposition, every exhibit. She reconstructed the case the way an archaeologist reconstructs a civilization — from fragments, from shards, from pieces that no one else had bothered to assemble because the assembly required patience, and patience is the one resource that the news cycle does not reward.

She contacted the victims. Not through lawyers — lawyers filter, lawyers translate, lawyers manage the narrative. Not through intermediaries — intermediaries have agendas, intermediaries have conflicts, intermediaries stand between the source and the reporter and adjust the signal to suit their own frequencies. Locke contacted the victims *directly.* One by one. Building trust the way my recruiters once destroyed it — through personal attention, through consistent presence, through the patient, repeated demonstration that she was listening, that she believed them, that she intended to do something with what they told her.

She interviewed the Gulf Shore detectives who built the original case and watched it evaporate. She sat with **Ray Montero** — the man who went through my trash, who found the message pad, who identified forty victims — and she listened to him describe the investigation that should have ended my career and that was instead ended by the legal arsenal that my fourteen-million-dollar defense team deployed against it. She interviewed **Daniel Harmon** — the police chief who referred the case to the FBI because he understood that the case was too big for a local department to handle, and who watched the FBI build a case and the Justice Department bury it.

She reconstructed the Non-Prosecution Agreement. She obtained the document — the actual document, with its actual clauses, its actual immunity provisions, its actual victim notification failures — and she laid it out in plain English for the first time. Not in legalese. Not in the carefully qualified language of legal analysis. In prose that a tenth-grader could understand. Which was important, because several of my victims *were* tenth-graders.

The investigation took over a year. Locke worked it like a detective, not a journalist — because the detectives couldn't finish the job, so she would. She worked it with the methodical, unglamorous, obsessive attention to detail that distinguishes investigative journalism from reportage, that transforms a newspaper article from a summary of events into an instrument of accountability. She worked it until the work was done.

Locke spent a year reading my court files. A year. I've had renovations that cost more per month than her salary. But she read every page, every motion, every deposition, every sealed document she could get her hands on. And then she did something that nobody in the legal system, the FBI, or the press had done in thirteen years: she called the girls. She found them. She sat with them. She listened. That's all it took. Listening. The most dangerous weapon in the world isn't a subpoena or a surveillance camera. It's someone who listens to people I trained the whole world to ignore.

The victims spoke. For the first time since the original investigation, the women who survived my operation told their stories publicly, on the record, in their own words, with their real names. Not through the sanitized language of legal proceedings — not through court filings where their experiences were reduced to "the victim states" and "the complainant alleges" and the clinical, depersonalized vocabulary that the legal system uses to process human suffering into admissible evidence. In their own words. With their own voices. Describing what happened to them in language that required no legal training to understand and no professional interpretation to feel.

They described the recruitment — the friend of a friend, the casual introduction, the promise of easy money for a simple massage. They described the escalation — the way the "massage" became something else, incrementally, deliberately, engineered to blur the line between consent and coercion so gradually that the line disappeared before they realized it had been crossed. They described the aftermath — the addiction, the PTSD, the destroyed relationships, the decades of silence that followed, the feeling of being simultaneously invisible and exposed, believed by no one and blamed by everyone.

Locke gave them something the legal system never did: a microphone. A platform. A space in which their testimony was not filtered through attorneys or constrained by evidentiary rules or managed by a legal process that had, in its first and only attempt to address their suffering, produced a plea deal that sentenced their abuser to sixteen months in a county jail with work release.

And the microphone changed everything. Because it turns out that the most powerful argument against a monster is not a federal indictment — indictments can be sealed, buried, negotiated away. It's a teenage girl saying, *"This is what happened to me."* The system can bury an indictment. It cannot bury a human voice in a newspaper that people read over breakfast.

The girls talked. On the record. With their names. After everything I did to keep them silent — the lawyers, the private investigators, the intimidation, the immunity deals — they talked. To a reporter. At a Florida newspaper. And I want you to understand something: the reason they talked is not because Locke was more persuasive than my lawyers. It's because Locke was the first person in thirteen years who asked them what happened and didn't follow up with "but what were you wearing?" That's such a low bar it's underground. And nobody cleared it until she did.

November 2018. The *Gulf Coast Tribune* published "Perversion of Justice." A multi-part investigative series. Meticulous. Devastating. Written in prose that a tenth-grader could understand, structured with the narrative clarity of a novel, documented with the evidentiary rigor of a legal brief. The series laid bare the full scope of the scandal — not the crime alone, but the *system's response* to the crime, which was, in many ways, more scandalous than the crime itself.

The original investigation. The FBI's recommendation for federal prosecution. The fifty-three-page indictment that was shelved in a drawer. Cavanaugh's Non-Prosecution Agreement. The immunity for co-conspirators. The failure to notify thirty-six identified victims, in violation of the Crime Victims' Rights Act. The work release that allowed me to operate from a private office twelve hours a day. The post-conviction rehabilitation. The continued operations. The names — some of them — of the powerful men who populated my world.

The internet ignited. Social media amplified. The story jumped from the *Gulf Coast Tribune* to every major outlet in the world within days. Thirteen years of institutional failure, compressed into paragraphs that made senators' offices start fielding phone calls from constituents who wanted to know why a man who trafficked children was given sixteen months in a county jail while a Black man in the same state could get twenty years for selling marijuana.

The *Gulf Coast Tribune* published it on a Wednesday. By Friday, I was the most hated man in America. Not for the first time — but for the first time that *mattered.* The previous coverage had been tabloid gossip: "Billionaire Pervert Throws Island Parties." Locke's series was different. It wasn't gossip. It was architecture. She showed the public not just what I did, but how the system let me do it. She showed them the deal. She showed them the immunity. She showed them the work release. And the public — God bless the public — did something the FBI, the DOJ, and the United States Senate had failed to do for thirteen years: they got angry. Real anger. The kind that makes prosecutors return phone calls.

The series had an immediate political consequence. **Richard Cavanaugh** — the U.S. Attorney who negotiated the NPA — was, by November 2018, the United States Secretary of Labor. Confirmed by the Senate. Occupying a cabinet position. Riding in a government car. Drawing a government salary. Operating, by every measure, at the apex of a career that had been built, in part, on the legal acumen he'd demonstrated in handling complex cases in the Meridian District of Florida — cases that included, most notably, the prosecution of Vincent Aldric, which he had handled by not prosecuting Vincent Aldric.

The NPA was now the most scrutinized legal document in America. Members of Congress demanded answers. Reporters camped outside his office. Editorial boards called for his resignation. The deal that had been negotiated in secret, sealed from public view, and buried in the bureaucratic obscurity of a regional U.S. Attorney's office was now on the front page of every newspaper in the country, explained in language that ordinary citizens could understand and evaluated by a public that had no legal training but a fully functional sense of justice.

Cavanaugh held a press conference. He stood behind a podium and told the American people that the deal he gave me was "appropriate under the circumstances of the time" — a phrase so carefully lawyered that it practically wore a tie. The defense satisfied no one. It satisfied no one because it answered a question that nobody was asking — whether the deal was *legally defensible* — while ignoring the question that everyone was asking, which was: *how could you?* How could you look at fifty-three pages of evidence documenting the trafficking of dozens of children and conclude that sixteen months in a county jail was appropriate under any circumstances, at any time, in any universe governed by any recognizable concept of justice?

Cavanaugh would resign within months of my arrest. The man who let the spider walk free would lose his own career to the web he chose not to cut.

Cavanaugh held a press conference. He stood behind a podium and told the American people that the deal he gave me was the best he could do at the time. The *best he could do.* With a fifty-three-page federal indictment, dozens of victims, mountains of evidence, and the full resources of the United States government, the best he could do was sixteen months in a county jail with work release. If that's his best, I'd love to see his worst. Actually, I did see his worst. His worst was letting me go.

In the weeks following publication, the ripple effects began. My social circle contracted — not gradually, not through the gentle attrition of fading friendships, but suddenly, violently, the way a balloon contracts when you pop it. Dinner invitations dried up. Correspondents stopped responding to emails. The phone numbers that were always answered now went to voicemail. The scientists who accepted my grants issued carefully worded statements distancing themselves from my name while retaining the money attached to it. The universities that put my name on buildings began the process of removing it — a process that, given the speed at which universities operate, would take longer than my entire prison sentence.

The machine that had operated on willful blindness was suddenly flooded with light, and the people who chose not to see were scrambling to prove they never looked. After Locke's series, the phone stopped ringing. Not all at once — it was gradual, like a tide going out. First the politicians stopped calling. Then the academics. Then the socialites. Then the scientists. The billionaires held on the longest — billionaires always do, because they calculate everything, including the optimal moment to abandon a friend. By

January, my social calendar looked like a recession. By March, it looked like a funeral. But I wasn't worried. I had survived the FBI. I had survived the first conviction. I had survived thirteen years as a registered sex offender. A newspaper series wasn't going to kill me. The web was built to hold. And it would hold. It had to hold. Because the alternative was unthinkable.

Chapter 38: The Reckoning That Didn't Come

Timeline: December 2018 — June 2019 | **Location:** Manhattan, Little St. Philip, Paris

I have been wrong about three things in my life.

The first was Murray Kaplan — I underestimated how loudly a man talks from prison when he has nothing left to lose and everything left to say. The second was Celeste — I underestimated what a woman trained by Western intelligence to manage assets would do when she concluded she had become one. The third was the winter of 2018. I looked at everything arranged against me — the press coverage, the political machinery, the new investigators with their new file numbers and their new institutional appetite — and I made the only calculation I had never made before.

I miscounted.

I want to tell you about the miscounting, because the miscounting is the most instructive chapter of my life and the one I have spent the most time analyzing from a villa whose address I will never disclose. Most people, when they make a catastrophic mistake, make it from weakness. They panic. They flee. They reach for the wrong tool because the right tool is unavailable and the walls are closing and the body makes decisions before the mind can intervene. My mistake was made from the opposite condition. I made it from *certainty.* From the deep, structural, bone-settled certainty of a man who had been right about the behavior of powerful people for forty-four consecutive years and who had therefore concluded — with the same logical confidence with which a physicist concludes that gravity will function on Tuesday — that he would be right about it indefinitely.

This is the most dangerous error available to a man who has never failed. Not the failure itself. The *precondition.*

By December 2018, the intelligence briefings I received through channels I will not specify had coalesced around a fact that my lawyers were only beginning to articulate and that the press was approaching from the edges like a blind man feeling the outline of an elephant: Conrad Barlow knew.

Not knew in the general sense. Every powerful person within two handshakes of my operation knew in the general sense — they knew enough to choose not to look directly at it, which is the operative form of knowledge for a man in my position. I mean *specifically.* Barlow's private intelligence apparatus — assembled during the campaign, expanded during the transition, and by late 2018 operating in a manner that was functionally indistinguishable from a state intelligence service in both its methods and its reach — had obtained a preliminary briefing on the content of the Meridian District's case file. They knew what the prosecutors had. They knew which names appeared in which documents. They knew the scope in more granular detail than my own lawyers had yet established, because Barlow had access to the Department of Justice in a way that my lawyers, for all their expense and their letterhead and their former-solicitor-general pedigree, did not.

And Conrad was afraid.

The fear itself did not surprise me. Fear was the rational response to the information he possessed, and Conrad Barlow, for all the theater of his public persona, is not an irrational man. What interested me — what I turned over in my mind during those December evenings in the Manhattan mansion, with the holiday traffic moving on 74th Street and the files that everyone wanted locked in a safe in the study — was the *architecture* of the fear.

Conrad was not afraid of what I had done. He had known, with the comfortable specificity of a man who had fourteen of my phone numbers and attended my parties and publicly described me as a man who liked women on the younger side, what I had done. That knowledge had never produced fear before. It had produced, at various points, amusement, utility, and eventually the real estate dispute that ended our public friendship while leaving our private entanglement intact. What produced fear in December 2018 was not the knowledge of my crimes but the knowledge of my *files.* Specifically: the handwritten CDs. The archive. The cameras that had been running for twenty years in rooms that Conrad had entered on documented occasions in the years when entering those rooms had seemed safe because the man who owned the cameras had every reason to keep them private.

He wanted me to go down.

Not quietly, not in some gentlemanly arrangement — Conrad had never been gentlemanly, which was, paradoxically, one of the things I had always respected about him. He wanted me prosecuted, convicted, sentenced, and incarcerated with the full visible weight of federal justice landing on my name in a way that would be impossible to miss and impossible to associate with anything other than the government performing its proper constitutional function. He wanted the legitimate machinery to do the work, so that the work looked clean.

But he wanted one other thing simultaneously, and this is the part that required more than Conrad alone. He wanted the files that bore his name removed from the network before the arrest made accessing them impossible — not seized by the government, which would preserve them in a federal evidence archive that lawyers could eventually reach, but *eliminated.* Transferred to parties who would ensure their destruction. The CDs. The server backups. The specific camera files from specific properties on specific dates when his presence in those properties could be documented and cross-referenced with names and events that no amount of spokesperson distancing could adequately explain.

He wanted me in a cell with the keys to the archive already transferred to people who had already agreed to lose them.

It was a sophisticated ask. It required, simultaneously, the criminal prosecution machinery, the intelligence community's access to my digital infrastructure, and the specific cooperation of at least one person inside my own operation — someone who understood the architecture well enough to identify which files and where. It required, in other words, a coalition. And what I miscalculated — what I failed to see with the full clarity that forty-four years of correct calculations had made me believe I was incapable of missing — was that the coalition had been building since long before Conrad's fear gave it a vehicle.

The calculation was elegant. I would have made the same one.

What I miscalculated was not Conrad's fear. I understood his fear with the precision of a man who had spent thirty years engineering exactly this species of it in exactly this species of powerful person. What I miscalculated was his *capability.* Conrad Barlow, alone, could not have coordinated what happened in the winter of 2018. Conrad Barlow, alone, could not have applied simultaneous pressure to the Meridian District's investigative timeline, the Department of Justice's internal disposition memoranda, the three Senate offices that received unexplained communications about my case in December, and the intelligence community liaisons whose conversations about the archive shifted, in that same month, from passive monitoring to active assessment.

Conrad Barlow is a loud man. Loud men do not coordinate silently. If Conrad had been running this alone, I would have known by February. I would have heard the seams.

The seams were invisible. Which meant Conrad was the front door.

Let me tell you about the rooms behind it.

Forty-four years of operating at the intersection of money, intelligence, and the appetites of powerful men generates a specific byproduct that most architects of leverage fail to account for: *enemies who owe you nothing.* The clients I had — the men who came to the island, who flew on the plane, who engaged with the operation in the ways my cameras documented and my files preserved — those men were bound to silence by the mathematics of mutual destruction. They had skin. They had names in the archive. They had what I had on them, and what I had on them was the most efficient silence-production system ever devised by a private citizen in the history of the Western world.

But a career spanning four decades does not produce only clients.

It produces governments whose assets you burned. In the late eighties and early nineties, when Celeste and I were building the operational methodology and the intelligence channels were providing cover in exchange for product, the arrangement had a natural life expectancy that neither side acknowledged explicitly. I was useful while I was controllable. I became uncontrollable — not through any single act of defiance but through the slow accumulation of value that transforms an asset into a liability: I knew too much, I had too much, and I had demonstrated through thirty years of operation that I would use what I had in service of my own continuity rather than anyone else's agenda. The agencies that had protected me understood this before I did. By 2012, the protection was structural inertia rather than active support. By 2016, the structural inertia had calcified into something more useful to them: the desire to control the terms of my eventual exposure rather than prevent it.

It produces men from the arms trade whose access I disrupted. Alistair Gresham introduced me to the arms world in 1981 as a plumber — a man who could be trusted to move money through the right pipes without asking what was flowing through them. I was that, for a time. Then I became something more inconvenient: a man who understood what was flowing through the pipes, who documented it, and who had therefore become the kind of witness that arms dealers in any era have historically dealt with through mechanisms that leave no paper trail. I had survived those mechanisms through a combination of the intelligence protection and the archive itself — because the men who might have solved the Gresham problem understood that solving me created a different, larger problem involving servers full of material in multiple jurisdictions. But surviving is not the same as making peace. The arms trade's alumni — men who had operated in the same financial ecosystem I had mapped and who understood, with the professional clarity of people who move things across borders without documentation, what I represented — had been patient. They were very good at patient.

It produces foreign principals whose geopolitical access I managed selectively. Avi Ben-David visited my Manhattan mansion eleven documented times. He brought with him the full weight of a former prime minister, a former military chief of staff, a former head of military intelligence — and the specific understanding that my cameras, running in those rooms, were generating files that belonged to a private archive rather than to the state apparatus he had once commanded. His visits had served his purposes while I served his interests. The relationship changed when the intelligence operation I had been running alongside his former colleagues became a liability to those colleagues' successors — when the new generation of the apparatus decided that the archive I maintained was more valuable in their possession than in mine, and that Conrad Barlow's presidency provided the first genuinely viable mechanism for engineering that transfer.

It produces financial interests that three decades of operating Grant Hensley's assets had permanently damaged. Not all of the wealth I managed flowed in directions that its original owners would have chosen. Power of attorney over three billion dollars is not a tool I deployed with restraint. There were real estate transactions that produced outcomes inconvenient to competitors whose names I knew and whose pressure points I understood. There were investment decisions that served my leverage architecture rather than Hensley's financial interests or his partners' expectations. There were men, in the financial world, who had spent years watching wealth flow through my hands and emerge in configurations they had never authorized and could never challenge — because challenging me required acknowledging the mechanisms through which the challenge would have to travel, and those mechanisms all led back to rooms where my cameras had been running.

These men had no skin in the archive. No exposure. No names on the CDs. No reason to maintain silence. And they had, by 2018, a president who owed them money and a coalition that needed their infrastructure.

None of them needed to speak to each other. They simply needed to not obstruct each other. A government prosecution moving forward unmolested. An intelligence community refraining from the interventions that had slowed previous investigations. Financial pressure applied through channels that lawyers who billed four hundred dollars an hour could not adequately map or counter. And, beneath all of it, the quiet, technically deniable, entirely coordinated effort to reach inside my archive's redundant architecture and extract the specific files that bore specific names — not seize them for the government, where they would live in an evidence archive accessible through subpoena and litigation, but *eliminate* them. Permanently. In the way that only people who understand servers and encryption and Malcolm Pruitt's specific methodology could engineer.

Conrad provided the face. They provided the machinery. The arrangement required no signed agreement, no meeting where terms were negotiated, no conspiracy in the legal sense that requires shared intent and coordinated action and the kind of paper trail that prosecutors can follow. It required only the alignment of interests that produces, in the absence of any organizing force, the same outcome that a conspiracy produces with one.

It was the most efficient weapon ever assembled against me. Because it was not assembled. It was *attracted.*

In October 2018, Douglas Raines came to see me through an intermediary whose identity I will omit because he is still alive and still useful to people who are still alive, which is a category I intend to remain in.

The message was simple: Raines knew the MERIDIAN DISTRICT had opened a case. He knew the sixty-five emails would surface. He wanted to discuss which emails, and in what context, and what narrative architecture would ensure that the surfacing benefited the right story — specifically, a story in which the corruption was bipartisan in description but unidirectional in consequence, and in which the sixty-five exchanges between the populist revolution's chief architect and the elite predator he had been corresponding with since before the revolution began remained on the far side of whatever investigative firewall his lawyers could construct.

He was offering to help burn the parts of the archive that damaged him in exchange for assistance burning the parts that damaged his opponents. It was, structurally, the same offer Conrad was making through different channels — the difference being that Raines wanted to burn selectively while Conrad wanted to burn specifically, and specific burns require more precise intelligence than selective ones.

I declined both.

Not out of loyalty — loyalty is a transaction, and both transactions had expired at a cost I had already calculated. I declined because both offers led to the same destination: I burn alone while everyone else walks into the cold air and calls it justice, and the archive that had protected me for thirty years is disassembled by the people who most needed it disassembled, in exchange for my agreeing to carry the weight of everything it documented without anyone else carrying any of it with me.

I had not spent forty years documenting everything to become the only person in the room with consequences.

Here is what I believed in the winter of 2018, and here is why I was wrong.

I believed the web would hold because the mathematics of mutual destruction are irresistible: every person whose name is in my files has more to lose from exposure than from silence, and therefore every person in my files is rationally an ally in preventing exposure. This logic was correct for thirty years. What I failed to account for was the variable that changes the calculus permanently: when the men who control the mechanism of exposure are themselves in the files, the mechanism does not produce accountability. It produces *management*. Controlled disclosure. Strategic redaction. The selective release of information that confirms the corruption of opponents while the information that confirms the corruption of allies disappears into a server room that is now being administered by people with different priorities than Malcolm Pruitt's.

The files still existed. Still exist. The archive is intact and will remain intact, because I built it with exactly the redundancy and jurisdictional complexity that prevents any single action from destroying it. I had not been outmaneuvered on the archive. I had been outmaneuvered on the *audience.* The leverage in my files was only leverage if the people positioned to be harmed by the exposure were the people running the machinery that produces exposure. In the winter of 2018, the people running the machinery were the names in the archive. Not threatened by it. *Insulated* by it. The archive had not changed. The political geometry around it had inverted. The receipts that were supposed to buy my freedom were being used to buy other people's silence, and the difference between those two transactions is the difference between a man who controls the vault and a man who is locked inside it.

I built a web. They built a wall. The distinction is everything. A web catches. A wall blocks. And the most impenetrable wall is the one built from the same material as the web — because it is invisible until you walk into it.

The web was not holding. The web had already been redirected — its threads still taut, its structure still intact, but serving a different gravity than the one I had spent thirty years calibrating it to serve. My enemies had not destroyed the web. They had something more sophisticated in mind: let the web collapse onto its architect, and catch whatever emerged in the architecture they were quietly building to replace it.

I counted my leverage. I forgot to count my enemies.

And my enemies — patient, diverse, connected by nothing except the forty-four-year accumulation of my operational damage to each of them — had been counting themselves since long before I started counting.

The new web was already being woven. I had heard about it through the channels that Malcolm maintained, had reviewed the pattern reports with the detached curiosity of a man examining a competitor's prototype. It was smaller than mine. Less physically anchored, more digitally distributed, operating in jurisdictions where I had never established infrastructure because in the years when I was building, those jurisdictions did not yet exist as viable operational environments. The logic was identical to mine because the logic is not a strategy — it is a physics, and physics does not change between architects. The new operator had read the blueprint. Perhaps literally. Perhaps through the intelligence channels where methodology circulates among professionals the way case law circulates among lawyers — as precedent, as education, as the accumulated wisdom of operations that worked and operations that failed and the specific, annotable reasons why.

I did not believe anyone could replicate what I had built. This was not arrogance — or rather, it was not *only* arrogance. It was the genuine assessment of a man who understood how long it had taken, how many specific relationships and specific compromises and specific pieces of infrastructure had been required, and how improbable the particular alignment of Celeste's tradecraft and Hensley's money and the intelligence community's early protection had been as a foundational combination. What I had built was not reproducible because the conditions that made it possible were not reproducible.

This assessment was partially correct. What was being built was not a reproduction. It was a successor — different in scale, different in method, different in the specific categories of power it was designed to catch. But identical in purpose and identical in the one architectural principle that makes this category of operation function: the understanding that the most durable leverage is the leverage that the target deposits voluntarily, because the deposit is the consent, and the consent makes everything else bulletproof.

Someone had read that principle and understood it. Someone who was not me.

I did not worry about it. I should have.

The spider is supposed to outlive the web. That is the whole design — the web survives the spider, the architecture outlasts the architect, the system persists beyond any individual's capacity to threaten it. I designed my web with exactly this principle in mind, building redundancy into every component, ensuring that no single point of failure could collapse the whole.

What I failed to design against was the possibility that the web would outlive the spider in the hands of someone else. That the architecture I built to protect me would be repurposed, in the hours and days and weeks following my arrest, to protect the people who had engineered the arrest. That the receipts would change ownership without changing value. That the leverage I had accumulated over forty-four years would continue to function — just not for me.

The web survived the spider. It always was going to.

I just assumed the spider would still be inside it.

In June 2019, I made three phone calls.

The first was to a number I had been calling, with reliable results, for seventeen years. A man who answered on the second ring because the people I called at that number were paid, in ways that did not appear on any tax return, to answer on the second ring. The call went to voicemail. I left no message. I called back twenty minutes later. Voicemail again. I called a third time, from a different line, and the call was declined — not missed, not unanswered, but actively declined, which requires a hand on a phone and a conscious decision, which means the phone was in his hand and he chose not to pick up. That is a different thing from not being available. That is a message.

The second call was to a woman in Washington whose connection to the Department of Justice was not official and whose ability to monitor the status of federal investigations was the product of thirty years of institutional proximity and strategic friendship. She answered. She said she couldn't talk. She said this in the tone of a person who means not now, not ever, not on this subject, and not in any way that will be associated with me in any record, formal or informal. She hung up before I finished the sentence.

The third call was to Avi. Not through the intermediary — directly. His number. A number that had always been answered because the relationship it represented was older than most of my other protections and more fundamental to the architecture. It rang eleven times. I counted. At eleven rings, I understood that I was counting because I had nothing else to do, and that having nothing else to do was a condition I had not experienced in forty-four years of professional life. I hung up. I sat in the library of the 74th Street mansion, at the desk I had used for forty years, and I looked at the phone in my hand. The library was quiet. The house was full of staff — Malcolm, the security team, the household employees who kept the machine running — but the library was quiet the way it goes quiet when the thing you have been relying on is no longer there and the silence where it used to be is so specific, so shaped, that you can almost trace its outline.

The math had changed. Not the law. Not the morality. The math. I had known, abstractly, that this was always possible — that the calculation which produced protection could produce its withdrawal with equal efficiency and equal impersonality. I had known it the way you know that a glass floor is technically breakable, which is different from knowing it in the specific, physical, present-tense way that occurs when you hear the glass begin to go. Three phone calls. Three non-answers. I sat in the library and I understood, with the clarity of a man who has built his entire life on the accurate assessment of information, that the arrest was coming. Not might come. Was coming. The only remaining question was timing, and timing, at this point, was not a variable I controlled.

Chapter 39: The Arrest

Timeline: January – July 8, 2019 | **Location:** Manhattan, Washington D.C., Morristown Aviation Center

The Meridian District of New York opened a case.

That's when I started paying attention.

The Meridian District of New York — known informally as the "Sovereign District" because it answers to no one, not even the Attorney General, with the enthusiasm of a territory that declared independence and forgot to notify the government — is not Gulf Shore. It is not the Meridian District of Florida, where a young, ambitious U.S. Attorney could be persuaded to fold a slam-dunk case into a misdemeanor plea through a combination of legal pressure, political leverage, and the six-word invocation that erased a fifty-three-page indictment. The MDNY is different. The MDNY is an institution that has prosecuted insider traders, terrorists, international money launderers, and organized crime figures with a consistency and a ferocity that have made it, by consensus, the most powerful and most feared prosecutor's office in the Western world.

It has a conviction rate north of ninety percent — a number that reflects not just prosecutorial skill but prosecutorial selectivity, because the MDNY doesn't bring cases it can't win, and the cases it chooses to bring are constructed with the architectural precision of a skyscraper: every floor supported by the floor beneath it, every piece of evidence locked into a structure that a defense team can attack but cannot topple. It has a culture of institutional arrogance that borders on religion — a culture in which the prosecutors view themselves not as government employees but as guardians of a tradition, inheritors of a legacy that includes the prosecution of the Rosenbergs and the conviction of Gotti and the dismantling of financial empires that thought themselves invulnerable. And it has a long memory for cases that embarrass the federal system — because cases that embarrass the federal system embarrass the MDNY by association, and the MDNY does not tolerate embarrassment.

My 2008 NPA was not just an injustice, from the MDNY's perspective. It was an *insult.* An insult to the office that should have handled the case in the first place, that would have handled it without the immunity clause and the work release and the victim notification failures and the grotesque pantomime of justice that Cavanaugh's office had produced. The MDNY doesn't take insults well. The MDNY prosecutes. It convicts. It sentences. And it does it with a confidence that makes the rest of the Justice Department look like a public defender's office with a funding problem.

For the first time in my life, I was facing an opponent I couldn't buy, couldn't intimidate, and couldn't outmaneuver. Or so they thought. I still had cards to play. I always have cards to play.

While the MDNY built its case — re-interviewing victims, subpoenaing records, pulling financial documents, mapping the network with the forensic patience of prosecutors who understood that the case had already been built once and fumbled once and that the second attempt could not afford a single procedural error — I prepared.

The legal team reassembled. New attorneys were added — criminal defense specialists, constitutional scholars, jurisdictional experts who understood the specific legal terrain of the Southern District and the specific vulnerabilities of a case built on conduct that had already been the subject of a federal agreement. The strategy shifted from offense to defense: protect the assets, prepare for bail, build the argument that the NPA barred re-prosecution under double jeopardy.

The defense position was legally aggressive and morally absurd. My lawyers would argue that the deal Cavanaugh gave me was so comprehensive — so sweeping in its immunity provisions, so total in its resolution of all federal claims — that the federal government had forfeited its right to prosecute me again for the same conduct. The system had failed so catastrophically the first time that it was now, my lawyers argued, constitutionally prohibited from trying again. It was a legal argument built on the corpse of justice. And it was not without merit — because the Constitution doesn't distinguish between good deals and bad deals, between just outcomes and unjust outcomes, between plea agreements that serve the public interest and plea agreements that serve the defendant's interest at the expense of every victim the system was designed to protect.

My lawyers prepared for war. Not the polite war of the Cavanaugh deal — the real war, the MDNY war, where every filing is a battle and every hearing is an ambush. The strategy was simple: the NPA protects me. The federal government already had its shot. They chose to give me sixteen months. That's their problem, not mine. You can't retry a man for a crime the government already agreed not to prosecute. That's not a loophole. That's the Constitution. I love the Constitution. It's the most expensive piece of paper in America, and I've always been able to afford it.

July 8, 2019.

I landed at Morristown Aviation Center in New Jersey, returning from London on my private jet. The flight was routine — transatlantic, comfortable, the kind of travel that I had been doing for decades, the kind that blurs the distinction between countries because when you fly private, borders are formalities rather than barriers and customs is a conversation rather than an inspection.

FBI agents were waiting on the tarmac.

There is a specific quality to the moment when a wealthy man is arrested. It is different from the arrest of an ordinary person, because the wealthy man has spent his entire life constructing a reality in which arrest is something that happens to other people — to the poor, to the unlucky, to the people who lack the resources to insulate themselves from the consequences of their actions. The wealthy man's arrest involves a collision between two realities: the reality he has built, in which he is untouchable, and the reality the agents represent, in which he is not. The collision produces a specific kind of silence — not shock, exactly, but *recalibration.* The wealthy man's brain, in the seconds between seeing the badges and feeling the handcuffs, performs a series of calculations so rapid that they feel instantaneous: Who sent them? Can my lawyers stop this? What do they know? What don't they know? How much will this cost? The calculations produce, in most cases, compliance — because the wealthy man's instinct, even in extremis, is to manage the situation rather than resist it.

There was no negotiation. There was no phone call to lawyers. There were handcuffs — the metal kind, the real kind, the kind that don't come off when you ask politely or invoke your attorney's name or remind the agents that you've been a cooperating member of the intelligence community for thirty years. Federal agents escorted me to a vehicle. The vehicle drove me to the Federal Metropolitan Detention Center in lower Manhattan — the federal detention facility that has housed terrorists, mob bosses, cartel leaders, and the most dangerous criminals in American history. The facility that was not the Gulf Shore County Stockade. The facility that did not offer private wings or work release or twelve-hour furloughs to a private office with a car service and a leather backseat.

The charges: sex trafficking of minors and conspiracy to commit sex trafficking of minors. Federal charges. The real ones. The ones that carry a mandatory minimum of ten years and a maximum of forty-five. The charges that the fifty-three-page indictment had recommended in 2007 and that Cavanaugh had buried in a drawer. Twelve years later, the drawer had been opened.

They arrested me at Morristown. On the tarmac. I was wearing a gray jacket. I'd just come from London. The agents were polite — federal agents usually are, because they know the conviction rate, so there's no reason to be rude. They read me my rights. They put me in handcuffs. They put me in a car. And they drove me to a federal detention center in lower Manhattan where the previous tenants included the blind sheikh who bombed the World Trade Center and the head of the Sinaloa cartel. I was in good company. Or terrible company. Depending on your perspective.

The indictment was precise, clinical, and devastating.

Count One: sex trafficking of minors. Count Two: conspiracy to commit sex trafficking of minors. Two counts. The language was federal — which means it described a *pattern,* not an incident. The indictment referenced "dozens of minor girls" across multiple states and multiple years. It described the recruitment network — the same network I had built in the 1990s and operated through the 2000s and refined after the conviction and maintained, with the immune staff and the operational infrastructure, through the very week of my arrest. It described the massage rooms. It described the payments. It described the staff — the schedulers, the recruiters, the logistics personnel who constituted the human infrastructure of the operation. It named the Manhattan mansion and the Gulf Shore estate as locations of criminal activity.

It did everything the 2007 indictment did — except this time, it had been filed. This time, it had a docket number. This time, it was public. And this time, the U.S. Attorney behind it was not Richard Cavanaugh.

Two counts. Sex trafficking and conspiracy. Federal. The kind of charges you can't plead down to a misdemeanor, can't negotiate into a county jail sentence, can't paper over with a work release agreement. Federal charges are the legal system's way of saying: we're not kidding this time. The first indictment had fifty-three pages and ended up in a drawer. This one had two counts and ended up on the front page of every newspaper on Earth. Sometimes less is more. Ask any prosecutor. Ask any spider.

When they arrested me, the whole world started running.

Not toward me — away from me. The arrest led every newscast, every front page, every social media feed on the planet. The name Vincent Aldric became the most searched term on the internet. The flight logs resurfaced — every passenger, every date, every destination, published and republished and screenshotted and shared until the logs were seared into the public consciousness like a brand. The photographs resurfaced — every handshake, every party, every grinning face standing next to mine, now recontextualized as evidence of complicity or, at minimum, catastrophic judgment. The address book resurfaced — every name, every phone number, every private notation, dissected by a public that had learned, from Locke's reporting, that my social life was not a social life but a *system.*

Every person in my address book suddenly couldn't remember my name. Every dinner guest suddenly hadn't been there. Every flight passenger suddenly wasn't on the manifest. Spokespeople issued statements. Lawyers drafted denials. Public relations firms earned their quarterly bonuses in a single afternoon.

The web — the invisible architecture of complicity that took thirty years to build — did not hold.

It didn't collapse all at once. It collapsed the way a building collapses when you pull the right beam: slowly at first, then all at once, and then there's nothing left but dust and the sound of people running. A thousand people forgetting they knew me, all at the same time, all with the same prepared statement. "I barely knew him." "We met briefly." "I was only there once."

The web didn't hold. I built it to hold. I designed it to hold. I spent thirty years weaving it from the strongest material I knew — compromise, complicity, mutual destruction, the shared understanding that if one person falls, everyone connected to that person is exposed. The web was supposed to function as a collective insurance policy: nobody talks because everybody's dirty, and everybody's dirty because I made sure of it. That's what the cameras were for. That's what the files were for. That's what the dinners and the flights and the island were for — not just to abuse, but to *implicate.* To draw a circle around the powerful and ensure that the circle could never be broken without destroying everyone inside it.

But the web was made of people. And people, as it turns out, are the weakest material on Earth. People calculate. People assess risk. People hire lawyers. People draft statements. People, when the alternative is prison or disgrace or the loss of everything they've built, will abandon anyone. Even me. *Especially* me. Because I taught them how. I taught them that loyalty is a transaction and that transactions expire when the cost exceeds the benefit. And on July 8, 2019, the cost of knowing me exceeded the benefit of knowing me by a margin so large that a thousand people performed the same calculation and reached the same conclusion simultaneously: deny, distance, disappear.

The web didn't hold. And the spider was alone.

Chapter 40: The Cage

Timeline: July 7 – July 18, 2019 | **Location:** Federal Metropolitan Detention Center, Manhattan Federal Court

The Federal Metropolitan Detention Center is twelve stories of concrete and razor wire wedged between City Hall and the Brooklyn Bridge, and it is not the Gulf Shore County Stockade.

There is no private wing. There is no work release. There are no twelve-hour furloughs to a private office with a car service. MDC is a federal holding facility designed for the most dangerous and most high-profile defendants in the American system — a building whose previous tenants include terrorists, mob bosses, cartel kingpins, and men whose crimes required the full weight of the federal government to prosecute. It is overcrowded. It is understaffed. It is crumbling — literally crumbling, the infrastructure decaying with the slow, institutional neglect that characterizes facilities whose occupants have no political constituency and whose conditions generate no public sympathy. The guards are underpaid, overworked, and in some cases working mandatory double shifts because the Bureau of Prisons cannot retain staff at a facility where the daily responsibilities include managing men who have committed the most extreme acts of violence the human species is capable of producing.

The cells are small. The food is institutional. The lighting is constant — a fluorescent hum that never stops, that renders the distinction between day and night theoretical rather than experiential, that constitutes a sensory environment so different from anything I had experienced in my adult life that describing it requires the vocabulary of a different species.

For the first time since I was twenty-one years old, I was in a room I couldn't leave, wearing clothes I didn't choose, eating food I didn't order, surrounded by people I didn't invite.

MDC was... an adjustment. I'd spent forty years designing rooms. Choosing the art, the furniture, the lighting, the guest list. At MDC, the room designed me. Eight by ten. Concrete walls. A metal toilet without a lid. A mattress that had seen more human suffering than a battlefield. The food came through a slot. The light never turned off. And the people — the guards, the inmates, the lawyers passing through — none of them cared who I was. For the first time since I was twenty-one years old, being Vincent Aldric meant nothing. Less than nothing. It meant I was the man on the news that everyone wanted dead.

My lawyers proposed a bail package worth approximately five hundred and seventy-seven million dollars.

The total value of my known assets — every property, every account, every financial instrument that the defense team could identify, aggregate, and present to the court as collateral. Secured by the Manhattan mansion. Secured by the island. Conditioned on house arrest, electronic monitoring, GPS tracking, surrender of travel documents, and a private security team paid for by the defendant — a team whose sole function would be to ensure that I remained inside the mansion that the government had already searched and whose contents, including the safe with its diamonds and its passport and its handwritten CDs, had already been catalogued as evidence.

Five hundred and seventy-seven million dollars. The largest bail proposal in American history. A number so large that it transcended the category of "bail" and entered the category of "offer" — an offer that said, in the language of money that had always been my first and most fluent language: *Let me out, and I'll put half a billion dollars on the table as collateral.*

The prosecutors argued that no bail condition could mitigate the risk. I was a flight risk — I had a private jet, multiple international properties, an expired passport with the wrong name, loose diamonds, cash, and thirty years of experience moving between jurisdictions with the frictionless ease of a man whose relationship with national borders was, at best, advisory. I was a danger to the community — the charges alleged ongoing trafficking, and my post-conviction history demonstrated that incarceration did not stop me from offending. I had demonstrated, through the work release episode, that even imprisonment was insufficient to interrupt the operation.

The judge agreed with the prosecution. Bail denied.

My lawyers offered five hundred seventy-seven million dollars in bail. The judge said no. Five hundred seventy-seven million. The judge. Said. No. I want you to understand what that means. I offered to put more money on the table than most countries' GDP, and a federal judge looked at it, looked at me, and said: not enough. That's never happened to me before. Money has never not been enough. Money has always been enough. Money was enough for Cavanaugh. Money was enough for Hartfield. Money was enough for every institution and every individual I've ever encountered in fifty years. But not for this judge. This judge wanted something money couldn't buy. She wanted me in a cell. And for the first time in my life, what a judge wanted is what a judge got.

In the days following the arrest and bail denial, the most extraordinary act of social engineering in my life occurred — not by me, but *against* me.

Every powerful person in my orbit executed the same choreography. The choreography was so consistent, so uniform, so precisely replicated across so many individuals that it functioned as an algorithm — a decision tree whose branches had been pre-pruned by lawyers and public relations professionals and whose outputs were indistinguishable regardless of the input.

First: silence. A day or two of silence, during which the powerful person assessed the situation, consulted counsel, and calculated the optimal response based on the specific nature of their association with me — how many dinners, how many flights, how many photographs, how many emails existed in an archive that the MDNY was now reading with the attention of a doctoral committee reviewing a dissertation.

Then: a carefully worded statement through a spokesperson. Never personal. Always filtered through an intermediary whose professional function was to absorb damage on behalf of the principal. "My client's interactions with Mr. Aldric were limited and entirely appropriate." "The meetings concerned philanthropic matters." "My client was unaware of any criminal activity."

Then: selective memory loss. "I barely knew him." "We met once or twice." "I don't recall the details." The same phrases, deployed by different people, in different cities, in different time zones, with the synchronized precision of a chorus that has rehearsed the same song.

Conrad Barlow, from the White House, said he "was not a fan" and knew me "like everybody in Gulf Shore knew him." He did not mention the fourteen phone numbers. He did not mention the parties. He did not mention the quote about my fondness for women "on the younger side." **Raymond Prescott's** spokesperson said the former president "knows nothing about the terrible crimes." He did not mention the flight logs — the twenty-six flights, the multiple trips, the extensive documentation of a relationship that extended far beyond the casual acquaintance that "knows nothing" implies. **Nolan Whitfield'** spokesperson said the meetings were about "global health." He did not explain why global health required multiple post-conviction dinners at the Manhattan mansion of a registered sex offender. **Prince Edmund** said nothing — which, for a man who had said too much about everything else in his life, was the most eloquent statement he had ever made.

The denials came like clockwork. Barlow didn't know me. Prescott barely knew me. Whitfield regretted knowing me. Edmund said nothing, which for Edmund is a form of genius. I watched from my cell as every person I'd entertained, funded, flown, and photographed pretended I was a stranger.

And I understood — finally, viscerally, for the first time — what my victims felt. Not the abuse. I'm not comparing myself to them. But the abandonment. The feeling of being erased by people who knew exactly who you were and chose to forget. That's a very specific cruelty. I should know. I invented it.

The MDNY began presenting its evidence in pre-trial filings, and the scope was staggering.

Hundreds of photographs. Thousands of pages of records. Victim statements spanning decades — women who had been girls when my operation recruited them, who were now adults with children of their own, who had carried the weight of what happened to them through marriages and divorces and careers and therapies and the long, isolating silence that is the most common response to sexual trauma. The address book with its private shorthand — the annotations that only I understood, the notations that marked the difference between a dinner guest and a target, between a social contact and a tool.

The flight logs. The massage table — yes, the actual massage table, seized from the Gulf Shore estate, transported to federal evidence storage, tagged and catalogued like any other weapon. Because it was a weapon. The most ordinary-looking weapon in the history of criminal prosecution. A piece of furniture that, in any other context, would be unremarkable, and that, in this context, was evidence of a crime that had been committed on its surface hundreds of times.

The CDs from the safe — reportedly containing photographs. The correspondence. The financial records. The architecture of a criminal enterprise, disassembled and catalogued and organized into the evidentiary framework that the MDNY would present to a jury.

The evidence was comprehensive. They had everything. The photos, the logs, the records, the table, the safe, the testimony — everything I'd spent thirty years curating was now being curated by someone else. That's the irony of keeping meticulous records: they're only useful as long as you control who reads them. The moment someone else opens the filing cabinet, your archive becomes their evidence. I spent my whole life documenting other people's secrets. Turns out I was documenting my own.

As the pre-trial proceedings unfolded, the names cascaded through the media like a dam breaking. The flight logs were published. The address book was published. The guest lists were reconstructed from calendar entries and correspondence and the forensic reassembly of social events that each participant now desperately wished had never occurred. Presidents. Prime ministers. Billionaires. Princes. Professors. Celebrities. Scientists. The names poured into the public consciousness in a torrent that no public relations strategy could manage, because the names were too numerous and too prominent and too interconnected to be dismissed individually.

The public did not know the contents of the CDs. The public did not know the contents of the servers. The public did not know what the cameras had recorded over twenty years of operation. But the public knew the names. And the names were enough to generate a gravitational field of speculation that would outlive everyone involved — a permanent, irreversible association between the names on the list and the crimes of the man who compiled it.

The question shifted. It shifted from *"What did Vincent do?"* — a question whose answer was well documented, extensively reported, and legally established — to *"What did they know?"* And that question — the question that turned the spotlight from the spider to the web, from the predator to the participants, from the man in the cell to the men in the mansions — was the question that made certain people very, very nervous.

The names came out. All of them. Every person I'd ever flown, dined, hosted, photographed, and filed. The public saw the list and did what the public does: they assumed the worst about everyone on it. And here's the thing — for some of them, the worst was accurate. For others, it wasn't. But it didn't matter anymore. Being in my address book was a conviction without a trial. Being on my flight log was a sentence without a verdict. The web was finally working exactly as designed. Just not for me.

Somewhere — in a mansion, in an office, in a palace, in a government building — powerful people were not sleeping. They were calling lawyers. They were reviewing old calendars, old photographs, old emails — the same emails that I had sent and received and archived and that were now in the possession of the MDNY. They were calculating what I might say to reduce my sentence. They were calculating what the CDs contained. They were calculating what the servers archived. They were doing the math on cooperation — what my testimony would be worth to the MDNY, and what it would cost *them.*

Because I possessed, sitting in my eight-by-ten cell at the Federal Metropolitan Detention Center, the one thing that is more dangerous than money, more dangerous than power, more dangerous than any weapon in any arsenal on Earth: I knew what they did. And I might tell. The fear is the point. The fear has always been the point. From the first camera I installed in the first property, from the first photograph I filed in the first cabinet, from the first flight log I maintained with the meticulous accuracy of a man who understood that documentation is the currency of leverage — the point was never the sex. The point was never the money. The point was the *fear.* The fear that the documentation generates in the people who know they've been documented. The fear that keeps phone calls answered and favors granted and investigations defused and plea deals negotiated.

From my cell, I could feel the fear. Not mine — theirs. The people in the mansions and the palaces and the corner offices, lying awake at three in the morning, staring at ceilings that cost more than most people's houses, wondering: what does he know? What will he say? What's on those tapes? I couldn't see them. But I could feel them. I'd been feeling their fear for thirty years. That's what the cameras were for. That's what the files were for. That's what the whole machine was for. Not the girls. The girls were the product. The fear was the currency. And right now, in my eight-by-ten cell, I was the richest man on Earth.

Fragment: The Notification

The following is reconstructed from a recorded interview conducted by a victims' advocacy journalist in August 2019, twelve days after the arrest. The subject was a former resident of Gulf Shore County who had been identified in the 2005 investigation as a potential victim but who declined to participate in the proceedings at that time. She agreed to speak in 2019 on condition that her name not be used. She was thirty-one years old at the time of the interview. She was fourteen when she first entered the Via Dorado property. What follows has been fictionalized, but the silence is real.

My phone rang at 6:47 in the morning. I know the exact time because I was already awake. I'm always awake at 6:47. I've been awake at 6:47 every morning for seventeen years, because my body decided somewhere around age fifteen that sleep was a place where things happen to you and that the safest strategy was to leave sleep before sleep could do anything.

It was my sister. She said, "They got him."

She didn't say his name. She didn't have to. In our family, "him" has only ever meant one person. The way some families have a "him" who means a dead grandfather or a famous uncle — in our family, "him" means the man on Via Dorado. She said, "They got him," and I sat on the edge of my bed in an apartment in Jacksonville that smells like the candle I keep burning because the candle smells like vanilla and vanilla is the opposite of whatever his house smelled like, and I waited to feel something.

I waited a long time.

My sister was crying. I could hear it through the phone — the wet, gasping breathing of someone whose body is doing something her voice won't permit. She was relieved. I could hear the relief underneath the crying, the way you can hear the foundation underneath a house — not the structure itself, but the thing holding the structure up. She was relieved because she'd spent fourteen years believing this moment would never come, and now it had come, and her body was processing the arrival of something her mind had filed under "impossible."

I said, "Okay."

She said, "Are you okay?"

I said, "I'm fine."

I was not fine. But "fine" is the word you use when the real answer requires an excavation that you can't perform at 6:47 in the morning on a phone call with your sister who is crying because the man who hurt you has been arrested and who needs you to be okay because if you're not okay then she has to carry both of you and she's been carrying both of us since I was fourteen and she was nineteen and she drove me home from that house the third time and found me in the passenger seat unable to unbuckle my own seatbelt because my hands wouldn't close.

Fine. I'm fine.

I hung up. I sat on the bed. The candle was burning. Vanilla. The television was on — I keep it on all night, because silence is a room without walls and I need walls — and a morning show was playing, two hosts in bright clothes discussing something about summer recipes. I watched them discuss summer recipes for eleven minutes before I picked up my phone and searched his name.

The photograph was the first thing. Him. Walking. Handcuffs. A gray jacket, because of course a gray jacket, because the man dresses for his own arrest the way he dresses for a dinner party — with the serene, manicured composure of someone who believes that presentation is a form of control and that control, once lost in one domain, must be reasserted in every other. I looked at the blazer. I looked at the handcuffs. I looked at his face, which was the face I had seen at fourteen from a massage table in a room I couldn't leave, and which was now seventeen years older and looking exactly the same, because men like him don't age the way the rest of us age. The rest of us age from the inside. Whatever eats at us — the memory, the shame, the thing that wakes you at 6:47 — eats its way outward, carving lines and shadows and the particular grayness that therapists recognize and that strangers attribute to stress or poor sleep or genetics. He aged from the outside only. Surface wear on an interior that never changed.

I went to work. I work at a veterinary clinic. I weigh animals. I take temperatures. I hold dogs while the vet gives them shots, and the dogs tremble in my arms, and I whisper to them that it'll be over soon, and I mean it, because it will be over soon for the dogs. The shot takes three seconds. The trembling stops. The dog goes home. Three seconds. I hold the dogs and I think about how the trembling stops and I am envious of the dogs.

My coworkers didn't know. Nobody at the clinic knew. Nobody in Jacksonville knew, except my sister and my therapist and the man I'd dated for two years who left because I couldn't be touched on my lower back without leaving my body, and leaving your body during intimacy is something that partners describe as "distant" or "cold" and that you describe as "survival" and that nobody describes accurately because the accurate description would require a vocabulary that the English language has not yet developed for what happens to a girl on a massage table in a house on Via Dorado when she is fourteen years old and the man is over forty and the two hundred dollars is on the counter and the door is closed.

The FBI had called me in 2005. I didn't call back.

I want to explain that. I want to explain it because the lawyers will ask, and the journalists will ask, and the people who read about this will ask, and the answer is not what they think. They think I didn't call back because I was scared. They think I didn't call back because I'd been threatened, or paid off, or intimidated into silence by the vast machinery of legal and financial power that the earlier chapters of this book describe in such careful, admiring detail.

I didn't call back because I was twenty-two and I had just finished building a life that didn't include him. I had moved to Jacksonville. I had gotten a job. I had an apartment with a candle that smelled like vanilla. I had constructed, brick by brick, night by night, therapy session by therapy session, a version of myself that could function — could go to work, could eat dinner, could watch television, could sleep until 6:47 — without the thing that happened at fourteen being the first fact of my existence. I had buried it. Not forgotten — you don't forget; forgetting is a fantasy sold by people who've never had anything worth forgetting — but buried. Placed in a sealed room in my mind, behind a door I'd locked with every tool my therapist had given me, and the FBI phone call was a hand on the doorknob.

I didn't call back because calling back meant opening the door. And opening the door meant being fourteen again. And being fourteen again meant the massage table and the two hundred dollars and the sound of his voice saying "good girl" in a tone that I have spent seventeen years trying to unhear and that I will spend the rest of my life trying to unhear and that I will die still hearing, because some sounds don't live in your ears. They live in your spine.

So I didn't call back. The investigation went forward without me. The plea deal happened without me. The sixteen months happened without me. The work release happened without me. The entire arc of American justice — such as it was, such as the word "justice" can be applied to sixteen months and work release and immunity for co-conspirators — happened without me. I wasn't part of it. I was in Jacksonville, weighing dogs.

And now he was arrested again. And my sister was crying. And the morning show hosts were discussing summer recipes. And I was sitting on the edge of my bed at 6:47 in the morning, waiting to feel something.

Here is what I felt, eventually. Not immediately — immediately I felt nothing, because nothing is the body's factory setting when the alternative is everything. But eventually, over the course of that day, between weighing a Labrador and taking a cat's temperature, I felt something I did not expect.

I felt tired.

Not relieved. Not vindicated. Not triumphant. Not hopeful that justice would finally be served, because I had seen what justice looked like in 2008 and justice looked like sixteen months and work release and a man walking out of a county jail and going back to the same house and doing the same things to different girls who were fourteen the way I had been fourteen.

Tired. The bone-deep, cellular exhaustion of a woman who has been carrying a sealed room inside her mind for seventeen years and who has just been told that the room is about to be opened — not by her, not on her terms, not with her therapist present and her candle burning and her television providing the wall of sound that keeps the silence from getting in — but by the federal government, on the federal government's schedule, in a federal courtroom, in front of cameras, in front of journalists, in front of the entire country, which will watch the proceedings and form opinions and argue about the implications and turn her sealed room into a public exhibit and her fourteen-year-old body into evidence and her worst day into everyone else's content.

That's what I felt. Tired. Because it was starting again. And this time, the whole world would be watching.

I called the FBI back. In 2019, seventeen years after I didn't call back. I called and I said I was ready. I said I would testify. I said I would open the door.

The agent was kind. She said they appreciated my courage. She said my testimony could make a difference. She said the case was strong.

He died five weeks later.

The door I'd spent seventeen years sealing shut, the door I'd finally agreed to open, the door that I'd walked toward with every molecule of courage my body could produce — that door became irrelevant. He died and the trial evaporated and the testimony I'd prepared — rehearsed in my therapist's office, practiced in front of my bathroom mirror, refined into sentences that a jury could hear without flinching because the witness had already flinched enough for everyone — that testimony went into a file.

A file. Next to thousands of other files. In a cabinet that nobody will open because the defendant is dead and dead men don't stand trial and the living men whose names are in the adjacent files have lawyers whose hourly rate exceeds my annual salary.

I went home. I lit the candle. I turned on the television. I sat on the edge of my bed.

6:47.

The subject completed her interview in a single session lasting approximately ninety minutes. She did not cry during the interview. She held a cup of coffee throughout and did not drink from it. When asked if she wished to add anything, she said: "I want people to know that the worst part isn't what he did. The worst part is that I was ready. I was finally ready. And the system took that from me too." The interview was published in a digital outlet with a modest readership. It received approximately twelve thousand views. On the same day, a cable news segment debating whether the death was suicide or murder received fourteen million.

Chapter 41: The Watch

Timeline: July 19 – August 9, 2019 | **Location:** Federal Metropolitan Detention Center

On July 23, 2019 — seventeen days after my arrest — I was found in my cell with marks on my neck.

Semi-conscious. On the floor. My cellmate — a former police officer awaiting trial on a quadruple murder charge, a man whose own capacity for violence was a matter of federal record and whose assignment to my cell raises questions that have never been satisfactorily answered — reported that he found me in that condition. He said he discovered me. He did not say he caused me.

The incident was classified as a possible suicide attempt. That's the official version — the version that generates the appropriate bureaucratic response, that triggers the appropriate protocols, that initiates the appropriate paperwork in a system that runs on paperwork the way a combustion engine runs on fuel.

I told my lawyers something different. I told them I was *attacked.* That someone — my cellmate or someone else, someone who entered the cell in the hours when the distinction between "cell" and "crime scene" depends entirely on who's watching — tried to strangle me. The marks on my neck were consistent with both interpretations. A man trying to kill himself and a man someone else is trying to kill leave similar marks. The difference is intent, and intent is invisible on skin.

The two accounts are contradictory. Both are possible. Neither was investigated with the rigor that a potential murder attempt inside a federal facility should demand. The former police officer was transferred. No charges were filed. No formal inquiry was opened. The incident was logged and forgotten — the way inconvenient things are always logged and forgotten in institutions that prefer not to know.

Following the incident, I was placed on suicide watch.

The federal protocol for inmates deemed at risk of self-harm is specific, detailed, and designed to make death by self-harm physically impossible. Constant observation — a trained counselor stationed outside the cell, eyes on the inmate at all times, documenting the inmate's status at intervals measured in minutes rather than hours. Paper-thin bedding — no sheets, no blankets, no fabric of any kind that could be fashioned into a ligature. The cell is stripped to its irreducible minimum: a mat, a paper gown, and the unblinking presence of another human being whose sole function is to ensure that the inmate survives the night.

Suicide watch is the most restrictive environment in the federal system — more restrictive than general population, more restrictive than solitary confinement, more restrictive than any condition I had ever experienced in a life that had, until seventeen days ago, been characterized by the absolute absence of restriction. I had spent forty years moving through the world with the frictionless ease of a man whose money dissolved every barrier and whose connections neutralized every constraint. On suicide watch, the barriers were concrete and the constraints were human and the money was irrelevant.

For a man who spent thirty years watching *other* people — filming them, recording them, documenting their most private moments with cameras they didn't know existed — the reversal was structurally appropriate. I was now inside the camera instead of behind it. And I can tell you: the view is terrible.

They put me on suicide watch. Which means someone sits outside your cell and stares at you, around the clock, while you lie on a mat thinner than a beach towel with no sheets, no blankets, and a light that never turns off. It's the opposite of my life. I spent thirty years watching other people. Now someone was watching me. For thirty years I had watched other people from behind the glass. Now I was the one on display, in eight-by-ten feet of concrete, under a light that never turned off. The reversal had a structural logic I could appreciate even while despising it.

On July 29 — six days after the incident — I was removed from suicide watch.

Six days. A man who was found with marks on his neck — who either attempted suicide or survived a murder attempt, and in either case demonstrated that the cell was not safe — was removed from the only protocol specifically designed to prevent his death after less than a week.

The decision was made by a staff psychologist at MDC. The rationale was documented in records that would later be scrutinized, debated, litigated, and found insufficient by virtually every independent expert who reviewed them. The psychological assessment that cleared me for removal from suicide watch was conducted by a mental health professional operating in a facility so understaffed that the assessment itself was likely compressed into a fraction of the time that a thorough evaluation would require — because MDC did not have the resources to provide thorough evaluations, because the Bureau of Prisons did not have the budget to staff MDC adequately, because the federal government did not have the political will to fund the Bureau of Prisons at a level that would prevent the exact series of failures that was about to occur.

Six days. The protocol says you remain on suicide watch until a qualified psychiatrist determines, through comprehensive evaluation, that you are no longer at risk. A determination was made. The determination was made quickly. The determination will be called premature by some and convenient by others, and the distinction between "premature" and "convenient" is, in this case, the distinction between tragedy and conspiracy.

They took me off suicide watch after six days. Six days. I'd spent more time waiting for a table at Nobu. The speed of the decision was either a testament to my psychological resilience or a testament to something else entirely. I'll let you decide which. But I'll give you a hint: I am many things, but psychologically resilient has never been one of them. I'm a man who controlled everything, and now I controlled nothing. That is not a person who recovers in six days.

After the removal from suicide watch, my cellmate was transferred out.

The replacement had been in position for fourteen months before I needed him.

Not *a* replacement — *the* replacement. Specific. Selected. Vetted the way I vetted everything: by specification first, then by availability, then by the progressive elimination of candidates who failed the one criterion that separated the workable from the useless. Institutional identity verification is a documentation problem, not a visual one. A federal medical examiner working a night shift in an understaffed facility does not look at a body and think: *is this the man?* He looks at the intake photograph attached to the file and thinks: *is this consistent?* Consistent. That is the operational word. Not identical. Not a twin. Consistent — close enough in age and proportion and the general architecture of a face that nobody who has already decided what they're looking at will think to look again.

He was sixty-four. Six foot one. One hundred and ninety pounds within twelve months of a sustained dietary protocol that I had, through channels whose names I will not write, managed to monitor. The facial structure — the jaw, the orbital distance, the specific geography of features that a file photograph reduces to a two-dimensional pattern — was sufficiently proximate that a surgeon I will also not name made three targeted adjustments over eight months to close the remaining gap. Not transformation. *Calibration.* The photographs in my file were taken on the morning of my arrest. I was tired. The lighting was institutional. The frame was tight. The result was an image that, compared to a man whose face had been calibrated toward it by a careful hand and adequate time, would pass every check that a documentation-dependent system performs.

The system would look at the paperwork. I had arranged the paperwork.

This is what thirty years of operating inside institutional logic teaches you: every system has a verification threshold, and the threshold is always lower than the system believes it is. You don't defeat institutional verification by overwhelming it. You defeat it by being *just* sufficient. Just sufficient is invisible. Just sufficient looks like confirmation. Just sufficient makes the night-shift examiner sign the form and go home, because the form is what he was asked to sign and the man on the table is what he was told to expect and the cameras — I know cameras — are not recording anything useful.

I had learned this from a building full of senators who thought they were choosing to attend my dinners.

Nobody chooses anything. They confirm what they've already been told to expect. The confirmation is the system. The system was always mine.

On August 9th. The night before I died.

In a federal facility where overcrowding is so severe that inmates sleep on the floor, where double-bunking is the norm, where cells designed for one hold two or three as a matter of routine operational necessity — I slept alone. On the night of August 9th, 2019. The night before the most important federal inmate in America would be found dead.

The transfer was not explained. The timing was not explained. The decision to leave a recently suicidal inmate — a man who had been found with marks on his neck seventeen days earlier, who had been placed on and then removed from suicide watch, who was facing federal sex trafficking charges carrying a mandatory minimum of ten years — in a cell *by himself,* in a facility that was supposed to check on him every thirty minutes, was not explained. It was, however, *documented.* Because everything in MDC is documented. Transfer logs. Cell assignment records. Administrative memos. The paperwork exists. The paperwork always exists. And documentation, as I know better than anyone, is only as useful as the person reading it.

My cellmate was transferred out. The night before I died, I was alone in a cell in a federal detention facility where nobody sleeps alone because there aren't enough cells. But I slept alone. In a building where they're supposed to check on you every thirty minutes. The distinction between "where they check" and "where they're supposed to check" is the most important distinction in this story. It's the space between policy and practice. Between what the rules say and what the guards do. I built my entire career in that space. I just didn't expect to die in it.

Two guards were assigned to my unit on the night of August 9th, 2019.

They were required by federal regulation to conduct rounds every thirty minutes — walking past each cell, visually confirming the inmate's condition, and logging the check. The rounds are the most fundamental safety protocol in the federal detention system. They are the mechanism by which the Bureau of Prisons fulfills its constitutional obligation to ensure the safety of inmates in its custody. They are the line between a detention facility and a death chamber.

The guards did not conduct rounds. They did not check on me. They did not check on anyone. According to the subsequent investigation, both guards fell asleep at their desk and failed to perform any rounds for approximately eight hours. Both guards later admitted to falsifying the check-in logs — signing off on rounds they never made, documenting observations they never conducted, certifying the safety of inmates they never saw.

One of the guards was working his fifth consecutive overtime shift — a schedule that would be considered dangerous in any profession and that, in a profession whose responsibilities include ensuring the physical safety of human beings, constitutes a structural failure so profound that it implicates not just the individual guard but the entire administrative chain that authorized the schedule. The other was not a regular corrections officer but a fill-in employee — a person who was assigned to the unit not because of specialized training or demonstrated competence but because the facility could not find anyone else to fill the slot.

These were the two people standing between me and whatever happened in the night.

Two guards were assigned to watch me. Two guards fell asleep. Both of them. For the entire night. In a facility that has housed terrorists, cartel leaders, and mob bosses without a single comparable lapse. Both guards, on the same night, in the same shift, at the same time. Asleep. If you believe that's a coincidence, you believe in coincidences. I don't. I've spent my entire life engineering situations that *look* like coincidences. I know what a real coincidence looks like. And I know what a manufactured one looks like. This looks manufactured. But I'm biased. I would say that. Wouldn't I.

The federal detention facility has security cameras covering the exterior of every cell in the Special Housing Unit. On the night of August 9th, 2019, two cameras with a view of my cell malfunctioned. Both of them. Simultaneously.

The footage is described variously as "unusable," "corrupted," and "insufficient" — the precise term depends on which federal agency is asked and on what day the question is posed. The footage is not missing in the sense that it was never recorded. It is missing in the sense that what was recorded cannot be used — cannot be played, cannot be analyzed, cannot tell the story of what happened in the hours when the guards were asleep and the cellmate was gone and the spider was alone in his concrete box.

In a building where security footage is the primary accountability mechanism for inmate safety — where the cameras are the institutional memory, the only witness that cannot be bribed or intimidated or transferred — the two cameras covering the highest-profile inmate in the facility both fail on the same night that both guards fall asleep and the cellmate has been removed.

Each individual failure has a mundane explanation. The cameras are old — MDC's infrastructure is aging, underfunded, maintained with the institutional indifference that characterizes facilities whose occupants have no political advocate. The guards are overworked — the Bureau of Prisons' staffing crisis is documented, studied, and unfixed. The cellmate transfer is routine — inmates are moved between cells constantly, for a variety of administrative reasons.

But the simultaneous convergence of *every* failure, on *this* night, for *this* inmate — the removal from suicide watch, the cellmate transfer, the sleeping guards, the falsified logs, the malfunctioning cameras — that is not a mundane explanation. That is either the most catastrophic coincidence in American corrections or something else entirely.

I've spent my life in the surveillance business. I know cameras. I know what "malfunction" means when it happens to one camera: bad luck. I know what "malfunction" means when it happens to two cameras on the same night in the same hallway covering the same cell of the most high-profile inmate in the federal system: it means someone made a decision. Cameras don't malfunction. They're turned off. By people. With keys. On purpose.

Chapter 42: The Voices—Nine Testimonies

Timeline: 1984–2025 | **Location:** Everywhere

You've heard my version. You've sat in my dining room, flown on my plane, walked through my properties. You've listened to me explain the architecture — the cameras, the money, the blackmail, the appetites. I've been a generous narrator. I've given you more than any prosecutor ever extracted, more than any journalist ever published, more than any of them ever knew.

Now listen to them. They lived inside it.

I'm going to be quiet for a while. Not because I want to. Because they've earned this.

I. The Spa Girl

I was sixteen and I thought I was lucky.

That's the part nobody understands — not the journalists, not the lawyers, not the therapists I've been seeing for two decades. They all want to start with the bad part. They want the horror story. But the horror story doesn't make sense without the lucky part, because the lucky part is how they get you. The lucky part *is* the trap.

I was working at the spa at the resort. Towels. Locker room. Minimum wage plus whatever the members tipped, which wasn't much because rich people are the worst tippers on earth — that's not bitterness, that's data. I'd been bounced around. Group homes. My father's house, which was worse than the group homes. The streets, which were worse than my father's house. By sixteen I'd already learned that the world was a series of rooms you survived until you got to the next room, and the spa at the resort was the nicest room I'd been in so far.

She found me there. The woman. Elegant. British accent. Hair like she'd just stepped off a yacht, which she probably had. She watched me fold towels for a few minutes before she spoke, and when she spoke, she said the words that every girl in this story heard in some version or another: *I know someone who can help you.*

A massage therapist position. Real training. Travel. The man was a philanthropist — he helped young women get started. He was connected to everyone. He was generous. He was kind.

I believed her because I wanted to believe her, and because I was sixteen, and because when you've spent your whole childhood being told you're worthless, the first person who tells you you're special owns you. That's not a metaphor. That's the mechanism. They don't recruit girls who feel safe. They recruit girls who are drowning and they throw what looks like a rope and is actually a leash.

The first visit to the townhouse was almost normal. Almost. The building was enormous — the biggest private home I'd ever been inside, and I'd cleaned houses for cash so I'd been inside some big ones. But this was different. This was a museum that someone lived in. Paintings on every wall. A grand piano nobody played. Framed photographs of the man with people I recognized from television — presidents, actors, scientists. The photographs were placed where you couldn't miss them. I understand now that the photographs were the first weapon. They said: *This man is important. This man is connected. This man is protected. Who are you going to tell?*

The woman showed me around. She was warm. Sisterly, almost. She touched my hair and told me I was beautiful and asked about my family and listened with what I mistook for compassion. She was cataloging me. She was checking my inventory — no stable parents, no money, no support system, no one who would come looking. I passed inspection.

The man was charming. Funny. He asked about my life and seemed genuinely interested. He told me about his foundation, his scientists, his plans to change the world. He made me feel like I was being invited into something important — like my presence mattered, like I wasn't just another damaged teenager but someone with potential that the right mentor could unlock.

That's the trick. That's always the trick. They don't drag you into a van. They open the door to a mansion and they tell you you belong there.

The training started. The "massages" started. What they actually were started. And by the time I understood what was happening, I was on an airplane and the airplane was in the air and below me was the ocean and on the other side of the ocean was a country where I knew no one and had no money and didn't speak the language and the woman told me in that warm sisterly voice that I should be grateful, that other girls would kill for this opportunity, that the man I was about to meet was very important and very powerful and that I should do for him what I did for her employer.

The man was royalty. Real royalty. Title, castle, family on the currency. We went to a nightclub. He danced badly and laughed too loud and acted like a man who had never been told no in his life because he hadn't. Later, in the car, the woman gave me my instructions the way you'd give a caterer the menu.

I was seventeen by then. Old enough to understand what was happening. Too deep to get out.

They'll tell you we could have left. That's what they always say — the people who've never been on a private island with no phone, no passport, no money, and a staff that works for the man who brought you there. Try leaving. Try walking to the airport when there is no airport. Try calling the police when the police have been to dinner at the house.

I got out eventually. I married a good man. I moved as far from that world as geography allowed. I spent fifteen years building a life and twenty years trying to destroy the people who stole the first one. I founded an organization. I testified. I sued. I fought every day until the fighting was all I had left and the fighting wasn't enough.

There's a photograph of me. I'm seventeen in it. There's a man's arm around my waist — a royal arm, worth more than my entire bloodline in the economy of inherited power. We're both smiling. The camera flash preserved evidence that would take fifteen years to matter, and even then, he settled and I settled and nobody went to prison and he kept his name until he didn't and I kept my rage until I couldn't.

I chose a blue butterfly as the symbol for my organization. Blue is the international color of human trafficking awareness. Butterflies represent transformation — the victim becoming the survivor. I liked that. I needed that. The girl who folded towels becoming the woman who testified before Congress.

I'm not here anymore. I died on a farm on the other side of the world, in a country where the sky is big and the ground is flat and nobody knew my story unless I told them. I was forty-one. I fought for twenty-five years and then I was tired and the tiredness won.

But I wrote it down first. I wrote everything down. And the book is out there now, with my name on it, and the names inside it are the names of the men who did this, and the book will outlast all of them.

Including me.

II. The Boy on the Yacht

I don't remember boarding the yacht. I remember leaving it.

I remember the dock. I remember my legs not working right — the way you walk when your body doesn't feel like your body anymore, when the connection between your brain and your feet has been severed by something you don't have a word for because you're fourteen and the word hasn't been invented yet for what happened in that room below deck.

The man who brought me was someone my family trusted. He wore a suit that cost more than our car. He told my mother I was gifted — that I had potential, that he wanted to mentor me, that the people on this yacht were investors and philanthropists who helped young people from families like ours.

Families like ours. That phrase. He said it the way you'd say "damaged goods" if you were too polite to say "damaged goods." He meant poor. He meant the kind of family where a missing boy wouldn't make the news. Where the parents would be too ashamed to go to the police, and too broke to hire a lawyer, and too beaten down by life to believe that anyone would listen.

They target us. That's the thing I need you to understand. This isn't random. This isn't opportunity. This is *selection*. They choose children the way a predator chooses prey — the weakest, the most isolated, the ones at the edge of the herd. Rich men in suits scouting poor neighborhoods for children whose parents are too tired or too desperate or too absent to protect them. That's not a conspiracy theory. That's a *business model.*

The yacht was beautiful. I'd never been on a boat that big. The wood was polished, the brass was gleaming, the glasses on the table were crystal. Everything was expensive and everything was clean and the cleanliness was the most disorienting part because the thing that was about to happen in that clean, expensive space was the dirtiest thing imaginable, and the contrast — the yacht and the act — is what breaks your brain. If it happened in a dirty room, you could file it where dirty things go. When it happens on a yacht with crystal glasses, your brain doesn't have a drawer for it.

There were other men. Some I recognized from the photographs in the townhouse. Older. White. Powerful in the way that only comes from a lifetime of never being questioned. They looked at me the way you'd look at a menu. Not with cruelty, exactly — with something worse than cruelty. With *nothing*. With the absence of recognition that I was a person. I was a feature of the evening. I was the entertainment.

They didn't tie me up. They didn't need to. We were on open water. Where was I going to go? The ocean was the restraint. The money was the restraint. The fact that nobody knew where I was and nobody would believe me if I told them — *that* was the restraint. They'd built a floating prison without bars and they knew it and I knew it and the knowing was part of it.

One of the men had a knife. Not a regular knife — something ceremonial, curved, old-looking. He showed it to me the way a collector shows you a painting. *This is very rare. Very old. Do you know what it's for?* I didn't answer. He ran it along the bottom of my foot. Not deep enough to scar. Deep enough to teach me that he could.

Afterward — and I'm not going to tell you what "afterward" contained because the afterward belongs to me and not to you — I sat on the deck and looked at the water and thought about jumping. The water was dark and cold and very deep and jumping would have been the easiest thing I've ever done. I didn't jump. I don't know why. Something in me that was too stubborn or too stupid or too young to know that what had just happened was going to follow me for the rest of my life decided to stay on the deck and wait for the yacht to dock.

It docked. I walked off on legs that didn't work. The man who brought me drove me home and told me that if I told anyone, he would explain to my mother that I had participated willingly, that I had been paid, that I had done things no boy my age should know how to do, and that my family would be destroyed by the shame of what I had chosen.

Chosen. He used that word. I was fourteen.

I didn't tell anyone for twenty-five years. In 2019, I walked into an FBI field office and sat down in a gray room with a metal table and two agents who had notepads and coffee cups and the specific facial expression of people who have heard a lot of terrible things and have been trained to hear more. I told them everything. Every detail. The yacht, the men, the knife, the water.

They wrote it down. One of them made a note in the margin of the report. I found out later what the note said. It said: *Unsubstantiated.*

They said I was emotionally unbalanced. They were right. Being on that yacht unbalanced me. That was the point.

III. The Model from Monterrey

They will tell you I was crazy. Remember that when you can't find me.

I was a model. Twenty-one. Working in Mexico City, Monterrey, sometimes across the border. The industry is a pipeline — you enter at one end looking like a girl who might be on a magazine cover and you exit at the other end looking like a girl who has seen things that don't go on magazine covers. In between, there are men. Always men. Men with money, men with connections, men who own the agencies and the hotels and the magazines and the governments and who look at a twenty-one-year-old model the way a butcher looks at meat — assessing weight, assessing value, assessing how much of you is usable.

I was introduced to a circle. That's how they phrase it — "introduced." As if it's a party. As if you're being welcomed. The circle included politicians, businessmen, cartel-adjacent men whose money came from places nobody discussed. Some of them were connected to the American network — the billionaire on the island, the operation with the planes and the cameras. The circles overlapped. The Mexican circle and the American circle shared clients the way neighboring restaurants share a supplier.

I went to a dinner. Private. Exclusive. A villa outside the city, gated, guarded, the kind of property where the walls are high enough to block the view and the staff are paid enough to block their memory. I was told it was networking. I was told the men at this dinner could make my career.

The dinner was wrong.

I knew it from the moment the plates were uncovered. I knew it from the smell — not a food smell, not any smell I could place, but a *wrongness* in the air, a chemical sweetness that my body recognized before my mind did. I looked at the plate. I looked at the faces of the men eating. They were calm. Some of them were smiling. One of them caught my eye and winked, the way you'd wink at someone who's in on the joke.

I wasn't in on the joke.

I left that dinner in a car that smelled like cologne and cigar smoke and I went back to my apartment and I sat on the bathroom floor for three hours. I didn't eat for a week. I started using — cocaine first, then whatever was available — because the drugs were the only thing that stood between me and the memory, and the memory was the kind that doesn't go away, the kind that lives in your body and surfaces when you smell certain things or see certain textures on a plate.

I kept quiet for months. They paid me. Not a lot — enough to communicate that I was now a paid participant, that accepting the money made me complicit, that the money was a receipt they could produce if I ever talked. *You were paid. You attended voluntarily. You ate what was served.* The money was a trap with a dollar sign on it.

Then one day in Monterrey, standing outside a hotel, I broke.

I don't remember deciding to scream. I remember the sound coming out of me — not words at first, just sound, the sound a body makes when it has been containing something it can't contain anymore. Then words. Words about what I'd seen. What they'd done. What was on the plates. I was pointing at people — at the police, at the bystanders, at the hotel doorman — and screaming that they were all part of it, that everyone was part of it, that the entire structure of power in this country was built on the bones of children.

Someone filmed it. Of course someone filmed it. We live in a world where everything is filmed and nothing is investigated.

The police came. They didn't ask me what I was screaming about. They asked me if I was on drugs. They asked me if I was having a psychiatric episode. They asked me every question except the one that mattered, which was: *What did you see?*

They handcuffed me. They put me in a car. The car drove away from the hotel and I watched the crowd disappear through the rear window and I knew — with the certainty that only comes from having seen how the system actually works — that I was never going to tell this story again. Not because I chose to stop. Because someone was going to stop me.

The video went on the internet. It circulated for years. People watched it the way they watch videos of UFOs and Bigfoot — as entertainment, as spectacle, as proof of nothing except that the world contains crazy people who scream outside hotels.

Put a true thing next to enough false things and the true thing becomes invisible. That's not a bug. That's a feature. And the men who ate dinner at that villa understand this better than anyone alive.

I'm not going to tell you where I am now. I'm not sure anyone can.

IV. Thirteen

My uncle said we were going on a boat ride.

I was thirteen. I was pregnant. I didn't really understand being pregnant except that my stomach was big and I was tired all the time and my uncle said I needed to be somewhere private until it was over.

The boats were on a big lake. There were yachts — I didn't know that word then, I just called them big boats. My uncle knew the men on the big boats. They wore nice clothes. They smelled like the cologne counter at the department store, all of them, like they all used the same bottle.

My uncle told me to be nice to them. He said they were helping us. He said the money was for my future.

There were other girls on the boats sometimes. Some younger than me. Some older. We didn't talk much. We looked at each other the way animals look at each other in the same cage — recognizing the shared situation without being able to name it or change it.

The men came and went. Some were regulars. Some I only saw once. One man was different from the others — he was the one who organized things, the one everyone else deferred to. He talked more than the others. He smiled more. He looked at me the way you look at furniture you're thinking about buying — checking for defects, estimating how long it would last.

I had my baby on one of the boats. There was no doctor. There was a woman who knew how to deliver a baby and she delivered mine and my baby was a girl and my baby cried and I reached for her.

They took her.

My uncle took her. He carried her up to the deck. I could still hear her crying — that thin, new sound that a baby makes when it's just arrived in the world and doesn't know yet what kind of world it's arrived in.

Then the crying stopped.

Then there was a splash.

Then there was nothing.

The man — the organizer, the one who smiled — was on the deck. I heard his voice through the walls of the cabin where they were holding me. He sounded disappointed. Not horrified. Not disgusted. *Disappointed.* Like a missed opportunity. He said something about his chef. He said something about what could have been done with the ingredients. The men around him laughed. Some of them laughed.

I was thirteen years old. I had just given birth. My baby was in the water. And a man on the deck above me was making a joke about eating her.

I went home. My uncle drove me. He told me that if I said anything to anyone, he would tell my mother I had been a prostitute and that the baby was the proof and that the shame would kill her. I believed him. I was thirteen and I believed everything adults told me because that's what thirteen-year-olds do.

I didn't tell anyone for thirty-six years.

In 2020, I filed a tip with the FBI. I wrote down everything. Every detail I could remember. The lake. The yachts. My uncle. The men. My baby. The splash. The joke.

They wrote it down. I don't know if they read it. I don't know if anyone investigated. I know that the document exists now, in a stack of three million pages, released to a public that will skim it and share it and argue about whether it's true and then move on to the next document, the next scandal, the next thing that trends for forty-eight hours before the algorithm replaces it with something else.

My baby's name was going to be Maria. I never got to call her that.

V. The Transgender Model

Let me save you the trouble: yes, I'm trans. Now can we talk about what he did?

I know how this works. I've been through it before. The moment my identity enters the story, the story stops being about a sixteen-year-old who was assaulted by a billionaire and becomes about a sixteen-year-old's chromosomes. That's the trick. That's always been the trick. When they couldn't discredit what I said, they discredited what I am.

I was sixteen. I was Latina. I was living in New York and I wanted to be a model — not an unusual dream for a sixteen-year-old, trans or otherwise. A man connected to the lingerie empire — you know the one, everybody knows the one, the brand that sold a fantasy of femininity to the entire world — told me he could get me in. He could introduce me to the right people. He knew a man who funded things, who helped young people, who had connections to every agency and every magazine and every door that mattered.

The townhouse on the Gold Coast was the biggest house I'd ever been in. The man was charming. He told me I was beautiful. He told me I was special. He told me I had a body that could make me famous. He used those words — "your body" — like it was a product he was evaluating, a thing separate from me, a thing he had opinions about.

He asked me to undress. He said it was part of the modeling evaluation. I'd been told that models undress for evaluations — that this was normal, professional, part of the business. I was sixteen and I didn't know that the business doesn't usually happen in a billionaire's bedroom with the door locked.

What happened next is mine. I'll give you the edges of it: I said no, and the no didn't work. I tried to leave, and the door didn't open. He was bigger than me. Older than me. Richer than me. More powerful than me. And when it was over, he handed me money the way you'd tip a valet and told me I had a great career ahead of me if I was smart.

If I was smart meant if I was quiet.

I was quiet for nine years. The quiet cost $28,000 — that's what they paid me to sign a piece of paper that said I would never talk about what happened in that bedroom. Twenty-eight thousand dollars for my silence. For context, that's less than he spent on a single dinner party. That's the market rate for a poor trans teenager's trauma in the economy of the extremely wealthy: less than the catering.

In 2007, I broke the silence. I filed a lawsuit. I named him. I thought — stupidly, beautifully, impossibly — that the system might work. That a courtroom might believe a girl over a billionaire.

The newspaper got the story. But they didn't write the story I told. They wrote a different story — the story of what was between my legs. "Gender-Bend Shocker," the headline said. They published my medical history. They published my HIV status. They published details about my body that I hadn't shared with anyone outside a doctor's office. They turned my lawsuit into a freak show and my assault into a punchline.

His lawyer went on record. He said — and I will carry this sentence in my body until the day I die — "It wouldn't surprise me if the next claim was from the Loch Ness Monster."

The Loch Ness Monster. That's what I was. Not a sixteen-year-old who had been raped. A mythical creature. An impossibility. Something that doesn't exist.

The case was dismissed. Not because I lied. Not because the evidence didn't hold up. Because the statute of limitations had expired while I was still trying to survive what he did to me. The clock ran out on justice while I was running from the damage.

Here's the part that keeps me up at night: I was one of the first. In 2007 — two years before the sweetheart plea deal, twelve years before the federal arrest, eighteen years before the files dropped — I stood up in a courtroom and said *this man assaulted me* and the world responded by investigating my genitals.

If they had believed me — one trans girl, one Latina, one teenager with nothing but the truth and a medical record and a $28,000 check with his signature on it — over a thousand girls might have been spared. The pipeline would have been shut down in 2007 instead of running for another twelve years. The girls who came after me — the ones who were recruited and transported and used and discarded between 2007 and 2019 — would have been safe.

But they didn't believe me. Because I was trans. Because I was poor. Because I was brown. Because the man was a billionaire and I was the Loch Ness Monster.

Remember that the next time someone tells you a story you don't want to believe. Ask yourself: Are you rejecting the story, or are you rejecting the storyteller?

VI. The Kid on the Poster

You know my face. You don't know this.

I was fifteen. Already famous. Already on magazine covers and billboards and the screensavers of a million teenage girls' computers. Already surrounded by adults who wanted something from me — money, access, reflected fame, the specific energy that radiates from a young person who has been told by the world that they are extraordinary.

A man in the industry — not my manager, not my producer, someone adjacent, someone who occupied the gray space between business and friendship that the entertainment industry creates and exploits — told me I needed to meet the right people. The *real* people. The ones who controlled things from above the level I could see.

"You're talented," he said, "but talent doesn't protect you. *Connections* protect you. These are the people who decide who gets protected."

I went to a party at a house in Manhattan. Private. Maybe twenty people. I was the youngest by a decade. The men in the room were old enough to be my father, my grandfather. They were in finance, politics, entertainment. They had the kind of confidence that comes from never having been told they were wrong — the kind that fills a room and uses up all the oxygen.

One of them looked at me and said something to the man standing next to him. I couldn't hear the words. I could hear the tone. It was the tone of appraisal. Of appetite. Of a customer examining merchandise. The man next to him nodded and looked at me and smiled and the smile didn't reach his eyes.

I should have left. I know that now. But I was fifteen, and fifteen-year-olds don't leave rooms full of powerful adults because fifteen-year-olds have been trained their entire lives to defer to authority, to be polite, to be grateful for the opportunity, to not make a scene.

The mentor took me upstairs. He told me what was going to happen. He told me it was how the industry worked. He told me that every star I admired had been through this — that this was the door everyone walked through, the price of entry, the thing you did once and never spoke about and then you were in and the career was yours and nobody would ever ask you about it.

He was lying about the "once" part.

I'm not going to tell you what happened in that room because the room belongs to me and I am keeping it. What I will tell you is this: I didn't say no because I didn't know how to say no. I didn't fight because fighting would have ended my career and my career was the only thing I had that felt real. And when it was over, the mentor drove me home and told me I had done well and that the men were impressed and that my future was secure.

My future. The years that followed — the drugs, the breakdowns, the public behavior that the tabloids called "erratic" and "troubled" and "off the rails." The videos of me crying in parking lots. The shaved head. The canceled shows. The interventions. The rehab. The comeback. The relapse. The comeback. The relapse. The endless, grinding cycle of a person trying to outrun something that happened in a room when he was fifteen.

They wrote about me constantly. The tabloids. The blogs. The entertainment shows. They analyzed my behavior the way sports commentators analyze a player's statistics — clinically, publicly, without ever once asking the question that would have explained everything: *What happened to that kid?*

I'll tell you what happened to that kid. A room happened to him. And he's been trying to leave that room for twenty years and the door doesn't open from the inside.

I've never said this publicly. I'm saying it now. Not with my name attached — not yet, maybe not ever — because the industry that did this to me is the same industry that pays my bills, and the men who were in that room are still in rooms like it, and the system that allowed it hasn't changed, it's just gotten better at keeping the doors closed.

But I'm saying it. That counts for something. A boy who was famous and broken is saying: they did this to me too. Not just the girls. The boys too. And the fame doesn't protect you. The fame makes it worse because the fame means everyone is watching and nobody is seeing.

VII. The Recruiter's Daughter

March 12. Today I signed the papers for the house. Three bedrooms. Half acre. John says we can get chickens.

March 15. Went to Home Depot. Picked out paint for the kids' rooms. Blue for the boys. Lilac for the girls. Lilac was my favorite color when I was fourteen, before everything. Still is, I guess. Some things survive.

March 18. Nightmares again. The mansion. The massage table. The woman's hands on my body, checking me like produce. "Great body type," she said. I was fourteen. Great body type for what?

March 20. Called Mom. She cried. Happy tears for once. She says she's proud of me. I don't know how to hold that — someone being proud of me. It sits in my chest like something too big for the space it's in.

I was fourteen when a friend — a girl from my neighborhood who was also fourteen, who had been there before, who had been taught to bring others — told me I could make three hundred dollars in an hour. Easy money. Just a massage. The man was rich and he liked massages and he paid cash and it wasn't weird, she said. It wasn't what I thought.

It was what I thought.

The mansion in Gulf Shore was the kind of place I'd only seen from the outside — the kind of place my mother cleaned for women who didn't learn her name. I walked in through a side door. The staff didn't look at me. They'd seen a hundred girls walk through that door and they'd learned not to look.

The woman met me in the hallway. Older. Beautiful. The kind of beautiful that requires money to maintain. She looked at my body the way a horse trader looks at a horse — checking the teeth, the legs, the overall condition. She touched me. My chest. My hips. She said I had a great body type for Mr.— and she said his name like it was a title, like it was something I should be impressed by.

I was fourteen. I was terrified. I was three hundred dollars away from being able to buy my mother groceries.

The massage wasn't a massage. The three hundred dollars was real. The man told me to come back. The woman scheduled my next appointment. And the next. And the next. For four years, I went back. Not because I wanted to. Because the money was the only steady thing in my life, and because by the second visit they had made it clear — not with threats, not with violence, but with the quiet certainty of people who have eliminated all your options — that leaving wasn't available.

I started using after the first year. Cocaine. Pills. Whatever stopped the replay in my head — the massage table, the room, the sounds, the three hundred dollars on the nightstand like a receipt for my childhood. The drugs were the only off-switch I could find, and I pressed it so many times that by the time I was eighteen I couldn't function without them.

March 25. John found the bathroom. I was using. He didn't yell. He just sat on the floor next to me and held my hand and said we'd figure it out. I don't deserve him. But maybe deserving isn't the point. Maybe the point is just surviving long enough to get to the part where someone sits on the floor next to you.

In 2021, I testified. I walked into a courtroom and sat in a chair and looked at the woman — the one who had touched my body when I was fourteen and said "great body type" — and I told the jury what she did. What he did. What all of them did. The defense attorney said I was a drug addict. That I was a liar. That my criminal record made me unreliable. As if the criminal record and the drug addiction and the unreliability weren't caused by the thing I was there to testify about.

A juror said later that my testimony was the most gripping thing he'd ever heard. He said: "She told the truth every step of the way."

I told the truth. The woman got twenty years. I got a settlement check and a new house and a chicken coop and three bedrooms and lilac paint and the first twelve months of peace I'd had since I was thirteen years old.

May 22. North Carolina is beautiful. The chickens arrived yesterday. The kids are in love with them. John is building the coop. I watched him from the kitchen window and I thought: this is what normal looks like. This is what they stole from me and I stole it back.

May 23.

That's the last entry.

They found her in a hotel room in West Gulf Shore. Fentanyl. Her husband found her. Her children were in the next room.

She was thirty-six. She had survived the mansion and the massage table and the woman's hands and the drugs and the courtroom and the cross-examination and the defense attorney calling her a liar and the twenty years of damage. She had survived all of it. And then the surviving stopped.

She is the second survivor from that county to die of an overdose. The first was twenty-nine.

Their mother said: *"Do you know how many days I've sat in my room crying? She was ecstatic. She had a new house. She was clean. And then she was gone."*

The chicken coop is empty now.

VIII. The Woman Who Worked for Him

I was employee number four. My job title was Executive Personal Assistant. My actual job had no title because the English language hasn't invented a word for what I did.

I was eighteen. Legal. That distinction mattered — it was the crack in the wall that separated me from the girls, the hairline fracture between "victim" and "participant" that the legal system and the press and eventually my own conscience would use to sort me into a category that felt wrong but was technically accurate. I was an adult. I was making choices. The choices were made inside a cage, but the cage was invisible and the door appeared to be open.

My first week was normal. Scheduling. Travel arrangements. Phone calls. The man was demanding but professional. The woman — his partner, his coordinator, his whatever she was — trained me on the systems: the calendars, the properties, the staff protocols, the flight manifests. It was corporate. Organized. The efficiency of a well-run operation that happened to be the most prolific sex trafficking enterprise in the Western Hemisphere.

The first request that wasn't normal came six weeks in. "Find someone." That's what she said. "He needs someone for this evening. Young. Pretty. New to the city." I thought she meant a date. I thought I was doing what executive assistants in New York do for wealthy bachelor bosses — finding appropriate dinner companions, making restaurant reservations, the glamorous administrative work that movies tell you about.

I made a call. I found someone. The someone was nineteen, fresh off a bus from the Midwest, working at a café in the Village. I told her what I'd been told to tell: a wealthy philanthropist, a beautiful home, good conversation, career connections. I heard the hope in her voice — the same hope I'd had three months earlier when I accepted this job.

She went. She came back changed. Not crying — something worse than crying. She was *flat*. Blank. Like someone had erased something behind her eyes. She collected the cash and left without speaking and I never saw her again.

The second request came the following week. The third, the week after that. By the sixth month, "find someone" was the core of my job. I stopped thinking about what the phrase meant. I stopped connecting the request to the result. I developed the specific professional numbness that allows people to do terrible things inside bureaucratic structures — the same numbness that allows prison guards to walk past cells, that allows administrators to process paperwork for systems they know are destroying people.

I scheduled girls the way I'd schedule meetings. Monday at 4, Wednesday at 7, Friday at 3 and again at 6. I used first names only. I kept notes on preferences — not mine, *his* preferences. Hair color. Body type. Age. Ethnicity. The notes were organized in a filing system that I maintained with the same meticulousness I'd have applied to a client database at any legitimate corporation. I was good at my job. I was exceptional at my job. That's the part that haunts me.

The man never threatened me. He didn't need to. The threat was structural. I knew what the girls went through because I'd gone through a version of it — milder, because I was staff, but enough to understand that the line between employee and victim was a line he could erase whenever he chose. I knew about the cameras. I knew about the files. I knew that every person who passed through those properties was documented, recorded, stored — and that the documentation was the leash that kept everyone in orbit.

I could have left. Technically. The door was right there. But leaving meant admitting what I'd done — the calls I'd made, the girls I'd sent, the system I'd maintained. Leaving meant becoming a witness, and witnesses in this operation had a way of becoming victims or suspects or both. Leaving meant starting over with nothing and no one and the knowledge that I had been, for years, the smiling voice on the phone that lured girls into the building.

There's a legal term for what I became: unindicted co-conspirator. Named publicly. Not as a victim. Not as a survivor. As a *collaborator*. And the term is accurate. I was. I collaborated. I was also eighteen years old and terrified and embedded in a system designed by a genius of manipulation who understood that the most effective way to trap someone is to make them complicit in their own entrapment.

Was I a monster? Was I a hostage? Was I a victim who became a perpetrator who was still, underneath, a victim?

I don't know. I've been asking myself that question for twenty years and the answer changes depending on which face I see when I close my eyes — mine, or theirs.

I'm not asking for your forgiveness. I'm not sure I'd accept it if you offered. What I'm asking is for you to hold both truths at the same time: that I was used, and that I was useful. That I was trapped, and that I helped build the trap. That I am sorry, and that sorry doesn't fix anything, and that the man who designed this system — the man who could turn an eighteen-year-old girl into a cog in his machine in six weeks flat — understood human nature better than anyone I've ever met.

That was his real genius. Not the money. Not the blackmail. Not the cameras. The genius was the ability to make everyone — the victims, the staff, the scientists, the politicians, the princes — complicit. To spread the guilt so thin that no single person bore enough of it to act. To build a web so intricate that pulling any single thread would bring the whole thing down on top of the person pulling it.

We were all trapped. Some of us more than others. The difference between me and the girls I sent into that room is a matter of degree, not of kind. And the man who created that system — who calibrated the degree of each person's entrapment with the precision of an engineer — is the only one who ever fully understood what he built.

He's dead now. The machine isn't.

IX. The Boy from the Ranch

I'm missing two fingers on my left hand.

People ask. They always ask. In job interviews. At the grocery store. On dates, when dates still happened, before I stopped letting people close enough to see the hand, which meant close enough to ask, which meant close enough to hear the answer, which meant close enough to leave.

I tell them a farming accident. Thresher. Grew up in the country. People accept that. People accept farming accidents the way they accept weather — as something that happens to other people in places they've never been. Nobody asks follow-up questions about threshers. Nobody wants the details of agricultural machinery. The lie is boring enough to be true, and boring lies are the safest kind.

The truth is a ranch in New Mexico. The truth is a room with a medical table. The truth is a man in surgical scrubs who treated my body the way a mechanic treats a car — with professional interest, with technical precision, with absolute indifference to the fact that the car is screaming.

I was fifteen. I came from a family that didn't have the money or the connections or the language skills to ask where I'd gone. I was picked up. I was transported. I arrived at a property that was so far from anything that the silence had texture — thick, dense silence, the kind of silence that tells you that there is no one to hear you. That the nearest human ear that isn't in on it is forty miles of desert away. That the landscape itself is complicit.

The surgeon was calm. I want you to understand that. He was *calm.* He wasn't nervous. He wasn't rushed. He wasn't a man you'd picture doing what he did. He looked like a doctor. He smelled like antiseptic. He had clean nails and steady hands and he explained what he was going to do — not to me, to the men watching — with the composed, clinical vocabulary of a man presenting at a medical conference. He used terms I didn't know. He referenced procedures. He described recovery timelines.

Recovery. Like I was going to recover. Like the plan included an after.

The drugs kept me awake. That was the point. The surgeon calibrated the dosage — I could feel him adjusting, the way a sound engineer adjusts volume, finding the exact level where I couldn't move and couldn't scream but could *feel* and could *see.* My body was pinned to the table by chemistry.

My mind was pinned to my body by the surgeon's expertise. He had done this before. The calibration was too precise for a first attempt.

I felt it. I felt everything. I felt things that the human nervous system is not designed to process and that my brain handled by splitting into pieces — one piece in the room, on the table, experiencing what the surgeon was doing; another piece somewhere above, watching, the way you'd watch something happening to a stranger on a screen; and a third piece — the piece that kept me alive, the piece I didn't know I had — in my grandmother's kitchen. In Nogales. In the house with the yellow door where she made tortillas on Saturday mornings and the flour hung in the air like dust in a church.

I went to the kitchen. I stayed in the kitchen. While the surgeon worked and the men watched and the sounds my body made filled the room with something that the men apparently found *interesting* — I heard one of them say "fascinating," the way you'd say it at a museum — I stood in my grandmother's kitchen and I watched her hands press the dough and I smelled the oil heating in the pan and I said the prayer she taught me, the one I'd forgotten, the one I didn't know was still inside me until the moment I needed a place to go that wasn't the table.

Dios te salve, María, llena eres de gracia.

The men took turns. Not with what the surgeon was doing — with what came after what the surgeon did. The surgeon's work produced something, and the something was taken to the kitchen — the real kitchen, the ranch kitchen, where a chef I never saw prepared it the way a chef prepares anything, with heat and oil and seasoning and the professional indifference of a man who has been paid enough to not ask what he's cooking.

They ate in the next room. I could hear them through the wall. The sounds of dinner. Silverware. Conversation. Someone discussing wine. Someone discussing a business deal. The ordinary sounds of men eating dinner, except the dinner was a piece of a boy who was still alive on a table in the next room, listening to them eat him.

One of them came back. He looked at me on the table and he said — and I will carry this sentence in my bones for the rest of my life, in the space where the bone used to connect to the fingers that aren't there anymore — he said: "Exquisite."

He said it the way you'd compliment a chef. He said it to the surgeon. And the surgeon nodded. Professional courtesy. The quiet pride of a man whose work has been appreciated.

This happened across four days. The surgeon monitored. He adjusted the IV. He checked vitals. He kept my body running the way a mechanic keeps an engine running — maintaining the machine so the machine can continue to produce what the machine is designed to produce. My body was a machine. The surgeon was the mechanic. The guests were the customers. And what the machine produced was an experience so far beyond the boundary of what most people believe is possible that the men who consumed it became, in consuming it, permanently bonded to each other by the knowledge that they had crossed a line that cannot be uncrossed.

That's why they did it. Not for the taste. For the *bond.* I understood that later — years later, when I was old enough and distant enough and medicated enough to think about it without the wall in my mind collapsing. The meal wasn't the point. The shared secret was the point. The shared knowledge that every man at that table had participated in something that would destroy them all if it became public — that was the adhesive. That was the mechanism. My body was the raw material for a contract that none of them could ever break.

I survived. I don't know why. The surgeon, I think, was too good at his job. He kept me alive past the point where the guests were finished, and once the guests were finished, killing me would have required a decision, and decisions require someone to take responsibility, and the entire architecture of the operation was designed to ensure that no single person was responsible for anything. So I survived. I was transported. I was deposited somewhere. I woke up in a hospital in a city I didn't recognize with injuries that the emergency room doctors cataloged with the stunned, nauseated professionalism of people who have been trained to treat the body without asking what the body has been through.

The medical records describe "traumatic amputation, left hand, digits 4 and 5, with evidence of surgical precision inconsistent with accidental mechanism." Surgical precision. Inconsistent with accidental mechanism. That's the medical profession's way of saying: someone did this on purpose, with training, with tools, and they knew what they were doing.

Nobody called the police. The hospital filed a report. The report went into a system. The system processed the report the way systems process everything — slowly, automatically, without urgency or conscience. The report was filed alongside thousands of other reports of unexplained injuries, in a bureaucracy that treats paperwork as the equivalent of action and filing as the equivalent of investigation.

I'm thirty-eight. I work with my hands — or the hand I have left, and the three fingers on the other one that still work. I do carpentry. I build things. I build shelves and cabinets and tables and there is a specific kind of peace in building a table, in constructing a flat, solid surface where people can eat meals that are made of food and served with love and consumed in the company of family, and the table is just a table, and the meal is just a meal, and nobody at the table is bonded by anything except the ordinary, beautiful, unremarkable bond of people who care about each other. I build tables. They ate off a table. The word is the same. The world is not.

My grandmother died in 2014. I didn't go to the funeral. I couldn't go to Nogales. I couldn't go to the kitchen. Because the kitchen is the place I went to survive, and going there in my body — physically standing in the room where I stood in my mind while the surgeon worked — would collapse the wall between the two kitchens, the real one and the one that saved my life, and if those two kitchens become the same kitchen then I lose the only safe place I have left. I say the prayer sometimes. At night. When the hand that isn't all there anymore aches in the way that absent things ache — the phantom pain, the nerve endings still firing signals to fingers that don't exist, the body's refusal to accept what was taken from it.

Dios te salve, María, llena eres de gracia. She would have understood. She wouldn't have asked about the hand. She would have made tortillas and the flour would have hung in the air and she would have said the prayer with me and that would have been enough.

It would have been enough. There. Now you've heard them.

Nine voices. Nine rooms inside the building I constructed. Nine people who lived inside the architecture I described for you in my own charming, self-aware, wryly self-deprecating voice — the voice that made you forget, or almost forget, that the architecture was built on the bones of children and the silence of everyone who walked through the front door and chose not to look at what was happening in the rooms upstairs.

Are you satisfied? Do you feel righteous? Good. Hold onto that feeling. You'll need it.

Chapter 43: The Night

Timeline: August 10, 2019 | **Location:** Federal Metropolitan Detention Center, Cell

Here is what the record says.

The last verified observations of Vincent Aldric alive come from the evening of August 9th.

I met with my lawyers. We reviewed documents. We discussed strategy — the specific, granular, operationally detailed strategy of a defense team preparing for a federal trial that would be the most scrutinized legal proceeding in a generation. We discussed evidence — which pieces the prosecution would present, which pieces could be challenged, which pieces would require expert testimony to contextualize. We discussed the trial timeline — the months of pre-trial motions, the jury selection, the opening statements, the prosecution's case, the defense's case, the closing arguments, the deliberation.

I was, according to those who saw me, focused, engaged, and working on my defense with the intensity of a man who intends to fight. I had not written a suicide note. I had not given away possessions. I had not said goodbye — not to lawyers, not to family, not to anyone. I had, however, signed my will two days earlier — the will that names Theodore Marsh as primary executor and Anton Segura as backup, the will that routes five hundred and seventy-seven million dollars through a trust designed to be impervious to civil claims from the victims whose lawsuits would, inevitably, follow the criminal proceedings.

The will is either the prudent estate planning of a wealthy man facing a long trial and an uncertain outcome, or the final arrangement of a man who knows the trial will never happen. Both interpretations are supported by the evidence. Neither can be proven.

I met with my lawyers on the evening of the 9th. We discussed strategy. We discussed evidence. We discussed the trial timeline. I was not a man who was giving up. I was a man who was preparing to fight the most important legal battle of my life. Or I was a man performing preparation for an audience of lawyers who would later testify about my state of mind. Both of those men look the same from the outside. The difference is on the inside.

And nobody will ever know what was on my inside. That's the last privilege I have. The last thing I control. My own ending.

The silence woke me.

Not a sound — the *absence* of sound. Eight hours of silence in a building where silence should be impossible, where the metallic clanging of doors, the murmur of inmates who cannot sleep, the footsteps of guards making rounds they are required by law to make — all of it should have formed the ambient noise of a federal detention facility at night. None of those sounds occurred. The guards were asleep. The cameras were dark. The corridor was empty. Eight hours during which the most important defendant in America existed in a blind spot — a gap in the record, a hole in the archive, a missing tape in a life defined by tapes.

I lay on the bunk and listened to the nothing. The building had never been this quiet. Even on the first night, when I'd been too wired to sleep, there had been sounds — the distant argument on another tier, the clank of a food cart, the wheeze of ventilation. This silence was different. This silence had been arranged.

I knew what arranged silence sounded like. I had arranged it myself, many times, on the island, in the mansion, in the rooms where the cameras ran and the guests didn't know and the only sound was the soft, almost imperceptible click of equipment doing exactly what it was designed to do. Silence is not the absence of activity. Silence is the sound a system makes when every variable has been controlled.

I should have been afraid. That's what a normal person would tell you — that lying in a concrete cell in the middle of the night, in a silence that felt engineered, you should have been afraid. But I wasn't a normal person. I was a man who had spent thirty years engineering silence for other people. A man who understood, professionally, what silence meant: that somewhere, someone had decided what would happen next, and that the decision had already been made, and that the silence was not the prelude to the event but the *first act* of it.

The lock turned at 2:14 a.m. I know this because I was looking at the clock. Not because I was keeping time — what would be the point? — but because the clock was the only thing in the cell that moved, and when you are lying in the dark listening to a silence that has been built for you, your eyes settle on the only thing that proves time is still passing.

2:14.

The door opened. Not fast, not slow. The way a man opens a door when he has been told exactly how to open it — with the calm, practiced efficiency of a person executing a procedure. Not breaking in. Not sneaking. *Entering.*

The way a janitor enters an office after hours. The way a stagehand enters a theater before the audience arrives. With the quiet authority of a man who belongs in the room because someone has made it his room.

He was not a guard I recognized. He was not wearing the standard uniform of the Federal Metropolitan Detention Center — or rather, he was wearing *a* uniform, but it fit him the way a costume fits an actor: technically correct, functionally convincing, but worn by a man whose body language said *military* and not *corrections officer*. The difference is in the shoulders. Guards slump. Soldiers square. This man's shoulders were architecture.

He didn't speak. Not yet.

He closed the door behind him. The lock engaged — from the outside, which meant someone was on the other side of the door, which meant this was not a solo operation, which meant the silence in the corridor was not an accident of sleeping guards but the product of a cleared hallway, which meant — and this is the part where the narrator of this book, the man who has been explaining power structures and leverage systems and intelligence operations for forty-two chapters, finally arrives at a conclusion about his own life that he has been avoiding since the first sentence of the first page —

It meant I was not going to trial.

The man moved to the bunk. He was efficient. I'll give him that. I spent my career surrounded by efficient people — Diane with her schedules, Jenna with her calendars, Malcolm with his servers — and I can recognize competence when it enters a room, even when the competence has come to kill me.

I opened my mouth to speak. To say something. To deploy the only weapon I had ever truly possessed — language, persuasion, the ability to make any man in any room believe that I was the most important person he would ever meet and that harming me was the worst decision he could make. I had talked my way into Prescott Academy. I had talked my way onto the trading floor at Meridian Sachs. I had talked my way into the confidence of billionaires and presidents and princes. I had talked my way out of a fifty-three-page federal indictment. Talking was the whole thing. Talking was all I had. Talking was —

He put his hand over my mouth.

Not violently. Not with the dramatic force of a movie villain. With the firm, practiced pressure of a man who has done this before and who understands that the mouth is a problem to be managed, not a threat to be feared. His hand smelled like latex. Gloves. The detail registered somewhere in my brain — the part of my brain that was still cataloging, still filing, still doing what it had always done, which was observing the behavior of powerful men in private spaces and storing the information for later use — and the absurdity of that reflex, the absurdity of my dying brain still trying to build a file on the man who was killing me, struck me as the last and greatest joke of my entire life.

I couldn't talk.

For the first time in sixty-six years, I couldn't talk. The man who had narrated his way through every crisis, who had talked his way past every obstacle, who had built an empire on the understanding that language is the most powerful tool in the human arsenal — that man was lying on a prison bunk with a latex glove over his mouth, and the tool didn't work. The weapon was jammed. The machine had encountered the one input it couldn't process: a man who didn't want to hear what I had to say.

He leaned close. Close enough that I could feel his breath on my ear. Close enough that I could smell coffee and something antiseptic. Close enough that the intimacy of it — the terrible, unwanted intimacy of a stranger's face next to yours in a dark room — reminded me, with a clarity that I did not welcome and could not suppress, of the intimacy I had forced on hundreds of girls in hundreds of rooms across two decades. The proximity. The breath. The understanding, arriving too late to matter, that being the body in the room rather than the man standing over it changes everything about how the room feels.

"You know who says thank you for your service," he said.

That was it. Eight words. No name. No explanation. No monologue. No villain's speech revealing the conspiracy and the conspirators and the chain of command that led from some mahogany office to this concrete cell. Just eight words delivered in a voice that was calm and flat and utterly without drama, the voice of a man completing a task, not performing one.

You know who says thank you for your service.

I did know. That was the worst part. I knew exactly who. Not one person — many. A list. The same list that was on Malcolm's servers, on the flight logs, in the address book, in the files. The people who had visited my island and attended my dinners and flown on my plane and done things in my rooms that my cameras had recorded with the patient, mechanical fidelity of equipment that does not judge. They were all saying thank you. Every one of them. Thank you for your service. Thank you for your silence. Thank you for dying before the trial. Thank you for taking the names with you. Thank you, Vincent. Thank you.

The sheet was already in his hands. I don't know when he'd taken it from the bed — during the sentence, maybe, or before he spoke, while my brain was still processing the glove and the coffee smell and the squared shoulders. The sheet was cotton. Thin. Standard issue. The kind of sheet that inmates on suicide watch are not permitted to have, but that inmates who have been *removed* from suicide watch receive as a matter of routine. Someone took me off suicide watch. Someone gave me the sheet. And now someone was using the sheet for the purpose that the suicide watch protocol was specifically designed to prevent.

The irony is not poetic. The irony is *structural.* I built a machine that ran on surveillance. The machine that was supposed to surveil me was turned off at the exact moment it mattered. And the tool that killed me was provided by the same government that had spent twelve years failing to prosecute me. The government gave me the sheet. The government removed the safeguards. The government cleared the corridor. And then a man who was not a guard walked through a door that should have been locked and did what the government had been too compromised to do at trial: he closed the case.

The sheet went around my neck. His hands were professional. Quick. The knot was tied to the upper bunk frame — the ligature point that would, in the morning, suggest a self-inflicted hanging. The staging was meticulous. Of course it was. Whoever sent this man understood staging. They had watched me stage scenes for thirty years.

I want to tell you that I fought. I want to tell you that the man who built the web, who controlled presidents, who held the secrets of the world's most powerful people in a filing system maintained by a man named Malcolm — I want to tell you that this man did not go quietly. But I would be lying. And I have told you, from the first page of this book, that I would tell you the truth. Not the whole truth — never the whole truth — but the truth about the things I choose to disclose.

I did not fight. I couldn't. Not because I was restrained — though I was — but because fighting requires the belief that fighting will change the outcome, and I had spent my entire career studying the outcomes of fights between individuals and systems, and the system always wins. Always. I built a system. It protected me. And now a bigger system — older, more powerful, with more resources and more patience and the one thing my system never had, which is the ability to kill — was dismantling me with the same efficient professionalism that I had applied to every operation I'd ever run.

The pressure increased. Something cold entered my arm — not the sheet, not the hands, but a needle. Small. Professional. The kind of needle that a man carries when the objective is not death but *disappearance.* The chemical hit my bloodstream with the warm, spreading numbness of a substance designed to simulate exactly one thing: cardiac arrest. My heart rate dropped. My breathing slowed to a frequency that a guard checking from the doorway — if there had been a guard, which there wasn't — would have measured as absence. The world — the cell, the clock, the smell of latex, the sound of my own pulse — narrowed to a point.

The point went dark.

And I understood, in the final compression, the thing that every girl I ever trafficked understood the first time she walked into one of my rooms: that the room belongs to the man standing up. That the body on the bed has no voice. That the architecture of the room — its locks, its cameras, its silence — serves the man who controls it. I had spent my life on the standing side. Now I was on the other side. And the other side is exactly what I always knew it was: it's nothing. It's the end of the sentence. It's the period that someone else places after your last word.

Or so I thought.

What I know about the next two hours I was told, in the matter-of-fact briefing of a professional completing an after-action report, by the man on the boat was the man arranged the body. My body. The sheet positioned to suggest suspension. The bunk frame staged to bear weight it was never designed to bear. The cell restored to the appearance of a scene that would tell one story — suicide — while concealing the other story, which is the story you are about to read, which is the story that nobody will ever believe because the cameras were off and the guards were asleep and the corridor was clear and the only witness is a man the world believes is dead.

He left the cell. The door closed. The lock engaged.

And somewhere between the closing of that door and the discovery of my "body" at 6:30 the following morning, a second team entered through a service corridor that the Bureau of Prisons blueprints don't include on their public filings. They brought a gurney. They brought a body bag. And they brought something else — a body. Not mine. A body that was close enough in height, weight, and general physical description to pass a visual identification by guards who had been told to expect a corpse and who would see exactly what they expected to see, because human beings are remarkably cooperative witnesses when the institution they serve has already written the narrative.

The switch took eleven minutes. I know this because I was told later, by a man whose name I don't know and whose face I never saw clearly because my vision was still blurred from whatever compound had been injected into my arm four hours earlier. Eleven minutes to replace a living man with a dead one. Eleven minutes to transform Vincent Aldric from a federal inmate awaiting trial into a corpse awaiting autopsy.

I woke up on water. The gentle rocking of a boat — not a yacht, nothing glamorous, a working vessel of the kind that moves between Caribbean ports carrying cargo that customs officials are paid not to inspect. My wrists were zip-tied. My head felt like someone had filled it with wet concrete and shaken it. The man sitting across from me was not the man from the cell — different build, different posture, the relaxed bearing of a professional who has completed the dangerous part of the assignment and is now managing the logistics.

"Where," I said. My voice sounded like gravel being dragged across a chalkboard.

He didn't answer the question. He answered a different one — the one I should have asked first.

"You're alive because the archive is more valuable with a living operator than a dead martyr," he said. "The people who arranged this want the files accessible. They want the passwords. They want the encryption keys. And they want a man who understands the system well enough to maintain it."

You know who says you're still useful.

That was the deal. Not freedom. Not mercy. Not a reward for services rendered. Utility. The same currency I'd traded in my entire life — usefulness, indispensability, the understanding that a man who can provide something no one else can provide is a man who stays alive. I had used that currency to survive for thirty years. Someone was now using it to keep me breathing.

The boat docked at a port I didn't recognize. I was transferred to a vehicle. The vehicle drove to an airstrip. The airstrip had a plane. The plane had no markings I could identify and a flight path I was not told. I slept, or lost consciousness, or existed in the pharmaceutical twilight between the two, for what might have been hours or might have been days.

I woke up in a room with white walls, white sheets, and a window that looked out on a coastline I had never seen. Mediterranean, I thought. Or possibly Adriatic. Somewhere warm enough that the light coming through the window had the specific golden quality of southern latitude, the kind of light that real estate agents in Manhattan describe as "natural" and that actually exists only in places where the sun has nothing to prove.

A man entered. A doctor — or a man dressed as a doctor, which in my experience amounts to the same thing. He examined me with the brisk efficiency of a professional who has treated patients in circumstances that medical school does not prepare you for.

"You'll need surgery," he said. "Facial reconstruction. New documentation. A recovery period."

He said it the way a mechanic describes an oil change. Routine. Expected. Part of the service.

"How long?" I asked.

"The surgery, six hours. The recovery, three months. The new identity..." He paused. "The new identity is permanent."

Vincent Aldric died in a federal cell on August 10, 2019. That's what the record says. That's what the world believes. That's the story that launched a thousand conspiracy theories and a single, devastating, universally held conviction: *Vincent Aldric didn't kill himself.*

They're right. I didn't kill myself.

But I didn't die, either.

At approximately 6:30 a.m. on August 10, 2019, a guard making a round that should have been made hours earlier finds my body in the cell.

Unresponsive. Not breathing. The body is positioned in a manner consistent with hanging — a bedsheet fashioned into a ligature, attached to the top bunk of the cell's bunk bed. Medical personnel are summoned. Resuscitation is attempted. The attempt fails. Vincent Aldric is pronounced dead at age sixty-six.

The cause of death, pending autopsy, is described as "apparent suicide by hanging." The official record will say I hanged myself. The official record is a beautifully staged scene, and I should know — I staged scenes for thirty years. Whoever arranged that cell understood composition the way I understood composition. The sheet positioned just so. The body angled to tell a story. The knot tied with a precision that suggested either a man determined to die or a professional determined to make it look that way.

I was found at 6:30 in the morning. That's what the record says. *Found.* As if I were a set of car keys or a missing glove. "We found him." Found implies lost. I wasn't lost. I was exactly where they left me.

The autopsy was performed by the New York City Chief Medical Examiner. The body on the table was not mine, but nobody in that room knew that, and the medical examiner was not looking for evidence of substitution — she was looking for a cause of death, and the cause was written clearly enough in the staged ligature marks and the carefully broken hyoid bone.

The findings are clinical. Death by hanging. Asphyxiation. The mechanism documented in medical language that reduces the final moments of a human life to a sequence of physiological events: compression of the airway, interruption of blood flow to the brain, loss of consciousness, cessation of cardiac function. The body tells a story. The story the body tells is: this man died from a ligature around his neck. The story is technically true. The story is also incomplete. But incomplete stories are the specialty of every institution that ever dealt with me.

The hyoid bone — a small, horseshoe-shaped bone in the throat — is broken. In the medical literature, hyoid bone fractures are more common in strangulation homicides than in suicidal hangings. The fracture pattern is, according to multiple forensic studies, more consistent with the application of external pressure by another person than with the suspension of body weight from a ligature point. You already know why the bone is broken. I just told you why.

But the medical examiner doesn't have the story I just told you. The medical examiner has a body, and a cell, and a sheet, and the institutional expectation that the simplest explanation is the correct one. The medical examiner ruled the death a suicide.

A forensic pathologist hired by my brother, **Dennis Aldric**, examined the same evidence and reached a different conclusion. The injuries, in his professional opinion, were more consistent with homicide. Two medical professionals, examining the same body, reaching opposite conclusions. One of them is wrong. I'll let you decide which one, now that you know what happened at 2:14 in the morning.

The news broke on a Saturday morning.

Within hours, five words became the most common phrase on the internet: "Vincent Aldric didn't kill himself."

The phrase crossed political lines. It crossed ideological lines. It crossed every line that American society had drawn to separate left from right, red from blue, conspiracy from consensus. Conservatives believed I was killed to protect Prescott. Liberals believed I was killed to protect Barlow. Libertarians believed I was killed to protect the intelligence agencies. Everyone — left, right, center, and fringe — believed that the system killed me to protect itself. For the first time in a generation, the American public achieved consensus on a single proposition: a man was killed in a federal cell to prevent him from testifying about the crimes of the powerful.

Whether this is true is, in a sense, irrelevant. What matters is that *no one believes the official story.* Not the victims. Not the public. Not the press. Not the politicians. Not even the people who benefit from the official story — because the people who benefit from the official story understand, as I always understood, that the believability of a narrative is a function of the institution telling it, and the institution telling this narrative had spent twelve years demonstrating its inability to manage a case involving a single defendant.

The death of Vincent Aldric is the moment when American institutional credibility — already damaged by decades of corruption, incompetence, and the systematic failure to hold the powerful accountable — suffers a wound from which it may never recover.

Within hours of my death, the whole world agreed: I didn't kill myself. That's remarkable. Not because it's true or because it's false — I'm not going to settle that debate from beyond the grave. It's remarkable because it's the only thing Americans have agreed on in twenty years. The left thinks the right killed me.

The right thinks the left killed me. Everyone thinks the system killed me. And the system can't prove otherwise because the cameras don't work and the guards were asleep. The most powerful system on Earth, undone by two sleeping guards and two broken cameras. Or: the most powerful system on Earth, executing a plan that required exactly two sleeping guards and two broken cameras. Same facts. Different stories. Welcome to my legacy.

The novel's narration arrives at the question it cannot answer.

The first-person voice that has carried you from a Brooklyn classroom through Garrison Brothers, through the Ponzi years, through the mansion and the island and the cameras and the girls and the presidents and the prince and the arrest and the cell — that voice arrives, now, at the edge of what it can tell you. Because the narrator is either dead by his own hand or dead by someone else's, and neither answer resolves the larger truth.

The question is not: *Did Vincent Aldric kill himself?*

The question is: *Who benefits from his silence?*

And the answer to that question is a list so long that it reads like my address book. Presidents. Princes. Billionaires. Intelligence agencies. Governments. Institutions. Every name on every flight log, every face in every photograph, every guest at every dinner — all of them benefit from the silence. All of them are safer because I cannot testify. All of them sleep better because the CDs will never be played and the servers will never be accessed and the cameras will never be reviewed in open court.

The web that I built was designed to ensure that the powerful could never escape. The web was my insurance — the thing that kept me alive, because the information I held was too dangerous to let me die. But insurance only works if the policyholder is alive to make the claim. Somebody decided that the claim was too expensive. Somebody decided that the premiums were too high. Somebody decided that the cheapest option — the most elegant, the most efficient, the most *permanent* option — was to cancel the policy.

I built the web. But someone else held the scissors. And on the night of August 10, 2019, in a cell with no cameras and no guards and no witnesses, the scissors closed.

Chapter 44: The Autopsy of a System

Timeline: August 2019 | **Location:** The Aftermath

The Department of Justice opened an investigation into my death at the Federal Metropolitan Detention Center.

The investigation would determine that the two guards falsified records. That the cameras malfunctioned. That the facility was chronically understaffed. That the removal from suicide watch was premature. That the cellmate transfer was unexplained. That the Bureau of Prisons had failed, at every level, to fulfill its most fundamental obligation: keeping the inmate alive long enough to stand trial.

The investigation would determine all of these things, and the investigation would be correct about all of these things, and the investigation would result in criminal charges against the two guards — the two underpaid, overworked, exhausted human beings who fell asleep at their desk on the night that the highest-value defendant in America died in his cell.

The charges against the guards were eventually resolved through a deferred prosecution agreement. The terms of the agreement required community service.

Community service. Two guards who were supposed to protect the highest-profile federal inmate in America falsified records on the night he died, and their punishment was community service. Hours logged at a nonprofit. Supervised tasks performed under the watchful eye of a probation officer. The kind of sentence that a judge assigns to a teenager caught shoplifting, applied to two federal employees whose failure — or whose cooperation — contributed to the death of a man whose testimony could have implicated presidents, princes, and billionaires.

The echo of my own sweetheart deal reverberates through the outcome. Sixteen months for trafficking dozens of children. Community service for failing to prevent a death in federal custody. The system investigates itself and finds that mistakes were made. The system punishes itself with a slap on the wrist. The system moves on.

They investigated my death the way they investigated my crimes: thoroughly enough to check a box, insufficiently enough to change anything.

The guards got community service. Community service. Sixteen months for trafficking children. Community service for failing to prevent a death. The American justice system doesn't have a sentencing problem. It has a *seriousness* problem. Nothing is taken seriously because the people in charge of taking things seriously are the same people who benefit from nothing being taken seriously. It's a beautiful system. Self-sustaining. Self-protecting. Self-pardoning.

The victims learned that the man who abused them was dead.

The women who survived my operation — who had been girls when they entered it, who had carried the weight of what happened to them through decades of silence and therapy and the slow, grinding work of reconstructing a life that a predator had dismantled — learned the news the way the rest of the world learned it: from a screen. A phone notification. A news alert. A text from a friend who had read the headline and remembered, perhaps for the first time in years, that the woman she was texting had once been one of the girls.

The reactions were not uniform. Some felt cheated — denied the trial they had been promised, denied the testimony they had prepared, denied the verdict that would have validated what they endured. They had waited. Some of them had waited decades. They had cooperated with investigators, with lawyers, with journalists. They had told their stories — the most painful, most private, most difficult stories a person can tell — to strangers in official capacities, and they had done it with the understanding that the telling would lead somewhere. To a courtroom. To a jury. To a verdict. To the word that the legal system uses to say: *you were right.*

The verdict they had earned. The single syllable that would have transformed their testimony from allegation into fact, their suffering from private wound into public record. A dead man cannot be convicted. A dead man cannot be cross-examined. A dead man cannot sit in a courtroom while twelve citizens render the judgment that every one of those women had spent years preparing to hear.

Some felt relief. The man was gone. Whatever form justice takes, whatever inadequate substitute the civil courts and the estate proceedings and the institutional apologies provide, he will never hurt anyone again. The body is in a coffin. The threat is neutralized. The relief is real, even if it is incomplete, even if it carries within it the knowledge that relief is not justice and that the absence of a threat is not the presence of accountability.

Some felt nothing. The numbness of people who stopped expecting anything from the system a long time ago. The system failed them when it gave me sixteen months. The system failed them when it granted my staff immunity. The system failed them when it let me operate from a work release office. And now the system had failed them one final time, by allowing the defendant to die before the trial could deliver the one thing the system was supposed to provide: a reckoning.

The girls — the women now, the survivors — learned I was dead and felt... what? I don't know. I can't know. I never knew what they felt. That was the whole problem, wasn't it. I never knew and I never cared and now I never will. But I can tell you what they were denied: a trial. A verdict. A moment in a courtroom where a jury of twelve people looked at the evidence and said: guilty. That word — *guilty* — is the most powerful word in the English language for a victim. It means: you were right. You were telling the truth. We believe you. I took a lot of things from those girls. But the system took that word. Guilty. Nobody will ever say it about me in a courtroom. That's not my victory. That's my final crime.

My death triggered a legal chain reaction.

Civil lawsuits continued — the estate was liable even if I was not, and the victims' attorneys moved with the accelerated urgency of lawyers who understood that the estate's assets would be the only available source of compensation and that those assets were protected by the same offshore architecture that had shielded them throughout my life. The **Natalie Brennan** case moved forward. Sealed documents began to unseal — slowly, through litigation, through judicial orders, through the grinding procedural mechanics that govern the release of information in a legal system that defaults to secrecy and requires affirmative action to produce transparency.

Some of the names emerged. Not all of them. Some. Enough to generate headlines. Enough to fuel speculation. Enough to demonstrate that the web extended further than the public had imagined and that the people caught in it included names that the public recognized.

But the full scope of what I knew — what the cameras recorded, what the servers stored, what the CDs contained, what the files documented — all of that died with me. Or disappeared. Or was taken. The distinction between "died with me" and "was taken" is the distinction between suicide and murder, between tragedy and conspiracy, between the official story and the story that no one believes.

The FBI raided the island within days of my death. They arrived by boat and by helicopter. They removed hard drives, computers, and documents. They catalogued the contents of the buildings. They photographed the interiors. They processed the property with the methodical thoroughness of investigators who understood that the evidence they were collecting was simultaneously the most valuable and the most politically dangerous material in the federal system.

What they found — and what they didn't find — is classified, sealed, or otherwise inaccessible to the public. The most comprehensive surveillance archive in modern history is now in the possession of the same government that gave me immunity, that fell asleep while I died, and that cannot explain what happened in my cell.

Ten days after my arrest — and within the gravitational pull of my death — **Richard Cavanaugh** resigned as Secretary of Labor.

Cavanaugh resigned. Stood on the White House lawn and gave a speech about how much he cared about the victims. The same victims he didn't notify about the plea deal. The same victims whose case he buried in a drawer. He resigned with dignity, which is a phrase that means "he resigned before they fired him." And then he disappeared into private law practice, where the billing rate is high enough to cure any public servant of whatever conscience survived the government. The door closed. The system moved on. The system always moves on. That's the system's superpower: it has no memory.

In the weeks and months following my death, investigators, journalists, and the public all turned their attention to the same question: *where are the files?*

The cameras recorded for twenty years. The servers stored for twenty years. The backups existed for twenty years. Twenty years of footage. Twenty years of documentation. Twenty years of the most powerful people on Earth doing things they would pay anything — and perhaps did pay anything — to keep hidden.

Malcolm Pruitt — one hundred and fourteen emails, the most frequent correspondent in the entire archive, the man who maintained every camera, every server, every backup drive, every encryption protocol — is the only person alive who knows the full architecture of the system. He knows where the servers lived. He knows where the backups were stored. He knows which files were on which drives. He knows the encryption keys. He knows the access protocols. He knows who is on the tapes. He knows everything.

And Malcolm Pruitt says nothing.

He cooperates with investigators only to the extent required by law — answering questions when compelled, producing documents when subpoenaed, performing the minimum legal obligations of a citizen subject to a federal investigation. He does not volunteer information. He does not write a memoir. He does not sell his story to a journalist or a publisher or a documentary filmmaker. He does not appear on television. He does not post on social media. He does not participate in the public conversation about the web or the cameras or the files or the death.

The man who maintained the spider's surveillance system becomes the last mystery in the spider's web — a technician who holds the key to every secret and who has apparently decided that some doors should remain locked. Whether this is loyalty, or fear, or a calculated understanding that the information he possesses is more valuable as a secret than as a disclosure — whether Malcolm Pruitt is a man protecting a dead employer or a man protecting himself or a man who has been threatened into silence by the same forces that may have silenced me — is, like everything else in this story, a question that generates two contradictory answers and cannot be resolved.

I told you at the beginning that I had met four genuinely dangerous people. The first was me. The second was Celeste. I never told you the third and fourth. The third was Malcolm Pruitt. He was dangerous the way a foundation is dangerous — invisibly, structurally, and in ways you only understand when the building starts to move. The fourth was a teenager from a Gulf Shore spa who couldn't afford a lawyer and knocked on locked doors for eleven years. Her name is Natalie Brennan. I built a system to protect me from the powerful. I never built anything to protect me from a person with nothing to protect.

I have one more thing to tell you. And then I'm done.

I'm writing this from a villa whose address I will never share, in a country whose name I will never speak, with a face that my own mother wouldn't recognize and a passport that belongs to a man who has never existed. The surgery took six hours. The recovery took three months. The new identity took a week to fabricate and will take the rest of my life to inhabit.

I watch the aftermath on a television that receives satellite news from six continents. I watch the investigations. I watch the lawsuits. I watch the conspiracy theories bloom and multiply and merge and contradict each other in the grand American tradition of disagreeing about everything except the one thing everyone agrees on: *Vincent Aldric didn't kill himself.*

They're right. But they don't know how right they are.

I've spent forty-four chapters being the smartest man in the room. I've explained the architecture. I've named the parts. I've shown you how the machine was built, how it ran, how it was fed, how it was protected, and how it survived every attempt to dismantle it. I've been articulate and analytical and occasionally funny, because articulate and analytical and occasionally funny is the performance I've been giving since I was twenty-one years old, and the performance is all I know how to do.

But here, at the end, I want to drop the performance for exactly one paragraph.

I was not the architect. I was the blueprint.

The machine I built — the cameras, the leverage, the bipartisan web of complicity that protected the powerful at the expense of children — I did not invent it. Grank Thelden ran it on North Heron Island before I was old enough to shave. Porman ran it out of Dallas with thirty thousand index cards. Roman Harlow ran it across two continents with a media empire as his shield. The machine existed before me. It will exist after me. I was the most efficient operator it ever had — the man who refined the model, who digitized the leverage, who turned the handshake deal into a surveillance archive — but I was not the origin. The machine is older than I am. The machine is older than anyone alive. The machine runs on the simple, immutable, structurally permanent fact that powerful men will exploit children if the architecture permits it, and the architecture always permits it, because the architecture is designed by powerful men.

I didn't build the machine. I *was* the machine. And now the machine has moved on without me.

The archive exists. Somewhere. I know where. That's the leash. That's why I'm alive — not because anyone cares whether Vincent Aldric breathes, but because Vincent Aldric is the only man alive who knows every password, every encryption key, every backup location, every failsafe that Malcolm built into the system on my instructions. The people who extracted me from that cell didn't do it out of mercy. They did it because a dead man can't enter passwords. A dead man can't navigate the architecture. A dead man can't maintain the most valuable collection of secrets in the modern world.

I am alive because I am *useful.* The same currency I traded my entire life. The same principle that protected me for thirty years. Usefulness. Indispensability. The understanding that a man who can provide something no one else can provide is a man who keeps breathing.

But useful to *whom?*

I know the answer. I recognized it six months into this exile, in a message from an intermediary who used a phrase I had never written down — a server notation, a specific timestamp format, a piece of internal vocabulary that existed in exactly one place: the messages between me and the man in the basement. I have not acted on this recognition. I will not act on it.

The people who extracted me operate through intermediaries. I don't know their names. I don't know their government. I don't know whether the archive is being used for intelligence purposes or diplomatic leverage or simple, old-fashioned blackmail on a geopolitical scale. I know only that they need me alive, and that the need is the only thing standing between this villa and a second cell — or a second death scene, this one real.

The spider is not dead. The spider is in a cage made of sunlight and false passports and the knowledge that the web he built is now someone else's weapon. The spider can see the web from a distance. The spider can watch the web catch flies. The spider cannot touch the web. The spider cannot control the web. The spider can only sit in his villa and watch the television and understand, with a clarity that no prison sentence could have provided, what it means to build something so powerful that it consumes its creator.

The leverage was *mine.* The files were *mine.* Every president, every prince, every billionaire in those cameras — they were in *my* cameras, doing things that gave *me* power, generating leverage that *I* controlled with the precision and the patience and the strategic discipline of a man who understood that information is the only asset that appreciates indefinitely.

And now the information belongs to someone else. And the someone else owns not just the files but *me* — the man who built the filing system, maintained as a living key to a digital vault, kept alive not by grace but by *necessity.* I am the most expensive piece of infrastructure in the operation I created. I am a server that breathes. A hard drive with a heartbeat. The most sophisticated filing clerk in the history of organized crime, sitting in a Mediterranean villa, watching conspiracy theories about my death on satellite television, and understanding — finally, completely, with the devastating clarity of a man who has no audience left to perform for — that I was never the spider.

I was always the web.

One last thought. And this one is for the girls.

Not an apology — I am not capable of apology, and offering one would be the final performance, the final con, the final deployment of language designed to make the listener feel something the speaker doesn't feel. I will not insult you with a fake apology. You've been insulted enough.

But I want to acknowledge something that nobody else in this story has acknowledged, including me, across forty-four chapters of detailed confession: you were not extras. You were not supporting characters. You were not the "massage girls" or the "victims" or the "Jane Does" or the anonymous entries in the civil lawsuits filed in the Meridian District of New York. You were the point. The entire operation — the mansion, the island, the ranch, the plane, the cameras, the scientists, the presidents, the princes, the seven thousand five hundred emails — all of it existed because of you. All of it required you. All of it was built on the understanding that you would walk through the door, and that you would be too young to know what the door was, and that you would not be able to leave.

I built a machine that consumed children and produced power. That is the sentence. That is the whole book in twelve words. Everything else — the clever analysis, the cynical narration, the dark humor, the structural commentary about systems and followers and media architecture — everything else is camouflage. My last act of camouflage. Because I've been camouflaging the truth for thirty years, and I can't stop, even in exile, even in a confession that is supposed to strip the camouflage away. The truth is twelve words long and I buried it in a hundred thousand.

You were children. I was the machine. The machine is still running. The machine will still be running when everyone alive who was ever in one of my rooms is dead. The machine doesn't need me. It never did. I know this now, from a villa with the wrong name on the door, watching the conspiracy theories cycle on satellite television and understanding the one thing that forty-four chapters of explanation have been avoiding: the machine was never about leverage. Leverage was just the mechanism. The machine was about the appetite. The appetite that brought the men to the rooms. The appetite that made the rooms necessary. The appetite that is older than me, older than Grank Thelden, older than the network, older than the concept of a private island in the Caribbean where rules don't apply. The appetite is the machine. I just built it a house.

The End

About the Author

Jordan Wright, M.Ed., didn't set out to write a book about how power really works. That happened by accident — or by observation, which is the same thing if you've been paying attention long enough.

With a background in education and a career spent studying how systems shape behavior — how institutions teach people what to value, what to ignore, and what to tolerate — Wright became increasingly interested in the question that lives at the center of *The Spider's Web*: not how bad people do bad things, but how entire structures of otherwise decent people learn to look the other way. The answer, it turns out, is architectural. It's designed. And it works because the people inside it are never shown the blueprint.

Wright writes fiction that pulls the blueprint out of the wall and lays it on the table.

The Spider's Web is the first book in The Loom Series — a body of work that examines how networks of influence, exploitation, and institutional silence are constructed, maintained, and protected across decades. The series is less interested in the monsters at the center of these systems than in the systems themselves: the mechanisms that allow a single individual to operate in plain sight, surrounded by people who know and choose not to act, because the cost of acting is higher than the cost of silence. It is fiction built on the understanding that the most dangerous architecture in the world is not hidden. It is merely ignored.

Wright's approach to storytelling is rooted in a simple conviction: that fiction can go where journalism cannot. A novel can put you inside the mind of a person no interview would ever reach. It can show you the logic of a system from the perspective of the person who designed it — and force you to sit with the uncomfortable realization that the logic makes sense. That it was always going to make sense. That the system was built by someone who understood people better than most people understand themselves, and that understanding is the weapon the rest of us never see coming.

Before writing fiction full-time, Wright spent years in education — designing curriculum, studying how people learn, and developing an unhealthy fascination with the gap between what institutions say they do and what they actually do. That fascination turned out to be the foundation for everything that followed. The classroom became a lens. The lens became a novel. The novel became a series.

Wright publishes through Humbolton Press and lives in a state of perpetual caffeination, surrounded by manuscripts in various stages of completion and a whiteboard covered in the kind of diagrams that would concern a therapist. When not writing, Wright is probably reading, arguing with a draft, or staring at a wall in a way that looks unproductive but is, in fact, the most important part of the process.

The Loom, Book Two of The Loom Series, is forthcoming.

Other works by Jordan Wright include *Mayor Mayhem: She Ran for Office and Took Out Corruption with a Safe Word* (co-authored with Ibrahim Roble).

For more information, visit humbolton.com.

www.ingramcontent.com/pod-product-compliance
Lightning Source LLC
LaVergne TN
LVHW030908080826
845145LV00010B/2806

* 9 7 8 1 9 6 6 7 0 3 3 1 0 *